APACHE KNIGHT

APACHE KNIGHT

CAROL FINCH

KENSINGTON BOOKS

KENSINGTON BOOKS are published by

Kensington Publishing Corp.
850 Third Avenue
New York, NY 10022

ISBN 0-8217-5299-5

First Zebra Paperback Printing: October, 1994
First Kensington Hardcover Printing: September, 1995

Printed in the United States of America

This book is dedicated to my husband Ed and our children Christine, Jill, and Kurt. With much love . . .

A very special thank you to my editor, Ann LaFarge. Your support and enthusiasm are greatly appreciated!

Part One

A book of Verses underneath
    the Bough,
A jug of Wine, a Loaf of
    Bread—and Thou
Beside me singing in the
    Wilderness—
Oh, Wilderness were Paradise
    enow!

        —Omar Khayyám, *The Rubáiyát*

Chapter One

Globe City, Arizona Territory
Spring, 1881

Shane Stafford ambled down the street of the rowdy mining town, feeling all eyes upon him. It was an unwelcome but familiar sensation to Shane. The citizens of this five-year-old community had an uncanny way of reminding Shane that he was different. To them, he would always be an outsider, the mysterious stranger even in a land that was his by right of birth.

Conversation faded into silence as Shane strode along the boardwalk. He maintained a high profile in Globe. His mere size commanded the kind of attention he didn't want or need. He was a spectacle, the subject of speculation aplenty and gossip galore.

The moment Shane passed a group of miners lounging in the shade, he could hear whispered conversations resume. Those who knew him delighted in identifying him to newcomers. Shane could hear his life story being passed by word of mouth, tellers embellishing the tale until he was more of a legend than a man. Because of the circulating gossip that left him larger than life, he was well known to all by sight, and ironically, he was understood by no one.

Shane veered toward The Cottage set on the outskirts of town. Only the faint creak of the door heralded his arrival. Again, all eyes turned toward him, watching him with a wariness that was as tangible to Shane as the spoken word.

The Cottage was the favorite haunt of prospectors, cowhands, and businessmen. The customs of this establishment were ones that Shane still could not appreciate or fully comprehend, even after years of forced indoctrination into what was considered "civilized" society. In Shane's estimation, O'Connell's Cottage was a haven for men who diminished themselves in shallow pleasures, saturating their senses in free-flowing whiskey and perfumed harlots.

And the white man called himself civilized? Shane scoffed derisively. He rather thought the *Pinda-lick-o-yi*—or white-eyed men, as the Apache referred to the offensive intruders—suffered delusions of their own grandeur. There were times when Shane wondered who was the real savage and who was the true gentleman.

With what seemed to the occupants of the ornately decorated parlor as an absent glance, Shane absorbed all that transpired around him. Portraits of scantily-clad females hung on the walls that were papered with gaudy red, velvet, and gold. The tufted chairs and plush sofas that lined the spacious parlor were occupied by male patrons and the "nymphs du prairie" who wore more paint on their faces than an Indian war party. The gaily-adorned prostitutes lounged in the laps of their lusty suitors. The chummy couples groped at each other without any pretense at modesty or respect.

To his left, Shane could see the dining area in which another congregation of men and their harlots ate and drank their fill, flirting outrageously in the first phase of their crude mating rituals. Phase two was performed in the expensively furnished parlor where more whiskey flowed like a mountain stream.

The soiled doves cast glances in Shane's direction, but he

ignored the appreciative feminine stares. His obsidian eyes were focused on the bulky form of the carrot-haired proprietor.

Keery O'Connell ricocheted off the walls of the hall, making enough racket to wake the dead. Keery's red-streaked eyes narrowed on the towering mass of masculinity who filled the doorway to overflowing. With a foul curse, Keery glared mutinously at Shane and then propped himself against the wall for support and chugged another swig of whiskey.

"What are you doing here, half-breed? You know you aren't welcomed at The Cottage. You think just because your daddy got himself between a squaw's legs that you've got rights in this town?" Keery snorted drunkenly and downed another swallow of liquor. "As far as I'm concerned, you're no better than the Chinamen who swarmed in to work the copper and silver mines. They aren't allowed in my house and neither are you!"

All eyes darted to the swarthy giant who loomed by the door, gauging Shane's reaction to the degrading remarks. Shane's bronzed face was a well-schooled mask that revealed not one single emotion. He had so little use for Keery O'Connell that the man's opinion meant nothing whatsoever. When Keery was sober he was a barely tolerable bastard. When Keery was drunk—and he usually was—he was at his obnoxious best. Because Keery stood over six foot tall and had utilized brawny muscle to survive in his early years, he perceived himself as invincible. Although he was two years Shane's junior, Keery considered himself the half-breed's superior. But then, so did all the Americans who had invaded Arizona Territory like a conquering horde, outnumbering and driving the Apache off land that had been theirs since the beginning of time.

Keery's lips curled and his bloodshot eyes riveted on Shane. "Get the hell out of here, you stinking savage."

Shane's expression never altered. He gave not the slightest indication that the insult fazed him. He simply met Keery's loathing gaze with unblinking black-diamond eyes. "I came to fetch my men and I'm not leaving without them, O'Connell."

"*Your* men?" Keery slurred out. "You have no men, half-breed." His abrasive voice echoed around the parlor and filtered into the adjoining dining area, bringing all conversation to a halt. "White men don't take kindly to hearing a filthy savage refer to them as if they were his slaves."

Keery staggered across the parlor toward the half-breed who was dressed in buckskin and moccasins. "Get out of my sight, you disgusting son of a bitch, before I throw you out."

"Keery."

The woman's sultry voice gave Keery slight pause. He glanced sideways to see Royal Winston emerge from the office on the east side of the parlor.

Shane spared the voluptuous brunette a quick glance. Royal was partially responsible for the hostility Keery O'Connell felt for Shane. Two years earlier, when Shane had come to fetch his pleasure-seeking cowhands, Royal had flirted openly with him. That had not set well with the possessive Keery O'Connell, who had designated this provocative madam as his private property.

In one of his many drunken rages, Keery had picked a fight with Shane—a fight he had not been able to win. The humiliation caused by the incident had festered in Keery each time Shane crossed his path. The bad blood between the two men was compounded by the fierce prejudices O'Connell had formed during his stint in the Army.

Old grudges were about to erupt once again. Keery, like a possessive bull protecting his herd, charged toward Shane. If this was Keery's attempt to impress Royal, he was making a bad showing, Shane thought to himself. The man was stumbling drunk, and Shane had tolerated as many scathing affronts as he planned to endure. If Keery had his black heart set on another battle, Shane would gladly accommodate him.

Most folks had the good sense to give Shane Stafford all the space he needed—and then some—without unnecessarily provoking him. But Keery had allowed the excessive amount of whiskey he consumed to go to his head. He deemed himself to be Shane's match and attempted to prove it once and for all.

When Keery coiled an arm and threw a punch that connected with nothing but air, the patrons and their paramours made the mistake of bursting into laughter. That incensed Keery, his

Irish temper exploded. With a sneer and a guttural growl, he lowered his head and rammed Shane broadside.

"Savage bastard! I'd like to send you to hell where you and the rest of your breed belong!"

When Keery tried to mow him down, Shane doubled a fist and buried it in Keery's fleshy face. The blow snapped Keery's head backward, and he collided with the imported liquor cabinet in the corner. The expensive piece of furniture wobbled and crashed to the floor, catapulting whiskey bottles and shot glasses across the room. The alarmed occupants of the parlor shrieked and dodged the flying debris.

"Stop it this instant!" Royal screeched.

Keery hauled himself clumsily to his feet. Glass crunched under his boots as he sprang at Shane with blood in his eyes and truculent curses on his lips.

"I said . . . stop this nonsense at once!" Royal blared.

Keery wasn't listening. He concentrated on his primary objective—beating this brawny half-breed to a pulp for making him a laughingstock in front of Royal and his customers.

Shane was ready and waiting. Problem was, the door swung open, catching him in the back, momentarily knocking him off balance. Keery's lowered head slammed into Shane's belly, propelling him backward. Bodies leaped off the sofa before Keery and Shane crashed upon it. The couch reared on its hind legs and plunged to the floor, sending both men rolling in a flurry of damning curses and flying fists.

Sheriff Eli Nelson, who had heard the commotion when he passed the brothel, had entered in time to see Shane raise a doubled fist that connected with Keery's puckered face. Swiftly, Eli flipped the Colt over in his hand and slammed the butt against the first head within his reach. The head happened to belong to Shane. Despite the pain that pulsated through his skull, Shane managed to throw a well-aimed punch, but the second blow from Eli's pistol put Shane out like a doused lantern.

Cursing the air blue, Keery squirmed to free himself from

the two-hundred-some odd pounds of dead weight that pinned him to the floor. "Get this filthy barbarian off me!"

Several men scurried over to roll Shane's limp body away and upright the couch that was missing a hind leg.

"What happened?" Eli demanded to know.

"The half-breed wrecked my place," Keery said out the side of his mouth that wasn't swollen twice its normal size. "I told that bastard to leave and he refused. I want him locked up before he demolishes the rest of The Cottage."

Eli's pale gray eyes darted to Royal Winston, who remained transfixed in the doorway of the office. After an assenting nod from Royal, Eli pivoted toward the male patrons to enlist assistance. "You men haul Shane to jail so he can cool off."

Keery was none too happy that Royal's silent nod carried such weight with Eli Nelson. Keery's drunken gaze bounced back and forth between his seductively lovely business partner and the sheriff. With a slurred curse Keery hauled himself to his feet, dusted off his elegant garments, and massaged his stinging jaw.

"I expect to be reimbursed for the damages. But what I prefer is to extract my payment out of this half-breed's hide."

"Calm down, Keery. You ought to be thankful you're still in one piece," Eli said, watching blood trickle from Keery's swollen lips.

The blow Shane had delivered looked to be painful. Eli was glad he hadn't been on the receiving end of it. Over the years foolish men had picked fights with Shane. None of them had fared well, not well at all. Keery O'Connell was the only man foolish enough, and drunk enough, to attempt the feat more than once.

"Calm down?" Keery howled. "Look at this place. That bastard was only here five minutes. I told him never to come near me or The Cottage, but he defies me every time he has the chance. By damn, he'll pay for it this time!"

"Melody, why don't you help Keery get cleaned up," Royal suggested as she swept forward in a swish of silk and petticoats. To Keery she said, "I'll handle this unfortunate affair."

Once Melody Bright had herded Keery off to tend his wounds, the patrons set about restoring the demolished parlor to reasonable order.

Taking Eli's arm, Royal escorted the sheriff outside. "The man is making a complete nuisance of himself," Royal confided.

"Which one?" Eli grumbled, watching the four men haul Shane's unconscious body down the street to jail.

"Keery," Royal replied.

"I don't know how you tolerate Keery. His drinking sprees cause as much disturbance as vagabonds and rowdy miners who try to blow the lid off this town. Keery's ongoing feud with Shane is getting out of hand. He dreams up excuses to belittle Shane and provokes him into fighting."

"Unfortunately Keery is my partner and I have to endure his drunken rages."

When Royal heaved a long-suffering sigh, causing her ample bosom to strain against the confines of her daring neckline, Eli savored the tantalizing display of creamy flesh. He had the pleasure of spending a great deal of time in private with Royal since her arrival. Despite Keery's possessive nature, Eli and Royal had become intimate, but extremely discreet.

Of course, there would have been little Keery could have done, except pick a fight with the sheriff. If he did, Eli would employ the power of his position and threaten to close down The Cottage. O'Connell's Cottage remained open for business because Eli had developed a fond attachment for Royal. If not for the shapely brunette, Keery would have been out of business.

Royal had formed a liaison with Eli in order to establish good relations in Globe City. She had learned her lesson in years past. The sheriff in Phoenix was an arrogant bully much like Keery. Royal and her girls had been ordered out of town when she refused to cater to the abusive lawman, who demanded to take his pleasures with whomever pleased him, as often as it pleased him—free of charge.

Nowadays, Royal made it a point to promote amicable relations with those in positions of authority. She patronized Keery because he owned the majority of the stock in The Cottage. She had blandished him into allowing her to invest in the brothel he had built with money he had collected from his days as a prospector. Royal had also formed a working alliance with Eli to ensure she was not forced out of Globe City. Luckily, Eli was much easier to manage than the sheriff in Phoenix.

In short, Royal had both Keery and Eli wrapped around her finger and she planned to keep it that way. Most men catered to her because of her stunning beauty and her expertise in her profession. There were a few exceptions however. Shane Stafford was one of them. The first time Royal laid eyes on the sinewy giant she had been intrigued by him.

The idea of taming and bedding Shane appealed to the daring side of Royal's nature. He was like a forbidden fantasy that Keery denied her. Not only did Shane Stafford hold title to the prospering ranch north of Globe City, but he was one hundred percent male. Royal would have taken him as one of her lovers, if not for Keery's unreasonable jealousies. But Royal had to maintain a business as well as intimate relationship with Keery O'Connell. To that end, Royal was forced to hold her fantasies in check where the powerfully built half-breed was concerned. For certain, Royal would not have denied Shane entrance to The Cottage if *she* were the sole proprietor. Unfortunately, Keery's deep-seated prejudices against all Apaches, and his vicious jealousy, made the intriguing possibility too dangerous.

"I wish there was something I could do to remedy the problem with Keery," Eli murmured, jolting Royal from her pensive reverie.

"So do I, Eli," she murmured. "So do I . . ."

Offering Royal a consoling smile, Eli strode off to see that his prisoner was settled comfortably in his cell.

Chapter Two

Before Royal could re-enter The Cottage, Keery stormed outside, looking like black thunder. The cold cloth Melody Bright had applied to Keery's head and jaw had not cooled his legendary Irish temper. He was a mass of boiling fury on a quest for revenge.

"I want that half-breed hanged!" Keery bellowed.

"There will be no hanging. You got exactly what you deserved," Royal said without an ounce of sympathy.

"You're still harboring that ridiculous infatuation for that savage, aren't you?" Keery muttered in question. "What is it with you women anyway?"

"Perhaps a savage like Shane is not such a savage in a woman's bed. I'm curious to know if that might be the case."

Keery grabbed Royal's arm in a vise grip. "If that bastard ever dared to lay a hand on you, I would kill him. And you don't want to know what I would do to you if you let him touch you."

"Let go," Royal hissed. "You are hurting me."

"Not as much as that heathen bastard would hurt you, I expect," he snapped.

"That remains to be seen." Royal's flashing blue eyes drilled into his battered face. "You do not own me, Keery. We are business partners—"

"And lovers," Keery took excessive pleasure in reminding her.

Royal pried Keery's fingers from the sleeve of her gown and stepped back apace. "That can change rather suddenly. Now, if you will excuse me, there is a mess to clean up—"

"Thanks to that wild savage," Keery scowled.

"Thanks to *you,*" Royal corrected. "And if you don't change your annoying ways, and soon, I will tell Eli that you were responsible for the damages The Cottage suffered. Indeed, it was you who started the fisticuffs."

"You would side with that stinking Apache?" Keery stared at her in astonishment.

"In a minute," she said without hesitation. "Shane Stafford might make the most intriguing bedfellow." On the wings of that goading remark, Royal lifted her skirts and returned to The Cottage.

Swearing ruthlessly, Keery glanced toward the jail. He had never been able to tolerate Shane Stafford and he never would. Shane was a constant reminder of the atrocities Keery had witnessed at the Apache's hands. For two years, Keery had served with the Army of the West, assigned to relocating various bands of Apaches on their reservations. During that time, he had come upon several small regiments of dragoons who had been attacked by hostiles. One of the men had been Keery's closest friend. By the time the Apache war party finished with the young soldier, there had barely been enough left of him to fill a pine coffin.

The mere thought of the horrors Keery had observed caused his stomach to twist into a knot. As far as he was concerned, the world would be a better place if every Indian and their half-breed bastards were annihilated.

Keery had no complaints about the massacres the Army inflicted on the Apaches. The fact that Shane Stafford was allowed to flit around, free as a bird, agitated Keery to no end. Knowing Royal Winston harbored a fanatical fascination for the half-breed Apache irritated Keery to the extreme.

So help him, he would rid the world of that son of a bitch.

One day, Shane Stafford would push Keery too far and he would wipe that red-skinned giant off the face of the earth!

On that thought Keery marched off on his crusade of revenge. The crimson rays of sunset had splashed across the surrounding mountains by the time Keery caught up with Sheriff Nelson, who was making his nightly rounds.

"I want every cent of cash Shane Stafford has on him confiscated to pay the damages," Keery demanded.

"Now Keery, you know damned good and well that Shane isn't carrying extra money. He and the Linnox brothers rode into town this morning to gather supplies for the ranch. Their wagon is laden down with goods," Eli informed him.

"Then we'll sell all of his supplies."

Keery wheeled around and then halted abruptly when he spied the two saddle horses tethered beside the heaping wagon. When his gaze landed on the muscular stallion whose sleek coat gleamed blood-red in the twilight, a vindictive smile bordered his swollen mouth.

"Ah yes, the half-breed's pride and joy. Why didn't I think of it earlier?" Keery mused aloud.

Keery snickered as he appraised the devil stallion with its silky coat and contrasting cream-colored mane and tail. It was said that this magnificent stallion could chase the wind and catch it. There were as many tales circulating about this steed's phenomenal abilities as there were about the half-breed's incredible skills of survival in the wilds. And here was Keery's opportunity to seek fiendish satisfaction against Shane Stafford.

"I'll take the stallion in exchange for the damages to my establishment."

"Now hold on, Keery, you can't—" Eli tried to object, but Keery was already lumbering toward the hitching post. Hurriedly, Eli followed after him. "Keery, you know how Shane feels about that horse. He likes that stallion better than any human alive. He trained Sultan from a colt and breeds him to his herd of mustangs."

Keery paid no attention whatsoever. He jerked the saddlebags and rifle scabbard off the steed and carelessly tossed them on

the wagon. Sultan laid back his ears and attempted to kick, causing Keery to fling several curses at him. Snatching the reins,
Keery tugged the rebellious creature forward, only to be yanked
backward a time or three.

"Damned devil stallion," Keery scowled at the spirited animal. "What you need is a good beating."

"If you take a whip to that horse, he'll trample you to death,"
Eli cautioned. "You know that's what happened to the last man
who tried it."

Since Keery could not force Sultan to stir a step, he demanded
the attention of everyone on the street with a bugle-like voice.
Then Keery proceeded to hold an auction, promising to sell
Sultan to the highest bidder.

"Damn it," Eli muttered as Royal edged up beside him to see
what the commotion was all about. "If O'Connell goes through
with this, he is going to have more trouble than he can handle.
When Shane finds out about this, he'll beat Keery to a bloody
pulp. I might just look the other way and let him."

Royal tended to agree. Shane Stafford was the kind of man
who could make him suffer hell, times three.

Despite Eli's objections, Keery boasted the stallion's breeding
lines of Arabian and mustang cross. He informed the gathering
crowd of the steed's impressive speed and stamina, as if the
whole town wasn't already aware of the legendary Sultan, whose
keen senses testified to good breeding and rare intelligence.

Problem was, none of the residents of Globe City dared to
bid on the stallion for fear of repercussions. There were, however, four soldiers from Fort McDowell in town, quenching their
thirst at their favorite watering hole. They were unaware that
Keery was attempting to sell a steed that didn't belong to him.

"The highest bidder gets a free night with any one of my
girls at The Cottage," Keery baited the reluctant crowd. "What's
the bid, friends? Who wants to take two memorable rides in the
same night?"

The ribald remark earned Keery guffaws of laughter and four
bids from the unsuspecting soldiers. In no time at all, Keery
had a fine price for Sultan and compensation in hand for the

damages. Lieutenant Haskell and his companions led Sultan away—or rather they *attempted* to take Sultan where he didn't want to go. The feat was not accomplished without considerable difficulty. The stallion reared up, his shrill whinny piercing the night air. His flailing hooves sent men scattering for their lives.

A half hour later, the soldiers managed to tether Sultan to the hitching post in front of The Cottage. It was another hour before the indignant Sultan ceased his stamping, sidestepping, and snorting.

"Are you sure that stallion is tame?" Lieutenant Haskell questioned, warily scrutinizing the steed.

"Spirited," Keery clarified, tucking the cash in the pocket of his gold brocade vest. "Once Sultan grows accustomed to you, he'll perform superbly. He will more than compensate for the amount you paid for him, believe you me. There isn't a horse in the territory that can outrun Sultan when you give him his head. But don't ever take a whip to him. According to the story, he killed a man when he was a yearling for trying to beat him into submission. Sultan comes unglued at the mere sight of a quirt."

"He just about comes unglued at the sight of a man," Lieutenant Haskell declared. "I'm not sure I struck such a good bargain."

Keery wrapped a thick arm around the officer's shoulder and ushered him into The Cottage. "What you need is a good ride with one of my girls to bolster your confidence before you mount that devil."

Haskell beamed in anticipation. "Maybe I do at that."

Once Keery had put the four soldiers in competent feminine hands, he strutted back to the street to become the recipient of Sheriff Nelson's frown.

"That was one of your more foolish moves, Keery. Shane will chew you up and spit you out."

Keery shrugged carelessly. "I am pressing charges for assault. That half-breed will be spending the night in jail, learning to control his temper."

"And when Shane is released, he will come looking for you,"

Royal predicted. "I think you should buy back the stallion before Shane gets wind of it—"

"I own the majority of shares in The Cottage," Keery reminded her gruffly. "And what I say goes."

"Until you're *gone,*" Royal snapped back. "Which you will be when Shane gets through with you."

The fact that Royal believed the half-breed to be Keery's superior in every arena offended his colossal pride. " We'll just see about that, honey, now won't we?" He turned to Eli. "You keep that bastard locked up overnight. I'll deal with him in the morning when I have a clear head."

"When you have a hellish hangover is more like it," Royal muttered.

It was with cool tolerance that Royal allowed herself to be shepherded back inside The Cottage on Keery's arm. She knew what Keery wanted from her. He intended to remind her of his prowess in bed and prove his dominance over the half-breed he had unfairly sentenced to jail.

With one last glance at Eli, Royal closed The Cottage door behind her.

"Cocky bastard," Eli grumbled, pivoting on his heels to stalk back to his office.

The whole affair left a sour taste in Eli's mouth. He didn't appreciate knowing Royal would be appeasing Keery's lusts, or that Shane would be fit to be tied when he learned his stallion had been sold at auction. It was going to be one helluva long night. It would be a great deal shorter and more pleasant if Eli procrastinated in informing Shane of the events that had occurred that evening.

And that was exactly what Eli decided to do—procrastinate. He could use a few hours of peace and quiet. More than once Eli found himself wishing it had been Keery's head he had cracked rather than Shane's. Perhaps the evening wouldn't have evolved into such a disaster if Keery was the one who had been knocked senseless and tossed in jail.

Chapter Three

Shane groaned. A throbbing headache pulverized his skull. The last thing he remembered was that he had given way to the compulsive urge to hammer Keery O'Connell into putty.

Groggily, Shane pushed himself into an upright position on the cot and stared at the iron bars and glowing rays of dawn that slashed into his cell. Instinctively, Shane was on his feet, pacing the narrow cubicle, despising the feeling of confinement and smoldering with frustration.

There were times—like now, especially now—that Shane wished for the limitless freedom he had enjoyed as a child. He longed for that sense of inner peace, something he hadn't experienced in years. The only way to escape a world that was fraught with turmoil was to disappear into the majestic mountains and pine forests that had once been part of the *Apacheria*. And ah, if wishing could make it so, Shane would be there now.

Shane's life had changed so drastically the last decade that he had forgotten the meaning of happiness and contentment. Now he straddled the borderline between two contrasting civilizations. And thanks to Keery O'Connell, Shane had become a controversial figure in Globe City. He was accepted by very

few men and despised by many. He had become like the lone
wolf, constantly on the prowl, keeping to himself as much as
possible. The limited friendships he enjoyed could not compensate for the long-harbored resentments that ate at his soul. He
felt imprisoned in his own skin, forced to survive in a foreign
world and hating every minute of it . . .

The whining door jolted Shane from his pensive musings. He
wheeled around to see Sheriff Nelson ambling toward him with
a breakfast tray. White man's food—another reminder of a partially civilized renegade who had been forced to accept the ways
of the invading whites.

"I brought you some biscuits." Eli shifted awkwardly beneath
Shane's quelling stare.

"You eat them," Shane bit off, onyx eyes flashing.

"Come on now, Shane, you know I don't like this any better
than you do. Keery pressed charges for assault and battery."

"White men's charges. White men's lies," Shane insisted. "I
didn't start the fight. He did."

Eli shrugged a thick-bladed shoulder and knelt to slide the
tray beneath the bars.

"Cactus and Sticker Linnox are here to see you," Eli informed
him. "Shall I send them around when you're in a better mood?"

"I won't be in a better mood until you free me," Shane
growled.

"And I can't free you until your disposition sweetens considerably."

As if that was going to happen anytime soon, thought Eli. He
had yet to work up the nerve to tell Shane about his missing
steed, one which was already on its way to Fort McDowell with
a new owner.

"Shane?" Cactus Linnox poked his wiry brown head around
the corner to see the formidable giant looming in his cell like
a caged bear. "You okay?"

The slightest inclination of Shane's raven head was his only
response.

Eli shouldered his way between Cactus and Sticker. "You tell
him what happened. After he cools down, I'll let him go. You

boys are the only ones within a hundred miles who have any influence on him."

"Thanks a lot, Sheriff," Sticker grumbled. "I'd rather be the honored guest at my own hangin' than tell Shane about Sultan. He'll go through the roof."

Eli glanced ceilingward. "No, he won't. Those beams are a foot thick."

"So's Shane's head," Cactus insisted.

Shane grabbed the tray of biscuits and milk and forced himself to eat while Cactus and Sticker slinked into the room.

John Linnox—or Cactus, as he was affectionately called—was a lean, trail-hardy cowboy whom Shane had known since the day his father dragged him to the Bar "S" Ranch a decade earlier. Cactus was thirty-five or thereabouts, and his younger brother William—or Sticker as he had been nicknamed—was four years younger. Of all the ranch hands that had come and gone over the years, Cactus and Sticker were the only two men whom Shane regarded as friends. They were not bound by the prejudices that alienated Shane from the white man's world. They judged a man for what he was, not who he was by an accident of birth.

"We're awful damned sorry about this whole mess," Cactus apologized all over himself. "Me an' Sticker are to blame for your bein' here."

"Yeah, Shane, if I hadn't had this fierce cravin' for a poke, none of this would've happened," Sticker said miserably. "And if I hadn't been so involved in what I was doin', I would've come downstairs to help you beat the tar out of Keery, even if he banished me from The Cottage!"

"I needed no help with Keery."

"I wasn't implyin' that you did," Sticker hastily added. "I just would've been on your side, that's all."

Shane bit into the biscuit, wishing it was Keery O'Connell's thick neck. His keen sense of awareness keyed on the nervous mannerisms of the two men who kept shifting from one foot to the other like skittish colts.

Shane had noticed that same uneasiness in Sheriff Nelson's

demeanor a few minutes earlier. Something was wrong. Shane could sense it. "What happened?"

Both men flinched, as if hissing arrows had lodged in their backs.

"Damn it, Shane, sometimes that sixth sense of yours unnerves me," Cactus mumbled. "An' sometimes I swear you know what I'm thinkin' while I'm thinkin' it—"

"Get to the point," Shane demanded irritably.

Cactus nudged his brother with an elbow. "You tell him, Stick."

"No, you tell him, Cactus. You're the oldest."

"What the hell does that have to do with anything?" Cactus wanted to know.

"Tell me what!" Shane could not recall seeing the Linnox brothers quite so fidgety, not even in the middle of a stampede.

"Well—" Cactus gulped, causing his Adam's apple to bob up and down in his throat. "Keery demanded payment for the damages to his parlor."

"Damages *he* caused," Shane bitterly corrected.

"Keery says nothin' would've happened if you would've left when he told you to," Sticker finished glumly.

Cactus inhaled a fortifying breath, causing his chest to swell like a balloon and reluctantly blurted out, "Keery sold Sultan to pay the damages to The Cottage."

There. He had said it. With bated breath he awaited Shane's reaction. It was everything he expected and more. Shane vaulted off the cot like a human spring. He hurled the tin tray at the wall and kicked it when it crashed to the floor. His deep baritone voice boomed in a string of Apache phrases that invited no translation, followed by a barrage of white man's curses.

"That bastard!" Shane's huge body trembled with barely restrained fury.

That blood-red stallion was precious to Shane in ways no one could begin to understand, and he would prefer never to explain his feelings to another living soul, either. They were too private, too deeply imbedded.

Shane and Sultan had grown up together in a foreign world.

They were very much alike—both half-breeds who had been civilized by necessity but still free at heart. Sultan had become Shane's mode of escape so many times over the years that losing the steed was like losing his very best friend—his only true and loyal friend.

Before Shane realized it, he was pacing the cell like a brooding tiger. And suddenly it dawned on him why Eli, Cactus, and Sticker had been so apprehensive. They had anticipated his violent reaction to Keery's vindictive retaliation. It was the expectation of explosive rage that had prevented Eli from releasing Shane from jail. It was also that same wary trepidation that made Cactus and Sticker reluctant to impart the information to Shane. Although these men considered Shane their friend, they still viewed him as a dangerous threat, even when he customarily controlled his temper. They believed the savage side of his nature was lurking beneath the surface like a dormant volcano that could erupt at any given moment. He was an Apache, and none of these three men had ever allowed themselves to forget that.

During Shane's training as a warrior, he had been taught to outwit his enemies, to rely on stealth, cunning, and unpredictability. Cleverness and forethought were to be admired. Shane had obviously lived in civilization too long. He had forgotten the first rule of The People. If he no longer thought like an Apache then he was no longer an Apache. And if he was no longer an Apache, then he was not attuned to nature and its omnipotent powers. He became nothing. He had to get himself in hand—and quickly!

In baffled amazement, Cactus and Sticker watched the brooding giant rein in his temper. Shane's puckered brows returned to their normal arch. The malicious sneer that bracketed his mouth disappeared. The clench of bunched muscles beneath his buckskin clothes relaxed, projecting an air of indifference. Shane's expression could have disguised killing fury or boredom, and not another living soul could tell which. Even Eli Nelson, who had been eavesdropping on the other side of the partially opened door, was thunderstruck by the transformation from vicious savagery to well-disciplined control.

"Where is Sultan?" Shane asked in a deceptively bland voice.

"Keery sold the stallion to one of the four soldiers who was passing through town on his way back to Fort McDowell," Eli responded as he ambled into the room.

"Then I will have to buy Sultan back," Shane said in a pleasant tone.

Cactus glanced at Sticker who peered at Eli. Then all three men stared at Shane in stupefied amazement.

"And what about Keery O'Connell?" Eli queried. His gimlet-eyed gaze fastened on Shane, searching for a crack in his seemingly tranquil veneer.

With absolute control, Shane raised his dark head. His obsidian eyes revealed none of his churning emotions. "Keery O'Connell is still a bastard," he contended.

"And—?" Cactus prodded.

"And he will always be a bastard." No inflection of voice, only a flat statement of what Shane believed to be fact.

After scooping up the fallen tray, Shane unfolded himself like a graceful panther. "Let me go, Eli. I want to retrieve my horse."

"You can trade my piebald pony for Sultan," Sticker charitably offered. "The gelding can't hold a candle to your stallion, but he can hold his own on a race track."

Shane nodded silent acceptance.

"I don't want any more trouble," Eli declared, fishing into his pocket for the keys. "Your daddy was a good friend of mine, and I have no quarrel with you as long as you behave yourself. But if you cause problems, you'll be back in jail and that's a fact, even if I have to round up a posse to help me haul you in."

Shane didn't smile. He hadn't smiled in years. He stared at Eli with a look that was neither amicable nor hostile. "You will never see me behind bars again."

Eli unlocked the cell, hoping the time would never come when he had to drag Shane back to jail. The complete absence of emotion in Shane's voice was more unnerving than his previous display of temper. When a man's disposition turned sour, it made him vulnerable and pinpointed his weaknesses. When a man, who could be as cold and deadly as Shane, spoke without one smidgen of emotion, it was downright scary. This bronzed giant could project such a phenomenal air of invincibility that a man either had to be drunk or stupid to pit himself against Shane. In Eli's estimation, Keery O'Connell had been a lot of both!

"You just fetch your wagon of supplies and skedaddle out of town, Shane. And don't come back for another month," Eli ordered. "By then Keery will have calmed down."

Shane didn't give a damn if Keery ever calmed down. He had absolutely no use for that besotted bully. Keery deserved none of Shane's consideration.

Shane ambled toward the main office to collect the wicked-looking knife that he kept in his knee-high moccasins. Although his father, Robert Stafford, had insisted and ensured that his half-breed son learned to handle a pistol with deadly proficiency, Shane preferred the silence of the dagger, just as he preferred bows and arrows to noisy rifles. Shane had agreed to tote a rifle on his saddle because Robert had adamantly insisted. But when Shane fought, he chose the tactics of an Apache warrior, employing his skills in hand-to-hand combat. Furthermore, Shane would have preferred to live out his life as an Apache. But that choice had been stripped from him when his mother and the tribal council commanded him to accompany his father to the Bar "S" Ranch. Thus had begun Shane's rigorous indoctrination into the white man's civilization. And that, Shane remembered, was the day he had died inside. He was obliged to honor the vow he had given to the tribe, but he would always be an Apache at heart.

"I'll get the wagon hitched up," Cactus volunteered.

"I'll fetch my piebald gelding," Sticker offered.

Eli shot Shane a warning glance. "No more trouble."

There was no trace of a smile in those coal-black eyes or on those chiseled features that concealed years of untold torment. With nothing more than the slight inclination of his head, Shane walked away. Even the echo of footfalls did not betray his departure. He was gone like a breath of wind.

Eli Nelson sighed in relief. He held grudging admiration and respect for the brawny half-breed. Shane Stafford was a man to be reckoned with, and it was wise not to cross him. Spiteful provocation—the kind that Keery O'Connell delighted in manufacturing—was as dangerous as prodding a rattlesnake with a blade of straw. Eli had more sense. He wished he could say the same for Keery O'Connell.

Sticker Linnox graciously presented Shane with the reins to the pony that was marked with black and white patches on his shiny coat and a long, flowing black mane and tail. The piebald was stockily built, trained to run long distances, though not at the fantastic speeds Sultan could attain when given his head. Still, he was a sturdy, well-dispositioned mount, known for his gliding gait and endurance.

"When I get back to the ranch, I'll break another colt to replace my gelding, if that's okay with you," Sticker said. "If you can trade the piebald for Sultan, I'll consider my debt partially paid for the trouble we caused you."

Shane unfastened the saddle and dropped it on the back of the wagon. "Take any horse you want from the herd, Sticker."

After Shane swung onto the barebacked steed, he leaned out to scoop up his saddlebags. When he had situated the leather bags in front of him like a harness for the piebald, he reined away. And then, without warning, Shane gouged the steed in the flanks. The gelding plunged forward in a gallop.

When Shane made a beeline toward The Cottage, Cactus's and Sticker's unshaven jaws fell off their hinges. Hooves clattered across the boardwalk and thudded onto Keery's imported Belgian carpet.

"Holy hell!" Cactus croaked after he regained control of his vocal apparatus.

Holy hell was right! thought Sticker.

Keery O'Connell had awakened with his customary hangover, nursing a queasy stomach and staring at the world through eyes

that burned as if they had been soaked in kerosene. Two cups
of coffee and a hot bath later, he was still miserable and grouchy.

Lounging at his office desk, Keery drummed his square-
tipped fingers in rhythm with the tom-toms that pounded in
his head. He very nearly came out of his skin when there arose
such a clatter in the parlor that it sounded as if a herd of wild
mustangs had stampeded into The Cottage.

Before Keery could grab his pistol and bolt out of his chair,
Shane and the wild-eyed paint gelding barged through the door,
splintering woodwork and stirring dust. Keery fumbled with
his revolver, only to have it kicked from his hand by a moccasined foot. The pistol discharged, causing the panicky steed to
bolt sideways. The horse slammed into the side of the desk,
wedging Keery against the wall.

Shane dismounted onto the desk and jerked Keery up by the
lapels of his coat. In the batting of an eyelash, Shane snatched the
bulging pouch of coins from Keery's pocket—vest and all. The
garment dangled on Keery's heaving chest, parted at the seams.

Shane thrust his face into Keery's and snarled, "Be warned,
O'Connell. If you ever touch me or what is mine again, you are
a dead man."

"And if you come near me ever again, I'll fill your stinking
hide full of buckshot," Keery snarled back.

Shane wasn't certain what caused what happened next, but
the desk shot sideways. Shane and Keery tumbled from the desk
in a whirlwind of flying fists and clenched bodies. Shane suspected the piebald gelding had slammed around the narrow
quarters, knocking furniture out of the way, growing more skittish with each passing second. That was undoubtedly what had
sent Shane and Keery somersaulting to the floor. But no matter
how it happened, both men were instantly at each other's
throats—throwing and receiving teeth-rattling punches. The
taste of blood was on Shane's lips, intensifying his desire to
leave a lasting impression on this cocky bully who was rife with
so many prejudices he didn't know what to do with himself.

Years of suppressed fury energized Shane's taut body. He was
fighting for all those times when he had forcefully restrained

himself, fighting for all the times he wanted to bellow in rage at the tormented hell his life had become.

Furious hisses and curses spewed from Keery's curled lips as he jabbed Shane in the belly. "Damn your sorry soul, you son of a bitch!"

Shane struck out again, provoked by the insults Keery had heaped on him for two years. Because of this bastard, Shane's life had become an open book to the citizens of Globe City. Keery O'Connell had seen to it that public opinion turned against Shane. Shane blamed half his torment on his embittered stepmother, who loathed the sight of him, and credited the other half of his hell on earth to this drunken whoremonger.

The previous day, Eli Nelson had intervened before Shane could deliver several brain-scrambling blows. Today Shane had Keery exactly where he wanted him. Shane aimed his blow at Keery's tender jaw and derived excessive pleasure in watching Keery's head slam against the wall.

With a roar of rage, Keery heaved himself up. His wrath provided additional strength, and his fingers clamped around Shane's throat in a death grip. But Keery, even in his fit of blind fury, was no match for the cunning Apache in battle. Shane countered by uplifting his knee and planting it in Keery's soft underbelly. Keery reflexively doubled over to protect himself from another devastating blow. Venomous curses flooded from his lips in a pained whoosh.

The sound of splintering wood suggested that the piebald gelding had become even more frantic in its attempt to find a way out of a room that was overcrowded with furniture. Objects crashed against the walls and floor. Glass shattered everywhere.

Hell-bent on vengeance, Keery scrabbled across the floor to retrieve his pistol. When the weapon swung toward him, Shane delivered a hatchet blow to the arm. The stray shot plugged in the doorjamb, causing the flighty steed to buck and kick out with his hind legs. Shane caught sight of an oncoming hoof and instinctively ducked away. The flailing hoof caught Keery upside the head, flinging him backward into a limp heap.

When Shane heard the shouts from the parlor, he bolted up

to grasp the reins and leaped onto the steed in a single bound. The crowd that had congregated in the parlor parted like the Red Sea when Shane burst through the doorway and headed for the street, exiting in the same wild flurry in which he had entered.

"Damn it to hell!" Sheriff Nelson muttered as he watched Shane thunder down the street and disappear into the purple-hued mountains that surrounded the mining community.

"I knew O'Connell was askin' for trouble when he sold Sultan," Sticker declared to the sheriff and anyone else who cared to listen. "Nobody messes with that stallion without Shane's permission an' I mean *nobody*. To sell off that spirited steed is like invitin' a death wish."

It was at that moment that Royal emerged from The Cottage, her expression grim. "Keery O'Connell is dead!"

"Good gawd!" Sticker howled. He stared bleakly into the distance, seeing nothing but a fading cloud of dust.

Eli grumbled under his breath as he elbowed his way through the crowd to reach The Cottage. With Sticker and Cactus following in his wake, Eli scanned the office. Shane had reduced the bordello to ruin worthy of a cyclone's destruction. Sticks of furniture were strewn about like casualties. Canvas and splintered picture frames lay helter-skelter on the carpet. Keery's body was sprawled facedown, showing no sign of life. A huge purple knot swelled on his temple and blood seeped down the back of his carrot-red head.

Stepping over the dismantled chair in his path, Eli brushed his fingertips over Keery's neck. Pivoting on his haunches, Eli stared gloomily at Royal.

"I was hoping your diagnosis was inaccurate, Royal. Too bad it wasn't. But sure enough, Keery is as dead as a man can get."

Before Royal could reply, Cactus and Sticker wedged past her to stare down at Keery's prostrate form.

"Hell and damnation," Sticker grumbled, glancing helplessly at his brother.

Cactus heaved a miserable sigh. "If this don't drive Shane back to the mountains forever, I don't know what will."

"I wonder if Shane even knows how complete his revenge is" Eli mused aloud.

"What are you gonna do, Sheriff?" Sticker quizzed him.

Eli shrugged evasively. "I don't rightly know what to do. If I follow Shane into the mountains, my chances of finding him wouldn't be worth my time and trouble."

"Amen to that," Cactus added his two cents' worth. "You'd have as much luck tryin' to pluck a needle out of a haystack. Shane can lose himself in them mountains in the blinkin' of an eye, just like his Apache cousins. You'd never find him unless he *let* you."

"But one thing I know for certain," Eli said pensively, "Shane will go after that stallion." He rose to his feet and navigated around the demolished furniture that formed a maze in his path. "If I can catch up with Lieutenant Haskell, maybe I can find Shane."

"You aren't gonna charge Shane for murder, are you?" Cactus looked incredulous. "Hell, Sheriff, you know Keery hounded Shane without reason. He purposely made Shane's life hell when he came to town. Keery hated Shane for the accident of his birth."

"If you ask me, Keery got what he deserved," Sticker said with great certainty. "Stealin' a man's horse is a crime, too, you know. Keery stole Sultan an' sold him. He should've hanged. The way I see it, Shane simply saved you the trouble, Sheriff."

Eli didn't argue that point. He had buckled the previous night when Keery was in another of his drunken frenzies. Eli should have stood up to the man. Now he felt as responsible for what had happened as Cactus and Sticker did.

Royal laid her hand on Eli's arm, requesting his attention. "They're both right. Keery brought this wrath down on himself. Truth is, Keery was the one who started the fracas last night. Shane was only defending himself."

"Damned straight," Cactus insisted. "You can't charge Shane with murder because you should've already hanged Keery for assault an' horse thievin'."

"There are folks hereabout who wouldn't see it that way," Eli said. "Most people in these parts have no love for Apaches, even half-breeds. They think Shane should have been confined to the reservation with the tribes back in '76."

"An' whose fault is it that some folks think like that, I ask you?" Sticker demanded. "I'll tell you who—Keery O'Connell. Like I said before, Keery had been goadin' Shane for years. He finally got what he had comin'—accident or on purpose."

Again, Eli glanced at Royal, awaiting her assessment of the situation.

"Like the man said. Keery has been baiting Shane since I've known him," Royal testified. "If you are looking to me to press charges, I won't do it. I warned Keery not to sell that stallion. He wouldn't listen to me anymore than he listened to you, Eli."

"Then it's settled." Eli stepped out of the office to face the crowd of curious bystanders. "Accidental death," he proclaimed.

Eli turned back to the Linnox brothers, who breathed a sigh of relief. "You boys are going to stick around the rest of the day to back me up, just in case some of the townsfolk have different ideas about my decision. And if Shane goes on the warpath, doing something rash in order to retrieve that precious stallion of his, I won't be able to justify my lack of actions. If the commander of the fort comes to investigate, he'll sure as hell hear about this incident."

"Maybe Shane won't do anything rash," Sticker said.

Eli's brows flattened over his gray eyes.

Cactus grumbled half aloud. The chance of Shane simply confronting the lieutenant and explaining the situation was as great as Eli's success in taking a search party to track Shane down in the wild tumble of mountains and thick pines that separated Globe City from the communities to the north.

Damn that Keery O'Connell, Eli muttered to himself. His spiteful retaliation had roused a sleeping tiger. Where Shane Stafford would stop nobody knew. Nobody even wanted to hazard a guess. Eli could only hope Shane would behave in a civilized manner when he retrieved his stallion. Otherwise . . .

Eli didn't even want to think about *otherwise*. It could depress a man in one helluva hurry!

Chapter Four

Calera O'Connell stared out the stage window, marveling at the jagged precipices of granite that reached toward the sky like gnarled fists. A forest of Ponderosa pines skirted the towering peaks that plunged into spectacular V-shaped valleys and meadows that gleamed like a rainbow with wildflowers. Since leaving Philadelphia three weeks earlier, Calera had crossed through treacherous passes to rolling hills, through barren deserts and onto this panoramic wilderness that seemed to defy the effects of civilization.

With diploma in hand, and no one there to help her celebrate her graduation, magna cum laude, Calera had packed her bags and headed west. She hoped her brother would be surprised and as eager to see her as she was to see him. It had been six long years since Calera had tearfully waved farewell to Keery. She had been only fourteen when he struck off to seek his fortune, promising to send his young sister the money he could spare. Keery had been twenty-two—a confident, enthusiastic young man out to conquer the world and to provide for the sister he left behind.

Calera sighed, remembering those chaotic years, the emotional turmoil she had undergone during her childhood. It seemed as if her life was a kaleidoscope—ever-changing tests of her spirit and endurance. Her mother had died in childbirth when Calera was two. Her infant brother had survived barely a week. When Calera was five, her father had perished in a coal mining accident, leaving two young children in dire straits.

Aunt Myrna and Uncle Blayne had opened their home and their hearts to the grieving orphans and provided as best they could for them. Aunt Myrna was the only mother Calera had known and she had cherished the years she had spent with Myrna and Blayne.

But alas, history repeated itself, proving to Calera and Keery that they had not been blessed with that legendary Irish luck. Uncle Blayne had passed on when Calera was ten years old. The loss had devastated Myrna O'Connell. She had been a frail woman, prone to illnesses which prevented her from bearing children of her own. Losing Blayne had been the final blow. Aunt Myrna had not lived to see Calera complete her studies at the ladies' seminary.

Calera had shouldered the responsibility of laying all her family to rest—all but Keery. She and Keery were the last survivors of the Irish immigrants who had fled their homeland with dreams of hope and prosperity in America.

Well, at least there was Keery, Calera consoled herself. She would be reunited with her older brother after a long, painful separation. They would make up for lost time, and Calera would compensate for the cash Keery had sent to provide for her living expenses and education over the last six years.

According to Keery's letters—which did not come often enough to suit Calera—he had finally established himself as a successful businessman in Globe City, Arizona after the hard, laborious years of building steel rails westward, serving in the Army, and trying his hand at prospecting.

Now Keery claimed to own an elegant hotel and was enjoying impressive profits. Calera had come West with the savings she had collected from selling her aunt's home and the money she had made from her part-time job at a fashionable boutique. She planned to present her brother with her savings and become Keery's accountant at O'Connell's Cottage.

The time had come for her to sacrifice for her brother, to repay him for the generous concessions he had made in her behalf. Keery would be proud of her educational accomplishments and she would become his devoted employee. The family would be reunited at long last and her presence in Globe City would grant Keery more free time to find himself a wife and begin his family.

The thought of seeing Keery put a smile on Calera's lips. She had lived for the day of their reunion, dreamed of it, planned for it. When depression and loneliness engulfed her, she would remind herself of Keery's sacrifices and she would force herself to study and excel for the both of them.

Now Calera could return to her brother that which he had nobly forfeited for her sake. One of them had been allowed to become educated and refined. Very soon, Calera would employ the knowledge she had gained to better her brother's life . . .

Her thoughts trailed off when one of her companions snored so loudly that he woke himself up. Horace Baxter stirred like a plump June bug uprighting itself on the seat beside Calera.

Calera had noticed at the onset of the journey that Horace had been imbibing from the bottle he carried in his jacket. At each stage depot and swing station along the route, Horace would wander off by himself to guzzle as many drinks as time allowed. Although his breath was a mite offensive at times—and Calera wouldn't dare strike a match within ten feet of him for fear of blowing him and herself up—she liked the jovial Horace Baxter. He was a brilliant conversationalist who helped while away the long hours of traveling.

Horace was fiftyish—or somewhere thereabout. He was a rotund but amusing character with full jowls, pale brown eyes, and a bald spot on the crown of his head. He had come West to write a series of informative articles on gold and silver mining for the *Boston Herald*.

Horace yawned and stretched his stubby arms before peering out the window. "Mountains. Good. I was ready for a change of scenery. I had enjoyed the arid desert as long as I could stand."

Calera was ever so thankful for Horace's presence. However, she did not have the slightest use for the two foul-smelling ruffians who had boarded the stage in Denver to accompany them to Arizona Territory. The noxious fumes emanating from these two scalawags suggested they hadn't bothered bathing in at least three months. If it was true that cleanliness was next to Godliness, these two galoots had definitely been rubbing shoulders with the devil in his smelly pit. The closest either man had come to bathing had been the cloudburst that had descended on them when they made a mad dash toward the home station the previous night.

Ike Fuller was as skinny as a scarecrow and his tattered garments hung on his thin frame. A tuft of greasy brown hair dangled over his broad forehead, and his laugh reminded Calera of a whinny. His large front teeth were also reminiscent of an ill-bred, underfed horse.

Grady Flax was as stocky as Ike was thin. He was plagued with an enormous nose that overshadowed his other plain features. His snout turned up at the end, leaving the impression that he was constantly looking down at the world and everyone in it. His deep-set eyes reminded Calera of dark caverns set beneath the pronounced bone-ridge of his square forehead. His brows reminded Calera of wooly caterpillars. He had no neck to speak of and a missing tooth at the corner of his mouth. Handsome, Grady Flax was not! Pleasant? He wasn't that, either. Barely tolerable was nearer the mark.

When the straggly-haired hooligans were not peering at Calera as if she were a meal they longed to devour, they were conversing between themselves, employing ungentlemanly curses and slaughtering the English language with deplorable errors in grammar.

Calera had one very unnerving encounter with Ike and Grady the day after they boarded the stage. If not for Horace, Calera shuddered to think what might have happened to her. The two lusty rascals had cornered her outside the stage station, tossing crude and offensive propositions. Calera's temper had burst loose at first touch and she had whacked Grady across the cheek, flattening his oversized nose. When both men pounced on her, Horace Baxter rounded the corner and barked a loud protest. His booming voice caught the attention of the stage driver and guard, who chewed both men up one side and down the other for pestering one of the passengers.

Needless to say, the confrontation had earned Calera several rude remarks, and she found herself the recipient of a good many probing stares. Calera preferred not to dwell on what she thought they were thinking and *imagining* themselves doing to her. The possibilities were repulsive.

When the driver tooted his bugle, signalling the stage agent at the upcoming station of their arrival, Calera fluffed her wrinkled skirt and exercised her cramped legs. She was anxious to escape the confines of the coach. Her limbs were numb and her back was stiff. She was eager to enjoy the panoramic view of pine-covered mountains and broad, sweeping valleys, to survey the intriguing rock formations that loomed in the distance. She could not fully appreciate the scenery while she bumped along the washboard road that cut a primitive path through this rugged wilderness.

Calera poked her head out the window to see the adobe buildings setting on a flat plateau. The barn and corrals were situated against the perpendicular stone wall beneath a towering mountain peak that protected the station from fierce north winds. To the east, huge, craggy summits loomed against the sky. Parading clouds flirted with the sun like shifting spotlights, casting and engulfing shadows.

Just ahead, Calera could see five horses tethered in front of the station. One of them in particular caught her eye and held her attention. It was a sleek, muscular blood-red stallion with a cream-colored mane and tail. Even at a glance it wasn't difficult to tell that the animal was proud and spirited and that it objected to being restrained and wedged beside the other horses that obediently awaited the return of their riders.

The steed radiated energy as it tossed its head and stared at some distant point, as if there was something there that it could detect that Calera could not. The fidgeting movements of the steed caused satiny flesh to ripple over the well-tuned muscles of its body.

Calera was sorry that she had never learned to ride. But if she had, this blood-red stallion would have been her choice of mounts. Of course, there had been no one around to teach her equestrian skills, and she had been too occupied with her schooling and part-time job to enjoy the leisures of life. Perhaps now that she would be joining Keery at his fine hotel in Globe City, she could spare the time to broaden her limited horizons.

For sure and certain, Calera would have to adjust to life in the West. This world of Indian reservations and outposts on the edge of civilization would be an education in itself. But Calera would learn to adapt, just as she had adjusted to all the other drastic changes in her life. This time Keery would be at her side, instructing her while she instructed him in the knowledge she had acquired in her studies. She would embrace her new life with open arms, continuing to learn and to become a credit to the immigrant family who sought to make a name and a place for itself in this promising new land.

My, aren't we getting philosophical all of a sudden, Calera mocked herself. Despite her lack of experience in the wilderness, she was as eager and enthusiastic as Keery had been when he set out to find his niche in life. Well, she *was* enthusiastic and determined by nature. It was an inborn O'Connell trait. Calera had been forced to brace up to many of life's disappointments and had vowed never to let depression get the best of her. She was a survivor and she had endured more than her fair share of heartache over the years.

Calera had scoffed at some of the silly females she had met at the seminary who had no concern for anything in life but proper protocol and the elegant etiquette required to project just the right impression at grand balls. Some of those foolish females had only attended the seminary at their families' insistence. They had not taken their studies seriously, but rather utilized the situation to impress and attract their beaux. For some, the acquisition of suitors had become a profession in itself. Calera, however, had not had the time nor inclination to flirt and flaunt and waste valuable hours discussing the redeeming graces and inconsistencies of the male gender. She had stuck her nose in her books and kept it there.

Of course, in her younger years, she had not been tempted by male distractions because men rarely noticed her, except to subject her to their cruel teasing. Calera had been as plump as Horace in adolescence and plagued with scads of freckles. She had also been cursed with a mop of red-gold hair that was so curly and kinky that it defied a brush. The term "ugly duckling" had been a favorite taunt of her male acquaintances. Their remarks had cut to the quick and Calera had responded by burying herself deeper in her books and avoiding those of male persuasion as much as possible.

And then the transformation began three years past—from frizzy caterpillar to graceful butterfly. Her long hair had relaxed into wispy curls, no longer kinky corkscrew ringlets, unless her hair was damp or humidity got the better of it. The freckles had faded and the baby fat had melted away. Suddenly, those same young men who had teased her unmercifully were bowing and scraping over her, vying for the attention they hadn't wanted a few years earlier.

Calera had never forgiven those young men for their complete about-face after the metamorphosis of her body. She was the same person she had always been, but that was of no consequence to those of the male gender. They desired only the pleasure an attractive female body could provide. They cared not one whit about a woman's intelligence, her personality, or her opinions on various topics. Calera had scorned the male half of the population for their shallow interests. Switching from cruel insults to effusive flattery only affirmed her belief that men sought only selfish pleasures of the flesh so they could boast of their feminine conquests.

Consequently, Calera had become a woman unimpressed by her own good looks and suspicious of those who dwelt on her outward appearance. She considered romance to be a waste of time, remaining polite but distant and never forgetting the painful lessons she had learned about the desires of men and their true opinions of women. Furthermore, she intended to put her acquired knowledge to good use in Keery's hotel, for she had not come West to find a husband. She had come to indenture herself to Keery until she had repaid him for the opportunities he had granted her.

When Horace leaned over to unlatch the door, Calera jerked herself to attention, anticipating the chance to exercise her legs instead of her mind. This exhausting overland journey was taking its toll. She was weary and yet so anxious to reach her destination. In another two days she would surprise her brother by arriving at his grand hotel. It would be worth the exhaustion, the unappealing meals that churned in her stomach, the cramped quarters, and unpleasant company she had been forced to keep.

"Lord-a-mercy, my legs feel like noodles." Horace levered himself off the seat and stepped outside to shake his legs and work the kinks from his back.

Before Calera could slide off the seat and balance on the step, Ike and Grady rudely barged in front of her.

The faintest hint of a smile bracketed Horace's mouth as he raised a proffered hand to assist Calera to the ground. "What considerate gentleman we have as traveling companions, don't you agree, my dear? And such stimulating conversationalists as well."

"They are indeed charming company," Calera muttered, casting Ike and Grady condescending glances. "I am beginning to wonder if I have already met Arizona's crop of rattlesnakes. Goodness me, I was under the naive impression that reptiles native to this territory were legless."

Horace chuckled at Calera's dry wit. But the smile evaporated from his pudgy features when a most extraordinary sound reverberated around the chasm.

Calera glanced over her shoulder to see a nightmare unfolding behind her. Three bare-chested savages, mounted on horseback, appeared from out of nowhere. Streaks of paint slashed across their dark cheeks and rows of bones and beads dangled from their necks. They clutched fierce-looking knives and thundered directly toward the coach, their intentions horrifyingly clear.

"Dear God!" Calera croaked.

Before Calera and Horace could seek refuge in the stage station, the savages descended. Calera was certain all that saved her and Horace from instant death was the volley of gunfire that spat from the door and window of the adobe station. Men scattered, groping for pistols to provide cover for the hapless victims who had been caught outside when catastrophe struck.

One of the whooping warriors reached out a muscled arm and slashed the leather straps that held the luggage atop the coach. Trunks and carpetbags tumbled to the ground, splattering their contents like broken eggshells. The lead rider swooped down to clutch the scattered garments that belonged to Horace. Horace, however, voiced not one objection to the looting of his luggage. At the moment, his scalp and his life were his greatest concerns. He headed for the station, his stubby legs churning like a locomotive, dragging Calera behind him like a caboose.

In her haste to escape disaster, Calera tromped on the hem of her skirt and skidded on her knees. She wormed her hand from Horace's grasp to brace herself before she skinned her chin on loose pebbles. Before Horace could pivot around and hoist her to her feet, one of the copper-skinned warriors charged his steed between them, snatching Calera up by the nape of her gown.

Damnation! Calera had taken great care in purchasing this particular travelling ensemble. Now the brown velvet riding habit was torn at the seams and ripped at the elbows and knees. Her dainty hat, with its peacock plumes, set askew on her head and red-gold curls tumbled from the neat coiffure to dangle around her face in disarray. And worse, she was being whisked off by the first Indian she had ever laid eyes on in her life! *Dear, dear God!*

"Miss O'Connell!" Horace took one bold step forward before his self-preservation instincts prompted him to take two steps in retreat. A second warrior, with his face skewed up in a threatening growl and his dagger poised to hurl, was heading straight toward Horace. The sound of the warrior's menacing howl and the murderous expression in those black eyes sent Horace scrambling for the safety of the station as fast as his legs could carry him.

The fusillade of gunfire ceased the instant Calera was hauled up in front of the gloating brave. The Indians were using Calera as their shield while they raided the fallen luggage. The braves seemed only interested in men's garments, for they selected shirts, breeches, and jackets rather than pilfering Calera's unmentionables and gowns.

Calera was so terrified that she thrashed like a wild bird in captivity, desperate for escape. Her flailing arm slammed against her captor's jaw, drawing his vicious sneer. He retaliated by backhanding Calera across the cheek. Whimpering in pain, she squirmed to free herself from the steely arms that clamped around her like a beaver trap. Despite her valiant efforts, all she succeeded in doing was flinging herself off balance and startling the wild-eyed steed.

This was another first for Calera. She had never met an Indian, though she had heard stories of captives whisked off to endure horrible tortures. She had never been on the back of a horse until this moment, either. Neither experience was proving to be pleasant!

The warrior put a stranglehold on Calera when she flopped forward and rammed her head against the steed's neck. The horse reared, spun around, and darted off in the opposite direction.

Out of the corner of her eye Calera spied the magnificent blood-red stallion, dancing tight circles around its tether, its eyes wide and its nostrils flared. It dawned on Calera just then why the stallion had been so apprehensive. The steed must have caught the scent of the bronze-skinned raiders. Its nervous action had been a forewarning, but Calera had not been experienced enough to decipher impending doom.

Now it was too late and her hindsight was all for naught. She was being carted off by three whooping, hollering braves, never to reach her destination. Keery would never know she was even in the same territory until she was long past dead. Her luggage might arrive safely, but she wouldn't. Dear God, after all the years of preparation and anticipation she would never see her beloved brother again.

Oh, yes you will! came that determined voice inside her. *Somehow, you will survive this calamity as you have survived all else.*

The thought provided inspiration, but stark reality questioned her ability to endure. The jarring motion of the galloping steed was pounding every ounce of breath out of her. The muscled arm that held her formed a vise grip on her hip, cutting off the circulation in her legs. And worse, the treacherous path the warriors had chosen to make their escape nearly frightened Calera out of her pantaloons!

From her jackknifed position on the steed, the steep incline and jagged boulders that tumbled down to the swift-moving stream below gave Calera a nerve-shattering view of the world. There were places along the perilous path where one miscalculated placement of a hoof could have meant instant and fatal disaster. In less than a heartbeat, Calera could have plummeted over the boulders to wind up dead by the edge of the stream . . .

The thought ignited a spark of ingenuity. Calera gave herself a mental slap to cease her futile whimpering. Instead of lying there screaming her head off she should have been paying close attention to her surroundings. If she was going to survive this disaster which could prevent her from being reunited with her beloved brother, she was going to have to rely upon her ingenuity and intellect. She was also going to have to disguise her intentions in order to throw her captors off guard. Thus far, she had been floundering and yelping like any self-respecting captive might have done. If she did *not* continue to do so, her captors might second-guess the reason for her sudden silence.

Bearing that in mind, Calera resumed yowling and floundering like a fish out of water. But all the while, she was assessing the path and the towering ledge above the river. The moment Calera spied the spot where the trail was least dangerous, because of the perpendicular rock wall that dropped to the stream, she abruptly arched backward. Her swinging arm caught her captor across the face, momentarily obstructing his vision. Simultaneously, she jabbed her knees into the steed. The horse responded as it had earlier, just as Calera prayed it would. Sure enough, the steed reared up, forcing its rider to cling to the reins for support. Calera pushed away, hoping the stream below was as deep as its dark-blue color suggested it might be. If it wasn't . . .

Well, time would certainly determine whether the plunge would kill her. For certain, these three raiding savages would eventually get around to it. In Calera's estimation, she had no choice but to take this risk.

An instinctive scream tore loose from her throat when she plunged through the vast expanse of nothingness. In vain she tried to twist her body so she could see where she was about to land, but because of her billowing skirts, Calera didn't see the water coming until she landed with a *kersplat* on her back. The forceful impact knocked the breath clean out of her. Her backside stung as if she had been whipped. Huge black dots blurred her vision and sent her head spinning. She floundered in panic as the fast-moving current dragged her over the boulders that were imbedded in the stream.

A sense of horror overcame Calera before she managed to snatch a breath to prepare for tumbling through a chute of frothy rapids. She lost all sense of direction when the force of the water sent her rolling over like a log. As brilliant and successful as her escape had been, there was still one small hitch Calera had overlooked. It was a little late to recall that she didn't know how to swim!

"Dear God!" she gurgled before the swirling current sucked her beneath the surface . . .

Chapter Five

From his lookout point on the pine-clad ridge above the stage station, Shane Stafford had watched the untimely events of the afternoon unfold. He had finally caught up with the soldiers who had purchased Sultan. They had waylaid at the stage station to take their meal, leaving the stallion unattended. Shane knew Sultan had caught his scent and also detected trouble by the way he was straining against the restraining rope.

Shane had been hiding in a clump of trees, awaiting the opportune moment to retrieve his steed when he heard the bugle announcing the arrival of the stagecoach. He had resorted to the white man's curses when he spied the three renegade Tonto Apaches who had come to raid the station. Shane had employed another string of profanity when he saw the warriors snatch up the white woman and carry her off to be abused and molested at their leisure.

As for himself, Shane didn't have much use for white women. Dealing with his hateful stepmother had cured him for life. And yet, there was something intriguing about the female with red-gold hair. Her pitiful wail for assistance called out to him like the tormented spirit of the newly-damned. The white woman no more deserved to be abducted and mistreated than Shane deserved to walk this lonely, tormenting path.

All Shane really wanted was his stallion, but fate was not known for its good timing. If not for this inconvenient abduction, he could have set his plans in motion without injury to anyone. Now the situation had changed. His steed was just a stone's throw away, but the white woman was in grave danger. The fact that she had relied upon cunning, as any clever Apache would have done, impressed Shane. For all appearance and pretense she was squirming and squawking. But she had shrewdly waited until the perfect moment to launch herself away from her captor and dive into the river.

Very commendable, but exceedingly dangerous, thought Shane. The creek raced through a chain of rapids that led to a tumbling waterfall. The woman's chances of survival were decreasing with every passing moment. She couldn't keep her head above water long enough to see the danger that awaited her.

Shane glanced from his pawing stallion to the bedraggled female in the stream below fighting for her life in the treacherous channel of rapids. The scene reminded him of his own turmoil in life. The stream was symbolic of his tormented existence—the constant struggles he underwent. The opposing banks of the river represented two civilizations—the white man's and the red man's. Shane, like the hapless female, was caught in crosscurrents, unable to reach either side. And she, like Shane, had been an innocent victim, battling to survive.

Shane cast one last glance at Sultan. If he had given a sharp whistle, Sultan would have attempted to answer his master's call. Even if Sultan could have snapped the reins and restraining rope, Shane might have been forced to encounter the Tonto braves who had taken to raiding remote settlements and stage stations to display their belligerence at being confined to hated reservations. Shane had no intention of revealing his whereabouts to the renegades or to the soldiers in the stage station.

With a scowl, Shane turned his back on Sultan. As much as he wanted to retrieve his stallion, Shane felt obliged to rescue the white woman before she plunged over the twenty-foot falls onto a ledge of jagged boulders. He reined the piebald pony around and retraced his path down the mountain to reach the creek. There would be another time and place to retrieve Sultan, but the white woman had only one chance of survival and limited time to be rescued. Indeed, she could very well be dead before Shane could fish her out of the river. But at least he would have appeased his nagging conscience.

Calera swore she was on the verge of drowning at least three times in the course of . . . Her mind faltered as water swamped and buffeted her. It was impossible to measure the passage of time while she was preoccupied with the exhausting task of staying alive. Although she couldn't swim a lick, she needed to do no more than grasp an occasional breath. The swift channel kept her afloat while it sped over the rocks and broken stumps of decaying trees.

The rains from the previous day had filled the creek to overflowing and water rushed through the valley in torrents. Calera was dragged along at a dizzying pace, bumping and scraping against every object in her path. Her left arm ached something fierce and the burning sensation in her hips and knees suggested they had been scraped raw. Once she thought she felt blood on her lips, but an onrush of water quickly wiped that taste away.

Had she escaped her savage captors, only to be dragged over a torture rack of rapids while swallowing several gallons of water? Was she going to die without ever seeing her beloved brother again?

Calera O'Connell, you are not giving up that easily! came that unfaltering but waterlogged voice. *You will survive! You must! You shall!*

The jagged edge of panic chipped at her determination. "I can't," Calera choked out before another wall of water slapped her in the face.

Oh yes you shall! Damn your bruised hide, girl. You will survive!

The encouraging thought resounded in her soggy brain, prodding her to battle and overcome impossible odds. Although her left arm felt as if it had been yanked from its socket, Calera pushed away from the rocks and attempted to gain her feet. The force of the moving water shoved her sideways, flinging her off balance. A pained yelp gurgled in her throat when she crashed into another sharp obstacle and went tumbling with the current.

Calera felt like a human punching bag that had been beaten to a pulp and tossed in the river. Her gown had been ripped to shreds. Her arms and legs were numb from overexertion and there was nothing but an endless sea of water to fill her starved lungs. Only divine intervention would save her from a watery death.

Just as the sun peeked out from behind a fleeting cloud, bringing a ray of hope, *HE* appeared, sitting like a bronzed knight upon his painted pony, wearing so few clothes, that Calera first thought he was naked.

A gargantuan knight upon his painted pony? Calera would have laughed at her absurd thoughts, but she couldn't afford to swallow another ounce of water. She would sink like a stone. This was not her knight in shining armor; it was another damned Indian, come to lift her scalp and take whatever else he wanted from her. But even if another captor whisked her off, at least she would escape her watery grave. She would deal with the upcoming crisis when she confronted it.

In a silent plea for assistance, Calera uplifted her good arm. Inhaling and exhaling snatches of breath, she thrust her face out of the water. "H E L P ! ! !" *Gurgle, gurgle.* "D E A R G O D . . ."

Shane nudged the reluctant steed into the creek. The gelding scrambled to keep his feet when the raging waters hammered at him. The stream-bed was deep, swirling around the gelding's chest, causing him to shift apprehensively. Shane cooed at the frightened animal in the Apache tongue while he focused his absolute attention on the rumpled object that floated toward him. In the distance he could hear the roaring falls that tumbled into the canyon, reminding him that this was his one and only opportunity to rescue the white woman.

After the stream veered around the bend, the channel became even more treacherous before it cascaded over three ledges of rock. If Shane couldn't grab hold of the white woman now, he would have to give her up for lost. She would plunge to her death on the rocks and there would be nothing he could do about it.

Concentrating on his task, Shane urged the steed forward, wishing it was Sultan beneath him. The stallion, for all his wild spirit, had a heart of gold. Sultan also possessed additional strength the piebald gelding lacked.

Doubling over, Shane anchored himself to the gelding's mane and reached out to grasp the soggy fabric of the woman's gown. The garment gave way, forcing Shane to clutch at her leg before she was swept out of his reach.

Calera inhaled a quick breath before she was flipped upside down, held by one aching leg. She reared back, sucking in air to supply her burning lungs. The instant she felt her body collide with the muscled form beside her, she latched onto Shane like a barnacle to a ship, refusing to let go until the terror ebbed. Her teeth chattered so that she couldn't force out a single word of gratitude. She could do nothing but hang on for dear life. She could see nothing but the mop of hair that dangled in her eyes, hear nothing but the pounding of her heart,

Making no attempt to struggle, Calera waited for her rescuer to toss her upon the nervous steed. She half-collapsed, sputtering, coughing, and inhaling air in great gulps before lapsing into wheezes.

Calera had been in for a rude awakening when she reached the last outposts of civilization, and she had learned her lessons well the first time: Screaming and fighting accomplished nothing. Calera recalled reading that savages were impressed by displays of courage and valor rather than fear. Indians respected those who did not cower and beg for mercy.

This gigantic warrior may have rescued her for his own selfish purposes, but she was going to treat him with the kind of respect and consideration she demanded in return. She would see how this new strategy worked out. The bolder the better, she reckoned.

With her arms encircling the bronzed warrior's neck and her head buried on his shoulder, Calera waited until they had reached solid ground before daring to speak. When she opened her mouth, only a gurgle and cough tumbled free.

Shane glanced down at the curvy body of the half-dressed female in his arms. His gaze slid to the bruised but shapely legs that were encased in tattered pantaloons. The ripped waistline of the gown sagged on her hips, exposing her derriere through the damp cotton fabric. Shane willfully ignored the tantalizing sensations that luscious body aroused in him. His first order of business was to head for higher ground and elude the Tonto warriors who were searching upstream for their missing captive.

Without a word, Shane hooked his arm around Calera's waist and dragged her up in front of him so he could navigate around the boulders and take cover in the forest of Ponderosa pines. Their precarious route required concentration and silence. Unfortunately, Calera had recovered her powers of speech and was all set to blurt out a grateful "Thank you." Shane hurriedly clamped his hand over her mouth and pulled her back against him to keep her quiet.

The feel of solid bare flesh meshed to her soggy garments caused Calera to flinch. She felt surrounded by formidable strength and potential energy. Never had she been this close to a man, and certainly not a man who was so skimpily dressed! Dear God, between his bare flesh and her clinging garments it was as if they were both naked!

This warrior was dressed much like his counterparts—barechested, wearing knee-high moccasins. But in contrast, this savage wore only a loincloth that left little to the imagination. His imposing size and stature set him apart from the other renegades who had attacked her. He was huge and his arms were like inescapable bands of steel! Calera felt like a kitten tucked beside a tiger. Her quavering body was situated between the muscular columns of his bare thighs and braced against the rock-hard wall of his massive chest. Calera could feel his heart thudding against her shoulder, feel his warm breath against her neck. She was overwhelmed by the scent and feel of this voluminous mass of masculinity, and she sorely wished she wasn't quite so aware of him, wished she could place a respectable space between them.

When Shane clamped his hand over the lower portion of her face, Calera assumed he intended to stifle what he expected to be a bloodcurdling scream, rather than words of appreciation for his assistance. She sat there like a slug, determined to brazen this ordeal out, somehow or another. She would display her spirit and determination, demand this powerful warrior's respect, and impress him with her fortitude. She might even befriend him to the point that he would think twice about killing her or using her for his own lusty purposes.

Of course, Calera reminded herself, she knew so little about Indians that her tactic might be a waste of time and effort. But on the other hand, what did she have to lose?

With shaky hands, Horace Baxter retrieved his whiskey bottle and took a fortifying drink. Already, he had cursed himself for failing the lovely damsel in distress. Horace had sought to spare his own chubby hide. Fear had paralyzed his thought processes and put wings on his feet. He had been crouched inside the stage station before he could think straight. By that time, Calera was gone, abducted by murdering renegades.

Lieutenant Haskell stood with feet askance, staring down at the rattled journalist who was drinking liquor in huge gulps. "Mister Baxter, what can you tell me about the young woman who was kidnapped?"

"Her n-name was . . . is . . . C-Calera O'Connell," Horace replied in a trembling voice. "I believe she said she was headed to Globe City."

"O'Connell?" The officer frowned ponderously. "I know a man named O'Connell. Was she joining her husband?"

"I—I don't know."

Horace racked his brain for pertinent information. At the onset of the journey, Calera had mentioned her destination and spoke of beginning her new life in the West. Unfortunately, Horace had been imbibing liquor at the time and his memory was fuzzy. After that, he and Calera had conversed on numerous topics—from the arts to great poets, to politics. She had proved to be an incredibly well-informed young lady and they had not spent much time discussing their personal lives.

"You spent more than a week in the lady's company and you know nothing about her?" Haskell looked astounded.

Horace glared at the uniformed officer. "I know she is well-read, superbly educated, and prefers classical music. What am I supposed to know about her? Her favorite color? Her life history?"

Haskell heaved a troubled sigh. "Forgive me, sir. I did not mean to insult you. I'm afraid my own frustration is showing. The possibility of rescue in this neck of the woods is very slim indeed. There is no wilder country in Arizona than this region of forests and mountains between the Gila and Salt Rivers. I suspect Miss O'Connell's captors were the hostiles from the Tonto Apache tribe. A few of the more rebellious warriors escaped the reservation last month to pillage and plunder at will. Locating the renegades has become quite tedious. My men and I have spent three weeks on a foray that turned out to be futile."

"Well, surely you intend to search for the poor lass!" Horace hooted. "Those renegades can't have gone far!"

"Not far," Haskell concurred. "But in which direction? Tell me, Mister Baxter, have you ever tried to track Indians who know the wilds well enough that they can trek across this rugged terrain in the dark?"

"Of course not."

"Then take my word for it, traveling through this labyrinth of canyons and mountains is next to impossible without Indian scouts as assistants. By the time I return to Fort McDowell to gather scouts, those Tonto braves could be anywhere."

"You have to try to find her," Horace insisted.

"I will try, sir. But in a few hours it will be dark." Haskell performed a perfectly executed about-face and walked off.

When the soldiers exited the station, Horace slumped in his

chair and swallowed another gulp of whiskey. The drink didn't ease his anxiety so he downed another sip. Calera was probably suffering untold tortures at this very moment and no one could do a solitary thing to save her.

Bitterly, Horace glanced at Ike Fuller and Grady Flax, who were swallowing down their meal like starved pythons. If those two mongrels had been the least bit courteous, Calera would have been the first one off the stage. She could have made the dash to the station without being overtaken by the renegades. But no, these unrefined hooligans had left Calera to a plump old man who had not been able to save her from calamity.

Horace guzzled another drink. He had spent hours listening to the sound of Calera's melodic voice, imagining how many eager suitors she was going to attract in the West. Any dreams she might have had for a promising future had evolved into a horrid nightmare.

There was nothing for Horace to do but carry the grim news to Globe City. Those who awaited Calera's arrival with joyful expectation would face agonizing despair. Horace dreaded the upcoming encounter of informing Calera's family who were waiting to greet her.

To numb his own desolation, Horace took another drink . . . and then another, until his mind was too saturated to dwell on the disturbing incidents that left Calera fighting for her life.

"Damn, you're a handful, Sultan," Haskell grumbled as he strained against the blood-red stallion's reins. As of yet, Haskell had not dared to mount the spirited steed, choosing instead to lead him. Now, balking and rearing behind the procession of soldiers while Haskell searched for the missing woman, the cantankerous steed objected to going anywhere—period!

"I think O'Connell sold you this devil for spite," one of the soldiers declared. "This horse may be able to run like streak lighting, but he protests being mounted or led anywhere that he doesn't want to go."

"And I will remind Keery O'Connell that this steed was partially responsible for my inability to rescue his wife or one of his family members by hostile savages the next time I see him," Haskell muttered, jerking futilely on Sultan's reins.

After several minutes of watching Sultan toss his proud head and prance in circles, the cavalcade of soldiers finally trotted off in the direction the Tonto braves had taken. It was not, however, a pleasant journey for the soldiers. Sultan resisted and the warriors were nowhere to be found. When Haskell was very nearly jerked from the saddle by the contrary stallion, he called a halt to the unproductive search. It could take weeks to discover the whereabouts of Calera O'Connell. Haskell was not equipped for a lengthy trek through this wilderness. He had his hands full controlling the powerfully-built stallion that had become more rebellious—if that were possible—after the procession reached the stage station!

Chapter Six

The sun had begun its final descent, splashing shades of crimson, purple, and gold across the rugged precipices when Shane brought the weary gelding to a halt. Shane had employed a most difficult path to reach higher elevations in hopes of eluding the Tonto braves, but he could travel no farther without providing medical attention to the white woman. Earlier, when he noticed the bloody wound soaking through the sleeve of her gown, he packed sand on her arm and formed a makeshift tourniquet from the two strips of fabric he had torn from her petticoat. Now that Shane deemed it safe to stop, he needed to give the injury proper attention.

Hopping to the ground, Shane pivoted to pluck the white woman from the steed. It was his first opportunity to see her face at close range. Thus far, she had been propped in front of him while he kept his hand over her mouth, just in case she let loose with a squawk that alerted the braves to their location.

Shane's arms hung suspended in midair when he gazed up into bright green eyes in a porcelain face surrounded by a halo of curly ringlets. The shiny tendrils were neither red nor gold, but rather a fascinating combination of both colors that caught fire in the light of sunset. Despite the bruise on her cheek and the scrapes on her chin, the woman was bewitching by anyone's standards—red man or white. Her complexion was flawless and the heart-shaped curve of her lips made Shane's mouth water at the mere thought of tasting them.

This enchanting beauty reminded Shane of the elves and gnomes mentioned in the books his father had forced him to read while he was being tutored in the literature of the English-speaking world. Each feature on her oval face was exquisite—like the portrait of the angels Shane had seen in his father's family Bible.

Again, Shane's attention focused on that lush pink mouth which reminded him of a ripe, succulent peach. And again, he was tempted to take those dewy lips beneath his and savor the taste of her.

In the past, Shane had paid little attention to the white women with whom he had come in contact. He had been acquainted with Indian maidens, and Chinese and Mexican maids, while he was at his father's ranch. But this was the first close encounter he'd had with a white woman, other than his stepmother.

The white whores at O'Connell's Cottage wore paint like warriors in a war party, but this dazzling beauty needed no artificial makeup to enhance her appearance. Shane could well imagine that this bundle of shapely femininity had men dropping like flies at her feet. Beauty this delicate and rare, in a world that could be cruel and heartless, should never be destroyed. This woman, like the majestic waterfalls and towering peaks and buttes in the wilderness, was meant to be admired and preserved. The woman was a tribute to the natural wonders of this world.

Calera pasted on her most charming smile and gazed down at the ominous giant's inscrutable expression. Although there was something dangerously threatening about this muscular savage, there was something dangerously intriguing about him as well. He was, without a doubt, the most perfect male specimen she had ever clapped eyes on. This warrior was a living column of imposing strength, possessing well-proportioned shoulders and a chest like solid rock.

Hair as black as midnight framed his leonine features. Eyes like chips of black diamonds, fringed with thick lashes, set beneath his dark brow. In those eyes Calera perceived an incredible inner spirit, a fierce driving force—something she had always admired and aspired to possess. His face was tanned and rugged and his countenance was as rigid and immovable as bronze. There were no crinkles fanning from those fathomless black pools, no laughter lines bracketing his sensuous lips. This was a face that was not accustomed to a smile, Calera decided.

Years of hard living were stamped on his craggy but undeniably handsome features. His full mouth carried a cynical slant that left Calera wondering what ironic twist of fate carved this man into the hard, dynamic creature he was. For certain, constant danger and wary disdain were his ever-present companions in this wild, untamed land. Calera doubted this powerful giant depended on anyone but himself, and had no need to. There was an eerie aura that encircled him—one that suggested that even angels were leery of treading where this ominous man walked. Even the devil himself would be at risk, Calera suspected. This Apache knight looked as if he had been to hell and back countless times, but she doubted even his clash with demons had failed to find him a worthy opponent.

Her assessing gaze dropped from the broad expanse of his muscled chest to the solid columns of his thighs. Calera was not accustomed to viewing so much masculine flesh. Her lack of familiarity with the male of the species was revealed in the blush that worked its way up from her neck to stain her cheeks. The breechcloth which consisted of nothing more than a leather strap, fastened around the warriors hips, and a flap of buckskin covered his most private parts—just barely. The skimpy garment displayed every whipcord muscle and lean plane he possessed and emblazoned an unforgettable picture on Calera's mind. She had the feeling that when she closed her eyes she would still see rippling muscle and sleek, bronzed skin.

This man was definitely a credit to his Maker, a fascinating monument of finely-honed flesh. The savage stood tall in his splendor and glory, a magnificent Goliath of a man, and Calera could not conceal her admiration as she stared at him. Impolite though it was to gawk, Calera did just that. *Not* to admire such perfection was as impossible as overlooking the Seven Wonders of the World.

Calera finally gave herself a mental shake and concentrated on projecting an air of supreme confidence that commanded respect, despite the precariousness of her situation. She needed to communicate and befriend this handsome savage if she intended to survive!

"I did not have the opportunity to properly thank you, sir, but I am deeply indebted to you. I owe you my life and I will find a way to repay you."

Shane could think of one sure way to repay him for his trouble, but he said nothing. He was too dumbstruck by the siren's voice and her enchanting beauty. He merely glided his hands around her trim waist to lift her from her perch. When Calera bent forward to brace her arms on his shoulders, Shane's eyes feasted on the gaping neckline of her gown and the clinging chemise beneath it. The creamy swells of her breasts begged for his touch and his hands itched to determine if her skin was as soft and delicate as it looked.

A throb of desire pulsated through him as he set Calera to her feet. But as he had been taught during his training as an Apache warrior, he ignored the discomfort of the flesh and concentrated on mental control over his suddenly vulnerable body. Apache warriors learned to live with pain, discomfort, and even torture. This was a torture—to be sure—but of a far different nature than he had previously endured. Shane felt as if he were being burned from inside out, felt the intense heat consuming him until his skin crackled beneath the touch of her hands on his shoulders.

When Calera's curvaceous body accidentally brushed against his while she steadied herself on wobbly legs, Shane felt another uncomfortable ache fracturing his iron-clad willpower. He stepped back a pace, desperately trying to conjure up a distraction that would lead his thoughts down a safer avenue—one that didn't begin and end with the seduction of this green-eyed siren.

He had intended to save the white woman's life, nothing more. Too bad he had such difficulty remembering that!

Finally, finally! Shane regained his self-control. When his gaze dropped to the wound on her shoulder, he fished into his saddlebag to retrieve the healing herbs the Apaches had relied on for centuries. Silently, he prepared a poultice, refusing to glance at the bewitching nymph for fear he would become distracted all over again.

Calera commended herself for what was proving to be excellent strategy. She had displayed no fear of this formidable warrior and he had responded with respect rather than violence. There was obviously a language barrier between them, but if no apprehension registered in her voice, her companion would never know she was shaking on the inside.

"I'm afraid I am ill-adapted to the situations I have encountered, having just arrived from the East." Calera paused to flash Shane another blinding smile. When he didn't glance up from his task, she continued conversationally. "I was caught off guard when your friends whisked me away from the stage station."

Shane cast Calera a quick glance, but he did not inform Calera that he was not particularly fond of the hostile Tonto braves who had abducted her. Shane said nothing at all. He simply mixed the herbs and mashed them into a gooey substance. Since the woman seemed anxious to speak—a nervous reaction, no doubt—he let her.

"I suppose I startled your friends as much as they startled me. You see, I am not accustomed to being confronted in such an abrupt manner. Where I come from, ladies and gentlemen behave in a polite, reserved fashion. Well, most of them do, at least," she amended. "I must confess I have known a few rude individuals whom I have had to take to task for displays of vulgarity. Take those two hooligans on the stage, for instance. They treated me like a prospective prosti—"

Calera blushed and looked away. "Like . . . well, that is of no consequence now. I hope I never find myself in their disgusting presence again. And if Ike and Grady had not clambered out of the coach and left me sitting there, I would not have found myself in your friends' clutches."

Shane felt an unfamiliar sensation tugging at the corners of his mouth while the white woman rattled nonstop. It felt like a smile, if memory served. He suppressed the expression and concentrated on adding Jimson Weed leaves and Mullein plant roots to his concoction.

He had learned the necessity of restraining all emotion over the years. It felt awkward to buckle to any sensation—pleasant or otherwise. He recalled how he had lost his temper while he was confined to jail and he did not appreciate feeling out of control. Indeed, he was uncomfortable when he allowed anyone to know he was human, that he was vulnerable.

Calera had been chattering like a magpie in an attempt to project a casual air and relieve her nervous tension, but exhaustion was quickly catching up with her. The wound on her arm pulsated in rhythm with her heartbeat. The world wobbled on its axis and she struggled to keep her balance when her stomach flip-flopped. She had difficulty swallowing over her tongue, which felt as if it had swelled to twice its normal size, and her mouth felt as dry as dust.

"I'm afraid I feel a mite faint. I have never fainted in my life, but I fear I'm about to now—"

Shane managed to set the potion aside before Calera wilted like a dainty flower in the scorching summer sun. Her head drooped at an unnatural angle on her shoulder and her knees buckled beneath her. Shane caught her just before her skull clanked against the nearby boulder. Scooping her limp body up in his arms, Shane strode toward a patch of plush grass that grew beneath a rock ledge and gently lay her down upon it.

Now, while he would not be observed, Shane drank in the alluring sight of hair that danced like living flames and skin as soft as rose petals. Impulsively, he reached out to trail his forefinger over the luscious curve of her lips. And even more impulsively did his gaze follow his fingertip as it drifted over the delicate line of her jaw and tracked along the swan-like column of her throat. Although his conscience nagged him unmercifully, his palm splayed over the full mound of her breast, his thumb encircling the taut bead beneath the damp fabric.

Another ache, one far more profound than the others, riveted him. Shane peered down at the sleeping beauty and frowned in thought. Wasn't there some sort of fairy tale about a charmed prince and a drowsy beauty? Shane recalled something to that effect. All fantasy, of course. An Apache warrior and an Eastern debutante were nowhere near a perfect match. He and this nymph were not only worlds apart, they weren't even in the same galaxy! Shane would work himself into a frustrated frenzy if he ever let himself forget that this white woman was off limits to him. He was playing the good Samaritan and that was the beginning and end of it.

Shane had never gained much respect for white women after his many confrontations with his stepmother who despised the sight of him and never failed to remind him of it. He had even less respect for O'Connell's whores. Their affection came with a price tag and lasted no longer than the time it took for them to spread themselves beneath their customers and collect their profits.

Casting off his meandering thoughts, Shane unfolded himself from the ground to gather the poultice. With the silent tread of a panther, he returned to Calera and knelt beside her. He carefully peeled away the sleeve of her gown and grimaced at the deep gash that cut to the bone, marring what had once been absolute perfection. In the process of removing the garment to treat the wound, the gown dipped over her breasts, revealing the lacy chemise that did more to entice than conceal.

Shane gritted his teeth against the surge of hungry desire. He yearned to savor every inch of silky flesh and devour those petal-soft lips. Damnation, he should have opted to retrieve his stallion and let this female take her chances in the river. For certain, the enticing visions that were gathering in his mind would come back to haunt him.

Cursing his lack of willpower, Shane tore a strip of fabric from Calera's petticoat to cleanse the wound. He was well aware of why she had fainted. She had lost a considerable amount of blood. After he applied the poultice, he pushed the dangling sleeve farther down Calera's arm in preparation for wrapping the bandage. It was at that moment that lashes as feathery as angel's wings fluttered up and green eyes widened in alarm. Shane feared his lovely patient would burst loose with a blood-curdling scream, but she quickly compressed her lips and collected her composure.

Calera awoke to find the muscular giant peeling off her clothes. She suspected that he intended to ravish her while she was oblivious to the world, but the instant she spied the milky poultice on her shoulder she realized the savage was administering first aid.

Calera tugged at the sagging bodice to preserve what little dignity the situation allowed. This handsome warrior had no idea what it cost her composure to lie there with her breasts half exposed, pretending nothing out of the ordinary had happened. Calera was determined to remain as calm as possible. She did nothing to invite a battle she could not possibly hope to win against this sinewy, bronze-skinned giant.

"I truly do appreciate your assistance, sir," she managed to say.

No one had referred to Shane as *sir* in all his thirty years. The white woman had him feeling respectable and accepted.

"I don't know what is in your potion, but it works like magic." Calera offered him another amicable smile. "It has a most soothing effect on my shoulder."

It occurred to Calera just then that if she was to communicate with this magnificent creature, she was going to have to toss a few words of English at him and make him understand.

"Arm." Calera pointed to the appendage and repeated the word slowly and distinctly. "Head." She tapped her skull and then clutched the mop of damp corkscrew curls that dangled around her face. "Hair."

Perhaps Shane should have been insulted by her attempt to teach him English, especially since he spoke three languages quite fluently. Instead, he was amused. This lovely sprite had yet to react as he had anticipated. She displayed no fear, only the kind of courteous respect which she expected in return. Instead of wailing in self-pity, she had tried to talk Shane's leg off. He had to admire her gumption and her spirit.

As a child, Shane had seen Mexican and white captives dragged to camp—screaming, crying, and begging for mercy. For that reason the Apaches had considered other races of people weak and incompetent. Apaches never cowered. It was beneath their dignity. They were trained to fight, to endure tremendous amounts of pain. The young braves were conditioned to run as much as seventy miles during the course of a single day to increase their stamina. They were denied food and drink until they reached their destination. The Apaches took pride in their ability to survive in an unforgiving wilderness.

"Foot." She wiggled her toes and continued with her English lesson. "F-O-O-T. Say it with me . . ."

With extreme effort, Shane stifled the makings of another smile, one that came so easily while he was beneath this imp's bewitching spell. If she wanted to play her little games to teach and tame the man she believed to be an illiterate savage, then he would let her. It might prove highly entertaining.

Shane, feeling a bit mischievous, tugged at the tattered gown, uplifting the hem to reveal her legs. Her cotton pantaloons still clung to her flesh like a second skin. Biting back his amusement, he gestured toward the shapely appendages.

"Legs," she informed him, even though it was difficult to lie there and have a man hike up her skirt as if it were an everyday occurrence!

Shane found himself taking full advantage of the situation. His index finger traced the beautifully sculpted contours of her mouth and he uttered the word in Apache tongue for her benefit.

"Lips." Calera said in a strangled voice.

Her breath clogged in her throat when the muscular warrior leaned close, his sensuous mouth only a scant few inches from hers. Dear God! He was studying her lips as if they were the first pair he had ever seen, as if he were intrigued by them. Her pulse hammered like a mad carpenter driving nails when she felt his warm breath whisper over her cheeks. Calera had been all too aware of this brawny mass of masculinity since the moment he had hauled her from the river and settled her all too familiarly against his bare flesh. Now, it was ten times worse! She could feel the potential strength emanating from him as he loomed over her, eclipsing the sunlight, filling her world to overflowing.

When she snatched a shaky breath and inhaled the masculine scent of him, a strange heat collected deep inside her. Butterflies rioted in her stomach when her lashes fluttered up to meet those fathomless pools of obsidian.

Dear God, Calera felt as if she were being absorbed into the depths of those spellbinding eyes, as if her energy were flowing into him like a swift current following the channel of a river. And when his full lips descended upon hers in the slightest whisper of a kiss, Calera felt herself melting into the grass.

His kiss was light and experimental, allowing her to test her reaction to him while he tested his response to her. For all his ominous strength and overpowering size, he did not force himself on her as he could so easily have done. He merely pressed his lips to hers, examining the soft texture of her mouth.

An exquisite pleasure caused the nameless knot to coil even tighter in her belly. Calera could not smother the quiet moan that vibrated in her throat when his tongue glided over her lips, silently commanding her to surrender to him. Ever so tenderly, he investigated the moist recesses like a honey bee gathering nectar from a rose. He slowly retreated, his lips brushing like a downy feather over hers, gauging her reaction.

As if she instinctively knew what he desired in return for his gentle embrace, Calera tasted him with her tongue, just as he had tasted her. It brought her the most fascinating kind of pleasure to return that which he had tenderly bestowed on her. He moaned softly, as she had done, assuring her that what affected her also affected him.

His muscular body momentarily glided over hers before he withdrew like an outgoing tide. Then he kissed her again, *really* kissed her. Calera felt a wild, uncontrollable tremor flooding through every nerve and muscle in her naive body. A wave of panic accompanied those soul-shattering sensations. Before she lost her composure, the warrior backed away, as if he knew by instinct that he had dared too much too quickly with one so inexperienced in the intimacies between a man and woman.

As for Shane, he rather thought he had dared too little. His body clenched with insatiable hunger. He glanced down into those intriguing eyes that were as green as the carpet of grass upon which she lay and he ached up to the roots of his hair.

Shane was mesmerized, bewitched. He wanted more of this forbidden pleasure, even when he knew it was best to keep his distance. He was playing with fire, but he didn't care if he burned alive. He wanted to know this fascinating nymph as well as he knew himself, to touch her and feel the flames dance in his blood.

Calera swallowed hard, trying to ignore the tingling sensations that spilled through her like bubbly champagne. She very nearly leaped out of her skin when Shane touched the peak of her breast and lifted a questioning brow. Dark eyes twinkled but no smile pursed his lips. Calera liked to have died of embarrassment at the familiarity of his touch. Battling down the profuse blush, she reminded herself that progress often demanded sacrifices. Her modesty was the price she had to pay to establish a bond of friendship between herself and this magnificent savage.

"Breast," she chirped, her voice failing her when she needed it most.

Shane could see her reaction to each new sensation she experienced in her animated features and expressive eyes and he smothered a grin. He couldn't remember the last time he had this much fun.

Calera flinched and her face went up in flames when his thumb drifted over the throbbing peak, causing fire to shoot through her, scalding every fiber of her being. "I'm sorry, sir. If you knew how difficult this is for me, I doubt you would continue. And although you seem more the gentleman than those two heathens I met on the stage—"

Her voice trailed off when Shane abruptly wheeled away. He vaulted up to his feet, jerking a mean-looking knife from his moccasin in one fluid motion. Calera gasped when she saw the

three warriors who had abducted her. They stalked forward,
fanning out to block all avenues of escape.

"We found the white woman," Gakayo growled at Shane. "She
is ours. If you return her to us, we will leave you in peace."

Shane had no particular quarrel with the Tonto braves though
he did not approve of the fact that these three renegades were
causing difficulty for their own clans by leaving the reservation
to pillage and plunder. Oh too true, the white man had promised
food, lodging, and supplies for the tribes that had been confined
like herds of cattle. Unfortunately, the government authorities
had not delivered what their useless treaties guaranteed. Bands
of Apaches were starving and desperate, and they were outraged
by yet another round of white men's lies. But this woman was
not going to become another innocent victim caught in the cross-
fire of turmoil. She was *not* going to be used to appease the lusts
of these renegades, not if Shane could help it.

"The woman stays with me," Shane replied in the Apache
tongue. "Do not force me to go against my own blood brothers."

It seemed Gakayo had taken quite a fancy to the flame-haired
beauty, especially after she had outwitted him and escaped. Obviously, Gakayo's pride was smarting a bit, too. His pride was
going to smart even more if he pressed the issue with Shane.

Gakayo snorted derisively and half-turned to slap his buttocks
in the Apache's customary gesture of mockery. "You think we
fear you? Do not flatter yourself. We are three and you are but
one." His hawkish gaze flicked toward Calera, who was watching
with rounded eyes, unable to translate what was being said. "You
are a fool if you would die for a white woman. I claimed her as
my captive and it is I who will take her first. If you want her,
then you can have your turn with her when we have finished."

Shane scrutinized the braves, who slowly closed in on him.
"If you think I fear you, then *you* flatter *yourself* too much."

For several seconds the braves circled like looming vultures,
seeking the opportunity to attack. Shane waited with well-disciplined patience while he assessed his foe. Strength and stature
was in his favor, though he was outnumbered. These warriors
were not to be taken lightly. They were trained in the skills of

in the skills of combat and they knew every technique the Apache practiced. Shane asked himself if the white woman was worth risking his life to protect. And then he reminded himself of his first impression of this green-eyed sprite. Beauty and courage such as this should be protected, even if this woman belonged in the white man's world.

Shane concentrated on Gakayo, who seemed to be the self-appointed spokesman and leader of the group. When Gakayo charged, Shane deftly leaped aside and kicked with the force of a mule. Gakayo stumbled, caught himself, and wheeled, his knife slashing with deadly accuracy. Shane parried the attack and steel clashed against steel before he shoved Gakayo away.

Calera held her breath when the second warrior, with knife poised, leaped from Shane's blind side. Frantic, she snatched up a rock and hurled it at the approaching brave. Her aim was so far off the mark that she caught the third Indian warrior on the head.

Calera's assistance was a waste of energy. As if he had eyes in the back of his head, Shane lurched around and uplifted his foot, catching his second combatant squarely in the groin. With a groan, the brave dropped to his knees, and Shane drove home the blade with the quickness of a striking snake.

A wave of repulsion washed over Calera when the wounded Indian pitched forward in the dirt. Shane recoiled, holding his bloody knife up for Gakayo's inspection. Gakayo wavered, his dark eyes darting to Calera, who had turned as white as a cloud.

Calera, who had never been prone to fainting spells, had the queasy feeling she was about to pass out twice in the same day. She had never seen such swift, lethal retaliation. Watching her dark knight in action was like seeing lightning strike. The brutality she had witnessed was nauseating and the wound she had suffered zapped what little strength she had left. It was all she could do to remain conscious.

"If you are wondering if I will be as merciless with you as I was with him, do not doubt it," Shane snarled at Gakayo as blood dripped onto his knotted fist. "This dagger speaks of death without mercy." To prove his point, Shane pounced. The blade pricked Gakayo's nipple, prompting him to leap away from the path of the blade. "You are my brother and I give you a choice. Make it now or you will join your friend in the spirit world."

Gakayo spat at Shane's feet in a gesture of disdain, but he retreated with his life and injured dignity. "I will fight the fork-tongued white man to the death, and I will return to carve you into bite-sized pieces to feed to the hungry wolves, This woman will be your curse. One day you will die because of her. That is my promise."

"And this is my promise to you," Shane sneered back. "If you stalk me, I will introduce you to a new brand of Apache torture that you will not live to remember. Today I spared your life. I will not do so again. Take your fallen brother and go before I change my mind and slit you open like a carcass of beef."

Calera could not help but admire the Apache knight who had saved her from certain disaster a second time. It was evident which of these savages possessed the greatest skills in battle. Her guard dragon had struck like a flash of lightning, never batting an eyelash when he plunged his dagger into human flesh. Despite the gentleness he had displayed earlier, Calera quickly reminded herself that she was in the hands of a deadly killer. His abilities spoke for themselves in the heat of battle. And for certain, Calera preferred to be this giant's friend, never his foe!

Dear God in heaven! How she wished the mountain would open up and she could drop back to Philadelphia. Calera was far out of her element, living a nightmare!

Calera watched the three Tonto braves retreat—one of whom had to be dragged away, never to rise again. She could only assume that this ruggedly handsome giant had staked his claim on her and had fought for the right to take what his Apache cousins wanted. Unless Calera managed to gain this savage's utmost respect, she would fare no better in his hands than she would have with the other men.

Even more determined to win the respect she so desperately needed, Calera peered up at the towering savage who had returned to her side, breathing no more heavily than if he had taken a Sunday stroll.

"I find myself indebted to you again," she said, rather shakily. "Of course, I'm not so sure the end result will be different, but . . . What do you think you're doing!"

Calera strangled a squawk when Shane crouched down to tug at her pantaloons. Damn him. Was he going to celebrate his victory by raping her? Valiantly, she forced herself not to fight him, determined not to display a smidgen of fear, even though terror sought to warp her veneer of calm reserve.

"Leg." Calera chirped and tried desperately to smile. "Two of them as a matter of fact. They come in pairs. I would like to keep both of them if you don't mind." She made a stabbing gesture with her forefinger. *"Arm. Head. Hair.* I am fond of my scalp as well. It would look ever so much better on my *head* rather than flapping in the breeze on the end of a lance. I have heard Indians are fond of ornamental tresses, but—"

Calera slammed her mouth shut, biting her runaway tongue in the process. Instead of yanking her legs apart as if she were a wishbone, and throwing himself down upon her, the warrior scooped up his potion and smeared it over the scrapes on her knees. Calera thought she detected a twinkle in those obsidian eyes, but the warrior's expression never altered while he tended her various injuries. Calera lay there, assuring herself no harm would come to her if she accepted his ministrations without putting up a fuss—which would get her nowhere fast.

"You have amazingly gentle hands," Calera noted, gracing him with another smile. The urge to jerk her skirt down to her ankles and shoo the savage away very nearly overwhelmed her, but she managed to contain the impulse. "And you have quite a magnificent body, if you don't mind my saying so. Indeed, you put the Roman gods to shame."

Shane had to employ extreme effort to camouflage his grin. And here he thought he had forgotten how to smile. This chatterbox amused him to no end. No doubt, she would never confess her private thoughts if she knew *he* understood English as well as *she* spoke it.

"To tell the truth, I have never seen so much bare flesh, except my own of course," Calera rattled rather nervously. "But then,

I'm accustomed to that. I am not, however, accustomed to having my skirt under my chin in mixed company. I'm sure you have seen an exceptional amount of bare leg in your day, but allowing you to see mine is not the easiest thing I have ever done, believe you me . . . Dear God, what now?"

Calera felt firm but gentle hands clamp onto her hips and roll her to her belly. She blanched when his fingertips descended on her calves to rub the potion on each abrasion she had sustained from riding the rapids and colliding with tree stumps and jagged rocks. Calera turned all the colors of the rainbow while her self-acclaimed physician sought out each bump and scrape and massaged her cramped muscles.

Shane had been forced to roll Calera over because he could no longer contain the grin he had been holding in check. With her back turned, Calera couldn't see the broad smile that he swore would crack his face, nor did he intend for her to. This nymph's disposition would undergo a drastic change if she saw him laughing at her. As long as he kept his mouth shut he could enjoy her. And enjoy her he most certainly did!

Under the pretense of seeking and finding each and every injury, no matter how insignificant, Shane permitted himself the luxury of investigating the smooth texture of her flesh, to memorize every shapely curve.

Calera's skin was so unlike his own. Firm and well-shaped though her body was, there were no bulges of muscle. She was exquisite—every scintillating inch of her—and Shane was having the time of his life ogling her while she was unaware.

Calera choked on her breath when those warm hands glided up the back of her thigh and swirled over her derriere. True, she had a knot on her hip, but she did not need this all-too accommodating giant to investigate any more of her body than he already had. His seeking hands had toured more unclaimed territory than Lewis and Clark! Calera had never permitted such familiarities. Indeed, a chaste kiss was all she had ever bestowed on a man. This was almost too much to bear! Besides that, the tender explorations were triggering the most unnerving sensations imaginable.

When she could tolerate no more, Calera reached around to grab the hand that rested on her rump. She turned her head, causing the mane of tangled red-gold curls to cascade over her injured shoulder. She battled to keep apprehension from registering in her eyes when she met his onyx gaze. But what she saw annoyed her to the extreme. The man was grinning. *Grinning!*

"You find this all so very amusing, do you? Well, why don't you lie down here and let me give you the once-over. I wonder if you would hold still for this kind of intimate exploration."

"Leg," Shane said as proudly as he knew how.

"And I think you're pulling mine, you devil," Calera muttered half under her breath. Jerking down her high-riding skirt, Calera rolled over and sat up. She poked her finger into the washboarded muscles of his stomach, causing him to grunt uncomfortably. "Belly." She stabbed her finger in his face. "Eye."

Shane blinked and swallowed a bubble of laughter. Before his amusement burst loose, he unfolded himself from the ground and ambled over to retrieve his dagger.

Calera found her gaze drifting over the wide expanse of his back and dipping to the breechclout that barely covered his hips. The last rays of sunshine gleamed on Shane's bronzed flesh, spotlighting his virile physique as he moved with the silence of a jungle cat.

When he disappeared into the shadows of the pines, Calera frowned, puzzled. "Dear God, you aren't leaving me here all by myself, are you?"

An owl hooted in the growing darkness. It appeared that Calera *was* to be left alone, at least temporarily. And indeed she was to be. Shane found it necessary to sink into the shallows of the creek for a few minutes. Actually, he could have used a half hour of cold soaking. His male body was aflame. His playful prank had backfired, leaving a burning ache that his conscience refused to let him appease.

For the longest time Shane sat there, feeling the cool water swirling around him. Grinning like a baked possum, he recalled how he had pretended to administer first aid when all he wanted to do was investigate each voluptuous curve and swell that green-eyed siren possessed . . .

Another coil of heat scorched him from inside out. Damn, Shane wasn't sure there was enough water in the creek to cool the flames of unappeased desire. If he kept tormenting himself like this, he would require a swim in the Arctic Sea to cure what ailed him!

Chapter Seven

By the time Shane had himself under control—to some extent, at least—and returned to camp, Calera had drifted into exhausted sleep. Shane wondered if she would have noticed if the mountains toppled down upon her. No doubt, weeks of traveling, compounded by her hair-raising ordeals, had gotten the best of her. She slept, oblivious to the world around her.

Shane studied the delicate form in the moonlight, feeling his entire body clench with the kind of obsessive desire he had never known before. Damn, this game he was playing with this gorgeous nymph was sure to kill him. He had pretended to be what she thought he was—the uncivilized savage. He had held his tongue, allowing her to spill her innermost thoughts. He was being deceitful, he knew. But for some reason Shane was reluctant to destroy this intrinsic bond that had developed between him and this beguiling beauty.

For so many years he had lived a strained existence that invited no pleasure, no smiles, no laughter. He had been trapped between two worlds, feeling like an extra soul in search of something he couldn't find. But here, in this wild tumble of mountains and pine forests, away from the tormenting influences of two civilizations, Shane had discovered a place out of time. He had also tasted the forbidden fruit of lips that were as intoxicating as white man's whiskey. He didn't care who this enticing nymph was, or who he was for that matter. The fact was that this flame-haired beauty appealed to everything masculine in him. Being with her was like living a dream.

Life below the mountains was hell for Shane. But here was paradise. His lost angel had taught him how to smile again. She triggered pleasurable sensations that had become forgotten memories in the turmoil his life had become. Why should he turn his back and walk away when he could not name one day in the past ten years that could compare to the enjoyment and contentment he had known with this alluring siren?

Although Shane knew this interlude couldn't last forever, he was desperate to cling to the pleasure and amusement he experienced. He wanted to learn to laugh again, to live rather than to exist in an austere world that forced him to pack his emotions in cold storage.

Calera curled up in a tight ball and shivered against the cool night air. Moving like a shadow, Shane retrieved the blanket from his saddlebags and spread one quilt in the grass. Then he scooped Calera's shivering body up to position her beside him. Instinctively, she molded herself into the warmth of his flesh while Shane drew the second blanket over both of them, forming a cozy cocoon from which he wasn't sure he ever wanted to emerge. His body reacted as it had since the moment he drew this delectable angel to him on the back of his steed. His awareness was growing more profound, more intense with each passing hour.

Shane knew full well that gentling this lovely green-eyed nymph demanded patience, the same patience required to tame his blood-red stallion. Sultan had learned not to fear Shane's presence because he had employed caution and gentleness. He had never taken a whip to Sultan as the white men had tried to do. First had come acceptance then trust. It had been a slow but rewarding process. And by damned, Shane vowed as he cuddled up to the shapely form beside him, he would acquire the respect and affection of at least *one* individual in the white man's world. It would be this lost angel's, he decided.

For a full day and a night Calera battled fatigue and the steady throb of the wound on her shoulder. She awakened for a few minutes at a time to sip water and munch the food Shane supplied for her. Then she would doze off again, feeling her Apache knight's protective presence beside her, feeling his gentle hands checking the wound before he withdrew to allow her the rest she so desperately needed.

When Calera stirred beneath the quilt, she felt the warm rays of sunshine tapping at her eyelids. Her body objected to movement. She was sore and sluggish and . . .

Calera jerked upright when she realized she was cuddled up to Shane as if they were on the most intimate of terms. She peered into his handsome face, watching the first smile he had allowed her to view spread across his craggy features. Rattled though Calera was by thought of spending the night in a man's arms—romantically or otherwise—she was fascinated by Shane's expression. It gave her an odd sense of pride to know she was somehow responsible for that becoming smile. It was ever so much better than that well-disciplined facade he usually wore, one that revealed absolutely nothing of his thoughts.

Calera could not imagine what overcame her at that moment, but she was in no great hurry to remove herself from this cozy nest, or from this man's dynamic presence. She had instinctively accepted his warmth and strength while he slept beside her. The fact that he had not forced himself upon her even once since their first encounter earned him her trust. Now she, like he, had become curious about the differences and similarities between the two of them.

Her fingertips itched to explore the smooth muscled plane of his chest. Calera didn't know what demon prompted her to touch what her eyes beheld, but she felt her hand automatically moving toward the living columns of flesh that glowed like burnished gold in the sunlight.

"Chest." She repeated the word a second time before her hand swept off on a journey of intriguing discovery. "And a fine *chest* you have, I tell you true. Some men are plagued with an overabundance of hair that reminds me of a gorilla.

"Did you know that a British scientist by the name of Charles Darwin has written a dissertation on natural selection, suggesting that our ancestors may have been related to apes? Darwin's grandfather was a physician who practiced medicine at the turn of the century. He did studies on man's anatomical similarities to other primates. It is a rather novel and shocking theory to the most intellectual of circles, I agree, but I have met a few specimens of the male gender who bear a strong resemblance to monkeys in appearance as well as behavior," she said with an elfish grin. "You, however, do not." Her eyes followed the path of her questing hands, feeling his hard flesh flex and relax beneath her curious touch.

It was deliciously wicked to caress this gargantuan giant as freely as he had touched her. Calera simply couldn't help herself, for she had always been extremely inquisitive. Until now, she acquired knowledge from books—hundreds of them. Suddenly, she wanted to expand her expertise on the subject of males—this powerfully-built specimen in particular.

"I swear you have shoulders like a bull," Calera declared. Her hand drifted up his collarbone to measure the broad width of him. Her fingertips skimmed over the crisscrossed scars that marred his shoulders and back, wondering how he had come to have them. But since he could not respond to her question in English, she didn't bother to ask. "When I was a child, there were dozens of times that I wished for your strength. There were a few obnoxious bullies I would have liked to bring to their knees for tormenting me."

Why, Shane wondered, would this beguiling female have to employ force on anyone? One of her disarming smiles could bring a brawny giant to her heels like an obedient puppy.

Calera smiled ruefully. "There was a time when I was as plump and homely as a possum. I had to fight back the tears when I was teased horribly. Oh, how I wanted to wrap my fingers around those cruel boys' necks and shake them until their stuffing fell out. And when I grew into a woman, those same rascals were there to praise this so-called beauty they claimed I now possessed. I wanted to wring their necks for that, too."

Calera's fingertips feathered over the column of Shane's throat to trace the strong line of his jaw, his high cheekbones. "If there is one thing I have come to detest, it is judging an individual by physical appearance alone." She grinned sheepishly. "All too true that I find you so easy on the eye. But it is not just your outward appearance that intrigues me so. It is the gentleness you display. I had not expected it, or even hoped that you would treat me like your equal, especially after your friends behaved so abusively. Now *that* expresses your true nature," she said with a nod of certainty.

Shane digested the information she had unknowingly provided. This lovely morsel was utterly fascinating. She possessed intelligence and a depth of character that Shane wasn't sure still existed on the planet. Since the vicious wars between the Apaches and whites had begun a decade earlier, there was vengeance, bitterness, and hatred on both sides. The white's greed for gold, silver, and fertile farm land had provoked them to drive off the Apaches who had been lords over these mountains and valleys since the beginning of time. The whites had broken one promise after another in their eagerness to seize the land. To the Apache, it was inconceivable that man could claim title to this wild country. To The People, dividing land was as impossible as selling off chunks of the sky and the air that gave life to all creatures great and small.

Because of their opposing outlooks on life and nature, the Apaches and whites had clashed constantly. The Apaches struck out to preserve their homes and their way of life, but they were hopelessly outnumbered and had been corralled on the hated reservations like livestock. And when the whites discovered new riches of gold, silver, and copper on the reservations, they altered the boundaries to accommodate themselves, offering none of their profit to the tribes from which it had been stolen.

The Apaches had retaliated with vengeance and outrage.

Their families had been massacred, confined, and even poisoned. The atrocities committed against the Apaches were ignored and overlooked. Yet, the bloody retaliations of a society of people who were fighting for their very existence were used as propaganda by the whites, turning every situation to their advantage.

Shane had grown into a man, experiencing those feelings of resentment and betrayal. He had been hauled away by his white father to observe life from the other side, to claim his so-called heritage. He had not been permitted to return to his mother's people and he had been ill-received by his father's people. But here in these remote mountains, he could escape the outside influences that tormented him. Here, he had met a woman pure in spirit, one who possessed great wit, warmth, and courage. She had ventured into unfamiliar surroundings from a distant civilization, unaware of prejudices like the ones that poisoned Keery O'Connell. He knew she would eventually be influenced by other whites, knew she would begin to view him from an entirely different perspective.

Calera had never been so comfortable and at ease in the presence of a man. It went to her head like wine, especially since she could speak so freely without fearing she would be understood and teased. At times, this language barrier was advantageous—like now.

"I have always wondered what it would be like to make love to a man," she said frankly. "I have heard it described in many ways by those silly ninnies at school. Some of them insist it is a woman's duty—a painful one—to propagate the species. Others claim it to be an indescribable experience. The little death, according to one French writer, though what that means I have no idea."

Calera frowned curiously when a mysterious smile caused Shane's eyes to twinkle like stars in a midnight sky. "You think me a babbling idiot, don't you? If you spoke my language, you would probably be a wealth of information. No doubt, you have known many women in the most intimate sense. Men seem to delight in boasting their conquests of the female persuasion."

Her index finger mapped the sensuous curve of his lip. "You kiss very well, you know. And if that is any indication of other seductive skills, I suspect you could send a woman's head a-swimming."

Another smile, one that was as wide as the valley that opened below them, pursed Shane's lips. His hand folded over her fingertips and his tongue flicked out to taste her. Moistening the pads of her fingertips, he drew them across the sleek terrain of his chest.

"Dear God . . ." Calera croaked, feeling another jolt of awareness sizzle through her when he allowed her to touch him so familiarly. "I'm going to talk myself into an erotic frenzy if I'm not careful. I look at you and my betraying mind begins to wander down the most scintillating paths. When I touch you and you touch me with such infinite care, I am tempted to explore this mysterious realm called passion. I must be too curious for my own good!"

When Shane rose up on an elbow to press his lips to her bare shoulder, Calera heard a moan gush from her chest. She had managed to stir herself up *but good* with all this talk of desire and lovemaking. And furthermore, she had aroused this handsome giant by daring to explore his masculine body.

Calera found herself gently drawn down onto the quilt. Hard muscled flesh half-covered her, heightening her awareness of this intriguing creature who was a paradox of tenderness and omnipotent strength. When his lips grazed her eyelids and cheeks, Calera sighed audibly. This man instilled an indescribable longing inside her. His gentleness stripped away her inhibition as if it never existed.

When his mouth slanted over hers in a tender but possessive kiss, Calera surrendered without a fight. He had taught her not to fear him, and she responded with an ever-growing sense of trust and a burning desire to investigate the mystical dimension of pleasurable sensations. When Shane's hands glided up her thigh, Calera swore her flesh was about to melt off her bones. His languid explorations spurred a need that was fast becoming an addiction. His caress was so gentle and unhurried that she

was helpless to object. Her mouth opened to the silent request
of his kiss. Their tongues mated; their breath merged. His hand
skimmed over her belly and Calera felt the warm tingles burgeoning inside her.

When he lifted his dark head to peer down at her, Calera
smiled up at him. "I swear you are a most perplexing devil."
Her voice was thick with the desire his kisses and caresses had
aroused in her. "I have never dared so much with any man.
Their long lines of flattery made me leery. But in your silence
you have bedeviled me . . ."

When his hand scaled the ladder of her ribs to swirl over the
thin fabric that covered her breasts, Calera felt hot desire riveting her naive body. She arched helplessly toward him, granting
him privileges he had not even requested. Lord-a-mercy! His
hands and lips were teaching her startling discoveries about
intimacy and she instinctively responded to them! What was the
matter with her? The way she shamelessly yielded to this man's
tender touch, one would have thought she had been a harlot in
another lifetime.

They were strangers in a forbidden fantasy and she had spoken
to him as if she were speaking to herself. Thank goodness he
couldn't translate her most private thoughts. She would die of
embarrassment . . . if she didn't die of frustrated passion first!

And where was this pain that some of her acquaintances insisted accompanied lovemaking? Thus far, Calera could only describe these kisses and caresses as exquisite torture. Perhaps there
would have been pain and torment if she had been forced to
endure the touch of those three barbarians who had whisked her
off the stage. But that was not the case with this patient savage.

Savage? Calera laughed at her own ridiculous description.
This bronzed Goliath was anything but a savage. He hadn't
abused her; he worshipped her. He touched her as if she were
a delicate flower to be cherished and handled with the greatest
of care. And because he treated her with such admiring respect
Calera could not deny him. Indeed, she fairly begged for him
to introduce her to the world of enthralling sensations.

Shane's hand trembled, evidence of the restraint he demanded of himself. The impulse to bury himself deep inside this lovely nymph very nearly overwhelmed him. If she had a clue how much restraint it required to proceed at such a slow pace—when he wanted to devour her—she would have been amazed, perhaps even impressed. But because she believed him to be some phenomenal creature who possessed gentle patience he *became* what she believed him to be.

Even though Shane was driven by the fierce urge to rip away the fabric that deprived him of viewing every delicious inch of her creamy flesh, he fought down the ravenous needs. He slowly drew the tattered gown and chemise down to her waist, exposing her full breasts to his appreciative gaze. Never in his life had he beheld anything so exquisite as this angel. Her flaming hair tumbled around her face like a pool of glowing lava. Her lustrous eyes reminded him of spring leaves glistening with raindrops. Her skin glowed in the golden light like warm honey.

Shane lowered his head to brush his lips over the soft pink buds of her breasts, savoring the texture and scent of her skin. His tongue flicked out to tease the rigid peaks and he felt her luscious body quiver in response. When he suckled the dusky crest, her body instinctively moved toward his. Her arm glided over his shoulder and she trembled with the need he had instilled in her.

"Is this the little death, do you suppose?" Calera whispered raggedly. "It's like being consumed by a fire and welcoming the searing flames. If this is what dying feels like, I can't imagine why anyone would fear it—"

Her breath lodged in her throat when his hands and lips feathered over her body, finding and sensitizing every inch of her flesh. Calera could form no protest when Shane pushed the tangled fabric out of his way to explore her completely. A flood of embarrassment stained her cheeks while she watched those onyx eyes travel from the top of her head to the tips of her toes. Sensations spilled through her just as surely as if he had reached out to caress her. Such a potent gaze, such an incredibly tender man, she thought to herself. Part of her was thoroughly ashamed at her lack of feminine reserve and another part of her defied conscience and restraint, aching to discover where these delicious sensations led.

Until this moment Calera had been naively unaware of the powerful undercurrent of desire that could drag a woman into its hazy depths and drown her. Neither did she have time to consider the consequences of what would happen if she didn't collect her wits—and quickly. The minute those warm hands and moist lips followed the erotic path of his gaze she knew she was lost and gone forever.

Just once in her life she wanted to cast caution to the wind, to live for the moment. For years she had buried herself in books, reminding herself that she was living for her brother, as well as her departed family who held such great expectations for their children. But now, for this instant that defied time and space, Calera wanted to escape the rigid confinement she had designed for herself. This was her fantasy of limitless freedom and she was yielding to what felt wonderfully natural, surrendering to these luscious sensations that spilled over her like sparkling flames.

Over and over again, languid kisses and caresses flooded over her flesh. Calera became the center of a pulsating awareness that throbbed in spellbinding rhythm. She gave herself up to the wild, mind-boggling sensations that had her swearing she had come to life for the very first time. She was astonished by the maelstrom of emotion she never knew existed and she ached for more of this wondrous torment.

A gasp tumbled from her lips when his caresses became far more daring and erotic. He guided her thighs apart with his knees and bent to spread a row of heated kisses over her belly and the curve of her hip. And when his hands glided lower, Calera completely forgot how to breathe or why she needed to. The remarkable sensations she experienced were more than enough to sustain her. Her body shuddered in uncontrollable spasms when his fingertips explored the very essence of her femininity. He stroked her, aroused her until she convulsed around him, lost in sweet, torturous pleasure. And suddenly his intimate caresses were not enough to satisfy the monstrous ache that swallowed her alive. Calera clutched at him, her nails digging into the scars on his shoulders. When she would have held him to her, he withdrew and rose to full stature.

Shane's gaze never wavered as he unhooked the leather strap that held his breechcloth in place. The skimpy garment fell away and he waited for Calera's eyes to register the shock of seeing a totally naked man at the height of arousal.

"Dear God . . ." Calera stared at Shane as if he were the first naked man she had ever seen—because he was! And what he was, was an unbelievable masterpiece of steel-honed muscle, bronzed flesh, and . . . Her incredulous gaze dipped lower. "Dear God . . ." This Apache warrior in a breechcloth had definitely been a sight to see. Without the breechcloth he was something else again!

Like a graceful panther Shane knelt beside her, but Calera was so busy staring in innocent wonder that he almost laughed aloud. Despite the intense need that hounded him, he waited for Calera to regain some degree of composure. It took a while. Her unguarded stare was a reflection of her thoughts, ones he could read with vivid clarity. Owlishly, she peered at the throbbing evidence of his need for her. With her jaw sagging, her gaze darted back to his face, but only for a moment before her eyes fell lower.

"There's no way . . ." Calera choked out.

Never in all his miserable life had he felt so much a man as he did now. His warlike skills and his imposing strength mattered not. It was this woman's wide-eyed gaze that inspired an odd sense of pride and pleasure. This delicious dream was nothing like the lusty romps Cactus and Sticker described in great detail when they trotted off like two hounds on the trail of their whores. This was unique and special. It was magical. It was a forbidden fantasy beyond the scope of reality. There were no boundaries of civilization to confine him. He was but a man who wanted this woman more than he had wanted anything in all his life. He longed to pleasure her as she pleasured him when she surrendered to his touch. He wanted to feel her silky flesh meshed to his, to communicate in ways that needed no verbal translation.

When Shane drew Calera's quivering hand across the velvet

length of him, the breath she had been holding gushed out in a ragged sigh. Touching him where he was most a man sent her senses reeling, escalating her own pleasure. She dared the inconceivable and yet it still did not satisfy this white-hot need that coursed through her. When Shane taught her to please him with her untutored caresses, she gave no thought to right or wrong, only to the compelling power of passion in its purest, most unselfish form. Shane groaned in response to her caress, and Calera reveled at this newfound power she held over this magnificent giant. For all his brute strength, he had become *her* slave, moving upon *her* command. It was as if he had begun to live through her touch. And touch him she did, with caresses and kisses that expressed her own need to return the ineffable pleasure he had bestowed upon her. She wanted him to know how he had affected her. She watched him succumb to her bold caresses as completely as she had succumbed to his.

"Sweet nymph, you have bewitched me," Shane murmured in the Apache tongue. "You give me life and make me breathe."

Shane rolled above her while she held the pulsating length of him in her hand. He ached to feel more than just the throbbing need of his desire surrounded by her fingertips. He wanted to become a part of her for one glorious moment that caught and captured time. His arms trembled as he held himself above her, refusing to frighten her and yet aching to devour her.

There were those who feared and despised Shane for who he was, but he couldn't bear to see those emotions in her expressive eyes. He wanted to see the glow of trust and the sparkle of passion mirrored in those emerald pools. And now, when he would have whispered soft words of reassurance that it was not his intent to hurt her, he was trapped by his own mischievous deceit. He had to communicate through silent tenderness and patience or he would destroy this moment that he craved more than life itself.

Ever so slowly, Shane settled exactly upon her. His mouth sought hers, imitating the intimacy that was to come. He felt her body tense beneath him and he stilled himself, despite the raging passion that exploded inside him. When Calera relaxed and her arms slid over his hips to stroke the taut tendons of his back, Shane pressed against her. He closed his eyes and clenched his jaw against the urgent need that sought to take command of his body. He would *not* destroy this one sweet dream in his life of torment. No matter what the cost of self-control and blinding hunger, he would take this enchanting nymph with him into the joyous dimensions of ecstasy, sharing each new sensation with her, savoring each newfound pleasure they offered each other.

Calera flinched when she felt the penetrating length of him searing her like velvet fire. Pain shattered the spell and she instinctively pushed him away. "No! Please . . . no!"

Shane had depleted every ounce of restraint he possessed. He could feel passion spurring him like a merciless rider. *This,* Shane decided, was the worst kind of torture known to man. As for himself, he preferred to endure the heat of a glowing branding iron on his flesh than to deny himself ecstasy that was so close and yet so unbearably far away. He could not hold himself in check a moment longer. His need had become so tangible that it crippled mind and body. He would make this lovely siren forget the initial pain when he swept her up with him to heights that overshadowed the lofty peaks of these mountains.

Calera swore her body had split asunder when Shane thrust deeply into her tender flesh. She couldn't draw a breath, couldn't move. The pain intensified as he glided upon her with steady, rocking motions that pressed her deeper into the carpet of grass. A hoarse cry tumbled from her lips, but Shane smothered it with his possessive kiss, sharing his breath when she could grasp none of her own.

And then the most paradoxical sensation claimed her—an exquisite pleasure born of pain. Calera could feel herself accepting him like a new blossom unfolding in the warmth of the morning sun. As if her naive body had suddenly acquired an instinct that was hitherto unbeknownst to her, she began to move in rhythm with him, meeting each hard, penetrating thrust. She was compelled by some nameless sensation that expanded at a phenomenal rate—like a ball of fire consuming all within its path, feeding on its own raging flames. Calera felt like a meteor blazing across the sky, charting a course to its own destruction. Sensation after inimitable sensation converged upon her until she cried out in the overwhelming wonder of it all. She swore she had left her mark on this muscled warrior when another spasm of rapture riveted her. Her long nails spiked into the tendons of his arm. Her legs curled around him, holding him, arching ever closer to the maddening need that engulfed her.

And then every ounce of self-control abandoned her. The hypnotic sensations had recoiled upon her, bombarding her in the same breathless moment. Wild spasms raced through every nerve and muscle and Calera clung to Shane as if he were the only stable force in a careening universe. Indeed, he was! She was living and dying in the same fantastic moment. When his powerful body shuddered upon hers, another wave of ecstasy crested over her, stripping every last fragment of thought from her mind.

For what seemed forever, Calera lay there, her body intimately joined as if she were a living, breathing part of this incredible force of strength. A lazy smile pursed her lips as her hand absently trailed across his hip to investigate the corded muscles of his back. Calera had always been one to form her own opinions, and why she had ever listened to the yammering of her foolish schoolmates she would never know. Passion definitely was not an endurance test, not by any stretch of the imagination. It was a sharing of phenomenal sensations and the relating of the most intimate of all secrets. And it was certainly not the little death that had been described. It was, instead, a wonderful new dimension of life. She imagined that passion accompanied by love would even exceed all bounds of human experience.

And ah, how very easy it would be to fall in love with a man such as this—this gentle giant. But that could never be, Calera told herself realistically. She owed her brother six years of indentureship for the sacrifices he had made on her behalf. She had obligations elsewhere, and she and this Indian warrior came from two different worlds. Yet, for this time in space, they shared a mystical existence that could never be duplicated.

Calera closed her eyes to bask in the warmth of the rising sun. This, she decided, was paradise. This was the place where nothing that had come before, and nothing that would come after, mattered. Here, beneath the jagged precipices that reached like stony fists into the limitless vault of blue sky, there was only unparalleled pleasure. This was where life existed without the complications of outside influences. Her harrowing experience at the stage station was a small price to pay for this glimpse of heaven, and she would cherish the memory all the days of her life.

On that contented thought, Calera drifted off to sleep to relive the erotic dream. And there, beyond the measure of time and space, she could see that handsome bronzed face and those twinkling black eyes reaching out to her from across a sea of delicious memories . . .

Chapter Eight

Calera roused to the feel of sinewy arms curling around her, uplifting her, and carrying her away. Her thick lashes fluttered up to see Shane staring down at her with a lip-twitching smile.

"Where are you taking me?"

Shane did not reply. He simply followed the winding path that led to a secluded cove at the bend of the stream. A trickling waterfall whispered over two slabs of rock, forming an inviting pool that was shielded by Ponderosa pines. It was another corner of heaven that Shane intended to enjoy with this angel in his arms.

"I don't know how to swim," Calera declared when she realized his intentions. "No swim!" She mimicked a paddling dog and vigorously shook her head. "Put me down."

Shane never even blinked an eyelash while Calera squirmed in his arms. He walked right into the water, headed for the deepest part that rose to his chin and ascended well over Calera's head. When he said what he had to say to her, he wanted to ensure she didn't try to escape him. She couldn't escape, not here, not when she had to cling to him to keep her head above water.

"Now you listen to me, you big ox. I'm serious!" Calera practically crawled up Shane's naked body as he walked deeper into the stream. She made a stabbing gesture toward the sandy shore. "Take me to the creek bank this instant. I am not a fish and I like my water several degrees warmer and only bathtub deep. I demand—"

"Paleface, don't you ever shut up?" he asked with a scampish grin.

"Dear God!" Calera was so astounded to hear that rich baritone voice communicating with her in English that she launched herself away from him, completely forgetting where she was. She landed with a *kerplop* and sank like an anchor.

Uproarious laughter resounded around the secluded cove. Shane snaked out an arm and hauled Calera up against him— flesh to naked flesh. "Easy, paleface, you'll drown yourself if you aren't careful."

Calera surged out of the water like a spouting whale, her long hair clinging to her peaked face. With a swipe of her hand, she raked the tangled mass away to give Shane the evil eye. "You scoundrel!" she seethed. "All this time I have been babbling like a blessed brook, saying things I have never said to another living soul. You deceived me!" Calera swatted his shoulder—one that shook in silent laughter. "You seduced me and let me think it was *my* idea. Damn your rotten hide!"

"You enjoyed your own pompous game, didn't you? So why shouldn't I?" Shane chuckled at the splotches of outrage that caused a smattering of freckles to appear on her upturned nose. "You took it upon yourself to teach the primitive, illiterate savage to speak English—"

"And you took full advantage of even that, curse your wicked soul!" Calera spluttered.

Oh, how she wished she could swim. She would paddle ashore and leave this lout to shrivel up like a prune. But that was the whole point of toting her into deep water, now wasn't it? He knew she couldn't swim and she was stuck with him.

"Why didn't you tell me you could speak English?"

"You didn't ask."

"Of all the . . . Oh!" Calera was in such a fit of temper that she couldn't formulate a complete sentence to save her soul.

"You fascinate me, paleface," Shane admitted. "You still do."

"You infuriate me, always will." She glared at him good and hard. "How in heaven's name did you learn the language so well? What a sneaky trick to play on a person!"

"I'm a half-breed," Shane told her as he tugged a recalcitrant strand of hair off her face.

Calera had noticed that his skin was not quite as dark as the three braves who had abducted her. But since she was not an authority on Indians she never gave it a thought. She didn't really have the time. She was too busy struggling with the arduous task of staying alive.

"I was born Apache, trained as an Apache warrior, and hauled off against my wishes to learn to be civilized," Shane explained.

"You didn't learn your lessons very well," she huffed. "Gentlemen do not lie."

"No?" One black brow elevated to a mocking angle. "The Apaches have treaty after broken treaty to prove that white men speak with forked tongues. And if memory serves—and mine serves me very well—you said I was more the gentleman than those hypocrite dandies who sniffed at your heels in Philadelphia."

Calera turned beet red. Dear God! The things she had said! "Well, I stand corrected. You are no gentleman to take devious advantage!"

Shane resituated Calera in his arms, exposing the ripe buds of her breasts to his appreciative gaze, distracting himself from his purpose. Damnation, he simply could not get enough of this fire-haired imp to satisfy himself. Once had not been enough. The splendor he had discovered had only whetted his appetite. He had become addicted at first touch. But now was not the time for his mind to wander down erotic avenues. There was something he had to say and now was the time to say it.

In the aftermath of passion, Shane had lain on the quilt, watching this angel sleep. His conscience had given him hell the whole time. He knew that even if she lost her temper—

which she most definitely had—he had to confess the truth. She had been doing all the talking because she didn't think he knew how. She probably would have talked his other leg off if he hadn't said something eventually.

And besides, there was the matter of Sultan with which to contend, Shane reminded himself. As much as Shane relished this interlude in paradise, he had to track the blood-red stallion down. His playful charade with this lovely nymph had to come to an end. Once she got over being irritated with him, they could proceed.

"What is your name anyway?" Calera demanded and then inwardly groaned. Dear God, she had been seduced by a man whom she couldn't even call by name. How utterly humiliating!

"*Si-ha-ney Das-ay-go.*"

"Which means?"

"Swift killer."

Calera flinched. This formidable warrior certainly lived up to his namesake. She vividly remembered how he had made short shrift of the braves who had attacked him. Death had come like a thunderbolt—quick and certain.

"And what is your white name?" she asked, too mortified to meet his steady gaze.

"*Si-ha-ney* has been condensed to Shane."

"Shane what?" she prodded.

"It doesn't matter. I am more Apache than white."

"Truly? And how can that be *Si-ha-ney Das-ay-go?*"

"What is *your* name, paleface?" he questioned her sarcastic question.

"Calera."

"Calera what?"

"Calera It-doesn't-matter."

If he wouldn't do her the courtesy of revealing his white heredity, then why should she? She could be as ornery as he was if she felt like it. Besides, she had already revealed far more about herself than she should have!

Shane felt the makings of another smile tug at his lips. This sassy sprite truly did amuse him. She was as spirited as his stallion—one that was slipping farther away with each passing hour.

"Well then, Calera It-doesn't-matter, would you like to learn to swim before I put you ashore?"

"No, I would prefer that you to teach me to handle your wicked-looking knife so I can stab you a time or two!"

Shane chortled at the flash of temper in those emerald eyes. "You would murder the man who saved you from horror at the hands of the Tonto Apaches? You would draw my blood when I risked my life for you?"

"For those courageous deeds you have been properly thanked." Calera uplifted her chin to stare down at him from the lofty heights of indignation. "It is for the other things that you deserve a good stabbing."

"What things?"

"You know perfectly well *what things*," she snapped, staring at the air over his raven head.

"Because we made love?" he asked point-blank.

Calera squirmed in her bare skin, annoyed that she was forced to cling to this ornery rake while she was in so far over her head—literally and figuratively. "Yes, for that."

"You enjoyed it."

Of all the nerve! "That is beside the point and it was before I knew what a devious snake you are!"

Shane cupped her chin, bringing it down a notch. Despite her attempt to avoid his gaze, he forced her to look at him. "I regret much about my life, Calera, but I will never regret what we shared. I could have taken you anytime it was my want and you could not have stopped me. But I wanted only what you gave freely, just as I offered you all that any man has to give—his spirit, his tenderness, and his—"

Shane stopped short, unsure that he should continue. He had said quite enough. In fact, he had said as much as he could without delving into the most private part of his soul.

This conversation was making Calera decidedly nervous. It was one thing to be lost in the heat of newly-discovered passion and quite another to discuss it so openly. Calera felt shamed and embarrassed. What had seemed so right and natural had turned sour very quickly.

"Kindly set me ashore," she insisted. "I would like to catch up with my luggage."

"No, not yet."

Her head snapped up and she peered bewilderedly at him. "Surely you don't think I plan to stay here with you after you deceived me, after you—" Calera cleared her throat and plowed on, "I have obligations elsewhere."

"As do I, but I need your assistance."

"*My* assistance?" she parroted. This competent man needed *her* assistance? Unbelievable!

Shane pivoted toward the sandy bank. "Thanks to a treacherous bastard of a white man, my stallion has been stolen and sold. I am going to retrieve my mount and you are going to help me. Only then will I consider your debt paid in full."

Calera rather thought she had more than compensated for having her life saved. She had already given him that which no man could take from her again!

Feeling terribly awkward and self-conscious, Calera tried to cover herself the instant Shane set her to her feet. It was going to be a long walk back to their camp on the bluff in the *buff*—a walk she did not relish making with Shane following after her.

"I would appreciate a few minutes of privacy," she demanded in a tone that brooked no argument.

He smiled at the ridiculous pretense of modesty at so late a date. Why did this nymph have such difficulty accepting what had been so pleasurable to both of them an hour earlier? They had been as intimate as a man and woman could get. Even denial could not alter that fact. Calera had surrendered her innocence, and he had cherished the gift that could be given only once in a lifetime. She could not retract the emotions she had experienced, nor could he. Nor did he want to. Why should *she*? Had the bond between them changed so drastically just because he spoke English? What difference did that make? Shane wished he knew!

"I will fetch our breakfast while you dress," he volunteered, granting her the privacy she desired.

"Naked?" Calera questioned as her gaze flooded over every whipcord muscle and sleek plane in helpless appreciation.

"Naked as the prey I intend to catch," he assured her with a wry grin.

The comment reminded Calera of another naked prey he had entrapped—her. Blushing profusely, she darted behind a clump of reeds and scurried up the path.

Calera was beginning to regret her momentary lapse of sanity. She supposed the ordeal with the Tonto renegades was to blame for her uncharacteristic behavior. Now she had to live with her mistake—one she would never repeat, believe you her! This had been a fleeting affair that never should have happened. She simply had not been herself the past few days. People were entitled to an occasional blunder, weren't they? The trick was learning to live with the mistakes. Unfortunately, that was going to take some doing, Calera realized with a grimace.

When Calera reached camp, her footsteps halted beside the blanket, noting the evidence of her lost virginity. Her face flamed as it had so many times the past half hour. Dear God, what had she done? For all her staunch beliefs and high ideals, she had turned a complete about-face in one whale of a hurry. *Dear, dear God!*

What she and Shane had shared had been a secret fantasy. She had lived out a forbidden dream, thinking her reckless experiment with passion was safe from the world. And just what did that say about her sterling character? It said her character was tainted with serious flaws, that's what it said!

Calera had once been a dreadful cynic who had passed judgment on her foolish classmates for their obsessive fascination with the opposite sex. Now she had become a shameful hypocrite and she hated herself. She had become bedeviled by a man who deceived her in order to take what he wanted, as if her innocence was his prize!

Yanking up her chemise and gown, Calera fashioned a make-shift toga to wrap around herself. She was still chewing herself up one side and down the other when she stamped over to the edge of the bluff to watch the buck-naked warrior snare their breakfast. To Calera's amazement, Shane tied a piece of lace from her petticoat around the limb of a seedling and then scrunched down in the tall grass, completely disappearing from sight.

In a few minutes, several deer—or *pinal* as the creatures were called in Apache—wandered into the clearing. At first the wary animals bolted away from the fabric that flapped in the breeze. Curiosity got the better of them—Calera knew that feeling all too well! The deer ventured too close to the spot where Shane had concealed himself—and didn't she know exactly what that was like, too!

Calera watched the deer amble about and then dart off—save one. As a young buck went down, Shane appeared like a naked genii rising from a bottle. Ah, such cunning! Such a splendid specimen of masculinity! Calera smiled reluctantly to herself. She had been irritated at that rascal, but it was difficult not to be impressed by his abilities. *Si-ha-ney Das-ay-go* was like no man she had ever met. He was intriguing, virile . . . and so astonishingly gentle.

Just why had he been so tender with her? she wondered. As he had said, he could have violated her as the renegades intended to do. But he hadn't. Why?

Calera's resentful thoughts faltered when she remembered the gentleness Shane had employed when he touched her. She recalled how he had tended her wound, fought for her, and provided food for her. He had become her gentle protector, seeing to her every need. Why had he taken care of her? Was it because he wanted to appease his lust when she had recovered from fatigue and injury?

For a woman who had learned to adjust to all life's pitfalls, she had not adapted well to the intimacy she and Shane had shared. Her volatile temper had exploded, revealing the feisty side of her nature. But at least she wasn't the type of individual who held a grudge for extended periods of time like her brother had a tendency to do, she congratulated herself. Calera could erupt in bad humor one minute and regret her outburst after she had time to puzzle out what caused the upheaval of her emotion.

And just what *had* caused her outburst? she asked herself logically. Was it her overactive sense of pride? Her conscience? Most likely, it was a combination of both. Perhaps what disturbed her was that *she* had made more of the romantic interlude than Shane had. She had met so many men who did *not* impress her or intrigue her that she had surrendered to the only man who did. And of course, what normal man would balk when a woman practically invited him to introduce her to passion?

No doubt, Shane was an expert at seducing women and making them revel in every moment spent in his arms. But Calera was not likely to forget that tantalizing encounter, even if she was just another somebody else who had foolishly yielded to him. Yes, her pride was smarting after learning she had been deceived. And yes, she was totally inexperienced in dealing with the nagging guilt that plagued her. But life went on. Hadn't she learned that at an early age? And wasn't it time for her to be completely honest with herself? Truth was, she liked Shane—a lot. She had kept the rest of those of the male persuasion at arm's length, except for this one man who utterly intrigued her.

There it was then—the ultimate truth. Calera enjoyed Shane and he seemed to enjoy her. They would continue to pleasure each other for as long as this sojourn in paradise would last. She was not going to sulk about, just because he hadn't dropped down on his knee to propose to her. She knew their liaison had no future and he obviously did, too. This tryst in the wilderness was a place out of time, Calera assured herself sensibly. She would leave for Globe City as soon as possible, but in the meantime, she was not going to make herself miserable by trying to undo what could not be undone.

Soon she would be reunited with her brother and compensate for the years he had provided funds for her. Until that time came, she was going to savor the moments spent with the only man who had come remotely close to pushing her past the point of no return. She may never meet another man who impressed her or interested her as much as this ruggedly-handsome giant did. She was going to cherish the delicious feelings he instilled in her rather than begrudge them.

After having a heart-to-heart talk with herself, Calera ambled off to gather wood to roast the meat Shane had provided for their meal. And when Shane returned, he was not going to confront a pouting female who demanded that he shoulder all the blame for what had happened. She could have refused him if she had truly wanted to. Calera hadn't wanted to. And *that* was the honest truth she had to learn to accept.

Shane arched a curious brow when he returned to camp to become the recipient of a disarming smile. He had expected to find Calera slamming about, refusing to acknowledge his presence after the tantrum she had thrown earlier. Obviously, he had misjudged this white woman. But then, Shane had never claimed to understand the workings of a white woman's mind, so who was he to say how she would react from one moment to the next?

Calera sat upon a stump, enshrouded in a ridiculous looking garment that lay diagonally across her breasts and flared around her hips. She was peering up at him with sparkling green eyes that indicated none of the hostility he had detected earlier. When her gaze boldly raked over him, Shane's brows jackknifed.

"I am duly impressed with your skills, O Great Apache hunter. But when you slink around without a stitch of clothes, wielding that nasty-looking knife, aren't you afraid you might miss your target and lop off something else by mistake?"

If he didn't know better, he would swear Calera was trying to make amends for biting his head off. Ah, the woman mystified him. She could change moods like the wind switching direction.

"A while ago, I had the impression you preferred that I lop something off," Shane said, dropping the small deer beside the logs Calera had gathered for the campfire.

With head downcast, Calera absently massaged her aching shoulder "I have an Irish temper," she humbly confessed. "Sometimes I overreact and think later."

"So it seems." Shane fastened the breechclout around his hips and stuffed his feet into his moccasins.

"No, I don't think you do," Calera begged to disagree. "I said things to you that I never dared to voice to anyone else. And what we shared—" She fought down a scarlet blush and plunged on, "I haven't ever—"

"You haven't been with another man," he finished for her, since she was struggling to prevent embarrassing herself to death. "I know. And I did not take it lightly, though you seemed determined to think it so."

Wide green eyes blinked up at him. "You didn't? Truly?"

Shane ambled forward to draw her to her feet. His hands framed her face, uplifting her soft mouth to his kiss. Instantly, his male body responded to the feel of her flesh pressed familiarly to his. He savored the taste of her, reveled in her instinctive response to him.

A quiet rumble vibrated in his chest when he felt the heat of desire blazing through him. What was there about this woman that fascinated him so? One kiss and he ached to rediscover the magic they had created. But this time he yearned to let his passions fly wild and free without the forced restraint he had maintained earlier.

Calera felt the evidence of his arousal pressing against her hip. One look into those coal-black eyes and she was entranced by the emotions shimmering there. Her arm looped over his massive shoulder, marveling at the instantaneous spark that leaped from her body to his and back again. She suddenly found herself wanting to retest her reactions to this powerful giant.

The first time she hadn't known where those nerve-shattering sensations would lead. Now she knew all too well and she wanted to relive that splendorous dream, to explore it completely. Was it Shane who intrigued her so? Or was it the mysteries of passion that fascinated her? She truly should discover the answer to that question, now shouldn't she?

When Calera's soft lips drifted over his shoulder and skimmed his male nipples, Shane sucked in a ragged breath. When her kisses feathered over his belly, his lungs collapsed.

Calera seemed very determined to explore every inch of him, as he had explored each exquisite inch of her silky flesh.

Shane was astounded by her bold seduction. The previous hour she had been blushing profusely at the sight of his bare skin and at the thought of what they had shared. And now, like an ever-changing kaleidoscope, she had become the seductress. Not that he minded, but he wasn't sure he could endure this tantalizing kind of torment.

His hand curled beneath her chin, uplifting her enchanting face. "If you push me past the limits of my self-control, and you are dangerously close to it already, I can make no promises about how I'm going to react."

Her tongue flicked out to tease the rippling flesh on his chest and she smiled impishly. "No promises, Apache? I am disappointed. For a man who managed to keep a straight face while I wagged my foolish tongue, I would have thought you were made of stone." She reached down to tug at the leather lacing and the breechclout dropped to the ground. "We shall see what secrets *you* disclose when I turn your clever seduction back upon you."

"Calera!" Shane strangled on a gulp when her seeking hands and lips descended down his body like a slow burning fire, setting every inch of flesh aflame.

"Heady stuff, Apache?" she questioned against his clenched belly, amazed by her own boldness. When she was with this man she was definitely not her old self! She lived a spellbinding fantasy.

"Very heady stuff, Irish," he croaked like a bullfrog. "Don't say I didn't warn you—"

Shane lost his voice. Another barrier of noble restraint fell by the wayside when her fingertips glided lower—teasing, arousing, enticing. Her lips followed thereafter and Shane wobbled on his knees. A groan of unholy torment gushed from his lips when she did the most incredible things to his body. Her untutored caresses were going to be the death of him, he was sure of it. So quickly had this nymph learned to shatter a man's control, enslaving him to his own explosive passions. Earlier,

Shane had made wild sweet love to Calera and now *she* was making love to *him*. Why?

Calera urged Shane onto the carpet of grass, enthralled by the pleasure that sizzled through her when she heard him whisper to her in a pained plea. But Calera couldn't be satisfied until she had learned every well-sculptured column of his body by taste and touch. She remembered how he had made her body glow when he caressed her, how she had trembled with such profound need that no sacrifice had seemed too great to satisfy it. He would know that same helpless vulnerability, that same maddening craving. This time, ah, this time, the wild Apache knight would be *her* possession. She would unravel his emotions until she turned him inside out, just as he had done to her with such disturbing finesse. And then perhaps he would begin to understand why she felt so self-conscious when she had bared her flesh and her very soul to him.

Shane felt as if he had been drawn upon a torture rack. His nerves danced beneath her light, but oh-so devastating caresses. Her slender fingers trailed hither and yon, her moist lips investigating the texture of his flesh until he melted into a pool of bubbling desire.

His self-control was nowhere close to as good as he thought it was. Calera was dragging him to the edge of oblivion, leaving him teetering on a crumbling ledge. He would have her now or he would die wanting her. It was as simple as that!

"Come here, Irish," he demanded.

"Come *where*, Apache?" Her teasing laughter plucked at his taut flesh like fingertips on harp strings.

Shane had the sinking feeling he was being repaid for deceiving her, and he was paying dearly. She was going to torment him until he burned into a pile of ashes that scattered in the wind. This was not a woman, Shane decided. This was a mischievous leprechaun and she was torturing him to the extreme!

When her fingertips and gliding tongue had measured the length of him, Shane could stand no more sweet torment. He was on fire and this elf had ignited the white-hot flames that

fried him alive. *Now* she would compensate for her playful teasing.

Calera found herself on her back in nothing flat. Shane
loomed over her, his bronzed body rippling, his dark eyes glittering with the wild hunger she had aroused in him. With rough
urgency, Shane jerked up her skirt and lifted her hips to him.
His arm hooked around her waist before he lowered himself,
plunging deeply into her. Calera reveled in the intensity of his
need for her—a need she had drawn from him. In an instant she
was caught up in the swirling current of uncontrollable passion,
matching him, accepting him, wanting him with every part of
her being.

Truly, she did not know which she preferred most—his amazing gentleness or this unleashed urgency that ignited a hungry
impatience of her own. But the end result remained the same.
That wild burst of sensations consumed her, catapulting her to
the peaks of ecstasy and holding her suspended for eternity.

Shane had never experienced such unbridled emotion. He,
who had learned to shut himself off from all the world, could
not shield himself from his own vulnerability for this feisty elf.
Calera had succeeded in destroying his willpower. She knew it
as well as he did. His tightly drawn body communicated the
ungovernable need, just as surely as if he had voiced it.

When the tidal wave of pleasure buffeted him, Shane gasped
for breath and held on for dear life. He was afraid he would
squeeze Calera in two, but he couldn't let go. He was paralyzed
with the side effects of all-consuming passion, shuddering in
tempestuous release.

In the aftermath of lovemaking, Shane dragged himself on
his elbows and peered down into those dancing green eyes and
pixie-like smile. The smug little imp was gloating at her power
over him. Shane returned her grin—a mite awkwardly. He was
beginning to understand why Calera had been self-conscious
after their first intimate encounter. It was unnerving to have
one's emotions strung out like laundry on a clothesline for
someone else to see. His response to her intimate caresses had
been so fervent and uninhibited that he had laid bare his soul

in his overwhelming need. He and Calera had been through each other with all guards down, exposing their innermost desires in shameless abandon.

Calera reached up to trace the new smile-lines that bracketed his mouth. "You understand now, don't you, Apache? The way it was for *me* was the way it was for *you.*"

Shane knew exactly what she meant. When passion this wild and complete stripped a man and woman down to their souls, there was nothing left to say, nothing left to hide. They had become obsessed in their needs, willing to do anything and everything to enjoy the ultimate satisfaction demanded by such ardent lovemaking. This, Shane decided, was the closest man could ever come to heaven without actually dying first.

Shane dropped a light kiss to her lush mouth before he rolled away to stare at the towering peaks that surrounded them like the impenetrable walls of paradise. Calera eased up beside him, dropping her good arm familiarly over his shoulder. Her gaze followed his, admiring the magnificent rock formations on the purple-hued mountains, and the clear stream that lay like a silver ribbon in the plush green valley below. Calera sighed at the beautiful yet untamed savagery of this wilderness.

"How long do you suppose it will last, Apache?" Calera questioned softly.

"Forever," he said with great confidence.

Calera rested her chin on his arm, her lashes sweeping up to survey his chiseled features. "I was talking about *us,* not this glorious wilderness that is reminiscent of paradise."

Shane grinned as he drew her down into the grass to appease the burgeoning need that consumed him all over again. "So was I, Irish, so was I . . ."

Without one moment's hesitation or feminine reserve, Calera yielded to the sultry magic of this spectacular wonderland, and to Shane's tender touch. There was no help for it. She was bedazzled by this magnificent man who matched this rugged wilderness.

Shane was right. This wondrous fantasy *would* last forever, as long as there was memory, as long as these mountains marked the boundary of their wild sweet dream. And no matter where the courses of their lives led them, Calera knew she would never forget the mystical splendor she had discovered in Shane's arms. The memory of him—like these pine-clad peaks and sweeping valleys—would endure throughout eternity.

Nothing could tarnish this special kind of magic or taint these glorious memories . . .

Or could it . . . ?

Chapter Nine

Shane stared pensively at the meandering road that stretched through the Mazatzal Mountains toward Fort McDowell. From his lookout point at Four Peaks, he scanned his surroundings, utilizing the skills he had acquired as a young warrior among the Apaches. An ambush of this delicate nature required deliberate forethought. Shane wanted his stallion back, but with as little fuss and conflict as possible.

Every time Shane reflected on Keery O'Connell's spiteful retaliation, his blood boiled. There were several white men Shane detested, but Keery was at the top of the list. Shane hoped that viper had suffered considerable pain from the blows he had received during their fisticuffs. Shane had grown to hate that man with a vengeance.

"What are you planning, Apache?" Calera questioned, surveying the abandoned stretch of road.

Shane glanced over to see Calera sitting atop the piebald, garbed in the extra pair of breeches and buckskin shirt he kept in his saddlebags. The garments swallowed her petite form, concealing her alluring curves and swells. Even so, there was no mistaking the fact that she was all woman, not with that en-

chanting face and those curly red-gold tendrils flaming like a
burning bush at sunset. Shane could become sidetracked just
looking at her, remembering the breathless passion they had
shared before he finally got around to preparing their meal.
And consequently, Shane was several hours behind schedule,

There was an unspoken bond between him and Calera now.
There was no more awkwardness; there couldn't be. They had
become each other's possession, while containing their own individuality. Shane was as content as he had been as a child, even
more so. This delightful imp with bright emerald eyes and the
face of an angel had given him back his smile, his laughter. She
made him feel whole and alive . . .

"Don't look at me like that." Calera flashed him a teasing grin.
"We had to waylay once already at those cliff dwellings your ancestors inhabited. For a man who claims to be intent on rescuing
his steed, you have not made much progress this afternoon."

Wasn't that the truth! Shane had paused so Calera could rest
at the Black Mesa ruins and Shane had found himself appeasing
the insatiable need for her—again. And Calera had responded
without one shred of feminine reserve—again. But surely Sultan
would understand the reason for the delay, Shane mused with
a wry grin. The stallion had a penchant for mares. He couldn't
keep his mind on much else when there was a mare within one
hundred yards of him.

"Dear God! That blood-red stallion isn't *your* horse, is it?"
Calera chirped when she spied the procession of soldiers on
the road below. "I should have known. A horse like that would
have to belong to a man like you."

"That's Sultan," Shane confirmed as he led the piebald gelding along the old Apache trail that followed the constant lookout
points on the high ridges.

Calera well-remembered her fascination for the muscular stallion, not to mention her obsession for the steed's master. These
two dynamic creatures belonged together. *Why* these dragoons
had confiscated the prized stallion, Shane had never explained
to her. In fact, he had avoided most topics that dealt with his
background or his past. His fierce desire to retrieve his stallion

was the only exception to the rule. But for certain, Shane wanted Sultan back. How he thought he was going to snatch the steed out from the soldiers' noses, she could not imagine!

"Perhaps you should ride down and demand the return of your property," Calera suggested and then frowned at the disparaging thought that popped to mind. "Or are you a wanted man?"

Oh, he was wanted all right, Shane mused. Keery O'Connell would have every bounty hunter in the territory gunning for him. Their last vicious encounter had been a declaration of war. They both preferred to see each other dead—the sooner the better. To this day, Shane still didn't know why he had allowed that bastard to live so long. He had been too generous with Keery, who deserved no consideration whatsoever.

When Shane didn't respond immediately, Calera stared somberly at him. "You *aren't* wanted, are you?"

Still Shane did not reply. His feud with Keery was part of that tormenting world below the mountains. He had no desire to let the hell he had known intrude in the paradise he had found with Calera. Unfortunately, reality and paradise were already fiercely entangled, far more tightly than Shane could have imagined.

Since Shane refused to discuss the incident that left his stallion in the dragoons' hands, Calera fell silent. She didn't know what Shane was planning, but she supposed she would find out in good time.

For the moment, she concentrated on the instructions Shane had given her on riding. He had taught her to clamp her legs tightly around the barebacked steed when it scrabbled up steep inclines and down treacherous grades. She, of course, had yet to master Shane's impressive equestrian skills, and her body was tender and sore from the wild ride through the river and the ardent passion they had shared. But Calera had adapted, accepting and cherishing the moments she had spent with Shane.

She wondered how well she would adjust when this adventure was over. Calera knew those she loved always had a habit of slipping away from her—all but Keery. Someday she would be forced to bid her older brother farewell, but that wouldn't happen anytime soon. The chance of seeing Keery again had provided inspiration for her over the years.

Thankfully, when Calera had to leave Shane and the wild mountain splendor behind, her brother would be there to console her. Calera was far too realistic not to realize she couldn't hold a man like *Si-ha-ney Das-ay-go* forever. It would be like clinging to a sunbeam, watching it fade into shadows. As long as Calera kept that sensible thought in the back of her mind she would endure.

Her pensive musings trailed off when Shane hooked an arm around her waist and pulled her from the gelding. Darkness had descended over the mountains and the soldiers had paused for the night. It was then that Shane intended to strike. Calera was certain of that.

"Let me check your wound before we—"

"It's fine," Calera insisted. Well, it wasn't exactly fine. Her arm ached and the wound was tender, but she knew Shane was anxious to retrieve Sultan. Her throbbing arm could wait a few hours.

With deliberate concentration, Shane watched the silhouettes move around the flickering campfire in the clearing below. The dragoons had selected a most vulnerable location beside the road. The white man's arrogance still miffed Shane. No self-respecting Apache would sprawl out for the night in the wide open spaces like ducks on a pond. White men, however, thought only of their own conveniences rather than their best protection. Their selfish reasoning was one of the many reasons Apaches like Geronimo were still on the loose, eluding scores of search parties. The Apaches acquired knowledge from the habits of the creatures that roamed this wild country. The Apaches conformed to the behavior of the creatures in the wilds, using the trees, arroyos, and concealing boulders for protection. They relied heavily upon their well-developed sixth sense, as well as the other five senses the Great Spirit had bestowed on them.

That unique and practical approach to life was one of the many reasons why the Indians and whites could not completely understand each other. They would have to put themselves in each others' skins, responding to learned behavior before they could see through each other's eyes. Even as fascinated as Shane had become with this lovely nymph, she did not fully understand him, nor he her. Shane had taught Calera the rudimentary skills of survival, but she would have perished without his guidance, just as he constantly struggled in the white man's world below these mountains.

Shane shook himself loose from his ponderous thoughts and drew Calera along with him while he surveyed the area in the darkness. Calera copied his movements, trying very hard to emulate his ability to walk with the silent tread of a cat. Once or twice she stepped on twigs—ones Shane miraculously avoided. He would pause and stand there like a statue, holding her closely against him, listening for sounds that alerted him to trouble before pacing forward. It took almost two hours for Shane to circumnavigate the perimeters of the soldiers' camp and return to the spot where he had left the gelding tethered. By that time Calera was more than ready to plop down and rest her weary legs.

"I'm simply not cut out for statue-standing and tiptoeing," she groaned as she massaged her aching muscles.

"You have to develop your skills of statue-standing, as you choose to call it," Shane insisted with a grin. "You also have to learn to see obstacles in your path."

"See obstacles in the dark?" Calera scoffed at such foolishness. "I don't have the keen sight of an owl. No one does."

"It is the *knowledge* of that lack of sight that assists the Apache."

Calera peered up at the looming silhouette beside her. "What on earth are you talking about?"

Shane stepped behind her, covering her eyes. "Now what do you see, Irish?"

"Absolutely nothing, of course."

"Where are you?"

"Setting on a rock that bores into my aching backside like a spike."

"And where am I?"

"Behind me."

His warm breath whispered over the column of her throat, sending goose bumps skiing down her flesh. "And how do you know these things when you cannot see?"

Calera began to see all too clearly what he was driving at. He wanted her to rely upon her other senses and set her eyesight aside since it was more hindrance than help in the darkness.

"Do you recall the boulders on the north side of the soldiers' camp, the ones that rose like spires? There were three of them. The jagged stone crumbled at your touch, remember?"

When Calera nodded affirmatively, Shane's hands fell away from her eyes and he sank down beside her to place the leather pouch of coins in her hand. "You will make your way to that landmark and wait until the right moment to dart toward camp. Leave the money on a pallet and retrace your steps. Return here the same way we came—in a sweeping circle."

"And what are you going to be doing while I'm skipping around like a disembodied spirit?" she wanted to know.

"Retrieving Sultan."

"And how do you intend to do that, if you don't mind my asking?"

"The same way I snared the *pinal* for our meal this morning," he quietly informed her.

"Ah, the ol' tall-grass-trick," she said with a teasing grin. "And of course, when I go romping into camp, the soldiers will be so stunned that they will grab their pistols and fill me so full of lead that I won't hold water. They won't notice Sultan's disappearance until he is gone. Very clever, Apache. You *do* know how to plan a surprise attack."

Shane dropped a kiss to the tip of her nose. "No, Irish. I like you better minus the bullet holes. Sultan will provide the distraction and lead the dragoons away from camp. The soldiers will have their backs turned when you appear."

"You are very methodical and thorough," she complimented him.

"Thank you, Irish."

"But if something goes wrong and I don't—"

"You will," Shane assured her with the utmost confidence.

"You won't be looking with your eyes. You will *FEEL* your way back to me."

"Right." Her voice lacked conviction.

Shane framed her moon-drenched face in his hands and stared deeply into the starlit pools that sparkled up at him. "Don't you believe in magic, Irish?"

How could she not? This wizard had transformed her from a reserved bookworm into an eager adventuress. He had revealed the mysterious world of passion that transcended the realm of her experience. He had taught her how to move without one sound, how to ride when she had never straddled a steed, how to believe in fairy-tales and fantasies.

"I believe in the Apache brand of magic because I believe in you," she told him before she wrapped her good arm around his neck and kissed the stuffing out of him.

Shane felt a fierce tug on his heartstrings. The simple and yet eloquent statement made *him* believe in things that had died in his world a decade ago—things like faith, hope, and trust. In the years to come, he would return to the wilderness and he would remember the magic he had discovered with this delightful imp.

Before Shane buckled to his obsessive desire for Calera, he surged to his feet and stepped away.

"Come, Irish. I think Sultan has grown tired of the company he is keeping."

"Perhaps he has, but I have not," she murmured to herself.

Concentrating on the task Shane requested of her, Calera circled the camp, following the darkened trail she and Shane had taken earlier. Her footsteps halted when she realized she had forgotten to ask if he would send her a signal when it was time to make her dash into camp. Of course, if Shane were here, he would have said something like—"Use your sixth sense to determine that."

The man had more confidence in her novice abilities than she did, that was for sure! True, Calera had always considered herself an easy teach, but she was a giant step away from her own element. Yet, within the course of a few days, she had discovered more about herself than she previously knew. Living in the wilderness was an insightful experience that forced one to truly understand oneself and tested one's abilities to their very limits.

There you go getting philosophical again, Calera admonished herself. Now was not the time for introspection. Now was the time for swift, efficient action, and the dependency on that mysterious *sixth* sense that Calera wasn't certain she could acquire on such short notice.

The instant Shane crawled within range of Sultan's keen senses, the steed whinnied a greeting and stamped around the lone tree where he had been tethered.

"Now what's eating that devil stallion?" Haskell muttered to the world at large.

He had just settled down on his pallet to sleep. It had been a long, tedious three days. Since the attack on the stage station, Haskell and his men had scoured the hillsides in search of the missing woman and the three Tonto braves. He and his men had turned up nothing for their efforts, except new calluses on their saddle sores.

The stallion had not made traveling easier. Sultan had been as jittery as a grasshopper while they tramped along the precarious paths that evaporated into nothing, forcing the soldiers to double back to chart another course into nowhere. Since the animal was so cantankerous, Haskell had half a mind to turn the stallion loose. The money he had paid for Sultan had become a costly lesson. *Never buy a steed that is all devil, no matter how swift of foot and indestructible the horse is reported to be.* Haskell's money could have been better spent on the prostitutes at The Cottage. At least he would have enjoyed some kind of satisfaction. In Sultan's case, Haskell couldn't even *mount* his money's worth!

Climbing from his bedroll, Haskell trooped toward the flighty steed that had been staked apart from the other horses. Sultan's wild eyes gleamed in the moonlight when Haskell ventured close. The spirited stallion demanded his own space and he had since the moment Haskell had taken the reins in Globe City.

Haskell eyed the skittish creature whose sleek blood-red coat glistened in the illuminating light of the campfire. "I would like to meet the man you ever decide to accept as your master."

Shane could have easily arranged for the lieutenant to have his wish since he was standing not two feet away from the place where Shane lay camouflaged by tall grass.

Haskell outstretched his arm to stroke Sultan's neck. The steed bolted back, but he did not step on his master, though he came close enough for his nostrils to flare at the familiar scent. If Haskell had had the foggiest notion that Shane had dared to sprawl anywhere near those prancing hooves, he would have sworn the Apache possessed suicidal tendencies. Haskell would not have entrusted his life to this contrary creature, not even for a second!

"Maybe you'll settle down when you are confined to a stall and come to depend on me for food and water," Haskell said. "And then again, maybe I should pawn you off on some unsuspecting soldier the minute I reach the fort."

Shane decided to take advantage of opportunity. Haskell had grabbed the restraining rope, trying to bring Sultan within arm's reach. The slack of the rope behind Haskell lay just beyond the length of Shane's arm. He glided forward like a snake to sever the rope. When Haskell attempted to touch Sultan, the steed balked. Haskell retreated when Sultan reared up, pawing the air, fighting the rope. When the steed realized he had plenty of slack, he wheeled in midair and galloped off, his cream-colored mane and tail waving like a banner in the breeze.

Haskell expelled a furious bellow when the stallion escaped. The other three soldiers bounded from their pallets and came running when they heard pounding hooves beating a hasty retreat.

Calera took her cue and raced forward to deposit the pouch on the bedroll. She felt excessively proud of herself for appearing and disappearing like a specter in the night . . . until she cut a short corner and slammed into the spire of rock and fell flat on her face. Another lesson quickly learned, thought she. One did not gloat over one's cunning success until one was comfortably seated in one's own camp.

The fall tore open the tender wound on her shoulder. Pain seared down her arm as she scraped herself off the ground and limped toward her destination, favoring the knee she had banged on the jagged edge of stone. She definitely needed more practice in the art of stealth and cunning. Her arm was killing her and her knee wasn't in too good shape, either!

Shane remained in his prone position in the grass while the dragoons chased after the runaway steed . . . until he heard the echo of Sultan's shrill whinny—one that was reminiscent of a mocking snicker. Shane well-remembered those first few months while he had worked with Sultan, developing the bond of trust and respect between them. There were times when that ornery horse would bolt away, and Shane swore the steed was *snickering* at him rather that *nickering.* But eventually, Sultan would tire of his prank and come prancing back, tossing his head in that superior way of his. Then he would permit Shane to pet him, speak to him in Apache. Sultan never had cared much for English. It was also *his* second language.

"Shall I fetch our horses?" one of the soldiers questioned the lieutenant. "We might be able to chase that devil down if we—"

"Forget him," Haskell muttered. "I'll take my grievances out on Keery O'Connell when next we meet."

"What in the hell—?" Haskell scooped up the end of the rope that lay in the grass. He held the strands up to the firelight. "This rope didn't snap. It was cut!"

His startled gaze scanned the darkness. Had there been some-one or, something, hovering beside him while he tried to calm the devil stallion down?

"What is *this?*" the young private questioned when he sank onto his bedroll to find an unidentified object beneath him. He plucked up the pouch and held it up to the firelight.

Haskell retrieved the purse and shook out its contents. To his astonishment, he counted out the exact number of coins he had paid for the stallion. Now how had this money gotten here at the same time that the wild-eyed steed had bolted off into oblivion?

Lieutenant Haskell did not sleep well at all that night. He kept jerking awake, certain specters were hovering around him. The fact that the ghoulish phantoms didn't attack came as a great relief, but he was beginning to wonder if there was any truth to the Apache legends of evil spirits lurking in the night. Damnation, Haskell couldn't wait to return to the fort. Too many days and nights in this haunted wilderness was enough to unnerve the bravest of men—of whom he wasn't sure he was one!

Calera stood aside to watch the reunion between stallion and master. Shane had let loose with a whistle that very nearly shattered her eardrums. Out of nowhere a darting shadow blazed across the moonlight meadow. Calera caught her breath, watching the magnificent creature whose shiny red coat and creamy mane and tail glowed in the light. The stallion was awe-inspiring as he raced forward like poetry in motion, gobbling up the distance at incredible speed. With head and tail held high, Sultan skidded to a halt in front of Shane who stood his ground, even when Calera wasn't sure Sultan meant to break stride.

The two silhouettes, standing against a backdrop of a crescent moon and glittering stars, drew Calera's silent admiration. She had never known the luxury of such devoted friendship. She had many acquaintances, but never felt as if she had a true and loyal friend, except during those years when she had cried on Keery's shoulder at the loss of each loved one. Keery had shared the heartaches with her, comforted her, reassured her. Her older brother had taught her to survive before he went West, leaving Calera to face the remainder of her grieving alone.

Shane had told Calera that he had trained the stallion when he went to live in his father's world almost a decade earlier. Now Sultan was in his eleventh year. And for ten years, Calera imagined that Shane had treated this steed as if he were human. At the moment Calera was prepared to swear the animal was, too. Sultan had edged beside Shane to rub his muscular shoulder against his master's hip and nuzzle his sleek head against Shane's arm like a puppy begging to be petted.

"So you had no desire to join the Army, did you?" Shane chuckled at the steed.

Sultan nickered, as if he understood what Shane had said to him in the Apache tongue. Calera wouldn't have doubted if Sultan actually did. And for several moments she wondered if Shane remembered she was waiting in the distance. He was completely preoccupied with brushing down the stallion, as if it was a part of a daily ritual. Shane murmured in his native tongue and Sultan nickered while he stood patiently beneath his master's ministrations.

When Calera ambled over to sit down on a chair-size boulder, Sultan pricked up his ears and glanced toward her. It was only then that Shane seemed to recall that she was on the same planet with him. She was playing second fiddle to a horse. How flattering!

"Come here, Irish. I want you to meet Sultan."

"I doubt he cares to meet me," she replied, massaging her throbbing arm and fighting the feeling of lightheadedness that had suddenly overcome her. "Sultan seems to have an aversion to all humans but you."

"He is especially fond of females."

"Ones of his own species, no doubt," she specified.

"True, he does have a noticeable weakness for mares."

When Shane ambled toward Calera, Sultan followed behind him. That seemed an impressive feat in itself, considering the stallion's feisty temperament. To Calera's astonishment, Shane snapped his fingers and Sultan got down on his knees in front of her like a knight paying respects to his queen.

"A very impressive trick," she complimented, hesitantly reaching out to brush her hand over Sultan's forelock.

"It isn't a trick," Shane contradicted. "There are times when a man can be pinned down by injury or gunfire and it is safer for his mount to come to him. By clinging to the side of your horse, you can thunder off without being detected. *This* is a trick."

When Shane gave two sharp whistles, Sultan rolled onto his back, hooves and head up.

"Sultan likes to play dead," Shane said with a grin.

"What else does this phenomenal creature do?"

Shane clapped his hands and the steed gathered his legs beneath him. "Sultan runs with his heart. When I ask for all he has to give, he complies." He spoke again in the Apache tongue and the steed ambled off to graze, but not before pausing beside Shane, awaiting an affectionate pat. "No man can be blessed with a greater friend than he who will sacrifice everything without expecting anything in return."

"My brother has done that for me," Calera said softly. "If not for him, I would not be what I am today—"

When the piebald gelding's shrill whinny pierced the air, Calera's words died into silence. Before she could blink, Shane wheeled around, calling to his stallion. Calera watched Shane grasp the stallion's mane and bound upward in one fluid motion. Like a graceful centaur he galloped toward the piebald gelding.

Calera circled the ledge that dropped to the valley below to view the scene that unfolded beneath her. A pack of wolves had surrounded the gelding that had been tethered to a tree. The piebald turned tail and kicked, but the pack continued to close in . . . until thundering hooves caught their attention.

Calera sat down before she fell down. The display of skillful horsemanship she observed in the next few minutes reminded her of the hand-to-hand combat Shane had withstood against the Tonto braves. From her vantage point on the cliff, she watched the blood-red stallion plunge into the melee with a vengeance. The wolves yelped and scattered when they collided with the deadly hooves. Amid terrified whimpers and injured howls, Shane swept down, clinging to Sultan with one arm and a leg hooked over his back. Dagger poised, Shane struck like a shadowed demon. The attack was so fierce and intense that the wolves retreated—those that had not fallen beneath hooves and the blade.

Shane steered the stallion over to untie the rope and led the gelding away. Calera giggled to herself when Sultan pranced and tossed his head. He was showing off, assuring the gelding who was boss. As if there was any question, thought Calera. Sultan's superiority went without saying.

After Shane set both steeds free to graze, he ambled toward Calera. She peered up at him and found herself suffering the worst case of hero worship imaginable. This wild Apache knight had become her icon, her dream come true. Her footsteps automatically took her toward him, even though she was still feeling a mite lightheaded. First a walk and then a run, until she had leaped into Shane's arms and planted a zealous kiss in the middle of his amused grin.

"What did I do to deserve that, Irish?" he asked, molding her petite body familiarly against his.

"I swear, Apache, every time I see you in action, it sends the oddest kind of tingles through me. You are a most remarkable man."

A rumbling purr reverberated in his chest as he sought her dewy-soft lips and made a meal of them. Ah, how quickly this lively nymph could take control of his mind and leave him to burn with the want of her. The fact that he had impressed her filled him with a rewarding sense of accomplishment. He had somehow earned Calera's respect.

Until there was Calera, Shane hadn't given a damn what anyone thought of him because he had so little respect for the whites he had known. But what this green-eyed leprechaun thought of him had begun to matter, to influence his thinking and his actions. She mattered way too much, in fact.

"If you keep dishing out those compliments, you are going to get far more than *gratitude* from me," he assured her with a roguish grin.

Calera flashed him an impish smile. "Mmm . . . I was hoping you would say something like that, Apache . . ."

Shortly thereafter, Calera made Shane *immensely* happy.

Chapter Ten

"Why didn't you tell me you tore open your wound," Shane scolded Calera, jolting her awake at the break of dawn.

Shane unwrapped the blood-soaked bandage and grimaced at the angry red wound and seeping infection. Stark naked, he rolled to his feet to fetch the poultice he had concocted a few days earlier.

Calera raked the tangles from her hair and propped herself up, wincing at the stab of pain in her shoulder. The world teetered sideways, and Calera lay back down to battle the dizziness that swirled around her. When she glanced up to see Shane approaching with the poultice in one hand and the dagger in the other, she strangled on her breath.

"Dear God! What are you going to do!"

"What I should have done that first night," he said grimly. "I had hoped it would not come to this, but now I have no choice."

Calera's alarmed gaze leaped from the unsightly wound to the long-bladed knife. "You aren't going to cut off my arm, are you?"

Shane set his medical supplies aside and fastened the breech-cloth around him. Without another word he hurried off to gather twigs for a small fire.

"Well, *are* you?" she demanded to know the very second he returned.

Shane placed a ring of stones around the fire and then thrust a small bottle of whiskey at her. "Drink this, Irish."

"I never touch the stuff."

"You will today," he insisted in a no-nonsense tone. "And you'll drink plenty of it."

The somber expression on his bronzed features warned Calera not to quibble over her aversion to foul-tasting liquor. A teetotaler, Calera was not prepared for the first swallow that set her throat on fire and burned holes in her empty stomach. She sputtered and wheezed to catch her breath, feeling sicker by the second.

Shane whacked her between the shoulder blades and then thrust the bottle to her lips. "More."

Calera swallowed, coughed, and sucked in her breath when the fiery liquid scorched her tongue and put tears in her eyes. "More."

"Damn it, Apache. You are a harsh taskmaster," she croaked before he shoved another drink down her scalded throat.

Calera didn't know how many gulps of liquor she had been forced to ingest before she had satisfied her self-appointed physician. But by the time Shane decided she had consumed enough whiskey to serve as an anesthetic, Calera's vision was fuzzy, her nose tingled, and her head felt as if it were full of wool.

Shane arose from his crouch to fetch a green twig and ordered Calera to bite down on it. When he dribbled whiskey on the festering wound, she nearly came apart at the seams. Shane cursed, removed the twig from her lips, and thrust the bottle at her again.

"Drink up, Irish, and don't stop until you can see two of me."

Calera tried to obey—she really did—but the shooting fire in her shoulder left her trembling uncontrollably. She felt as if she had stabbed her arm into the campfire. Years earlier, she had burned her hand on Aunt Myrna's cooking stove and it had throbbed for days. But it was nothing compared to the pulsating agony caused by the whiskey on her tender wound!

"Now how many of me do you see?" he questioned, rocking back on his haunches.

"You . . . who?" Calera slurred out.

A reluctant smile pursed his lips. Calera was exceedingly sluggish of movement and speech. Her red-gold hair was a wild tangle around her waxen face, making her eyes appear like emeralds floating on fresh cream. This leprechaun was not only drunk, but she was also in very serious condition. Shane cursed himself for being so distracted by his uncontrollable passions and his compelling need to retrieve Sultan. He should have paid more attention to this festering wound. Now what had to be done could not be avoided. He had not wanted to leave an unsightly scar on Calera's flawless skin unless absolutely necessary. Now he had no option left. If gangrene set in—and there was a strong possibility it would—Calera would lose her arm. The very thought unhinged him.

"Listen to me very carefully, Irish," Shane demanded.

Droopy lashes fluttered shut and Shane snapped his fingers in front of her face. Sultan, who grazed a short distance away, dropped to his knees. Muttering, Shane gave two sharp whistles and the steed returned to his feet. "Calera, pay attention. This is important."

Her eyes flicked open to see two magnificent warriors hovering over her. "Hello, *Si-ha-ney Das-ay-go,*" she mumbled groggily. "Which one of you is really you?"

Assured that Calera had ingested a sufficient amount of liquor, Shane focused on the grim task at hand. "Very soon, you are going to want to fight me, to escape the pain," Shane blared at her as if she were deaf. "You must focus on my eyes until you can see so deeply into me that you have shed the confines of your own flesh. Do you understand, Irish?"

Calera blinked heavily-lidded eyes, trying valiantly to comprehend the words that came to her through an echoing tunnel.

"Last night I taught you to see without your eyes. Now you must learn to transcend the pain until your mind is no longer a part of your body. It is a warrior's training *not* to feel, *not* to surrender."

She nodded tipsily. "More Apache magic . . ."

Shane slid the twig between her lips and pushed her shirt aside. "Concentrate only on my face," he instructed. "Look only into my eyes. Nowhere else." His muscular body settled upon hers. He braced both knees on her forearms, then scooted his hips over hers so she couldn't buck and writhe and fling him off balance during that critical moment.

Leaning sideways, Shane grabbed the knife he had been heating over the fire. He felt his belly twist into a tight knot and his hand tremble as he held the glowing dagger over the unsightly wound. Gritting his teeth, he laid the blade against her flesh.

Calera reacted instantaneously to the scent of seared skin and white-hot pain that exceeded anything she had ever experienced. Even the drugging effects of whiskey couldn't diminish the sickening sensations that burned through her. Calera screamed bloody murder, despite the twig that was clamped between her teeth.

"Look at me!" Shane snapped harshly, tormented to no end by the spasms of pain that claimed her ashen features. "Concentrate, damn you."

Squiggles of tears streamed down her cheeks, but she peered into his solemn face and focused on those black diamond eyes that marched before her—two by two. Calera desperately wanted to reach outside herself as Shane had demanded. But it was difficult not to become distracted by pain so intense that it stole her breath and her strength.

The second time he laid the glowing dagger to her shoulder, a bloodcurdling scream gurgled in her throat and she bit down hard on the twig. She tried to focus on Shane's obsidian eyes, but the blur of tears and nausea made the task impossible. Her body shuddered as she instinctively tried to launch herself away from the agonizing pain. She heard Shane's curses flying, felt his muscular weight bearing down on her, cutting off the circulation in her arms that felt as if they had ice water flowing through them.

Shane was still cursing a blue streak when he leaned over to re-heat the knife. He needed Calera's full cooperation to finish this, but watching her face turn another shade of pale was killing him by inches. Yet, there was more to be done before he had burned out the infection and cauterized the serrated flesh together. It would be a blessing to both of them if Calera would simply pass out, but she had not reached that level of excruciating pain yet, even if she was prepared to swear she had.

With grim determination, Shane cupped Calera's chin, tilting her face upward, watching her breasts heave as she panted to breathe. "It is crucial that you remain perfectly still and focus on my face, Irish. Must I tie you down?"

"No," she whispered brokenly.

Calera blinked, her eyes awash with tears. She fixed her gaze on Shane's craggy features and peered into eyes as dark as midnight. He was staring intently at her, calling out to her in the silence. She looked deeply, drawing herself into him, seeking solace in his strength, absorbing the energy that radiated from him.

Shane never glanced away from her as he extended his arm to grasp the glowing dagger. He did not speak to shatter the hypnotic spell. He called upon the Apache spirits as his forefathers had always done. To *believe* was to command the omnipotent powers of *Usen* and Earth Mother. Shane would *make* Calera believe in the powerful forces that controlled mind over matter.

This time, when Shane cauterized the wound with flaming steel, Calera froze in midbreath. She stared up at Shane until she became only the reflection in his eyes. She had escaped the pain, feeding on faith, relying upon trust until the unbearable pain crippled her body and her mind. Thankfully, she slipped into unconsciousness, consumed by the abyss that had once been the black diamonds of his eyes.

Shane inhaled a fortifying breath and completed the worst of the task. After he cleansed the wound and applied a poultice, he stepped back to study the lifeless beauty whose wild cascade of hair formed a glistening pool of lava around her pale face. Now the aftereffects of the whiskey would induce sleep and dull the ache in her shoulder.

While she lay oblivious to the world, Shane strode off to

gather herbs and hunt game. Calera needed the Apache's potion to counter the poison that had spread through her bloodstream and she needed food to generate her strength.

Casting a glance skyward, Shane quickened his step. The scent of rain saturated the air. He would have to transport Calera to shelter so she could recuperate. The location Shane had in mind was a good distance away, but it could be reached before Calera roused.

Shane quickly saw to his task of gathering herbs and berries and returned to camp. Swinging the limp bundle into his arms, he called to Sultan. With a snap of Shane's fingers, Sultan came to his knees and Shane slid onto the steed's back. Cradling Calera in front of him with her head nestled in the crook of his arm, Shane urged Sultan into a walk.

The sound of distant thunder prompted Shane to set a faster pace. The last thing he wanted was for Calera to suffer complications from exposure to inclement weather while she was battling fever and a serious infection. It was bad enough that this spirited beauty lay in his arms like a rag doll. The thought of losing her completely was intolerable. Shane didn't even want to consider a world without her in it.

Forcing that bleak thought aside, Shane stared at the bald granite peaks that jutted above the timber line. He would brew whatever Apache magic necessary to ensure Calera lived to smile at him again. He would not have their paradise shattered with grief and that was that! This bewitching Irish rose was his only touch with happiness and contentment.

Thunder rolled and lightning illuminated the night sky. Rain tumbled from the overhanging stone ledge that protected the crumbling adobe ruins from the cloudburst. Shane sat at Calera's feet, watching her stir to the orchestrated drumroll of the storm that turned creeks into raging floods and gullies into roaring rivers.

Another boom of thunder brought Calera from the depths of slumber. For a moment she swore the fierce vibrations had been caused by the throb in her head. But once she got her bearings—to some small degree—she was able to differentiate between the thud of her amplified pulse and the clash of thunder.

"Dear God . . ." Calera said on a tremulous sigh.

"No, Irish, it's only me," Shane whispered as he sank down to brush his lips over her feverish brow. He levered her up to offer her a sip of water.

"Please, no more whiskey," she rasped.

"It's water," he assured her. "I also mixed a potion of herbs for you to eat."

"Not hungry." Indeed, her stomach pitched and rolled like a ship tossed on angry waves.

"You'll eat and like it all the same," he insisted, grabbing a second tin cup.

Calera made an awful face when Shane shoved the foul-tasting potion in her mouth. She shivered repulsively and swallowed, but there was no relief forthcoming. Shane stuffed another spoonful in her mouth.

"I think dying would be a more pleasant alternative to poisoning," she choked out.

Shane bit back a grin and allowed Calera to wash down the pasty potion with the tea he had brewed. "The Apaches swear by these remedies," he informed her. "A potion of Pennyroyal and violet leaves mixed with wild peppermint will cure the chills. The boiled Poplar bark and Willow leaves battle the fever."

"Dear God . . ." she groaned at the thought of what he was going to force down her throat.

"These natural potions have been passed down through generations," he assured her.

"I don't know how that could be possible when all previous generations must have died from these horrid remedies—"

Shane spooned more potion into her opened mouth and chased it with tea. "Trust me, Irish. You will survive the ailments *and* the remedies."

Speaking and swallowing seemed to demand incredible energy, more than Calera could muster. She had exhausted her strength.

"I trust you, Apache," she confided before her lashes fluttered against her pale cheeks like butterflies settling upon a rose petal.

Shane gathered his potion and sank back to watch Calera slip into the compelling arms of slumber. She looked so weak and vulnerable, like a fragile fairy that had been stripped of her magical powers. Pensively, Shane glanced from his patient to the torrents of rain that poured off the ledge above the cavern. He was becoming far too attached to this emerald-eyed nymph. That could breed disaster for both of them.

He and this beguiling beauty would have to part company as soon as she recovered. The longer he kept Calera in the wilderness with him, the more attached he would become. This fantasy had to come to an end, even if the sweet memories lived forever in his mind. Shane had known from the first moment he had dared to touch Calera that he would come to regret it. Yet, she had bewitched him, triggered emotions that had been long dead and buried, and were better left alone.

After his infuriating encounters with Keery O'Connell, Shane had grasped at pleasure—no matter how hopeless or fleeting it might be. He had needed to live this fantasy, needed the reassurance that there were moments of heaven in the hell his life had become. But letting go of such contentment would be difficult because Calera had become a habit he didn't want to break.

Shane's dark eyes swung back to the shapely form beside him. He bent over Calera, pressing a kiss to her ashen lips. Even in sleep, Calera automatically responded to him. A soft sigh tumbled forth and Shane smiled, remembering each moment he had spent in her silky arms. Ah, if only he *could* hold her forever, ignoring life below these mountains. But Shane had learned to deal with reality long ago. He had to make preparations to return Calera to her own world.

No doubt, there were those who were concerned about her. As soon as she could travel, he had to take her back to the stage station and send her on her way. He could not ask her to share his life with him since he could barely endure it himself. No, this lovely woman deserved more than Shane could give her.

With her beauty, intellect, and rambunctious spirit, she was destined for better things than to be tied to a half-breed who was tolerated by some and shunned by most. The greatest favor he could do for Calera was to let her go back where she belonged, to end this whimsical fantasy before it became such an obsession that he *couldn't* let go!

For two days, Calera drifted in and out of consciousness, fighting the infection that sapped her strength. Each time she roused, Shane was there, whispering words of encouragement, cleansing the wound, applying fresh salves, and force-feeding her.

The second time Shane informed her that he would have to sear the infected area, Calera had nodded resolutely and gulped down the whiskey he pressed to her lips. Without further instruction, Calera peered up into his eyes and never blinked when he laid the glowing blade to the wound. She had placed herself in his hands, depending on him to provide the strength of spirit she needed.

It was that courageous, unfailing stare that went through Shane like a lightning bolt. No one had ever looked up at him quite like that. No woman had ever aroused the sensations that this lovely nymph had. And ironically, in that instant when Calera rose above the physical pain he had inflicted upon her to seek solace through him, Shane experienced the worst kind of hell he had ever known. He felt like one of the newly-damned, craving that which he knew he could never keep—a bewitching pixie whom he could never truly call his own.

In those following hours, while Calera recuperated from her latest bout with infection, Shane wandered the mountain wilderness, wishing he was not the man he was—a loner with each foot heavily entrenched in two contrasting societies. He had nothing to offer a gently-bred young woman like Calera. He would *never ever* wish the anguish he endured on another living soul, *especially* not this enchanting elf.

In those moments of frustration, Shane cursed Calera for making him so vulnerable to emotions he had vowed never to feel again. And yet, in the same breath, he thanked the powers above that he had been granted at least one glimpse of heaven before he returned to his own private hell . . .

Chapter Eleven

"Apache . . . ?"

Through the darkness Shane heard the hoarse sound of his nickname drifting down from the ancient ruins. He jogged up the pebbled path to find Calera braced against the stone wall, her glorious hair feathering around her face as if an unseen hand had lifted the ringlets to test their silky texture. The greeting smile that curved Calera's lips melted Shane into mush. He had never laid eyes on a woman who stirred him to such extremes, never wanted a woman the way he desired this vulnerable beauty.

"I thought you had deserted me," she whispered.

Calera outstretched her good arm and Shane was beside her in less than a heartbeat, scooping her up to cuddle her protectively against him. His lips grazed her forehead as she pressed herself to him in a response as natural to her as breathing. To his relief, the fever had broken. That was an encouraging sign. Calera was on the road to recovery.

"Were you planning to?" she murmured against his cheek.

Shane frowned as he carried Calera down the moonlit path. "Was I planning to *what*, Irish?"

"Desert me."

A quiet rumble of laughter reverberated through his massive chest. There were a score of things Shane ached to do to this bewitching sprite. Deserting her was not one of them. "I was scouting the area for game," he informed her.

Calera laid her head against his shoulder and peered into his rugged features. A host of tender emotions bombarded her, putting words on her tongue that had echoed through her mind far too often the past week. Her sleep had constantly been interrupted by dreams that centered around this bronzed warrior—her wild Apache knight. The emotions triggered by those hypnotic dreams burst loose before Calera could even think to bite them back.

"I think I love you, Apache . . ."

Shane missed a step and glanced down into her enchanting face and expressive green eyes. Calera stared at the expanse of his chest, her fingertips measuring the width of muscular flesh. She waited apprehensively for Shane to respond. The seconds crawled by at a snail's pace. Finally, impatience got the better of her and her lashes swept up to gauge his reaction to her carelessly blurted confession.

Shane knew the greatest kindness he could show this vulnerable beauty was to let her go without promises that neither of them could keep. Hearing Calera's softly uttered words were Shane's heaven and his hell. As usual, he was trapped in between.

When Shane reached the creek that rippled like quicksilver in the starlight, he set Calera down on a boulder to peel off her oversize shirt. "The wound has begun to heal," he observed.

Perhaps the injury on her shoulder had healed, Calera mused, but the pain that just stabbed into her heart left it to bleed. She had murmured words she had never spoken to a man because she had never felt this way about anyone in her life . . .

The thought prompted Calera to peer up at Shane while he carefully divested her of her clothes, an action she made no attempt to halt. Maybe her obvious innocence of men gave Shane cause to doubt the credibility of her admission. He knew perfectly well that he was the first man she had known in the most intimate sense. He probably thought this to be some starry-eyed infatuation. Well, maybe it was and maybe it wasn't. Calera supposed she had no experience to draw upon to determine if that was so. And yet, she had a good deal more experience in judging men than most women did. She had emerged through the clumsy caterpillar stage of her life, suffering ridicule and taunts from the very same men who had bombarded her with flattery when she grew into a woman. She had learned to see men for what they were, or at least she liked to think she had.

Shane was certainly not the average man. To describe him as such was laughable. He could be as fierce as a mountain lion and every bit as deadly, but he could also be gentle and caring. He matched the untamed mountains that loomed around him. He could have been everything to Calera, if only he could have returned the affection that had blossomed in her heart.

Was it possible to make a man believe in love? she wondered. Had this brawny Apache warrior ever been in love before? Or had he taken women to appease his male needs, wanting nothing more than temporary pleasure? Maybe she wasn't such an authority on men after all. Since Shane had revealed very little about himself to her, Calera knew nothing of his past, nothing about the various influences that made him what he was.

Well, none of that mattered, Calera assured herself. She loved this Apache knight who had rescued her from certain death, battled to protect her, and saved her from fatal infection. And she would prove her love for him. Even if there was no such thing as forever for them, there was love—at least on her part.

"I see that you do not believe." Calera smiled at him as he removed the remainder of her clothes for what appeared to be a bath in the stream.

His dark eyes flooded over her, worshipping the beauty that had been revealed to no other man until he had dared to touch her. "I see that you are breathtaking, Irish." His index finger traced her petal-soft lips and then trailed down her throat to glide between her breasts. "I see a woman so rare and exquisite that she knows no equal on this earth." His hand cruised over her belly and swirled over the velvety flesh of her thigh, leaving her to tremble beneath his tender touch. "I see a woman of remarkable courage—"

"But you refuse to see that I love you." Calera accepted that reality and vowed to change his perspective. Her need to convey these newfound emotions gave her the strength that illness had stripped from her. A provocative smile twitched her lips as she reached out to limn his tanned features. "Look into my eyes, Apache," she murmured.

He did. That was his downfall. In those sparkling depths, he saw the reflection of a man who was crippled with overwhelming desire. He felt himself drawn into those emerald pools to drown without any possible hope of rescue.

"Come to me . . ." Calera whispered, just as he had whispered to her before he laid the blade to her flesh and ordered her to surpass the unbearable pain by becoming a part of him. He had demanded that Calera call upon the limitless powers of the mind, and now she employed that same Apache magic to prove the strength of her affection for him. It was not a bath that she wanted. She desired this ruggedly-handsome giant. She yearned to love him as she had loved no other.

For a woman who had not spent a lifetime cultivating the ways of the Apache, Calera had learned to summon the great powers in one phenomenal hurry! Shane could feel himself being drawn to her like a moth compelled to a flickering flame. It had been his intent to bathe Calera, to tenderly nurse her back to health and allow her to recuperate, even if his male desires gave him hell for exhibiting noble restraint. But the touch of her hand on his flesh and the look in her spellbinding eyes assured him that his resolve was no match for the power this enticing beauty held over him. She had taken possession of him and he was lost . . .

A soft sigh whispered from Calera's lips when Shane braced both arms on the boulder and slanted his mouth over hers. Her senses reeled as profound need erupted inside her. All inhibition flitted away in the breeze that swept along the channel of the creek. Calera sought to prove that even in her innocence she knew love, even in her lack of experience she could communicate the emotions Shane had instilled in her.

Perhaps Shane would never love her back, but he would know beyond all doubt that what she felt for him was real. It was she who would have to accept the fact that a man as wild and free as this Apache warrior could not love her, even if she had learned to make him desire her. But for another precious moment out of time, she would scale the mountains and touch the sun. She would know paradise.

A groan echoed in Shane's chest as he gathered Calera to him and walked into the shallows of the stream. He knelt to lay Calera in the water, watching the red-gold tendrils melt around her exquisite face, undulating in the sparkling silver ripples. When he stared down at her, his thundering heart slammed into his ribs and stuck there. Water droplets, like diamonds in the night, sparkled on her creamy skin. Her lustrous green eyes offered him the vast expanse of this starlit paradise and he accepted.

"Irish, you have bewitched me," he murmured as he lay down beside her, wondering if the water of the stream could even begin to cool the sultry flame that sizzled through him.

"Have I?" She smiled and pressed her lips to his sleek flesh. "To what extent, I wonder."

Shane was almost afraid to find out! His huge body shuddered once, twice, when her hand and lips coasted over him like moonbeams caressing the pine-covered peaks, like dew drops kissing the leaves. Calera was drawing upon his strength, regenerating it as if it were her own, feeding the fire that was dangerously close to consuming him.

Calera rediscovered the muscular columns and lean planes of his magnificent body. She tossed the breechcloth ashore when it deprived her from gazing upon every steel-honed inch of him. Her kisses and caresses cherished him, aroused him by maddening degrees. She invented new ways to excite him, to assure him that she truly cared for him. If this was to be her first taste of love, then it would fulfill every last fantasy and sustain her in the years to come. If she and her wild Apache knight could have no future, then she could close her eyes and utilize the powers of the mind to transport her back to this mountain paradise to relive this wondrous dream.

When her hand splayed across the muscles of his belly, Shane gasped for air. He was allowing this imp privileges that were sure to be the death of him. She was branding her memory on mind and body, filling him with ineffable sensations. Suddenly, Shane was no more than a shell that housed scorching needs, but when he tried to reach for Calera to return the intense pleasure that engulfed him, she stilled his restless hands and urged him to his back.

"Not yet, Apache," she murmured as her lips trailed lower, her moist tongue flicking at the velvet tip of his manhood. "For now, if never again, you will know what you do to me when you touch me so tenderly. When you melt into the heat that radiates from the stars above, you will know where I am when I'm with you."

"I'm already there," Shane croaked in a gasping breath.

"Are you?"

He not only heard her playful laughter, but he felt it drifting over his heated flesh. "Can you still see each shining star?" she purred in question.

"They're blinding me," he assured her huskily.

"Mmm . . . how interesting." She smiled against his pulsating flesh, her hand stroking him until he shuddered and groaned in unholy torment. "But a wise warrior once taught me that you have to find your way through the darkness to discover where you really are. You can't always trust your eyes to guide you. Reach deep, Apache, challenge yourself a bit more."

"Irish—" Shane struggled to breathe, battling the wild, urgent need ignited by her intimate fondling. He realized, there and then, that he had committed a grave error in encouraging this intelligent nymph to practice the ways of the Apache. She had taken his teachings and altered them to suit her purposes. He had taught her to depend on all her other senses to lead her when she couldn't see. He had taught her to escape pain by reaching beyond the limits of the flesh. And now, this imaginative siren had challenged him to reach beyond the fiery glaze that burned him alive, to experience emotions she wanted to draw from deep inside him . . .

Shane derailed from his train of thought when gentle hands

and lips skimmed his flesh, teaching him new ways to burn alive. Her honeyed lips tasted him, tortured him beyond bearing. Desire—so fierce and overwhelming that he groaned aloud—avalanched upon him.

"Come here, damn you!" Shane groaned, clutching desperately at her.

Her hand stroked and teased him until his body curled up to meet each tormentingly-delicious caress. "Damned, am I? Those were not the words I had hoped to hear, Apache."

The ornery elf! She was devastating him with her erotic seduction. She had seized control of his body like a playful little demon, making him move at her command, forcing him to battle to retain his crumbling restraint.

"Do I please you?" she whispered as she measured the length of him with the gliding caress of her tongue.

"Do you even have to ask?" he gasped.

"Do you want me?"

"Beyond reason."

Her hand enfolded him and her lips followed. "That's not enough," she insisted.

"There is no more," Shane warbled. "I swear it!"

"No more?" Her damp hair glided over the taut muscles of his belly like a provocative caress. "Are you certain?"

"I can't want you more than I do . . . and live to tell it."

By now, Shane was absolutely, positively certain that he had made a crucial mistake in teaching Calera the secrets of the Apache civilization. She was going to kill him with his own knowledge, turning the forces of natural instinct upon him. She employed his own strength and burgeoning desire to defeat him.

Shane had been conquered as he had never been before. Passion reigned supreme, governing his mind, body, and spirit. Her kisses and caresses had driven him past the point of oblivion and straight into insanity. He couldn't see; he couldn't think; he could barely survive the maelstrom of sensations that pelted him like hailstones. He was so close to convulsive release that he couldn't muster the strength to move. But he had to move. He had to! If he was not allowed to return the imitable pleasure she had bestowed on him, he would die an unfulfilled death. If his pleasure was not hers, then he would know no true satisfaction. These incredible feelings were created to be shared, not selfishly taken.

Shane snaked out a shaky hand and clasped her fingertips, drawing them to his lips, tasting his own urgent need, inhaling her alluring scent. He eased Calera to her back and crouched above her. He saw victory dancing in her emerald eyes and the reflection of his own defeat.

"Witch," he growled playfully, watching her lush lips curve into another captivating smile. "When you tamper with Apache magic, you dare too much. Now we shall see if you have acquired the powers to counteract your own potent spell."

When his dark head descended and his sensuous lips came down on hers in fierce possession, Calera didn't fight the splendorous sensations that coursed through her body. And when his tongue delved into the soft recesses of her mouth, imitating more intimate pleasures to come, she parried thrust for thrust, sharing his very breath until they merged as one.

A shuddering moan echoed in her chest when his hands blazed a scalding path over her collarbone to graze the throbbing peaks of her breasts. His fingertips whispered over her like a wizard weaving incantations, tormenting her with maddeningly-sweet sensations, evoking the responses he desired from her. With patient deliberateness he tasted her, touched her, aroused her. His hands and lips were everywhere, memorizing each ultra-sensitive place she liked to be touched, returning the pleasure—sensation for sensation—that she had given him, until fiery emotions multiplied and fed upon themselves.

Calera felt her pulse pounding in her ears as he teased her until she cried out to him to end the torment and offer fulfillment.

"Are you down to begging, Irish?" he taunted playfully, reveling in his own power to leave her defenseless.

"Yes," she answered shakily. "I want you desperately."

He raised his raven head, seeing the blatant hunger in her eyes. "And I want all of you, just as you had all of me."

When his lips glided over her abdomen and he guided her

legs apart with his elbows, Calera felt the wild tremors spiraling through her blood stream. "No!"

"Why not?" His fingertips glided lower and lower still, setting off a tidal wave of sensations that left her quaking in his arms. "Too intimate? Too daring for even this brazen witch who casts such remarkable spells?" He tested the moistness of her need for him with his finger and felt the silky heat of her response. "I gave myself up to you, as I have to no other. I want to know you as I have known no woman. I want to make love to you in every conceivable way."

The sound of his voice and the touch of his hand were her undoing. Calera could not have denied this magnificent warrior anything. And when he lifted her to him to teach her the most sensual intimacies imaginable, Calera felt herself consumed to such incredible extremes that her entire body contracted beneath the force of them. His tongue sought entrance to the soft core of her femininity and she died a slow, sweet death, knowing she could never give herself so completely to another man. The wild intimacy of the moment would be forever blazed in her memory. She shivered as he brought her to ecstasy again and again. She whispered his name as she reveled in the depths of rapture she never believed possible. They shared untold secrets, the mere memory of which could ignite the wildest flames . . .

"Oh, please . . . no . . . !"

Tears swam in her eyes as her body clenched against the holocaust of fire that knew no beginning or end. Calera shuddered convulsively as the world split asunder, leaving her oblivious and yet starkly aware, leaving her satiated and yet achingly unfulfilled. But despite the phenomenal pleasure that crested upon her, she could feel Shane's lithe body gliding the full length of her, taut and quavering with needs he had miraculously held in check while she could not. His lips feathered over hers as his masculine body molded itself to her, though he was ever mindful of her mending arm, careful not to let pain intrude where the quintessence of pleasure reigned supreme.

"Now the taste of you has become the taste of me," he whispered as he settled exactly upon her. "We *are* each other, Irish. No matter what else, we *are* each other . . ."

When he thrust deeply into her, appeasing the monstrous ache that bombarded her, Calera understood the full extent of his words. His warm, scented mouth was upon hers, devouring her with a kiss as intimate as the throbbing possession of his body. She could not tell where her body ended and his began. She melted into him, unconsciously seeking more of him until they were one in flesh, in scent, in mind, and spirit. What affected him affected her. They were the echo of each other's ardent needs, moving in an instinctive rhythm of passion as pure as the mountain air and as overpowering as a spring thunderstorm.

Calera clutched him to her, oblivious to the stinging pain in her shoulder. Her nails clenched in his back, clinging mindlessly as the world spun out of control, launching her into orbit around the sun and into eternity. And when his masculine body contracted upon hers in helpless release, she felt herself letting go in ways she never had before. She was free-falling through time and space while the spasms of ecstasy shook the very depths of her soul.

She loved this man with every part of her being. He knew her as she had only begun to know herself, and she knew him as she wanted to know no other man. This was the way love should be, Calera assured herself. This kind of love knew no boundaries. The emotions were so fierce that they transcended all realms to create a world of their own.

Adoringly, she reached up to comb her fingers through the midnight hair that framed his bronzed face. "I don't *think* I love you, Apache. I *know* I do."

His mouth captured hers in an exquisitely tender kiss. "And you cast a most remarkable spell," he whispered back.

"Not potent enough, it seems," she said on a sigh. "I wanted you to love me back."

"Didn't I just do that?" he asked with a wry smile.

"For then, but not for now—"

He pressed his fingertips to her lips to shush her. "For—ever . . ."

"And how long is *ever*, Apache?" Her green eyes searched deeply into his.

"*Ever* is as long as you wish it to be." Shane rolled away and sat up in the shallows, watching the stream rippling along the channel that rushing water had cut through the mountain meadow which was a riot of colorful wildflowers glowing in the moonlight. "In the seclusion of these mountains and forests, there are only the two of us, with no past or future. We have left our brand on each other." Shane smiled rakishly, indicating the claw marks on his back—ones that mingled with the scars left by a biting whip. "This wilderness left its mark on us as well." His smile faded as he stared past the mountains to the world below. "But beyond this meadow is reality, Irish. Even in the beginning I think you knew that as well as I. We let it happen, you and I. We walked away from the worlds we had known—two very different worlds. We set it all aside and defied time. We made our own space in this untamed wilderness that knows none of the cruel influences of man—"

"If you are suggesting that the combination of your white and Indian heritage makes any difference to me, you are wrong," Calera assured him. "*You* matter to me. Nothing else."

"And you matter to me." Shane did confess that much. But it would be mental suicide to embrace wistful thoughts of things that could never be. "And because you make a difference, I will let you go."

"Even if I don't wish to be set free?" she asked with her heart in her eyes.

"There is no other sensible choice." He half-turned to torment himself with the visual picture of perfection. She was a goddess, a woman so full of passion and spirit that it tore out his soul to see her hurting in any way. The pain was unbearable to him when he knew that he was the one who brought sadness to her heart when she asked what he couldn't give. "You don't belong in my world, and I have never been comfortable in yours."

"That is nonsense!" Calera felt tears burning her eyes and she swiped irritably at them. "Why don't you just admit it,

Apache? Why spare my feelings? You don't want me, except in all the usual ways any man wants to use a woman's body."

"That's not true," he vehemently denied.

"You mean you didn't really want my body, either?" Shimmering green eyes, awash with tears, peered up at him. Her kiss-swollen lips trembled in attempt to regain her composure before she reduced herself to humiliating sobs. "Did I seduce you into desiring me for the moment, just as you first seduced me into giving you the one gift I granted no other man? Is that the way of it? Was I just the challenge conquered?"

"The *last* thing I wanted to do was hurt you," he told her.

"Yes, of course," she said caustically. "Deceiving me, stealing my virginity, and humiliating me all came *first.*"

"Calera—"

"Don't Calera me!" She surged to her feet to gather her clothes—his clothes. Damnation, she didn't even have her own garments to fasten herself into. Everything was his—her heart and body included. Double damnation!! "Well fine, Apache. If it's over, then it's over. *Now* is as good a time as any to end it all, to awake from this foolish dream."

She was right, of course. Shane had wanted to delude himself for a few more days, to revel in this wondrous fantasy, to cling to the impossible. But delay would only make parting more difficult. Hadn't he known that? Hadn't he already had one or two in-depth consultations with himself on the subject? And hadn't he come to the grim conclusion that he had to send Calera back to wherever the hell she belonged so she could get on with her life while he got on with his?

"Just one more thing—" Calera secured the baggy breeches around her waist and pivoted to stare at the awesome giant, who was still lounging in the shallows like a creature of the wilds. "I have paid my debt for each time you saved my life. I gave you my innocence and you taught me passion. You also taught me to expect nothing more than that which you offer for a fleeting moment." She uplifted her chin, defying the tears that scalded her cheeks. "But believe me, I learned very young how to deal with disappointment and rejection, despite what you probably think of the *so-called* sophisticated world from which I came. And do not fret that I will let this mountain fantasy ruin my life, for it most certainly will not!''

Her delicate chin tilted a notch higher, providing Shane with an unhindered view of rebellion personified. "If you can walk away without looking back, then so can I. So there!''

Shane bit back a grin when Calera made her theatrical departure. It was most fortunate the previous rainstorm had passed. Otherwise, she would have drowned—she with her nose flung high in the air and her back as rigid as a lightning rod.

It was better this way, Shane convinced himself. Calera was using her anger and hurt as her shield. There had been a time when Shane had practiced that same policy to cope with the crises his life had become. But no longer. He simply dug another grave to bury his wounded emotion, sealing the sepulcher with the stones of indifference. What he refused to let himself feel could not injure him, just as physical pain could not destroy the mind if one chose not to let it. That was the way of The People. *Si-ha-ney Das-ay-go* was one of them, even if he had a white father who forced his son to adapt to the white man's ways. But at heart, where it truly mattered, Shane was still Apache . . .

"Well, don't just sit there dawdling." Calera stared down at him from the ledge of the ruins. "Take me back to the stage station this instant."

Shane rolled to his feet and walked ashore to scoop up his breechclout. "Coming, Irish."

Calera felt her heart tumble over the rock bluff and plummet to Shane's bare feet. She loved him; he had used her. She hated that more than anything. She hated knowing that, even when she had given all she had to give, it was not enough to reach this man who seemed determined to pack his emotions in ice. She had gazed upon this wild-hearted creature, seeing only what she had wanted to see. She had let him make love to her in every conceivable way and now the mystery and challenge were gone. Once she had allowed him the most intimate of intimacies, there was nothing left. Shane had been intrigued by her for a time, but the infatuation had died a quick death. He had been kind and compassionate when she was injured and alone in an unfamiliar world. But he ultimately got what he wanted—temporary pleasure before seeking new challenges elsewhere. Now that he had expended all the emotion he allowed himself to give during this brief tryst in the wilderness, he was anxious to return to his world.

Well, damn him to hell and back! And damn her for being such a naive fool! Ah yes, he could whisper sweet lies as well as any other man when he felt like it. He had deceived her once, hadn't he? Did she think he wouldn't do it again? Did she think that just because she had fallen hopelessly in love that she could wave her arms and make the world a perfect place, make this Apache knight learn to love her back?

Thank the Lord that Keery would be there to help Calera pick up the pieces of her shattered heart and glue them back together. She could count on her brother when she could count on no one else. She would immerse herself in work and devote her time to compensating for the sacrifices Keery had made for her. She would pledge herself to Keery and forget *Si-ha-ney Das-ay-go* ever existed. Just see if she didn't!

Calera yelped in surprise when something warm and wet nudged her from behind, very nearly toppling her off the ledge. Frantic, she wheeled around to anchor herself to the first object within reach. It was Sultan's neck. The stallion bolted back, yanking the clinging bundle with him. For a moment, Sultan stood stock still, quivering with potential energy. Calera thought she was a goner for sure when she could no longer see anything but the whites of the stallion's eyes. His nostrils flared and she felt him tense beneath her desperate grasp. If he reared up, he would catapult her over the cliff. Either that, or those deadly hooves would pound her into putty.

To her stunned amazement, the powerful steed relaxed beneath the death grip she held on his neck. His muzzle brushed against her hip and his nostrils flared again. A soft nicker filtered between his teeth as he nipped at the buckskin fabric that belonged to Shane. Calera was convinced that, if she had been wearing her own garments, she would have been dead by now.

It was Shane's scent that calmed the steed's fears and soothed his fiery disposition.

Shane remained where he was, looking up at the ledge. He had watched the scene unfold in the light of the campfire, certain he would have to call Sultan off before he knocked Calera over the ridge. Shane had seen the flash of Sultan's rounded eyes, the bunching of muscles beneath that gleaming blood-red coat. But just as suddenly, the stallion had quieted. Shane was stunned to the bone. He knew Sultan better than anyone and he also knew it was not the scent of the clothes on Calera's back that had mollified the stallion.

Sultan was too intelligent a creature to fall for that trick. Indeed, some of the wranglers at the Bar "S" Ranch had once stolen a set of Shane's clothes, thinking to earn Sultan's trust by pretending to be the half-breed. The man who had garbed himself in Shane's garments and hopped on Sultan's back had taken the ride of his life, and suffered a broken arm when the steed sent him flying.

Sultan allowed no one to touch him without his permission. He was fussy about things like that. Even Cactus and Sticker had learned to observe a respectable distance unless they wanted a battle on their hands. Lieutenant Haskell could attest to Sultan's aversion to being manhandled. But it seemed this formidable stallion had no objection to being *woman*handled. Amazing!

By the time Shane weaved along the path to reach the ruins above Cherry Creek, Sultan the Great was sentimental mush in Calera's hands. It seemed she was establishing a newfound friendship to replace the one Shane had destroyed—for her own good, even if she could not view his rejection for what it was. Calera was cooing at Sultan, who was soaking up her affection like a giant sponge. She had discovered that sensitive spot on Sultan's neck that made him arch upward and extend his head. The next thing Shane knew Sultan would probably roll on his back like a pup, begging Calera to scratch his belly. This stallion, who had earned a reputation as a four-legged devil swathed in a blood-red coat, had bowed down to a woman's sultry voice and stroking touch. Shane would have laughed at the steed-turned-to-putty, if not for the fact that *he* had suffered the same reaction to this leprechaun.

When Sultan caught Shane's scent, the steed turned his head and pricked his ears. The stallion usually met Shane halfway, but not this time. Sultan was content where he was and didn't budge an inch.

"She is ruining your bad reputation." Shane said in Apache and then clucked his tongue at Sultan.

"May I ride Sultan?" Calera asked without glancing in Shane's direction.

"That is entirely up to him."

Calera laid her hands on either side of the steed's head, nuzzling her nose against his velvet muzzle. "Would you mind so much, Sultan?"

Shane rolled his eyes in disgust when Calera snapped her fingers and the powerful steed got down on his knees. With supreme satisfaction, Calera eased a leg over the steed and grabbed his cream-colored mane to steady herself. To Shane's further disgust, both Sultan and Calera peered at him, as if to say—We no longer need you.

Well fine, Shane could deal with a traitor of a stallion and a spiteful female. Hadn't he learned to deal with everything else in life? Hadn't he survived it all? He didn't need either of them. He needed no one. He stood alone like a towering pine in the forest, enduring the storms, the pounding rain, the lightning bolts.

"If you want him, he's yours," Shane muttered before he stalked off to gather his saddlebags and fetch the piebald gelding.

"No, he is mine for a time because he thinks I am yours," Calera contradicted. "Sultan inhaled your scent in the clothes. Besides, he wouldn't fit into *my* world. He wouldn't be at home in an elegant parlor or grand ballroom, now would he?"

The sarcasm, meaningfully delivered, was well-taken. Shane definitely got the point. Calera was flinging his own words back at him, as she was so fond of doing. Ah, just what Shane needed— another reminder of Calera's keen wit. A man never realized the force and effect of his own words until they were heaped back upon him. It was not always pleasant being on both sides of one's conversations. It reminded Shane of the proverb about how it was better to give than to receive. Boy, was that statement ever true!

"I'm ready to leave," Shane announced, sitting astride the gelding.

Calera stared into the distance. "Good. I'm ready to be gone."

With the lightest touch of Calera's knees, the stallion responded. His hooves thudded in the cave as he headed toward the winding path that took him and his new mistress back to civilization.

Shane watched them disappear around a looming boulder before glancing back at the ancient ruins of his ancestors that glowed in the golden light of the campfire. The Apaches claimed the spirits of this lost civilization still lingered in the adobe fortress. Shane swore he could see the incongruous shapes in the swaying shadows, sense their supernatural presence, feel the departed spirits stealing quietly along the crumbled walls of a world that had once been and would be no more. He likened that thought to his experiences with the emerald-eyed beauty who now harbored bitterness because he had refused to offer his love. But one day, Calera would thank him for making no promises that would have to be broken. One day she would realize they didn't belong together except in a world of forbidden fantasies.

He and Calera were like the two tragic lovers in the play his father had forced him to read—in the name of providing his half-breed son with culture and an education. Well, that Shakespeare fellow had made an important point, now hadn't he? A man and woman could not fight the feuding world for love. Look how Romeo and Juliet ended up—stabbed and poisoned. Maybe Shane should remind Calera of that mournful tale.

And then again, maybe he should keep his trap shut and let Calera make the comparison herself. Smart as she was, the thought would occur to her sometime in the near future. Then she would accept this wild mountain fantasy for what it was—a space out of time that should not have been and could never come again . . .

Part Two

Gone—glimmering through the dreams of things that were.

Lord Byron—*Childe Harold*

Chapter Twelve

Calera tugged on Sultan's mane when she spied the crude stage station tucked beneath the overhanging ridge of granite. It was as if there were an invisible boundary line which she was hesitant to cross to reach the other side—to return to reality.

Although she was the first to admit she had been peevish the past few days, purposely picking fights with Shane each time they paused to rest, he had refused to pick up the gauntlet. Wounded pride and heartache had a fierce and mighty hold on Calera, but Shane exhibited very little emotion, just as he had when she first met him. He merely tolerated her verbal abuse and pointed out scenic landmarks along the route, speaking of Apache legends and beliefs to distract her from her bitterness and resentment.

Shane's courteous but standoffish behavior assured Calera that the mighty warrior had withdrawn into himself. She had become nothing more than his companion in the wilderness. When they stopped for the night at the Black Mesa ruins, Shane had bedded down a respectable distance away, approaching only to cleanse her wound and pack on more poultice.

Now they stood at their journey's end, peering at the simplistic outpost on the edge of civilization. When Shane eased the piebald up beside Sultan, Calera glanced sideways. The smile that she had come to adore was gone from Shane's craggy features. He could have been carved in bronze and she wouldn't have been surprised.

"Go back to your world, Irish." He nodded toward the adobe structure with its surrounding sheds and corrals. "Your future awaits you."

"Do not think I won't survive it, either," she replied with resentful pride.

"Do not think I doubted for a minute that you would."

Blinking back the mist of tears that glistened in her eyes, Calera allowed Shane to lift her from Sultan's back. The feel of his hands encircling her waist was tormenting pleasure. It would be the last time he ever touched her. That haunting thought squeezed life's breath out of Calera's soul.

Shane gently set Calera to her feet and handed her the pouch of coins from his saddlebag. When she bristled, intending to make an issue of the gift, as if it were payment for the pleasure provided, Shane gave his dark head a warning shake.

"Take the money in the spirit with which it is given. It will tide you over if you need it."

"I—"

Her words evaporated when Shane cupped her chin in his hand and tilted her face up to his. He leaned down to press the slightest whisper of a kiss to her lips. Despite her firm resolve, Calera felt herself melt like butter in a hot skillet. Oh, damn him! He had rejected her love and caused her to behave like a spiteful shrew, left her holding a grudge as she had never done in all her twenty years. Didn't he know she would retract every scornful word if he could only bring himself to love her? Didn't he know she longed to bask in the warmth of his smile, to revel in the sound of his bright ringing laughter?

When he withdrew into his own space, leaving her to battle aching emptiness, it felt as if he had robbed her of vital breath. Shane reached across the distance that separated them, pressing his forefinger to her quavering lips. The pad of his finger traced the heart-shaped curve of her mouth and Calera closed her eyes against the soul-wrenching shudder that ricocheted through her.

"Good-bye, Irish," he murmured huskily.

A gnawing ache coiled in the pit of her stomach when Shane stepped back apace. Calera fought the onrush of tears when her Apache knight swung onto Sultan's back and grabbed the piebald's reins. Without so much as a backward glance, he trotted away, disappearing from sight in the blinking of an eye . . . as if he had never been there at all . . .

Dear God! How she wished she had never dared to dream that wild, sweet dream. How she wished she had never opened her heart and felt it break in two!

Calera inhaled a determined breath and strode down the hill toward the stage station. *Well, Irish,* she said to herself. *You have endured plenty of anguish these twenty years. You will get over this, too.*

On that resolute thought, Calera walked back to reality, leaving her mountain fantasy behind.

The instant Calera ambled into the stage station, the attendant dropped the skillet he had been holding. It hit the stove with a clank.

"Miss O'Connell?" Jed Warren crowed in disbelief.

There was no question as to *who* this woman was, not with that halo of curly red-gold hair and that enchanting face. Jed had seen Calera dragged away by the renegade Indians so he knew for sure *who* she was. *How* she survived the ordeal was what had him staring incredulously at the fetching young woman dressed in oversized men's clothes.

". . . Or is it missus?" he asked after a dazed moment. "We didn't know for certain . . . God-a-mercy! How did you survive a week in that forsaken wilderness?"

Calera had no wish to disclose the details of her ordeal. "When will the next stage to Globe City be arriving?" she inquired.

Hot lard crackled in the heating skillet. Jed absently tossed in the sliced potatoes and dried meat. "You're in luck, Miss . . . er . . . Mrs. O'Connell. The stage is due in here in two hours. You seem to have good fortune riding with you."

That was debatable, thought Calera. She didn't feel lucky. She felt as if someone had trounced all over her heart—because somebody definitely had!

"We didn't know what to do about your luggage so we left it here after the attack last week. Your satchels and trunks are in the back room. If you want to refresh yourself, feel free to use my room." Jed smiled, displaying a missing front tooth. "I'm sure glad to see that you're all right, ma'am."

"Thank you." Calera headed for the bedroom to don her own clothes. The symbolic gesture of doffing Shane's garments would rid her of every last remnant of that wild Apache and his tormenting memory—she hoped!

Calera was amused by Jed's attempt to pry information from her while he prepared the meal for the arriving passengers. Jed, who was thirtyish, had a penchant for yammering. He obviously spent a great deal of time alone and relished the opportunity of engaging in conversation. After he had given an account—in long-winded detail—of the soldiers scouring the wilderness without meeting with the slightest success, he tried to lure Calera into revealing what happened next. Calera avoided the subject by inquiring about Horace Baxter, Ike Fuller, and Grady Flax who had accompanied her on her journey.

When Jed realized Calera had no intention of revealing the details, he abandoned his interrogation. For that, Calera was eternally thankful. Jed then provided a welcomed distraction by reciting the chronicles of his wayward youth and his adventures during his quest for gold in the Southwest.

"I finally decided to settle down after I met up with a grizzly in the Rockies," Jed said, handing Calera a cup of coffee that was as thick as axle grease and tasted the same. "That mangy beast liked to tore my leg plumb off with one swipe of his paw. After that, I went looking for a job with a steady salary. Sometimes it gets a mite lonely out here, and there's always a threat of Injuns, but I manage—"

A bugle sounded in the distance. Jed heaved himself out of his chair and limped toward the door. "Excuse me, ma'am. I have to harness the fresh team of horses. Just make yourself to home 'til I get back."

When the stage arrived, the driver and guard were as astounded to see Calera as Jed had been. They pumped her for information and received nothing for their efforts. Calera was as close-mouthed as a clam. She continued that policy after she boarded the stage to continue where her journey had left off over a week earlier.

Her two traveling companions were not the kind of individuals Calera preferred to associate with. Marsh Layton was dressed like a gambler and toted a well-used pistol. Calera imagined Marsh was the type of rascal who followed the trail of mining camps to reap whatever profits were to be had from prospectors. Marsh was undeniably attractive, with his sandy blond hair and crystal blue eyes—ones that leaped in Calera's direction many a time. When Calera made a spectacular display of ignoring him, Marsh occupied his time by shuffling the deck of cards he retrieved from his red silk vest.

When Marsh tried to lure her into conversation, Calera remained distant and remote in her corner of the coach. She was not in the mood for idle chatter, not while she was wallowing in self-pity and brooding over the sweet taste of first love that had turned sour. In short, Marsh Layton didn't have a chance to woo her with his charming smiles. She had sworn off of men forever more.

The other man who sat across from Calera was a beady-eyed little character who was plagued with the most annoying habit of chewing on his upper lip and stroking the bristly moustache that hung above it. Neither of the men could begin to compare to Shane—

Calera chopped off the betraying thought and absently

rubbed her mending shoulder. She was *not* going to give that Apache another thought as long as she lived. She was on her way to Globe City to be reunited with her brother. She was going to begin her new life in Arizona and that was that.

Resolved to that purpose, Calera propped herself against the door and drifted off to sleep. She didn't care if she slept until the stage rolled into Globe. And furthermore, if the good Lord could see His way clear to omit the next two days of traveling from His calendar, Calera would appreciate it. And He could strike the previous week from the annals of history while He was at it. Calera just wanted to forget how shamelessly she had responded to a man for the first—and the last—time in her life. She would never *ever* leave herself vulnerable again.

Dear God! The things she had said and done. Perhaps that was what had repelled What's-His-Name. She had become such an easy conquest that Someone-Or-Other had quickly tired of her. And dear God, if it wasn't for the fact that her beloved brother awaited her at the end of this washboarded road, Calera wasn't sure she could face her future. The thought of Keery was all that kept her spirits from scraping rock bottom. Thank the Lord for Keery!

Calera made the last stage connection early Monday morning, acquiring a new coach and another driver for her descent through the Pinal Mountains to the valley in which the community of Globe City was situated. With high expectations, she craned her neck to catch her first glimpse of her new home.

Calera had taken time to change into the finest gown she owned—with the exception of the brown velvet traveling habit that had suffered irreparable damage during her ordeal in the wilderness. She wanted to look her best when she surprised Keery.

The instant the stage ground to a halt, Calera bounded down without awaiting assistance. Her gaze swept from one end of the primitive community to the other. The Cottage was obviously at the far end of town, and Calera was in for a long walk, laden down with luggage. Not to be discouraged, and fiercely determined to get on with her life, Calera gathered her belongings and marched off.

"May I be of help, ma'am?" Marsh Layton drawled as he hurried to catch up with Calera.

Calera was overly anxious to be reunited with her brother, and she accepted the gambler's assistance. Although she did not approve of Marsh's profession, he had behaved quite respectably after those first few speculative glances cast in her direction.

"Thank you. I could use an extra hand." Calera dropped several satchels and the trunk, which he accepted good-naturedly.

"I wanted to take the opportunity to apologize for . . . well . . ." Marsh flashed her a disarming smile. "For staring in your direction more often than you seemed to prefer. You are a very lovely woman. There was no insult intended, only rapt admiration."

"Apology accepted." Calera hiked down the boardwalk, counting the excessive number of saloons that lined the street. She could see why this town would be a gambler's haven. A man could play poker day and night and never have to frequent the same spot twice.

When Calera sailed past the finest hotel Globe had to offer, Marsh frowned curiously. "Would you mind telling me where you're going? The accommodations in Globe City get no better than this, or so I have been told. Or do you plan to stay with friends or relatives?"

Calera glanced distastefully at the clapboard building. Surely Keery's hotel was more elegant than the modest establishment than had been recommended to Marsh Layton. Keery had said The Cottage was the finest in the community.

"I'm moving into The Cottage," she informed her companion.

Marsh did a double take. "The Cottage?" That particular establishment had also been recommended to him. He could not imagine why such an aristocratic beauty would be interested in setting herself up in a brothel. But then, who was he to argue with his good fortune? Marsh was eager to schedule himself as this lovely courtesan's first customer.

"Yes, The Cottage," Calera confirmed. She could not fathom why this rake was smiling at her in *that* way again, especially after he had apologized for ogling her on the stage. "Is there something wrong, Mister Layton?"

"No." His smile widened as he fell into step beside her. "But since we are on the subject of The Cottage, I would like to set up my appointment at your earliest convenience. In fact, I would prefer to be your *only* client." He waggled his eyebrows at her.

My, what a strange man, thought Calera. "An appointment for what?"

She looked so blithely unaware of what he implied that Marsh stopped short and peered down at her from his advantageous height. "If we are not speaking of the same *Cottage* in which you are planning to set up business, I am going to be apologizing all over the place again."

"Is there more than one *The Cottage* in Globe City?" she inquired.

"Not that I know of."

"Then whatever are you talking about, Mister Layton?"

"Marsh."

"Very well, Marsh," she accommodated. "What are you suggesting?"

His full lips pursed in a grin as he leaned down to convey the information in a quiet voice. "The Cottage is a first-class brothel."

Calera was so shocked by the announcement that she lost her grasp on her satchels. They plunked at her feet. She stared goggle-eyed at her companion, who could not contain his chuckle of amusement.

"Obviously, I *do* owe you another apology."

Calera was so unhinged that her mouth opened and shut like a drawer. "A-a . . . b-bro . . . ?" she croaked.

"Mmm . . . yes, I'm afraid so."

Marsh grinned again. He had a nice smile—for a gambling man.

"Someone must have decided to play an ornery prank on you by recommending you to the place," he speculated.

In light of the startling information, Calera decided it best to veer into the hotel to seek accommodations. She was definitely *not* going to take up residence in The Cottage! But she *was* going to give Keery a piece of her mind when she got hold of him.

How dare he lie to her! And how dare he establish a bordello of all things! Why, their parents would roll over in their graves if they knew. Dear God! They probably knew and already had! How could Keery shame himself so? He had been raised better than that.

Calera found herself the recipient of fawning attention when she announced to the proprietor of the hotel that she would like a room indefinitely and penned her name to the register.

"Miss O'Connell?" the clerk chirped, his wide-eyed gaze running full length of her.

"Yes." Calera frowned, bemused. "Is something the matter, sir?"

The middle-aged man snapped his eyes back to Calera's face. "No, ma'am. Well . . . yes, ma'am. One of the passengers on last week's stage—Horace Baxter is his name—informed us that you had been abducted by renegades and we thought—" He shifted uncomfortably beneath her penetrating stare. "We had given up hope of your rescue. I'm relieved to see you are in such . . . um . . . good condition after your horrifying ordeal and I'm sorry about—"

"Thank you for your concern," Calera cut in, but the proprietor seemed determined to pour out his compassion. For what? She couldn't imagine.

"I'm really sorry. This past week must have been a most unbearable experience. Tragic, in fact. You have my utmost sympathy."

Calera accepted his gushing condolences with a faint smile and then trudged up the steps to her room.

"I rented the room next to yours," Marsh informed her. "In case you need my assistance, I will be a door away."

"You are very kind, sir—" When he arched a thick blond brow in disapproval, Calera amended, "Marsh."

"That's better." Another engaging smile curved the corners of his full mouth upward. "After all, we will be neighbors. Out West, we quickly dispense with formality, *Cali.*"

After Calera had unpacked her luggage and shook out her gowns to hang in the wardrobe closet, she returned to the hall to find Marsh waiting for her.

"I thought we might share our first meal in town. The food at the stage stations left a lot to be desired."

Did they ever! "Thank you, but I have business at The Cottage," Calera explained with an embarrassed blush.

Marsh grinned. "Applying for a position now, are you?"

Calera's back stiffened, as if her vertebrae had been fused together. Her Irish temper was on the verge of bursting loose. Before that happened, Marsh clamped hold of her arm and shepherded her toward the steps.

"I am only teasing you, of course. Or perhaps it is only wishful thinking on my part." He slanted her a wry glance. "You know I find you extremely attractive, Cali."

"And I find you to be a hopeless rake, sir—Marsh."

"Sir Marsh." He nodded thoughtfully. "I rather like the sound of that title. It makes me feel damned . . . darned respectable."

Calera shook her head in resignation. "You are incorrigible and completely *impossible.*"

"No, my dear lady, I am within *easy* reach," he said, suddenly serious. "All you have to do is say the word."

She inhaled a weary sigh and stared up into the sky-blue eyes that offered intimate promises. "Sir—Marsh, I think you should know—"

"There's someone else," he finished, deflated. "Just my luck. I have a knack with cards, but never with beautiful women who seem determined to judge me solely upon my profession."

Calera stared meditatively at the gambler. Odd, there was a time not so long ago that her innocence of men made her wary of the male half of the population. She had isolated herself until that handsome half-breed came along to turn her heart inside out. Shane had walked out of her life and shooed her on her way. She owed his memory nothing. If she decided to accept the attention of another man, then it was her prerogative. And maybe she preferred tall, blue-eyed rogues to powerfully-built, midnight-haired renegades like Shane.

And just maybe, if she made a conscious effort, Shane's memory wouldn't continue to haunt her. Perhaps she did need the distraction of another man. Calera decided to test that theory and see how it worked. She definitely needed someone to preoccupy her thoughts and her time.

It was also for certain that she was going to need alternative companionship since she was annoyed with her brother for misrepresenting his line of business and outright lying to her. Calera had no intention of allowing Keery to return to her good graces until after he apologized all over himself for prevaricating about the source of his newfound wealth and explained why he had stooped to investing in a cursed brothel!

"No, Sir Marsh, there is no one else," Calera belatedly informed him. "And if I have prejudged you because of your profession, I am dreadfully sorry. What a man is on the inside is what counts. I have learned that covers of books are not the true measure of the contents. Thus far, you have conducted yourself like a gentleman. Unless you behave in an offensive fashion which alters that opinion, I will continue to hold you in high esteem."

Eyes twinkling, Marsh dropped into a courtly bow and pressed a kiss to her wrist. "I am deeply honored, Lady Calera. I may be prone to teasing, but I do have the utmost regard for you. I am bewitched by your wit and your beauty and—" He rose to full stature to edge a fraction closer. "And I feel it only fair to warn you that I also have the most outrageous urge to kiss you right where you stand."

The man had an engaging sense of humor that Calera found she desperately needed at the moment. She smiled impishly before she stepped out of his reach and continued on her way.

"Then I shall remember not to venture too close, Sir Marsh. I would be chagrined if I were the one responsible for destroying a paragon of gentlemanly behavior."

Marsh paced off two steps at a time to catch up with Calera. "Just how good do I have to be to win your favor, Lady Calera?" he asked with a teasing grin.

"Are you in line for sainthood?" she playfully flung back.

"No, I'm sorry to say, I have never been within shouting distance."

"At least you are honest. That is a point in your favor."

"You prefer honesty, do you?"

"At all times," she assured him.

"Then you should know that I could easily fall in love with you if you let me."

Calera peered up at him from beneath a fringe of thick curly lashes. "And if I don't *let* you, what then?"

Marsh reached out to trail his forefinger over the delicate curve of her jaw, testing the creamy texture of her skin. "My dear lady, to be honest, I don't think it would make any difference if you encouraged me or not. As I said, I am bewitched."

"You also have a definite way with women," Calera noted, eying him in accusing consternation. "I suspect it was acquired from years of practice in the romantic arts. Just how long is the chain of broken hearts that you wear around your neck, Sir Marsh?"

Marsh Layton was becoming more captivated by the minute. He had known his fair share of coy maidens in Texas and plenty of rollicking calico queens in five territories, but he had never met a woman like Calera O'Connell. She seemed unimpressed by her own ravishing good looks, and she resented being judged by her outward appearance. But nonetheless, she intrigued him. She possessed a depth of character few women attained, and her companionship was delightfully entertaining. She made Marsh hunger for more than temporary satisfaction.

"Calera, when I stare into those lovely green eyes, I cannot remember any other woman but you," he murmured.

She flashed him a dubious frown. "I thought we just established the fact that I resent idle flattery and prefer the truth."

"I am being honest," he said with all sincerity.

"Then you must have, by nature, a very short memory."

With that, Calera breezed out the door, headed for The Cottage to confront her brother. Marsh was one step behind her.

"Do you mind if I ask what business you have in the town's
most noted brothel?"

"I wish I had no business there at all," Calera muttered. "The
painful truth is that my brother owns it. Unfortunately, he led
me to believe he had purchased a fashionable hotel. And unless
you wish to be on hand to hear the insults I intend to fling at
my brother for deceiving me, I suggest you find something else
to do."

"And miss the fireworks?" Marsh chuckled. "I should say
not!"

He was anxious to see this feisty beauty light into her brother.
With her command of the English language she would chew
the poor man up one side and down the other before spitting
him out.

With grim determination, Calera trooped toward the establishment that stood apart from the other buildings on the out-
skirt of town. The moment Marsh opened the door for her, she
recoiled in disgust. She was greeted by indecent portraits of
females in various states of undress, by gaudy red velvet wall
paper, and red velvet sofas.

"Dear God!" she gasped.

Keery O'Connell had backslid as far as a man could slide
from his proper upbringing. He was going to get an earful!

When one of the nymphs du prairie approached, casting
Marsh a come-hither glance, Calera stepped into the woman's
line of vision. "I wish to speak to Keery O'Connell immediately," she demanded.

Melody Bright blinked and stared at Calera as if she had
antlers sprouting from her plumed hat.

"I am Keery's sister from Philadelphia. Please inform him of
my arrival," Calera prompted.

Melody shifted awkwardly from one foot to the other before pivoting to scurry down the hall. In the meantime, Calera had drawn the attention of every customer and prostitute within hearing distance. They all gaped at her for reasons Calera could not guess.

Marsh whistled softly as his gaze circled the parlor, scrutinizing the portraits in gold-plated frames. "I have the feeling your brother is going to catch hell. I don't suppose you have ever been in a brothel before."

"Not hardly!" Calera harumphed. "And God willing, I will never set foot in one again!"

When a buxom brunette sashayed from the shadowed hallway, Calera waited impatiently for her brother to appear. Where was the man?

"Miss O'Connell?" Royal Winston moved gracefully forward, smiling apologetically. "I was very sorry to hear about your ordeal during your stage journey. I also regret to be the one to have to tell you that your brother isn't here."

"Then where the devil is he?"

Royal inhaled a deep breath, causing her ample bosom to come dangerously close to spilling from the daring decolletage of her lavender gown. "I regret to inform you that Keery was killed last week."

"Dear God!" Calera's knees folded like an accordion. If not for Marsh's supporting arm, she would have collapsed on the floor.

Royal gestured for Marsh to usher Calera into the office. A snap of Royal's fingers sent Melody Bright scuttling toward the liquor cabinet to fetch the distraught young woman a glass of wine. Calera was deposited in a chair and handed a drink. Stunned with shock, Calera took one sip, and then another, while the world spun furiously around her.

"My b-brother is d-dead?" Calera questioned the room at large. "Dear God!"

Chapter Thirteen

Royal Winston sank into the chair behind the desk and motioned for Marsh to plant himself beside Calera, whose complexion had turned the color of flour. "I am very sorry to have to be the bearer of such bad news, Miss O'Connell. We heard only a few days earlier that you had been abducted from the stage and that you were feared dead. It seems this entire week has been one of colossal tragedy for you. You have survived one traumatic ordeal, only to be flung headlong into another."

"How?" Was all Calera could manage between the onslaught of tears.

Dear God in heaven! She had lived for this day for six long years. She had kept her nose to the grindstone, vowing to acquire the finest education Keery's money could buy so she could make him proud of her, to repay him, to rejoin him. And now her world, and all her hopes and dreams, had come tumbling down around her like a rockslide, burying her alive. This sultry harlot who sat across from her didn't even know half the torment Calera had survived!

Calera had her wits scared out of her when she was abducted and she'd had her heart yanked out like a three-rooted molar by a man who could not return her love. On the heels of very nearly losing her life three times, and suffering a disappointing bout with first love, Calera had arrived in town to discover her beloved brother owned a bordello. And this final blow of learning Keery had died was positively the last straw! Every fanciful ideal Calera had believed in was gone like ashes scattering in the wind. She had embraced love and it had betrayed her. She had placed Keery on a pedestal and he had descended into decadence. And worse, he had not lived to see that his sister had become the product of his youthful hopes and dreams for her.

Marsh handed Calera his handkerchief to absorb the cloudburst of tears that gushed down her ashen cheeks. His heart went out to Calera. In the course of an hour this lively beauty had made him believe in all that was good in this world. Watching her crumble in grief and disillusionment was most disconcerting. The lovely lass was alone in a land that was unfamiliar to her. She had nowhere to turn for support and compassion. Protectively, he slid his arm around her shaking shoulders to give her a consoling squeeze. Words seemed inadequate so he merely held her against him while she cried her eyes out.

"Last week your brother got into an argument with a long-time enemy," Royal explained. "The disagreement came to blows and Keery demanded the man be placed under arrest for ransacking The Cottage after being ordered to leave the premises." Royal paused for a moment, inhaled another breath and plowed on. "When Mr. Stafford was released from jail, the feud erupted again. Keery's rival rode his horse right through the front door and into the office where Keery sat. Another battle ensued and the blows to Keery's head proved to be fatal."

"He . . . was . . . beaten to death?" Wide, haunted eyes fastened on the brunette. "Dear God!"

"I'm sorry," Royal murmured.

"And is this murderer scheduled to hang for his vicious crime? I should at least like to be on hand for that!"

Royal stared at the air over Calera's red-gold head, unwilling to meet her teary-eyed gaze. "Charges were not brought against

Mr. Stafford because Keery instigated the feud himself. Keery had carried on this private battle for more than two years."

Calera was outraged that these Westerners had shrugged off Keery's death. She wanted restitution for the horrible crime and she wanted it *now!* "I think a court of law should decide whether or not my brother's killer was provoked to such a vile act. It does not sound as if it was a case of self-defense if my brother was in his office, obviously minding his own business."

"I don't think you comprehend the situation, Miss O'Connell," Royal said gravely. "Mr. Stafford hails from a very influential family in these parts, and Keery held a grudge against him, partly because of me, I am sorry to admit. But Keery provoked Mr. Stafford into retaliation by unjustly accusing him of demolishing the parlor when it was actually Keery who struck the first blow. I witnessed the first confrontation and advised your brother not to send Mr. Stafford to jail since he was not completely at fault."

"Not at fault?" Calera vaulted out of her chair. "The man killed my brother. Keery did not kill himself, now did he?"

"No, but—"

"Then I shall see what the sheriff has to say about this." Fuming in frustration and overwhelmed by grief, Calera whizzed out of the office and stormed down the street. It no longer mattered that Keery had lowered himself to establishing a brothel, or that the money he had sent to Philadelphia to put Calera through school was tainted. What mattered most was avenging a senseless death that had left Calera totally alone in the world. If there was no justice, then life had no value. But by damned, there *would be* justice in this instance, even if Calera had to shake up this complacent mining town where crime obviously ran rampant and folks just looked the other way without getting involved.

This Stafford character would pay dearly for murdering Keery. Calera didn't care if the man was God's brother. He had committed the crime and he was going to pay penance! She would not rest until he did!

The sound of footsteps prompted Calera to glance over her

shoulder. Marsh Layton was following like her shadow, his handsome face puckered in a worried frown.

"I appreciate your concern, but this is not your battle. I do not expect you to fight it for me. Believe me, I have learned to stand up for myself over the years," she assured him.

"I have no doubt of that, Cali," he readily confirmed. "But all the same, I am offering my support in your hour of need."

True to his word, Marsh trailed Calera into the sheriff's office. Calera found Eli Nelson camped out behind the newspaper with his feet propped on his cluttered desk.

Calera glared at the officer with mounting disdain. "Sheriff, if I might interrupt your perusal of the daily news, I have a pressing matter to discuss with you."

Eli's feet slid to the floor and he lowered his paper to assess the comely young woman whose haunted green eyes were fixed on him. "How may I help you, ma'am?'

"I want to file murder charges against a Mr. Stafford for the death of my brother—Keery O'Connell."

"Keery?" Eli choked. "You're Keery's sister? We thought you were dead."

"As you can plainly see, I am quite alive. However, that doesn't hold true of my recently departed brother whose murderer is running around loose!"

"Ma'am, I know you are upset and I can certainly understand how you must feel."

The man didn't have a clue! Calera thought to herself.

"But there were extenuating circumstances involved in the incident that led to accidental death," Eli explained.

"I fail to see how there could be the slightest margin for interpretation here, Sheriff. Murder is murder! Beating the life out of another human being can hardly be considered *accidental,*" Calera snapped in contradiction. "I want the murderer incarcerated and I demand immediate castigation!"

Eli leaned close to Marsh. "Did she say *castration?*" he chirped in question.

"Not castration, cast*igation*—as in severe punishment," Marsh defined. "However, I imagine she wouldn't mind seeing that particular surgery performed, too, so I wouldn't mention it."

Eli glanced back at the furious young woman. "Begging your pardon, ma'am, but your brother—" He cleared his throat and carefully formulated his words. "I came to know your brother well the past few years. Perhaps you considered him blameless, I cannot say for certain, but Keery was—" Damn, how did a man tell a woman that her brother had pretty much gotten what he deserved and that he had practically asked for it?

"My brother was *what?*" Calera prodded.

"He was not without fault." That was as politely as Eli could describe Keery without shattering the young lady's obvious illusions.

"Fine, my brother was imperfect, just like the rest of us. I believe it is up to a court to determine who was at the greatest fault in this instance. I wish to press charges against Mr. Stafford."

Eli's shoulders slumped. "How long has it been since you last saw your brother?"

"Six years," Calera informed him, uncertain what that had to do with anything.

"People can change in that amount of time. I have a feeling Keery did. I know for a fact that he changed greatly from the first time I met him until I . . . buried him." He forced himself to meet Calera's barely composed expression. "I will issue a warrant for Mr. Stafford's arrest if you insist. But I think you should concern yourself with the disposition of Keery's personal effects and learn more about the man your brother had become over the past few years."

"And how am I to understand the man you insist my brother became when you haven't bothered with specifics? Thus far, you have spoken in vague generalities."

"I am trying to be polite," Eli said in exasperation. "There is also the matter of The Cottage to be considered. The majority of stock in the establishment belonged to Keery. Now the business falls into your hands—yours and Royal Winston's. She was Keery's partner."

Calera staggered back as if the sheriff had slapped her. Dear

God! She was part owner of a bordello? Did the sheriff expect her to become a resident madam? Hell would endure an ice age before that happened!

"Rest assured that The Cottage will be closed down," Calera told Eli in no uncertain terms.

"Closed down?" Eli clamped his sagging jaw shut. "Ma'am, I wouldn't suggest doing something as rash as that. I don't know if you are familiar with mining towns that consist of a high percentage of men, but that is not a good idea. You would earn instant dislike from the citizens of Globe City if you shut down The Cottage."

"I am not trying to win a popularity contest," Calera said flippantly.

Lucky for her that she wasn't, thought Eli.

Marsh bit back a grin. As much as he liked this feisty green-eyed imp, he had to admit that she had a knack of making instant waves on the calmest of seas. Beneath that veneer of bewitching femininity was a bedrock of assertiveness and fierce determination.

"I will weigh my decision carefully," Calera bargained, "*if* you agree to place Mr. Stafford behind bars until his trial."

Eli shifted uneasily. Calera O'Connell was a very intelligent young woman, that was easy to see. She had maneuvered Eli into an uncomfortable situation. His close association with Royal Winston motivated him to defend her interests. His knowledge of the incident leading to Keery's death also left him obliged to defend Shane Stafford's interests. Shane had been dealt an unpleasant fate in life, and Eli had no desire to jail Shane a second time.

A court battle would draw entirely too much attention, especially while Geronimo was on the rampage, stirring up old resentments between whites and Apaches. If Shane was convicted, the Apache tribes would swear it was because he was Indian. If Shane was proved innocent, the begrudging whites would swear it was because the courts were afraid to ignite another feud in Arizona. Damn . . .

"Well, Sheriff?" Calera pressed him.

After considering his options for a long moment, Eli nodded reluctantly. "All right, ma'am. After you have had a few days to cope with this tragedy, and if you are still adamant about a trial, I'll have Shane Stafford arrested. But with him being a half-breed Apache and all, it might cause—"

The emotional impact of Eli's words caused Calera to stumble back as if she had suffered a forceful body blow. Marsh darted forward to catch Calera when she tripped over the trailing hem of her skirt and teetered off balance.

"Cali?" Marsh frowned in concern when her elegant features lost all their color. "Honey, are you okay?"

Okay? OKAY? No, she wasn't okay! She felt as if the last patch of earth had been yanked out from under her, leaving her nothing to cling to. Desolation descended like a suffocating fog, depriving her of breath.

"Dear God," Calera whispered miserably.

Emotions were converging on her from so many fronts that she didn't know which one to fight first. This last bit of news was simply too much! Calera had not been granted the luxury of the passage of time before another disastrous upheaval in her life cruelly bombarded her. Every dream had been shattered, every hope dashed. She could not even cling to that one bittersweet fantasy because the man who had stolen her heart, broken it, and handed it back to her in pieces was the same man who had killed her brother. Shane had touched her with exquisite gentleness, but he had blood on his hands—her brother's blood . . .

The world spun. Calera buckled beneath overwhelming despair. For the third time in less than two traumatic weeks, Calera fainted dead away.

Before Calera wilted onto the floor, Marsh scooped her limp body into his arms. Grave concern etched his blond features. "I think Cali has suffered one too many shocks in too short a time," he diagnosed. "I'll take her back to the hotel so she can recuperate."

"I'll notify Doctor Broxton," Eli volunteered. "Lyle can come by and check on her, first chance he gets."

"My thanks, Sheriff." Marsh peered down into Calera's waxen features, his gaze filled with pity and concern.

"She's a friend of yours, I assume," Eli speculated.

"Yes. And right now, Cali needs all the friends she can get. I don't think she has many places left to turn."

"She was so wild with grief that I didn't have the heart to tell her what a scoundrel her brother turned out to be. When Keery wasn't hitting the bottle, he was arrogant and ornery. When he was drunk he was offensively obnoxious. Lately, he was drunk more than he was sober. His business partner kept him in line as best she could, but Keery had bullying tendencies and he roused a sleeping lion when he tangled with Shane Stafford that fatal day."

Marsh never took his eyes off the lovely bundle in his arms. "I can understand why you were hesitant to tell Cali the truth about her brother. But unless she knows, she will press the issue to the very limits, bringing more heartache upon herself."

"I know." Eli inhaled an enormous sigh. "I'll have to tell her eventually. But I don't want to tear her world apart again so soon."

"Waiting would be advisable," Marsh concurred. "Once she has adjusted to her loss, she can face the bitter reality about her brother."

By the time Marsh returned to the hotel, he had gathered a curious crowd. Word of Calera's arrival had spread through town like wildfire. Now, news of her collapse was on every tongue. Globe City's young doctor met Marsh in the lobby with satchel in hand, to accompany his patient upstairs. The instant Marsh situated Calera on the bed, Lyle Broxton waved smelling salts under her nose.

Calera didn't want to rouse to face another round of tormenting anguish. She wanted to die and be done with it all, but the infuriating physician was insistent. He hustled Marsh Layton out of the room to fetch a tray of food. When Lyle divested

Calera of her confining clothes, he discovered the wound on her shoulder.

"My dear lady!" Lyle gasped. "You should have contacted me the minute you arrived in town. This injury needs attention. It's a wonder you have survived at all."

It was a wonder that she cared if she had, Calera thought, thoroughly disheartened.

"Whoever tended the wound saved your life," Lyle declared.

And then he stripped me of my will to live, she silently added.

"I'm going to apply some salve to the wound and bandage it. I want you to change the dressing twice a day until it heals. If you notice the slightest indication of infection, come see me immediately."

After Lyle had rummaged through the drawers to locate Calera's nightgown, he eased her into the garment and tucked her beneath the sheets. Marsh arrived a few minutes later with a tray of food and Lyle demanded—in his most authoritative voice—that Calera consume every last bite. He had doused the food with laudanum to help her sleep and he intended that she swallowed the full dose.

After Calera drifted off to sleep, Lyle handed Marsh a vial of medication. "Make certain she takes another dose tonight," he instructed. "I think it best to keep Miss O'Connell sedated for a few days. From what I have heard, she has suffered incredible emotional stress. She needs rest and time to adjust."

"I'll see that she takes her medicine," Marsh promised faithfully.

Lyle surveyed the elegantly-dressed gambler for a long moment. "Are you her fiancé, Mr. Layton?"

Marsh had a pretty good idea why the young doctor had posed that question—one that had absolutely nothing to do with Calera's mental or physical well being. Calera had acquired another admirer who was trying to establish his territorial rights against his competition. Lyle Broxton had the advantage of disrobing Cali under the pretense of a medical examination. The sneaky rascal!

"She isn't my fiancée—yet," Marsh replied with a smug smile which was quickly returned.

"She is a beautiful woman," Lyle said as if he ought to know, and he definitely did. He may have been schooled in medicine, but he was still a man.

"I am well aware of her beauty," Marsh replied. "But thank you for bringing that to my attention—again."

"I'll be back to check on her this evening."

"I was sure you would be, but thanks for the warning."

Lyle pivoted to stare into Marsh's smug grin. "I'm sure her guard dragon will still be here, too."

"You can depend on it, Doc."

Marsh dropped down into a chair to enjoy a few minutes of solitude, but a rap resounded on the door, interrupting him. He found a rotund gentleman peering up at him through red-streaked eyes.

"Is she going to be all right? The poor little thing!" Horace Baxter invited himself into the room to assess Calera's condition. "I never thought I would see her again. How she survived that horrifying ordeal with those savages, I'd like to know! I'm sure it would make a sensational story."

"I assume you and Cali have met," Marsh deduced, watching the overweight man waddle over to stare down into Calera's peaked face.

Horace wheeled around to scrutinize the handsome gambler. "Met? Of course we have met. I was on the stage during the attack. I cursed myself a thousand times for failing Calera when she needed me. I was scared witless, and I couldn't save her from disaster because I was so terrified for my own life. If there is anything Calera wants or needs, just contact me. I have a room down the hall. And tell her I came by to check on her the instant she rouses. I want to talk to her."

"Done, Mr.—" Marsh waited for the slightly inebriated gentleman to fill in the blank.

"Baxter. Horace Baxter." He thrust out a stubby hand. "I am a reporter for the *Boston Herald*. I fully intend to write Calera's story. I'm sure letters will pour in to offer her condolences after this second tragedy."

"I doubt Cali is interested in fame and publicity. She doesn't seem the type."

"That is the beauty of this story," Horace insisted. "An Eastern aristocrat, alone in the world, making her place in the West, despite difficulties, will provide inspiration for other females. Knowing Calera as I do, I think she would like that."

"Perhaps," Marsh said thoughtfully. "But we will leave that decision to Cali, *when* she has recovered from the shock of losing her brother. The doctor advised bed rest and a peaceful environment. I am here to ensure his orders are carried out."

"And if you think I intend to hurt Calera in any way," he said, highly affronted. "You are sorely mistaken, Mr—"

"Layton. Marsh Layton."

"Well, Mr. Marsh Layton, I happen to like this girl quite a lot. I am also at her service!"

"I'll be sure to tell her you said so." Marsh ushered the tipsy journalist toward the door and heaved a relieved sigh when Horace wobbled on his way.

Damn, Cali was collecting men faster than a locomotive gathered steam. Marsh smiled to himself as he plunked into his chair. That really didn't surprise him. Since Marsh had been difficult to impress when it came to women, why shouldn't he expect that the female who had quickly captured his interest also attracted the devotion of a dozen other men? Marsh could deal with competition, just as long as he remained ahead of the pack.

And who knew? Maybe Globe City would be the place he settled down after ten years as a wanderlust in search of that elusive something he had never been able to find. This green-eyed siren could lure a man into putting down roots and contemplating matrimony.

Marsh's family owned a meat packing company in Fort Worth and he had learned to carve beef as expertly as he cut a deck of cards. He could become respectable in a hurry if he decided to. With the railroads rapidly approaching Arizona, the beef prices were sure to escalate because of the accessibility to markets in the East. Mining towns like Globe City would always need a butcher to process beef for hungry miners. Marsh could have set himself up in business in the batting of an eyelash.

His gaze darted toward the bed where Calera lay like Sleeping Beauty awaiting a prince's kiss. He was feeling more respectable by the second. For the love of a woman like Calera O'Connell, Marsh could settle down and learn to enjoy it. No doubt, a saucy nymph like Cali could fulfill a man's wildest dreams . . . And damn that lecherous doctor for sneaking a peek at the woman who might very well become the future Mrs. Marsh Layton!

Chapter Fourteen

Shane stared down from the towering Mogollon Rim that dropped seven thousand feet to the fertile valley that had become his father's coveted ranch thirty years earlier. Although there were times Shane cursed his father for the hell he had put his half-breed son through, Robert Stafford was the kind of man who saw his will done. He had been a shrewd, calculating adventurer. Robert had looked upon this plush valley with its life-giving source of water and he had set out to claim it as his own.

The man must have been an exceptional poker player, too, Shane imagined, for Robert Stafford had played all his aces to his benefit. By staking his claim on this magnificent country, and the water rights it provided, he had also seen to it that he could graze his vast cattle, sheep, and horse herds over thousands of acres that would have been otherwise useless. Controlling water was the key to Robert Stafford's success and his fortune.

The liaison Robert had formed with the Apaches had granted him land without the threat of attack. While other ranchers risked the wrath of Apaches by nesting on this land, Robert had not lived in fear. When the white man's government literally stole the Apache's land out from under them and crowded them

onto hated reservations, Robert had applied for the Homestead
Act of 1862. According to the legislation, anyone with ten dollars
for the filing fee could enter a claim for a quarter section of
land—one-hundred-sixty acres. If a homesteader lived on his
claim and made improvements, the land legally became his after
five years. Robert, of course, met all the qualifications.

Robert Stafford had shrewdly staked the land that held all
the valuable water rights and thereby acquired all the acres he
had been granted by the Apaches years earlier. Again, Robert
had succeeded while other white men failed. Now the Bar "S"
herds roamed across wide-spread meadows and drank their fill
in the mountain streams.

Shane alternately admired and hated his white father. The
past few years of Shane's life had been less tolerable than the
first eight he had spent at the Bar "S" Ranch while his father
was alive. For the last two hellish years, Shane found no reason
to smile, enjoyed no happiness unless he ventured into the remote valleys that lay deep in the pine-covered mountain wilderness. Shane's mother had ordered him to take his place in the
white man's world. He had obeyed her dying wish, and that of
the tribal council, when Robert came to fetch him.

Shane had endured nine kinds of hell, tolerating the cruel
teasing of spiteful ranch hands. He had fought with his fists,
knives, and pistols to earn the grudging respect of the wranglers. But nothing Shane had ever done could erase the smoldering hatred of his stepmother. Muriel Stafford could not
abide the sight of her husband's bastard son. Shane's presence
was an ever-constant reminder of Robert's infidelity.

Shane peered at the distant ranch house that set against the
panoramic north wall of the Mogollon Rim. He always dreaded
returning to the house, but he was even more reluctant to re-enter
the white man's world after he had sent that green-eyed sprite
on her way. Turning his back on Irish—as he had come to call
her—was the hardest thing Shane had ever done as a man,
equalled only to walking away from the Apache way of life.

Anguish twisted Shane's gut when the forbidden memories
of a week-long fantasy descended on him like a fog. *Ah, Irish,*

he thought with a pang of regret, *if only you could fully comprehend the torture of letting you go!* But Shane had to be cruel to that beguiling imp to show her the greatest kindness. Once again, he had been damned if he did and damned if he didn't.

Shane would not have wished his life on his worst enemy, and certainly not a woman like Calera. A rueful smile grazed his lips as he urged Sultan down the winding trail. One brief glimpse of happiness had been lost and a new kind of torture had begun. Shane was positively certain now that hell had nothing new to teach him. He was plagued by such vivid memories of the past week—of innocent emerald eyes and silky hair glowing like a living flame. Shane had forsaken Calera's love to protect her, and she had cursed him for it. He had her best interest at heart and she would never forgive him for hurting her.

Absently, Shane stroked Sultan's muscular neck. Well, at least he had retrieved the stallion that had ridden through hell with him the past few years. At least he did not have to part with his faithful companion. There had been a time when Sultan was the only creature Shane dared to call friend. They had been through a lot together, he and Sultan. The unusual bond of man and beast had made life more tolerable.

On his own accord, Sultan paused to glance back in the direction he had come, as if he had left something precious behind him. It definitely wasn't the piebald gelding that plodded in Sultan's tracks. The stallion had no use whatsoever for the young gelding.

"I know the feeling," Shane murmured as he followed Sultan's gaze and became lost to memories of a place out of time.

The closer Shane came to the ranch headquarters that was encircled by the spectacular rock walls of Mogollon Rim, the more aware he became of the undivided attention he was receiving from the wranglers who were branding the livestock. He was accustomed to the stares, the harbored resentment. He had adjusted by refusing to let himself care what anyone thought of him. He had learned to walk the lonely path that had not been of his choosing.

Shane received even more attention than usual this particular day. He supposed the wranglers had heard about his recently-renewed feud with Keery O'Connell. That would explain the glances. True, Shane had carried the grudge a mite too far this time. Having Sultan stolen while Shane was locked behind bars had snapped the trap on his temper. He had struck out with a vengeance, giving Keery several tastes of beefy fists in hopes the man would never be foolish enough to tangle with Shane again.

Over the past few years, Keery had dealt Shane all the misery he intended to tolerate. Shane would have torn that whole damned brothel to the ground and left Keery buried in its shambles if there had been time. Too bad there hadn't been. Shane hated Keery and all he represented—the drunkenness, the exploitation, the prejudice. Why Shane had tolerated that scoundrel to live so long he wasn't sure. Shane had certainly wished the man dead often enough.

Swinging to the ground, Shane led Sultan to the stables to rub him down. The ritual always had a calming effect on man and horse. After Shane dried Sultan with straw, he washed the steed down with whiskey and water and then thoroughly dried him. Only when Sultan was swathed in a blanket and munching contentedly on hay was Shane satisfied.

The lengthy procedure also delayed entering a house that teemed with hatred. And speaking of wishing people dead, Muriel Stafford would have seen Shane in his grave years ago. Indeed, if wishing could have made it so, Muriel would have exchanged one life for another a decade earlier.

Shane was quick to note the sudden silence of the farm hands who ambled around the barn, tossing hay to the livestock. Shane was the subject of speculative glances, until his gaze met those of his taciturn companions. Obviously, when word of the fiasco in Globe City reached the ranch, Shane's actions had been condemned. Those who customarily took a wide berth around Shane were giving him extra-added space today. Those who usually offered a few civil words of conversation had nothing whatsoever to say.

Damn, what had Keery O'Connell done to retaliate for being beaten to a pulp? Had Keery put a death wish on Shane's head?

Or was there a bounty for the acquisition of Shane's half-Apache scalp?

Having delayed as long as possible, Shane pivoted toward the house. After he tolerated Muriel's customary sneer of greeting, he would shut himself in his private quarters and avoid her every chance he got—just as he usually did.

Shane did admire his stepmother's perseverance. It seemed each of them was waiting for the other one to pack up and leave. Since Shane knew this ranch land had belonged to the Apache before the intrusion of white men, he felt justified in claiming his inheritance. Muriel, of course, believed the land her husband had purchased was hers and she considered Shane a trespasser. She wanted Shane to take up residence on the reservation, if a bullet or knife didn't plant him in the ground first. The latter option was preferable to Muriel, Shane suspected. She could not abide the sight of her deceased husband's bastard son.

That feeling, however, was mutual. Years of Muriel's hatred and ridicule had earned her Shane's seething disgust. Muriel was selfish, spoiled, and manipulative, even when she got her way. She could make life miserable for anyone when she *didn't* get her way.

Ah, this was Shane's life. It wasn't pretty or pleasant. It was an endurance test, a day-to-day challenge. The one bright spot in Shane's world was a bittersweet fantasy of a woman's love that was inaccessible to him . . .

"I have forbidden you from entering *my* home dressed like a barbarian. Put on some decent clothes this instant!"

Shane flicked a quick glance at Muriel. Her petite frame was rigid with disgust. Her salt and pepper hair was pulled back in a tight bun that accentuated the pinched expression on her features. She reminded Shane of hate personified.

Shane made no comment, nor did he give any indication that Muriel's disdainful frown or sharp words affected him in the least. He glanced sideways to see that the Mexican house servants had the good sense to fade into the woodwork before

Muriel decided to take her anger out on them as well. Shane ambled across the tiled foyer toward the staircase, refusing to be baited by his stepmother, especially on an empty stomach. He was not in the mood for Muriel's taunts.

Muriel wheeled around when Shane sauntered past her. "Do you have nothing to say for yourself? No, of course not. How can I forget?" Bitter laughter tripped from lips that were as taut as fence wire. "Apaches think it is beneath them to defend their actions. Isn't that right? But this latest bit of trouble you have brewed suggests what I have known to be true all along. Once a savage, always a savage. How long is it going to take for you to realize you will never fit into this world and you go back where you belong—back to where I wish you would never have left?"

Shane stood there, immovable as stone. These vicious tongue-lashings were reminiscent of the physical scars left by the whip in years past—a whip Muriel ordered to be used on him when his father wasn't around to intervene. Shane had endured the pain, employing the same techniques he had taught Calera.

"Get out of my sight, you heathen!" Muriel railed at him. "You have only been back a few minutes and already I am sick of the sight of you!"

Shane complied because it was *his* wont to leave, not because it was Muriel's decree. He had proven to Muriel years earlier that nothing she said or did affected him. He had grown calluses on his emotions.

Garbed in white men's clothes, Shane accepted the tray the Mexican housemaid placed in front of him.

Neva Sanchez glanced toward the partially-opened door that led to the hall from Shane's private quarters in the east wing, and then confided, "The señora is furious with you after your last jaunt into town."

"*Si*, but then she is always furious with me for one reason or another," Shane reminded her.

Neva shook her dark head. "I'm serious, amigo. The señora is worse than usual."

Shane glanced up from his tray of food to survey the somber expression on Neva's aging features.

"She ordered me to pack all your belongings while you were gone, and move them to the bunkhouse."

His gaze swept his chambers, seeing nothing out of place.

"I disobeyed her, of course," Neva said proudly. "The señora threatened to dismiss me, but the other servants promised to leave with me. The señora would never lower herself to doing domestic chores since she thinks common labor is beneath her."

"Perhaps I should move into the bunkhouse to lessen the friction you and the others have to tolerate when Muriel and I are under the same roof."

"No!" Neva adamantly protested. "You have fought her too long to give into her wishes now. She holds you responsible for something you had no part in. She resents the fact that *he* died and you were allowed to live. She curses you for being born. The señora is poisoned with hatred. That is her problem, not yours."

When Shane finished his meal, he thanked Neva for her efforts on his behalf. Why she remained friendly to him when Muriel constantly belittled him in front of the servants, Shane didn't know and he hadn't asked.

In long, lithe strides, Shane ambled toward the door, halting when Neva called out to him.

"Never buckle to that bitter woman," Neva insisted. "Your father loved your mother as he loved no other woman, despite what Muriel says to the contrary. I know, because your father confided the fact to me when he first brought you here, right after your mother passed on and he was overcome with grief. The señora knows that, too, and it has eaten away at her for years, making her even more resentful than she already was."

Her dark eyes fastened on the muscular giant who filled the doorway to overflowing. "No, Shane Stafford, you must never leave this part of your heritage behind. Sometimes a man must fight for what he wants, what he believes in, just as the Apaches fought for what was theirs. My own people were guilty of atrocities against the Apaches. I saw it with my own eyes. And because I have seen too much hatred that can tear all of us apart, I stood

up to the señora for you when you were not here to defend yourself. And if I would have had a son, I would have wanted him to
be like you. You have grown up to be your own man, because of
and in spite of your trials. Never curse what you are. You are a
man among men."

Half-turning, Shane smiled at the tiny old woman. The expression that softened his hard features caused Neva to stare at
him in surprise and delight.

"Who taught you to smile again, *hombre?* I thought you had
forgotten how," she teased him. "Whoever it was, I wish to thank
them. It has been too long."

"And now that I know how much a smile pleases you, Neva,
I will try to do it more often."

Neva eyed him craftily. "It is that smile of yours that could
ensure Muriel's defeat in this ongoing battle of wills. If she sees
you smile, she will know she has lost. And never forget that you
have friends here in this *hacienda* and in the bunkhouse, though
the señora would prefer that you think otherwise."

Mulling over his conversation with Neva, Shane strode down
the hall, intent on lending a hand in the roundup that had
begun in his absence. When Muriel glanced up from her half-
reclined position on the sofa, Shane tossed her a grin, just to
test Neva's theory. Sure enough, Muriel snarled at him and then
muttered to herself.

Shane felt better already.

The instant Cactus and Sticker Linnox spotted Shane ambling
toward the corral, they breathed a collective sigh of relief.

"I was afraid you would decide never to come back after what
happened," Cactus said when Shane paused beside him.

"Things were a little unnervin' in town after you high-tailed
it into the mountains," Sticker contributed before spitting an
arc of tobacco.

"We spoke to Sheriff Nelson in your behalf," Cactus added.

Sticker smiled proudly. "Me an' Cactus did some fancy talkin' to get you off the hook. You'd've been proud of us. We sounded like silver-tongued lawyers, didn't we, Cactus?"

"Damned sure did." Cactus grinned smugly before spitting an arc of tobacco that outdistanced his brother's. "Even Royal said you weren't to blame for what happened to Keery. She stood up for you. I always did think she had an eye for you, even if Keery wouldn't let her near you."

"I suppose Keery's out for blood now," Shane speculated. He frowned when he noticed the odd expressions that claimed the two men's whiskered faces. "What's wrong?"

"Don't you know?" Cactus queried, shifting uncomfortably.

"Don't I know *what?*"

Shane's dark eyes narrowed beneath flattened brows. He well-remembered the Linnox brothers' awkward behavior while he was in jail. They had been reluctant to tell him that Sultan had been sold. Cactus and Sticker were behaving just as curiously now.

"You tell him, Cactus. You're the oldest," Sticker insisted.

"Oh hell, Stick, you always say that when you don't have the nerve to give somebody bad news." Cactus muttered sourly.

"What bad news?" Shane prodded, glancing from one averted face to the other.

"I gave him the bad news last time," Cactus declared. "It's your turn, Stick."

Sticker inhaled a deep breath, causing the buttons to strain on his shirt. "Keery ain't out for your blood because he's as dead as a man can get."

Shane could not muster much sympathy. "When did this happen?"

Cactus and Sticker glanced at each other and then peered incredulously at the towering giant.

"It happened the mornin' you rode into his office," Cactus explained, as if Shane ought to know. "One of the blows you delivered to Keery's head was fatal."

Shane finally understood why Cactus and Sticker had been patting themselves on the backs, boasting of their intervention on his behalf. Shane reflected on the incident in which vicious kicks and devastating blows had been delivered. He remembered how the piebald had bolted in fright. A hoof had caught Keery in the head, flinging him to the floor. Was that the blow that ended Keery's life?

"Sheriff Nelson felt obligated to put out a warrant for your arrest, but we reminded him that Keery had stolen Sultan—a crime punishable by hangin'. After Royal added her two cent's worth, the sheriff backed off," Cactus reported.

"Ever'thing finally simmered down after the funeral, even though there were still a few folks debatin' whether the sheriff did the right thing."

That figured, thought Shane. He still had plenty of enemies left, ones Keery had sicced on him. Luckily, none of the others were as vocal and spiteful as Keery.

"We were just preparin' to leave town when the stage arrived," Cactus went on to say. "Some journalist from back East reported the stage had been raided. Horace Baxter said that some she-male named O'Connell had been kidnapped by Indians—"

Cactus stopped short when Shane turned as white as an Apache could get. "You okay, Shane?"

Shane felt as if someone had doubled a fist and buried it so deep in his belly that it slammed against his backbone. *No! It couldn't be!* His mind forcefully rejected the idea. Shane frantically searched his memory, trying to recall if Calera had mentioned . . .

His thoughts skidded to a halt when Calera's haunting voice whispered through his tormented brain. "My brother has done that for me," Calera had said when they were discussing the kind of friendships that offered everything without expecting anything in return. Shane had declared Sultan was man's best friend and Calera had insisted her brother was *her* inspiration— or something to that effect.

Irish . . . Shane's thoughts stumbled again. Keery was Irish and he had a temper as hot as a branding iron. Had Calera been on her way to Globe City to visit her brother? Damn it, why hadn't he noticed the family resemblance? Because there wasn't much of one, Shane realized. Keery was big and burly and homely and Calera was everything her brother wasn't. Sweet mercy, if only he had made the connection!

"Go on," Shane insisted, feeling sicker by the second.

"There ain't much more to tell," Sticker said. "Everybody in town was sayin' how ironic it was that the O'Connells had been wiped out in less than a week—first Keery, and then this woman who had been captured by renegades. The journalist didn't know if the O'Connell woman was Keery's long-lost wife, sister, cousin, or what. That's about all we know. Me an' Cactus headed back to the ranch an' we ain't been to town since."

Sticker frowned in concern. "Shane, are you sure you're all right. You look a little green around the gills."

Shane could not possibly look as horrible as he felt. No eyes could see, and no ears could hear the tortured voice of the inward hell he was enduring at this moment,

Shane expelled a tormented groan. "Dear God!"

The thought of sending Calera on her way to face the shocking news of her brother's death nearly brought Shane to his knees. He felt physically ill. Learning that Calera was Keery's sister left Shane feeling a zillion times worse than knowing he was the one who caused Keery's death. Not only had Shane rejected Calera's generous offer of love, but he had also taken her brother's life! When Calera learned who had killed her brother, she would condemn him to the hottest regions of hell. Damnation, of all the people in all the world, why did he have to meet up with Keery O'Connell's innocent sister? Shane could endure the hatred of everyone on this earth—except Calera!

"Dear God!" Shane burst out a second time.

Shane had tried to cut himself and that lovely siren off from the world below the mountains. He had wanted and needed that precious time with Calera to regenerate his immunity to the outside world. He had existed in a secluded universe he likened to paradise, refusing to think in terms of a past or future. He had wanted to cherish his fantasy, but he had inadvertently brought more anguish upon himself. He could not have hurt Calera more if he had plunged his knife straight into her heart. Rejecting her had not been enough. Oh no, he had killed her beloved brother!

Without a word of explanation to Cactus and Sticker, who were staring at him as if he had lost his mind, Shane lurched around and charged off to retrieve Sultan.

Cactus scratched his wiry brown head and watched Shane race toward the barn. "Since when did Shane start usin' *that* expression?"

"Damned if I know." Sticker stared at Shane when he burst from the barn at a dead run, leaping the wild-eyed stallion over the corral fence to thunder off, as if the hounds from hell were nipping at his heels. "Shane never did bother to explain how he managed to retrieve Sultan without tradin' the piebald, either."

Cactus was silent for a long moment before he glanced at his brother. "Do you think we oughta follow him? There's no tellin' what he's plannin' to do now."

"I reckon we oughta," Sticker said with a decisive nod. "We're to blame for makin' Shane's life more miserable than it already was. Shane would never have walked into The Cottage if it hadn't been for us."

The Linnox brothers beat a hasty path to the stables to saddle their horses. Unfortunately, Shane had a head start, and he was riding a stallion that some folks swore had winged hooves. But no matter what, Cactus and Sticker were determined to become Shane's guardian angels to compensate for the trouble they had caused him. The man could definitely use one!

Muriel Stafford dropped the window curtain back in place when Shane disappeared into the forest of Ponderosa pines. Supreme satisfaction brimmed her lips. Robert's bastard had left again, and none too soon to please her.

Judging from the direction Shane had taken, his destination was Globe City. Muriel hoped public opinion turned against that vicious savage and that Shane met a lynch mob when he rode into town. If Muriel had been on hand when Shane committed murder, she would have seen to it that he was fitted for the hangman's noose. She had waited years to be rid of Shane. That half-breed's existence had tormented her life and ruined her dreams.

This war of wills she and Shane had been waging since Robert's death had to come to an end—the sooner the better. It was driving her mad each time Shane walked through the front door, as if *he* owned the place. That disgusting Apache should never have been allowed to reside at the Bar "S" Ranch— ever. Muriel had never forgiven Robert for that, or for his infidelity, even on the day he died.

"Neva, gather my satchels," Muriel ordered as she swept into the foyer. "I have decided to journey into Globe City."

A spiteful smile swallowed Muriel's features. Keery O'Connell's murder was her opportunity to remove her stepson from her life. She would have a long talk with Sheriff Nelson about his responsibility as a law official. Just because Shane carried the Stafford name should not grant him special privileges. He had committed the crime and he should pay for it. If Shane wound up swinging from a rope or lived out his miserable life in that hell hole known as Yuma Penitentiary, Muriel could not have been happier. She was going to rout that half-breed out of her life once and for all, even if she had to employ drastic measures. She had tolerated that man's tormenting presence as long as she could stand!

Chapter Fifteen

For two days Calera drifted in and out of drug-induced sleep, waking to find Marsh Layton and Doctor Lyle Broxton fussing over her, urging her to eat. Horace Baxter had arrived upon the scene, amazingly sober, apologizing up one side and down the other for failing her in her hour of need. When Horace tried to interrogate Calera about the details of her dreadful ordeal, Marsh pushed the journalist out of the room in nothing flat.

Calera had not protested Horace's hasty departure—compliments of her self-appointed body guard. She was in no condition to answer questions or excavate the tormenting memories. All Calera wanted was time to adjust to the devastating blows of one tragedy avalanching into another.

Ah, what was that ridiculous adage about the luck of the Irish? If the agony Calera had suffered of late was *luck*, she shuddered to think what Irish *misfortune* entailed! How was she supposed to cope with this latest catastrophe? Dear God, how many more adjustments was she supposed to make? She had outlived every member of her family. She had buried them one by one. She had plumbed the depths of every human emotion a dozen times and still she was asked to endure.

Well, damn it, why should she even *try* to survive? Everyone she cared about was gone. And what was infuriatingly worse was that Shane—the very same man she had confessed to love—had murdered her last surviving relative! Dear God, how could she ever forgive Shane for that? Wherever that Apache warrior was, she hoped he could hear her cursing his black soul to the farthest reaches of hell!

"Feeling better, honey?" Marsh sank down on the edge of the bed to feed Calera her afternoon meal.

"I'm alive, if that's supposed to be some sort of credit to my stamina and character," Calera said dully.

"Life is not always kind," Marsh agreed, before waving a forkful of potatoes under her nose. "And not every hand is a fistful of aces."

Calera slanted Marsh a dour glance. "And not every gambler is a philosopher. Spare me the spirit-lifting sermons, Brother Marsh. I am not in the mood."

"I should have been a preacher," he said, undaunted by the cloudy frown she cast on his sunny smile.

"I should have been a nun."

"Perhaps," he said for the sake of argument. In Calera's present mood of gloom and doom, Marsh thought it best to humor her. "Eat your peas and drink your milk, love. Doc Broxton gave me strict orders to ensure you regained your strength. He'll have me whipped if I neglect my duties."

Calera chewed on the crisp peas and swallowed. They tasted like sour grapes. "Don't you have to be somewhere else right about now? Like maybe in a poker game? On second thought, maybe not. That blinding smile of yours would give your winning hand away. Maybe you should go stand outside and replace the sun when it darts behind a cloud."

"Ah, Cali, even your bad humor amuses me," Marsh declared with a chuckle. He thrust another forkful of food at her. "When the world turns sour, as it has a tendency to do at times, you have to look on the bright side to carry you through. You still have me, you know. And there's Doc Broxton, who seems ever-so hopeful that the two of you can enjoy something more meaningful than your doctor-patient relationship. And of course, there is Horace Baxter, who has pledged undying loyalty to you. Even though you have only been in town a few days, you have collected an impressive number of sympathetic friends. And, as a wise philosopher once said—A man can never have too many friends."

"And if the Good Lord could see His way clear to save me from my well-meaning friends, I think I can protect myself from my enemies," Calera muttered.

Marsh eased back to stare down into her pale features. "My dear lady, you are being unnecessarily pessimistic."

Calera heaved an enormous sigh and stared up at the handsome gambler from beneath a fan of thick lashes. "I'm sorry. This is my resentful phase. You have the misfortune of being within snapping distance. Since I'm such bad company, I will understand if you wish to leave. I am trying very hard to cope, but it isn't easy."

"All is forgiven," Marsh softly assured her.

When Marsh combed the hair away from her face and tilted her chin upward, Calera gazed into his engaging smile and saw another face—a chiseled, bronzed face that triggered memories that tore her in two. How could fate have played such a cruel trick on her? Now she despised the man she had once loved! She didn't care if she ever experienced another emotion so long as she lived. Feeling nothing was the only mercy to be had when life dealt such cruel blows.

The abrupt rap at the door jolted Calera from her pensive reverie. She watched Marsh unfold himself from the edge of her bed and stride across the room. He opened the door to find Royal Winston poised before him, dressed in a respectable gown that did not accentuate her ample assets. Calera did not miss the speculative glance Royal cast the handsome blond gambler. Anyone with eyes in her head could decipher Royal's look. It must have been a hazard of Royal's profession, Calera decided. To a woman like Royal, every man was a prospective client.

What a way to make a living, Calera thought to herself. Did Royal realize men used her for their own lusty purposes without a care for her feelings? Did that matter to Royal or was money her primary objective and motivation?

Well, other things besides money mattered to Calera, though why they should she was beginning to wonder! She had given herself to a man for love and now look at her. She had been rejected. And worse, the first love of her life had murdered the last of her family! Damn that man!

On second thought, perhaps Royal *was* the wise one, Calera mused. Royal did not allow herself to become emotionally involved with men. She walked away with her heart intact and a pocketful of coins. Maybe Royal was using men, rather than the other way around. Calera hoped the seductive madam broke a few male hearts. They all deserved it!

"May I speak with Calera?" Royal requested after she had given Marsh a thorough going over, obviously liking what she saw.

Marsh half-turned, doing Calera the courtesy of allowing her to speak for herself.

Calera nodded agreeably.

Royal sailed into the room in a swish of petticoats and a fog of cheap perfume. "I would like to talk to you alone, if you don't mind."

Marsh broke into his typical grin. "While you two are visiting, I'll wander down the street to brush up on my skills at poker, just as Cali suggested earlier."

"Why don't you do that," Calera said. "I'm sure you're tired of playing nursemaid."

The look Marsh tossed Calera indicated he had no complaints about the task he had volunteered to assume. But being the rake he was, Marsh did not overlook Royal before taking his leave. He flashed her a charming smile and closed the door behind him.

"You have an extremely attractive guardian angel," Royal observed.

"Yes." Calera frowned, bemused. "And for the life of me, I can't fathom why he has taken it upon himself to nurse me back to health."

"No?" Royal sank down in the chair. "Obviously you have not spent much time in front of a mirror. You are a lovely woman."

One delicate brow arched curiously. Was Royal buttering her up for some ultimate purpose, or simply stating what she believed to be fact? "What did you want to see me about, Miss Winston?"

"Call me Royal. Everybody does," she replied. "I realize you have been under a great deal of stress since you arrived in town. I have tried to give you time to recuperate, but there is a matter of business that should be resolved. Now that Keery is gone, his stock in The Cottage falls to you."

Calera did not need to be reminded of that appalling fact.

"I could tell from our first encounter that you did not approve of your brother's business venture; therefore, I do not imagine you approve of me, either." When Calera started to speak, Royal raised a well-manicured hand to forestall her. "Do not feel obliged to deny it. I have lived with ladies' disapproval before. I was hoping you might allow the establishment to continue as is, remaining a silent partner. Of course, the profit Keery has been making would become yours."

Calera glanced away to conceal her distaste. The thought of living off the profits from a brothel set on her stomach like one of the indigestible meals she had consumed at the crude stage stations. In truth, Calera had been tormented by so many other troubled thoughts the past few days that she hadn't got around to fretting over how she would dispose of her brother's disreputable business.

"You must realize how I feel about The Cottage," Calera responded belatedly.

"I was afraid you might still feel that way." Royal sighed audibly. "That was why I suggested a silent partnership. You could maintain a distant association with The Cottage while I managed the establishment."

Calera was totally disconcerted by the situation she found herself in. She had ventured West, full of wistful hopes and dreams, anticipating an occupation that would allow her to prove her skills and knowledge while repaying Keery. Now she was completely alone in the world, grieving her brother's death, saddled with a business she had no wish to own and wishing Keery hadn't, either, How could he have done such a thing!

"I was thinking of turning The Cottage into a hotel and restaurant," Calera announced impromptu.

"A ho—!" Royal clamped her mouth shut and said through gritted teeth, "I see."

The attractive madam did not look at all enthused about Calera's extemporaneous decision. In fact, Royal's mouth pinched to such a degree that it reminded Calera of a duck's bill.

"My brother misled me into believing he managed a hotel, and I had planned to assist him when I came to Globe City. I thought perhaps you might wish to sell your interest in the business to me, if we could come to a satisfactory agreement."

"I can't do that," Royal objected. "The cash I received would not purchase another building as spacious and luxurious to entertain customers. And I cannot possibly afford to buy The Cottage outright from you."

"Then we have a serious dilemma."

"Indeed we do," Royal contended. "We seem more or less stuck with each other."

"Not exactly." Calera cleared her throat and stared levelly at Royal, knowing the forthcoming comment was not one the madam wanted to hear. But fact was fact and business was business. "Since I now hold controlling interest, the decision to shut The Cottage down until further notice is mine. I cannot, in good conscience, allow the brothel to remain in operation. The savings I have accumulated will pay the expenses of refurbishing the building into a fashionable hotel and adjoining dining hall. Considering our competition—" She gestured toward the modest furnishings of the room. "We could monopolize hotel business."

Royal's chin tilted belligerently. "I do not wish to manage a hotel."

"And I have no desire to be associated with a bordello," Calera said just as adamantly.

"We are going to hire my girls as hotel maids then?" Royal smirked.

"Yes, if they agree to change their ways," Calera stipulated. "I want nothing to tarnish the good reputation I hope to build."

"If you maintain your position, you will make more than a few enemies in Globe," Royal warned.

"Are you referring to your *girls?*" Calera queried.

"The girls *and* their clients," Royal predicted. "Despite your feelings, the townsfolk, comprised mostly of men, have a particular fondness for The Cottage."

"Your girls and their clients will have to take their business elsewhere." Calera's chin tilted a notch higher. "Tomorrow I intend to shut the doors to The Cottage, sort through my brother's personal belongings, and check into the cost of refurbishing."

Royal rose from her chair and pivoted toward the door with her back as stiff as a flagpole. She exited the same way she entered—with a rapid swish of petticoats and a whirlwind of cheap perfume. Calera knew she had offended the business partner she had inherited, but right was right. Prostitution may have been the oldest profession, but it was not a respectable one. Calera did not have to tolerate that brothel. She was going to manage a hotel, not a house of ill-repute and that was all there was to it. The Cottage would become a sentimental memorial to her brother, reflecting what the establishment *should have been* and *would be* everafter. Royal could be the silent partner, not the other way around . . .

Another insistent rap at the door jostled Calera's thoughts. "Come in."

Lyle Broxton, with black leather bag in hand, breezed into the room and paused to survey his patient. "You are beginning to regain some of your color. Good." He sank down beside her for closer inspection. "Are you feeling better, Calera?"

"Considerably."

It was a lie. Calera was miserable. She was nurturing a full blown hatred for Shane Stafford for ruining her life and her brother's. She was annoyed at Royal Winston for refusing to relinquish her disreputable ways and she was irritated at the whole world for dealing her another lousy hand. Calera knew she would be a horrible poker player, considering her rotten luck.

"I thought perhaps you might like to join me for supper this evening," Lyle invited. "I could enjoy the pleasure of your company and you could use some exercise and fresh air."

Maybe she could at that. Moping about certainly hadn't improved her blue mood. These four walls were closing around her by inches. It was time for a change of scenery.

"It's doctor's orders. I insist!" Lyle said emphatically.

"Then I accept."

Lyle beamed in delight. "I'll come for you at seven, provided no emergency arises. In my profession, I have to be flexible."

"I understand."

Calera watched the physician stroll away. Lyle Broxton seemed to be a pleasant man. He saved lives rather than destroyed them—like some people she knew. Damn that Shane Stafford! She would never forgive him for everything he had done to her. He was forcing her to turn to other men for companionship because he had sent her away and had left her without the brother she had idolized for years. He had turned her life into living hell.

On that haunting thought, Calera scrunched under the covers, begging for sleep to deliver her from this nightmare her life had become. Thankfully, drowsiness overtook her—compliments of the dose of laudanum Marsh had been instructed to mix with her noon meal.

While Marsh Layton circumnavigated the hotel room in sulking strides, Calera gathered her clothes and stepped behind the dressing screen. She had asked Marsh to grant her privacy to dress for her dinner engagement, but he had refused.

"I cannot imagine why you are making such a big deal of dinner," Calera called from her concealed niche.

"Can't you?" Marsh grumbled. "I have spent the past few days feeding and caring for you. And when you feel up to venturing out of the room, you intend to do it on the arm of Lyle Broxton. I'm insulted!"

Calera peeked around the dressing screen to toss Marsh a cajoling smile. "I think you are making too much of nothing. Lyle invited me out and I accepted."

"If I had known you were up to taking your meal at a restaurant, *I* would have invited you," Marsh muttered, his blue eyes fixed on the bare shoulder that protruded from the screen. He wanted to see *much, much* more of Cali. He found this unfamiliar role of the perfect gentleman too damned restrictive for his tastes. But now that he had managed to earn Calera's trust and acceptance, he was hesitant to disappoint her by grabbing her to him and kissing her tempting lips off.

"How was your luck at the gaming table?" Calera questioned before slipping on a clean chemise.

She hoped to divert Marsh's attention and lure him from his brooding mood. She had enjoyed his company the past few days, even if he was a gambler. Calera had quickly realized that clumping gamblers into one category and disliking them all on general principle was an unfair judgment. Marsh Layton possessed many admirable qualities, despite his profession.

"As usual, I seem to have more luck with cards than women," Marsh grunted.

"You are sulking again," Calera pointed out.

"I am not!" Marsh huffed. "I only want to know what Lyle Broxton has that I don't."

"A medical degree?" Calera offered with a teasing smile.

"Besides that," Marsh demanded grumpily.

Calera tugged her lavender gown into place and wrestled with the lacings on the back. Stepping from behind the screen, she silently requested Marsh's assistance. He eagerly approached, standing closer than necessary to accomplish the task.

Immediately, Marsh caught the scent of freshly washed hair and fragrant skin. Damn, he was all-too aware of this enticing beauty. To see her was to want her and he was beginning to want her in the worst way. If Calera didn't cut him some slack, and quickly, he was going to have to accept the offer Royal Winston had offered him when he passed her on the boardwalk. The want of this green-eyed siren was causing his male juices to simmer.

"In case you haven't noticed, Cali, I have become very attached to you," Marsh murmured, his breath stirring against the wispy ringlets that cascaded over her shoulders. "I'm feeling the bite of jealousy."

Calera pivoted to peer up into eyes that were the wrong color. And oh, how she wished she didn't find herself making these frustrating comparisons! She wanted to seek solace from this emotional turmoil that churned inside her, but she was wise enough to know that, until she could put her haunting affair with Shane into proper perspective and smother this tormenting fascination, she could not be fair to any other man. That midnight-haired Apache had left his brand on her with his tender touch, and he had left invisible scars as well. She hated him. She loved him. She wanted revenge, and yet . . .

"Cali?" Marsh's quiet voice interrupted her mental tug-of-war.

Calera waited, knowing Marsh intended to kiss her. A part of her wanted to test her reaction to this charismatic blond gambler, to let him wash away the lingering taste of Shane's explosive kisses. But another part of her was afraid to find out just how strong the spell that captivated her. Calera waited too long to make her decision and Marsh made it for her. His lips claimed hers in a kiss that demanded no more than she was willing to give. Calera felt strong arms gliding around her waist, pulling her closer. She wondered if distracting herself with another man could erase the bittersweet memories of another time and place . . .

The door suddenly burst open and Calera glanced around Marsh's shoulder. A startled gasp burst from her lips when the bittersweet memories she had stashed on the top shelf of her mind threatened to tumble down around her. Her torturous dream materialized in front of her, and a knot of anguish clawed at her stomach. Seeing the rugged Apache warrior, whose eyes burned into her like glowing coals, caused Calera to stumble back apace.

If the look on Shane's craggy features was any indication of his mood, Calera swore she was about to meet her brother's fate. She knew all too well what a formidable foe Shane could be. She had seen him take another man's life with that vicious-looking knife he carried in his moccasin. And she knew what had happened to her brother when he had dared to match hand-to-hand combat skills with this man. Shane was an imposing figure, a muscular mass of sinewy strength and lightning-quick reflexes. He was dangerous and capable of violence. Calera cursed herself a thousand times for being awed by such destructive potential.

"Try knocking next time, friend," Marsh snapped, stepping in front of Calera like a protective shield.

The swarthy giant paid Marsh as much heed as a hunter ignoring a rabbit on his way to confront a mountain lion. Marsh frowned curiously when the dark stranger focused glittering black eyes on Calera, prompting her to retreat another pace. "I want to talk to you."

Shane's voice rumbled with smoldering irritation. For the life of her, Calera could not imagine what he was angry about. *She* was the injured party here, certainly not *he!*

When Shane took two bold steps forward, Marsh whipped the Colt from its holster with a practiced ease that told its own story. "Get out . . . now," he ordered with distinct menace.

Shane never took his eyes off Calera, never showed the slightest reaction that would indicate he was concerned about having a Colt trained on him. "I came here to talk to you, Irish. Call off your guard dog before he gets hurt."

Calera was instantly reminded of why Shane was such a deadly threat. When it was his wont, he could mask all emotion. Suddenly his face looked as if it were carved from granite—like a man of stone with a heart to match. He could use his entire body as a lethal weapon and he possessed incredible agility, striking before his enemy had time to react.

"Irish?" Marsh questioned, bumfuzzled.

Marsh didn't glance at Calera. His gaze was glued to the ominous mass of strength that loomed in front of him—one that displayed not even a hint of fear or caution. This was the most dangerous kind of man alive, Marsh reminded himself. The gigantic intruder had the look of a man who was determined to have his wishes carried out—or else. When a man was so obsessively intent on his purpose that he damned all consequences to others and himself, he became an unstoppable force.

Marsh had the uneasy feeling that he was trying to contain the raging waters of a flood and proving quite unsuccessful at it. Only a well-aimed bullet would halt this powerful giant who made Marsh feel inferior in size and stature, and Marsh was certainly no one-hundred pound weakling, not by any means!

"Tell your guard dog to leave," Shane demanded a second time, his voice as cold as a tombstone.

The click of the trigger echoed around the silent room. Calera gulped, struggling with the maelstrom of emotion that assaulted her at the sight of this foreboding giant.

"Obviously the lady prefers that *you* leave," Marsh growled in a venomous tone.

For the first time, Shane acknowledged the pistol that was pointed at his belly, but he did so in such a nonchalant way that Marsh felt as if he were holding a toy weapon carved from wood. Whoever this man was, he defied all authority and scoffed at deadly threats. Marsh found this formidable stranger unnerving, to say the least!

"I'm losing patience, Irish." Shane said in an ominous tone.

"Just who the hell are you anyway?" Marsh wanted to know.

"Her worst enemy," Shane answered for Calera without bothering to glance in Marsh's direction.

The comment served its intended purpose. Marsh spared Calera a quick glance, noting the lack of color in her face. That split-second distraction was all the time Shane needed. Like a striking cobra, he reached out to snatch the pistol from Marsh's hand. Instead of pointing the weapon at Marsh, Shane tossed it on the foot of the bed.

"Leave now, my friend. You and I have no quarrel."

Marsh Layton, who prided himself on possessing a poker face and nerves of steel, was stunned to find himself disarmed with such remarkable ease. Furthermore, he was mortified by the fact that he had been bested with Calera as witness.

Inhaling a shaky breath, Calera tried to get herself in hand. It was apparent that Shane wasn't leaving, and she had no wish to see Marsh injured trying to defend her.

"Marsh, will you kindly close the door on your way out."

Marsh peered at her as if she were utterly mad. "You would dare to remain in the same room with this man?"

Calera's helpless gaze swung back to those obsidian eyes that reached across the distance to entrance her, despite her defiance. She had been here before, feeling herself drawn into those black pools by fierce will alone.

"If he intended to hurt me, I'm sure he would have done so before now. I will be all right, Marsh."

"But—"

"You heard Irish," Shane prompted. "Leave us alone. I came to talk to her. That is all."

Marsh pivoted to grasp Calera's clammy hand in his own, feeling the quaking she could not control. Pressing a kiss to her fingertips, he met her haunted emerald gaze. "I'll be right outside the door if you need me, Cali."

"She won't need you," Shane assured Marsh icily.

With great reluctance, Marsh veered around the towering mass of masculinity and closed the door behind him. Marsh didn't know what the hell was going on or who that gargantuan intruder was. Neither could he imagine what business a man like that had with a proper lady like Cali. And when, Marsh wondered, could that lovely nymph have met up with such a rough-edged brute? Marsh vowed to have the answer to that puzzling question the first opportunity he had to speak with Cali alone!

Chapter Sixteen

Shane stood in the middle of the room, battling emotions he had refused to display. Since the moment he discovered Calera's identity, the memory of her had haunted him. He had ridden hell-for-leather, driven by the compelling need to see her. The sight of that blond-haired rogue holding this bewitching elf had struck Shane like a physical blow. Despite the tragic circumstances that now left him and Calera at such impossible odds, Shane could barely abide the sight of another man touching the woman who had become *his* possession, a woman who had professed to love him less than a week earlier. But there was no love in Calera's expressive green eyes now. There was a shimmering mist of tears, a spark of hostility, and a glint of hatred.

"What do you want?" Calera demanded, her voice nowhere near as steady as she hoped.

Shane put his own frustrations aside and watched Calera. She was holding her emotions inside, letting them fester and boil. Her face was void of color. This wasn't the woman he had come to know, and he was determined to see Calera become her old self again.

"I'm sorry, Irish," he said in a voice that registered no emotion whatsoever.

Calera, who had maintained her composure as best she could up to this point, came apart at the seams, just as Shane hoped she would. "Sorry?" she railed, near hysterics. "You saved my life just so I could live through this? Well, you needn't have bothered!"

Impulsively, she snatched up the closest object within reach and hurled it at the infuriating man. The wooden tray on which her noon meal had been delivered slammed against the buckskin shirt that covered Shane's broad chest. He made no attempt to dodge the oncoming missile and he never even blinked when the object struck him.

When the tray clattered to the floor, the door flew open. Marsh bolted inside to determine if Calera had suffered injury. His gaze fell to the upturned tray before it darted to Shane, who hadn't budged from the spot where he had been standing a minute earlier.

"Irish has a temper," Shane said without glancing back at Marsh.

Marsh frowned in total bewilderment. The sinewy giant had obviously taken a blow, but he refused to retaliate against the petite beauty in lavender silk. Calera was staring at the intruder with tormented eyes. Marsh would have dearly loved to know what was going on between this unlikely pair, but no one bothered to enlighten him. In exasperation, he retreated, wondering if Calera intended to throw the whole room at the mysterious stranger before she was through. He also wondered if the enigmatic giant intended to let her get away with it.

"Do you think empty words will heal my pain?," Calera sputtered, determined to keep her voice down. "Did you know who I was in the beginning? Did you know I had traveled thousands of miles to be reunited with my brother after six long years?" Calera inhaled a shaky breath, feeling her composure crumbling around her. "You killed him! Do you think your apology can compensate for the anguish you put me through?"

Calera plucked up the tin plate and threw it at him with gusto. Again, Shane stood his ground, taking the blow on the shoulder.

Outside in the hall, Marsh listened to the crash of falling debris, wondering what object would next find itself in Calera's hands.

"I've missed you, Irish," Shane told her in a bland voice.

Calera hadn't known what to expect when Shane burst into her room. And sure enough, the man proved to be completely unpredictable. She had hoped to hear his version of the story, or at the very least, a sincere request for her forgiveness. She was only offered lies. He didn't sound the least bit sorry and he hadn't missed her, either! Damn him! She wanted to throw things, including this raven-haired giant who caused her emotions to erupt after days of keeping them buried inside her.

"I hate you, Apache. I despise you! You have destroyed all that I held dear." Her voice became a quiet but hateful hiss. "You used me and, fool that I was, I let you! But I am no longer a fool. Don't think you can barge in here and pretend emotions you don't feel. I loved my brother and there is nothing you can say or do to bring him back. He was all I had left!" Calera swiped at the squiggles of tears that bled down her cheeks and her voice boomed with torment. "Because of you I have *nothing!* Do you hear me?"

Who couldn't, besides the drunk and the dead? Shane asked himself.

When Calera grabbed the empty glass and hurled it at him, Shane didn't move a muscle. The glass grazed his cheek and shattered on the floor. He said nothing. He merely allowed Calera to rave on, venting her bottled frustration.

With supreme effort Calera inhaled a deep breath and lowered her voice, vowing that Marsh would not be privy to the conversation inside this room. "How do you think I felt when I arrived in Globe to surprise my brother, only to learn I did not even manage to attend his funeral? In one week you have destroyed two lives—mine and Keery's. All that I am, I am because of him. He supported me and provided for me. And when I came to repay him for his generosity, I find him gone, just like the rest of my family. And if that isn't enough reason to loath the sight of you, you stole the only gift I had to give. Ah, how proud you must be to know that you could do no more to the O'Connells, short of killing me, too! Double damn you!"

Having exhausted her unusual arsenal of weaponry, Calera lunged toward the pistol. Half-crazed with desolation and despair, Calera aimed the Colt at Shane's massive chest. "An eye for an eye, isn't that how it goes, Apache? I should bring you to the same violent end that you decreed for my brother. Then I could avenge him and put his soul to rest."

"If that is what you want—my life for his—then pull the trigger, Irish."

Her wild gaze locked with his, her fingers quavering against the trigger. "Have you nothing to say in your own defense?"

Shane looked Calera straight in the eye and said, "If I killed your brother, then he deserved it."

"*Deserved* it?" Calera repeated incredulously. "Who appointed you the arbitrator of Judgment Day, I'd like to know! And what did a kind, generous man, who sacrificed six years of his life to provide for me, do to deserve death?"

Shane moved forward, despite the threat of the weapon that was trained on him. He never glanced at the Colt, only at the teary-eyed woman who held it. "That is the question you must answer for yourself, Irish. You knew your brother six years ago. I knew a very different man. Are you reaping vengeance for the man he *was* or the man he had *become?*"

Calera was caught off guard by the comment and the preceding question. A dozen emotions warred inside her. She wanted to kill this looming giant. She *should* kill him where he stood!

"Irish . . ." His head dipped toward hers, despite the cold steel between them. His arms encircled her, bringing her trembling body into familiar contact with his.

Calera swore her legs had turned to jelly when Shane wrapped her in his brawny arms and kissed the breath out of her. The taste of his kiss had remained locked in her mind, simmering just beneath the surface, no matter how deeply she tried to bury it. The embrace was tender and yet devouring, opening a vault of emotions inside her. She cursed her betraying body for responding, but nothing could halt the tantalizing sensations that mingled with those forbidden memories. Calera was every kind of fool, she knew. Shane was taking advantage of her, just to save his own worthless hide. He was trying to rekindle the flame he so easily ignited in her, hoping she wouldn't press charges and see him hanged.

He was using her again, but in a far crueler way than before. He was forcing her to chose between her brother and her wanton desire for him. He was trying to demolish her hatred by preying upon the love she had confessed for him. But it wasn't going to work! She had fallen in love with a dream, not bitter reality. Reality was that Keery died because of Shane. She could never forget that. She could not betray her brother's memory, not after all he had done for her. How could she live with herself if she did?

Calera twisted away, finding that Shane made no attempt to hold her when she rejected him. And damn this infuriating man! He behaved in such an impossible manner that she didn't know what to think of him.

Shane reached up to limn her lovely features, rerouting the tears that streamed down her cheeks. He lifted the hem of his buckskin shirt to retrieve the small jewel-handled dagger and offered it to her. For protection? Or did he expect her to use it on herself? Calera never knew with a man like Shane Stafford.

"Take care of yourself, Irish. This is a rough town."

Shane pressed one last kiss to her quivering lips and then spun on his heels, walking away without looking back. Calera wanted to pull her hair out by the roots! Curse the man! He was making her crazy!

"I still hate you for what you did and I will go on hating you until the day I die!" she flung at his departing back.

When the door opened and shut behind him, Calera collapsed on her bed. A coiling ache gnawed at the pit of her stomach. Shane had returned to the scene of his vile crime, playing with her fragile emotions, hoping to soften her while she was vulnerable. But she was not going to succumb to his overpowering presence or those forbidden memories of a dream-turned-nightmare. Hating Shane Stafford had become the driving passion in her life. She would never *ever* forgive him. He was not going to destroy the precious memory of her brother, either!

"Dear God!" Calera wailed before emotion erupted like an earthquake. In less than a heartbeat, unbearable torment had reduced her to blubbering tears.

When Shane appeared in the hall, Marsh pushed away from the wall against which he had been leaning. He extended his hand, even though Shane stared at it as if it were some peculiar object he had never seen. "My name is Marsh Layton. Who in the hell are you?"

Shane accepted the proffered hand. "Shane Stafford."

Marsh jerked his hand away as if he were touching live coals. "Stafford?" Owl-eyed, he gaped at the bronzed giant. "You're the man who—"

"Who killed her brother?" Shane finished since Marsh appeared incapable of speech. "Yes, I am."

Marsh's breath came out in a rush as he glanced toward the closed door. "It's a wonder she didn't shoot you. *I* would have."

The fact that Calera had not blown Shane to kingdom come was the only hope of reconciliation he had. "If she had pulled the trigger, I would have made no attempt to stop her."

Marsh shook his blond head, miffed by this powerfully-built *hombre* and the unexplained connection between him and Calera. For certain, they had met before. Marsh jerked up his head when a disturbing thought occurred to him.

"No, I wasn't riding with the renegades who abducted her," Shane contradicted the unspoken question in Marsh's eyes. "I rescued her from the Tontos, but I didn't know who she was, nor did she know me."

"The sheriff told me why he didn't press charges against you—because of the incidents surrounding Keery's death. But he didn't have the heart to tell Cali what kind of man her brother turned out to be."

Shane could sympathize with the sheriff's decision. He hadn't wanted to shatter the memory Calera had erected of her older brother, either. Shane could not bring himself to torment her more than he already had. He would have sacrificed his own life, if that had been her wont for compensation.

Shane glanced sideways when he heard footfalls in the hall. Lyle Broxton recognized Shane and stopped short.

"What has happened? Is Calera all right? Where is she?"

Shane's narrowed gaze flicked from the physician to Marsh. "There are two of you?"

It took Marsh a moment to comprehend what the bronzed giant meant. He broke into a grin. "The competition for the lady's affection appears quite fierce. It seems there are not two, but three of us." His brows arched over twinkling blue eyes. "No man would walk in where angels fear to tread unless he felt very strongly about something, or unless he is an idiotic fool. After our first encounter, I doubt the latter is true in your case."

Shane did not appreciate the fact that he was beginning to like this blond gambler who vied for Calera's affection. And furthermore, Shane could see why Calera might be drawn to this good-natured rake. Marsh had charm, style, and an easy smile—none of which Shane thought he possessed.

"Lord have mercy, you didn't go in there, did you, Shane?" Lyle questioned anxiously. "If you upset Calera after I just got her back on her feet, I'll never forgive you."

Shane eyed the overly concerned physician for a thoughtful moment. The man was as bewitched as Marsh. That was obvious. The feisty elf who had haunted Shane's waking and sleeping hours had also captivated both these men.

"Well, did you upset the poor woman?" Lyle demanded, casting apprehensive glances toward the door.

Shane shook his dark head. "I gave her the kind of medicine you could not provide. You tried to give her something to fight *for* when she could see nothing but loneliness and despair in front of her. I gave her something to fight *against*. I let her take her frustration out on its true source. She no longer holds her emotions inside to fester and boil."

When Shane ambled away, Lyle heaved a sigh. "I wonder why he dared to come here? Most men would not have ventured close under these circumstances."

Marsh watched the half-breed disappear around the corner before he said, "I have the inescapable feeling Shane Stafford is *not* most men."

"You've got that right," Lyle assured him.

Marsh did not need a second opinion to know that for a fact. But what really piqued his curiosity was what had transpired between Shane and Calera while the half-breed was returning her to civilization. Just how well had Shane come to know Calera? The speculation sent a surge of jealousy coursing through his veins. The same surge, Marsh predicted, that had coursed through Shane when he walked in unannounced, to see Calera in another man's arms. And then, of course, there was the good Doctor Broxton who had come to escort the fair lady to dinner. The competition around here was indeed fierce!

"If you will excuse me, I have plans for the evening." Lyle smiled in satisfaction.

Marsh gnashed his teeth until he very nearly ground off the enamel. The doctor looked too pleased with himself for Marsh's tastes. Before the night was over, Marsh's frustration was going to lead him into another woman's arms to satisfy this unfulfilled craving he had been harboring since he laid eyes on that shapely green-eyed siren. He could also use a drink . . . or four. Marsh wondered if Shane would like some company. He was willing to bet they both were being hounded by the same frustration.

Shane half-turned while he leaned on the supporting beam of the hotel, watching Marsh saunter outside.

The questioning lift of Shane's brow provoked Marsh to chuckle. "The lady has another engagement this evening, with Doc Broxton. Dinner and a carriage ride in the moonlight, I'll wager. Can I buy you a drink, friend?"

When Lyle Broxton emerged from the lobby with Calera on his arm, Shane found himself snubbed. It was quite a spectacular display, to be sure. He had been ignored plenty of times, but never as superbly as Calera was ignoring him now.

After Broxton escorted Calera down the street, Marsh chortled softly. "The doctor and I caught Cali at a weak moment. I don't think you were so lucky."

Shane had no doubt about that. He had never enjoyed a single stroke of luck, except the kind he made for himself. His competition held a distinct advantage over him. But then, Shane was accustomed to battling life the hard way. Yet, he had made a vow to himself while he rode toward town. No matter *what* it took, no matter *how long* it took, he was going to convince Calera O'Connell that he did care about her, despite their impossible conflict.

Not so long ago, Shane had vowed that saucy sprite would be better off without him. Now the situation had changed drastically. She was alone, much like he was. They were still worlds apart, joined only by a dream that had turned nightmare. But no matter what, the day would come when Calera realized Shane had never meant to hurt her.

"How about that drink, Stafford?" Marsh prompted his preoccupied companion.

"Are you sure you want to be seen with me, Layton?"

Marsh shrugged nonchalantly. "I'm in the habit of choosing my own friends on their merit, not their reputation."

Shane accepted the offer. Marsh was new in town and he obviously hadn't heard the tales that circulated about the halfbreed.

"You will not endear yourself to Irish," Shane pointed out as his long, graceful strides took him down the boardwalk.

"Like I said, I make my own judgments."

Damn, Shane hated liking a man who could very easily take away the one thing that was important to him.

And damn, Marsh did not appreciate his unexplained desire to befriend a man who might walk away with the very woman he wanted more than any woman he had wanted in a very long time. Marsh had the feeling he and Shane had just formed a friendship of grudging respect and mutual curiosity. But then, what else did they have to do while Doc Broxton was courting the lady who had intrigued them all?

"Calera, you really must eat," Lyle insisted after watching her shove the pieces of steak around her plate with her fork.

Eat? With her stomach tied in knots? Impossible! Shane's appearance and his baffling behavior had Calera's mind spinning in circles. She didn't know what to make of that man. They had once been as close as two people could get and yet she didn't know Shane at all. He had refused to talk about his life and had never pressed her for details about her past. All she knew was that Shane had mentioned someone had stolen Sultan. Was that someone Keery? Is that what had started the fracas that left Keery dead? Dear God, had her brother perished because of a blood-red stallion with winged hooves?

"Lyle, tell me about Shane Stafford," she requested after a moment.

Lyle frowned warily. "I don't think you should—"

"Please," she interrupted him. "I want to know about the man I am contemplating charging for murder."

Lyle toyed with the napkin in his lap. "Well, I have no quarrel with the man myself. Some people, who battled the Apaches or lost loved ones to raids, hold him personally responsible for their woes. And there were . . . are those who tried to influence the opinions of others against Shane."

When Lyle failed to meet Calera's direct stare, she frowned warily, noting that he had changed from past tense to present tense in midsentence. "Are you referring to my brother?"

Lyle looked decidedly uncomfortable. "Really, Calera, this is not good for you so soon after your collapse."

Calera was not to be put off. She leaned forward, forcing Lyle to meet her unblinking stare. "Is my brother responsible for the ill-feelings the townspeople bear toward Shane?"

Lyle released the breath he had been holding in a whoosh. "Yes, I'm afraid so." He rushed on, refusing to dwell on that unpleasant subject. "Shane Stafford, as the story goes, was the son of an Apache maiden. Robert Stafford befriended the Indians when he came west to stake land in the territory. Some say the liaison Robert formed with the Apache maid was a tactic to ensure peace and provide protection while other farmers battled the Apaches for land that originally belonged to the tribe."

"Are you saying it was a marriage of convenience?"

Lyle gulped and looked away. "I'm not saying the union was a marriage at all."

"I see." Calera sank back in her chair, waiting for Lyle to continue.

"As I have heard it told, Shane grew up among the Apaches. His father returned to the ranch he claimed in the fertile valley beneath the Mogollon Rim. It turned out that Robert Stafford already had a wife and a son. He sent for them after he had established good relations with the Apaches."

Calera inwardly groaned at the information. No wonder Shane refused to discuss his background. He was the bastard son of a man who had used an Apache maiden for convenience, leaving her and his half-breed son behind while he returned to his white family and the respectability they could provide. The man was heartless!

"When Shane was a young man, his half brother, Charles Stafford, who was five years his senior, was killed trying to train a wild stud colt. The animal trampled him when he resorted to using a whip."

Sultan. Calera knew that without asking.

"After Charles died, Robert decided to retrieve his half-breed son from the Apache village. Shane's mother was critically ill at the time. She and the tribal council gave consent for Robert to take his son. That was when Shane's indoctrination to the white man's ways began.

"Muriel Stafford was beside herself when she lost her son and she was outraged to learn her husband had fathered a child with an Apache maid. She refused to accept Shane and the family was in great conflict for years. But Robert was determined that his half-breed son would inherit part of the Bar "S" Ranch. It was a double blow to Muriel when Robert allowed

Shane to train the very stallion that had killed her son. It is the same steed that Shane rides to this day."

Lyle took a sip of wine to lubricate his vocal cords and continued, "There was always friction between Shane and Muriel, but conditions worsened when Robert died during an accident at roundup a few years ago. In short, Shane has had to battle his way through life, facing gossip, bitterness, hostility, and resentment."

Calera picked at her meal while Lyle obliged by relating incident after incident in which Shane had been ostracized by several citizens who held grudges after their dealings with Apaches. More and more, Calera was beginning to realize why the handsome warrior preferred the wilderness to civilization. The knowledge of Shane's hardship only made Calera's mental wrestling match more difficult.

Earlier, Calera had despised Shane, mustering a burning hatred to protect her shattered heart. She had lashed out at him, railed at him, unleashed the churning emotion she had bottled inside her. Shane had stood there and endured the physical blows, the insults, every accusation without defending himself. He had infuriated her with his bland comments and that well-schooled expression that masked his face . . .

Calera frowned at her plate and paused to analyze what had seemed very peculiar actions on Shane's part. Why, the man had invited her fury—promoted it, in fact. Who else did she know who had the gumption to make an appearance after all that had happened? Calera slumped back in her chair, astounded at how well Shane seemed to know her when she couldn't understand him . . . or at least she hadn't thought she understood him, until now.

As a child, Calera had turned her despair inward when her emotions underwent upheaval. She wondered if perhaps Shane was accustomed to doing the same thing and knew the torment of bottling frustration inside. He had made a bold entrance, shocking her, forcing her to confront her anger and grief. She had spewed at him like a geyser and she had felt ever so much better after screeching at him and having herself a good cry.

How could he have known what she needed if he had not been there many times himself . . . ?

"I know you have not asked for my advice," Lyle was saying when Calera got around to listening, "But I wouldn't file charges. The painful truth is that your brother was just as much at fault as Shane. Of course, there are those who do not share my opinion, those who would like to use Shane Stafford as a scapegoat for their own bitterness against the Apaches."

"I will weigh my decision carefully," Calera murmured before forcing herself to eat.

Dear God! There was so much to consider, and yet, the sense of duty she felt to her brother very nearly overwhelmed her. Quite honestly, she didn't know what to do. But for certain, this mental wrestling match was exhausting her!

While Calera was sorting out her emotions, Cactus and Sticker were turning the town upside down trying to locate Shane. They had feared the worst. But to their surprise and relief, they found Shane seated at a table in a saloon, conversing with a fashionably-dressed gambler.

"God, are we glad to see you," Cactus said with a relieved sigh. "We didn't know what to expect when we caught up with you."

"We nearly ran our horses into the ground tryin' to keep up with you," Sticker added, dropping tiredly into a chair.

After Shane made the introductions, the saloon girl set a full bottle of whiskey on the table. Cactus and Sticker wasted no time downing their portion.

"Well?" Cactus demanded after his third drink.

"Well what?" Shane inquired.

"Well, why did you thunder off like a bat out of hell?"

Shane picked up his drink, staring at the Linnox brothers over the rim of his glass. Straight-faced he said, "I was thirsty."

Marsh bit back a grin when the Linnox brothers muttered at the evasive reply. He had the feeling Shane was in the habit of keeping his own counsel.

"If that's all it was, you should've said so," Cactus grumbled. "I've got calluses on my saddle sores, thanks to you."

Sticker perked up. "Maybe a massage is in order." His gaze darted toward the door. "Since we're in town, maybe we oughta pay the girls at The Cottage a visit."

"Perhaps you should," Marsh concurred. "The Cottage will be closing down very shortly. The new owner doesn't approve of brothels."

"Closing down?" Cactus and Sticker crowed in unison.

Shane paused in mid-drink, staring at Marsh with slitted eyes. "What is Irish planning?"

"Who's Irish?" Sticker wanted to know as he wiped a drip of whiskey off his stubbled chin with his shirt sleeve.

"Calera O'Connell is Keery's sister. She now owns the majority of interest in The Cottage," Marsh reported. "She is thinking of turning the bordello into a respectable hotel, at least that is what Royal Winston told me. Royal invited me to The Cottage before it goes out of business."

"Close down The Cottage? Why it's a noted landmark!" Cactus protested. "I live for these visits to town!"

"And what about you, Shane?" Marsh questioned pointedly.

"Keery wouldn't let Shane in his high-class establishment because he's a breed," Sticker insisted between sips. "That's what started the feud years back. Shane was comin' to get me an' Cactus an' Keery tried to force Shane out."

"Now that Keery ain't around to put up a fuss, you wanna join us, Shane?" Cactus questioned.

Shane swirled his drink around his glass. "No, you two enjoy yourselves. I'll stick with the whiskey."

"It ain't no substitute for a warm, willin' woman," Sticker insisted, rising eagerly from his chair to follow his brother out the door.

No, it definitely wasn't, thought Shane. The woman he wanted despised him with a vengeance. Not even the effects of liquor could wash away that fact. Perhaps he should simply back away and let Marsh Layton court Calera, distasteful as that thought was. The gambler was personable and the community had readily accepted him. He would be good for Calera with his engaging smiles and easy laughter. Marsh could help Calera through the difficult times ahead of her and help her adjust to her loss.

"I guess I'll call it a night," Marsh announced. "I want to make sure Cali has been safely returned to her room."

"Layton, about what happened earlier tonight—" Shane began.

"It's already forgotten." Marsh grinned wryly. "Why do you think I decided to befriend you? When a man disarms me as easily as you did, I want to be on his side when fights break out."

When Marsh ambled off, Shane stretched his long legs beneath the table and leaned back, to down the remainder of whiskey in one swallow. He really should back away, giving Calera the time and space she needed to cope with the tragedy. Marsh Layton was willing and able to keep an eye on Calera. And so was Doc Broxton, for that matter. Calera was obviously getting plenty of tender, loving care. Calera would prefer that Shane leave her alone while she was making arrangements to have him hanged. Muriel would enjoy that. She had been trying to get rid of Shane for years.

Unfolding himself from his chair, Shane sauntered out of the saloon, sensing all eyes upon him—as usual. Ah, just once he would like to enter this town without feeling as if he were a spectacle on parade. But that wouldn't happen for years, not until the seeds of insult and the condemning gossip Keery had sowed were long forgotten.

Damn it! Didn't Shane have enough torment in his life already? Why did that lovely pixie with red-gold hair and sparkling green eyes have to be Keery's kid sister?

Chapter Seventeen

Calera tossed her wide-brimmed hat aside and unpinned her hair, letting it cascade to her waist. She had just unfastened her gown when a knock resounded on the door. Her back stiffened, wondering if Shane had returned to cause another upheaval of emotions.

"Who is it?"

"Marsh. May I come in?"

"It's open."

Marsh swaggered inside and stopped in his tracks when the lanternlight caught flame in the unbound red-gold tresses. Damn, this was one gorgeous woman! She had the face and body other females would kill for. Entranced, Marsh crossed the room to uplift a strand of living flames, inhaling the feminine scent that teased his senses.

"Have I told you how lovely you are, Cali?"

"Yes, but I long ago became immune to idle flattery." She removed herself from his close proximity. She had allowed Marsh to kiss her and that had been a mistake. Calera had found herself making unwanted comparisons. The policy of forgetting one man by falling into the arms of another had not proved the least bit effective.

"Something wrong, dear lady?" Marsh questioned huskily.

"No." Calera manufactured a smile. "I have a busy day ahead of me, that's all. I need to rest. Venturing out this evening took its toll on my strength."

"So the doctor's prescription caused a setback? I'll make it a point to tell him when he pays you another call."

"Marsh—"

"I'm leaving." He tossed her a bright smile. "I just wanted to check on you. It's become a pleasant habit I don't want to break."

Despite Calera's attempt to keep a respectable distance between them, Marsh cornered her. "Easy, honey. You know I won't hurt you."

His lips feathered over hers and Calera accepted the display of affection, reminding herself not to make comparisons.

"Tender, loving care," he whispered as he withdrew. "Doctor's orders, of course." With a wink and roguish smile Marsh took his leave.

Calera stepped behind the dressing screen to disrobe, humming an old Irish ballad that seemed strangely comforting to her, just as it had been when she was a child. When her life was in turmoil—and it had been plenty of times, she was sad to say—she always found something to cling to. Calera cautioned herself against clinging to *someone* instead of *something.* The someones in her life had a disappointing way of disappearing. But she was going to survive this latest pitfall that had swallowed her. She would establish a fine hotel that added a touch of Eastern elegance to this rowdy town. She would immerse herself in the project of refurbishing The Cottage and she would get on with her life.

On that positive thought, Calera emerged from the dressing screen and stopped short. Her heart gave a painful lurch when she saw Shane leaning negligently against the wall, his face masked in that customary expression that gave none of his thoughts away. Calera's bewildered gaze flew to the door.

"I swear you are as quiet as a cat. Somebody ought to tie a

bell around your neck. How did you get in without my hearing you?"

Shane hitched his thumb toward the window, his bland gaze never leaving her shapely form—one enticingly displayed in the sheer nightgown. Although Shane had gotten very good at concealing his emotions, he could feel the heat of desire burning through him. Days of unfulfilled wanting coiled inside him. Forbidden yearning was eating him alive, but Shane was wise enough to know he had to proceed at a slow pace, just as the suave Marsh Layton had done a few minutes earlier.

The only relief Shane had enjoyed, while he sat crouched on the ledge outside the window, was overhearing Marsh's remarks. Thankfully, that rake had not taken Shane's place with Calera— completely. Shane had been bitten by jealous nips since he arrived in town to find Calera surrounded by two attentive men, both of whom were a far better match for her than he could ever be. But still . . .

"How *did* you do it?" Calera questioned incredulously, peering out the open window. "There is hardly a spot out here to get a foothold."

Shane felt the makings of a smile purse his lips while he studied Calera's curvaceous backside which was jackknifed over the windowsill. "Do you think a roof and window form as great obstacles as trailing along mountain summits, Irish?"

"No, I suppose not." She turned to face him, fighting for poise, striving for a tone of voice that registered nothing but indifference. She was not going to stare at this swarthy giant as she once had—with her heart in her eyes. Those days were gone like the images of a dream. "Next question. *Why* are you here? If you came to discourage me from bringing formal charges against you, I have decided not to press them."

Shane's onyx eyes flooded over her before he dragged his gaze back to her exquisite face. "Why not, Irish? I thought you wanted me hanged."

Calera purposely avoided that spellbinding stare and glanced at the bare wall. "Lyle advised against it because he insisted that Keery was—" Her voice wavered on her brother's name. "He was as much at fault as you were. Lyle also said the trial might stir up old resentments between whites and Apaches that are better left alone."

When Shane took a soundless step toward her, Calera added, "But do not think for one minute that I have forgiven you. My feelings have not changed."

"Which feelings?" he whispered, reaching out to trail his forefinger over the delicate curve of her jaw. "The love or the hate?"

"That is a loaded question." Calera slapped his hand away as if it were a pesky gnat. "Now that you know you will not become a wanted man, you can leave."

"I've missed you, Irish."

Calera's back stiffened. There he went again, saying things she knew he didn't mean. "Missed me?" she burst out. "Of course you did. That's why you sent me away and never looked back. Just how stupid do you think I am?" She didn't allow him time to reply. "Well, I am not *that* stupid, at least not anymore. I know exactly why you're here."

"Do you?" He looked amused by her volatile display of temper.

"I most certainly do," she said with great conviction. "You wanted to know if I was planning to have you strung up and left to swing by your neck. And since you know I plan to stay in the area, you probably think you can waltz in here anytime you please and I'll fall at your feet. You think just because I said I loved you that I will accept you as eagerly as I once did. Well, now I know that I fell in love with a dream in the seclusion of the mountains. It was nothing more than a fantasy!"

Calera inhaled a huge breath, causing the peaks of her breasts to strain against the sheer fabric. Shane's eyes automatically dipped to devour what he had not allowed himself to touch.

"We can't go back, Apache. You destroyed every chance of that when you rejected me and murdered my brother," she finished in an adamant tone.

"So you turned to Lyle and Marsh to forget," he speculated, still refusing to venture too close for fear Calera would dart away like a wary doe.

Her chin elevated to a defiant angle. "I did not turn *to* anyone. I simply turned *away* from you. There is a difference."

"So you don't love me anymore, is that what you are saying?"

Calera raised her chin another notch, staring at the awesome mass of masculinity who eclipsed the lanternlight and engulfed her in shadows. "No, I do not. Now go away and leave me be. I will not become the place you come for temporary satisfaction when you happen into town. I don't ever want to be in love with anyone again. I don't want to let anyone so close that I miss them when they're gone, either. It's too painful."

Tears misted her emerald eyes and her lips trembled, but Calera plowed on in grim determination. "I'm going to become just like you. My face will be a mask of cool indifference. My eyes will become chips of ice. No one will ever hurt me again, especially not you. In fact, I can even say the words I once offered you without meaning them. "I love you. I love you . . . ! And stop grinning at me, damn you!"

Shane couldn't help himself. He burst out laughing at the spirited tantrum Calera was throwing. She was still releasing pent-up emotion, and Shane let her, because it cured what ailed her. Shane had wanted to do that very thing himself in his younger years, but no one had volunteered to become his scapegoat. Usually, it was the other way around. But Shane would gladly play the role of a whipping boy for this sassy imp if it made her feel better . . .

Shane instantly recoiled when Calera slapped him across the cheek. He had been too busy snickering at her to anticipate her reaction. "Feel better, Irish?"

The question only irritated her more. Shane was not taking her seriously, curse his handsome hide. "Not yet!"

She doubled her fist and slugged him squarely on the shoulder. With a wail of pain, she shook the sting out of her hand. Damnation, when she tried to hurt this Apache warrior, she only hurt herself. The man was invincible!

The hairline crack in her composure split like the fissure of an earthquake and emotion crumbled around her. The tears Calera had valiantly tried to hold in check came gushing out.

Even the good cry she'd had that afternoon hadn't released all
the bottled emotion she had harbored since she had learned of
Keery's death and Shane's part in it. Calera sank down on the
edge of her bed and held her face in her hands, giving way to
frustrated emotion that clogged her throat.

"Now see—" Sob, gulp, "—what you've done!"

Shane sank down beside Calera, pulling her quaking body
against him. "Just let it all out, Irish, every last ounce of it."

Calera collapsed against the wall of warm strength and bled
a river of tears, wondering why she was crying on *this* man's
shoulder instead of any other man's. It seemed Shane was the
constant battle she waged against herself and never won. She
couldn't stop hating him and yet she hadn't gotten over wanting
him, either.

When Shane cuddled her close, muffling her cries, it reminded her of the time he had comforted her when she was
frying alive with the fever of infection. Oh, why was she so
susceptible to this wild Apache knight's tenderness? He cast
spells she couldn't break, that was why. She had fallen in love
with him once upon a time in a world far away, and then this
bittersweet affair had become the curse of her life!

"Cali? Are you all right?" a voice called from the hall.

Calera lifted her tear-stained face from Shane's shoulder and
peered at the door. "I'm okay, Marsh." She bit back a sob. "I'm
on my way to bed."

Her dewy lashes fluttered up, only to become entranced by
eyes that gleamed like black diamonds in the lanternlight. All
her firm resolve melted like snow when Shane gently wiped
away her tears with his fingertips and then brushed them across
his own lips. He bent his raven head to take her mouth beneath
his in the tenderest kind of kiss. His lips were like liquid heat
upon hers, dissolving her resistance. Despite everything, this
man still possessed the ability to twist her insides into hot, aching knots and make her want him beyond reason.

Calera felt herself sinking into a hazy cloud, knowing all the
anger and resentment in the world couldn't compete with the
forbidden yearnings that this one man's kisses and caresses

aroused. She was a royal fool and she knew it. But just once more, just this one last time before she closed all doors on her past and looked to the future, she longed to dream that cherished dream of a mountain paradise. She would let this bronzed wizard weave his spell of Apache magic and transport her back to that fairyland of innocent fantasy. For this one space out of time there would be no past, no future, no bitter resentment. There would be only this unrivaled pleasure that spilled through her, drowning all thought.

Shane inhaled a shuddering breath and deepened the kiss when he felt Calera surrender to the pleasure they had shared a lifetime ago in the mountains. He kissed her until he couldn't remember what it was like *not* to be kissing her, touching her, holding her. All the tormented frustration Shane had endured these past few days evolved into hungry desire. Even the sweet memories couldn't match the delicious feel of this nymph's luscious body pressed familiarly to his. It was as if he had survived only for this moment. When he was in Calera's silky arms there was no right or wrong, no anger or torment. There was nothing but the hypnotic beat of her heart pressed to his, only the feel of indescribable longing pounding out her name in ragged whispers.

It seemed like weeks since he had held her. It seemed years since he had satisfied this wild hunger, awaiting the phenomenal pleasure he knew would follow. There was no doubt about it. He was addicted to this green-eyed elf. He wanted her despite everything, and at any cost.

Shane remembered what Neva Sanchez had told him about his father, how he had loved the Apache maid, even while he remained married to Muriel. Only now was Shane beginning to understand the torment his own father must have endured. If Robert Stafford felt the same way about Shane's mother, it had been pure and simple torture to keep his distance. Robert had loved one woman and lived his life with another out of obligation to the white man's proprieties. Shane wondered what his life would have been like if Robert would have found the Apache maiden before he married Muriel. A dozen times,

Shane had cursed his father, but now he retracted every harsh thought. Robert Stafford had also been trapped between two worlds, tormented by a forbidden love. The fact that Robert had brought Shane to live with him, despite Muriel's fury, had been an unspoken declaration of the truth of his feelings . . .

Shane's thoughts trailed off when Calera slipped her hands beneath his buckskin shirt and drew the fabric away. Her fingertips skimmed over the lean contours of his belly and the padded muscles of his chest. Her caresses were as gentle as moonlight and as fiery as the sun. God, he loved her touch! Despite the obstacles between them, she, too, remembered those days and nights of unequalled splendor. She, too, wanted to recreate those magical moments when they had no identity except that of each other.

"Irish—" He groaned when her caresses became more intimate, more arousing.

Her index finger grazed his lips to shush him. "Just take me back to paradise, if only for the night, Apache. I've learned not to expect forever. Just bring back yesterday."

A low rumble reverberated in his chest as he clutched her to him, drinking in the sweet taste of her, inhaling the alluring scent of her. His hands moved upon their own accord, divesting her of the garment that prevented him from savoring every satiny inch of her. Denial had burned itself into self-destruction. Shane swore he had lived for this moment for weeks on end. He had never known anything as lovely and exquisite as this innocent imp who had given herself to him in the mountains. Letting her go had been like another turn on a torture rack. Discovering she was Keery's sister had buried the knife that stabbed at his heart. But holding this angel now, rediscovering the wild breathless passion they had created, compensated for every moment of torment he had endured.

Shane had watched this bewitching maid become a woman in his arms. He had watched her come close to dying and had prayed to all the Great Powers That Be—Indian and white—to spare her life when she was injured. And now he felt Calera come to life, fulfilling every dream. Touching her so intimately left him to burn. Sharing her kiss was like having fresh new life breathed into him. For this moment that pursued and captured time, he was whole and alive again. He was above pain and torment. Even if he and Calera could be nothing else, they were lovers who, for a few cherished moments, were one beating breathing essence—living for each other, through each other.

"I need you more than I need air to breathe," Shane whispered against the rosy tips of her breasts. "You're in my blood, Irish."

A quiet moan tumbled from her lips when his moist breath skimmed her belly and misted her thighs. Calera felt her body arching toward his gliding caresses, his feathery kisses. Intense pleasure pulsated through every fiber of her being when he worked his gentle magic on her sensitive flesh. Suddenly she was drifting in those majestic, purple-hued mountains that were as close to heaven as she had ever come. There was nothing between her and this magnificent man except a passion so fierce and tangible that Calera could touch the depths of it . . .

"Please, Apache," Calera gasped when his skillful fondling reduced her to begging for him to end the wild torment of having him so close and so unbearably far away.

"Please what, Irish?" he whispered, smiling proudly at his ability to pleasure her as he had pleasured no other woman. "Please leave you?"

Calera shook her head, sending the red-gold curls splaying over the pillow like a waterfall of fire. "Please love me." Her thick lashes swept up to see his masculine body gliding over hers, glowing like bronze in the lamplight. Her gaze locked with the black coals of his eyes and Calera felt the magnetic pull of his incredible inner strength. As so many times before, Calera could feel her very soul surging up from its resting place to pour through those entrancing eyes until she was a part of that remarkable supply of energy and spirit.

Entranced, she watched him come to her, felt the driving thrust of warm velvet flesh invading her, felt the flame of the man who possessed her. He moved upon her, watching her watch him. She heard the softly uttered incantation calling to her heart until it, too, beat only for him.

She was lost and gone forever, no doubt about that. Even the hatred she had harbored was no match for the uncontrollable blaze of desire for this man. He had become her heaven and her hell. She was betraying the memory of her brother because she couldn't deny the forbidden love she had discovered in that mountain paradise.

"Come with me, Irish," he murmured as he moved to the melody of passion that strummed through him. "Make this night span eternity."

When his sensuous lips slanted over hers and he plunged deeply within her, Calera surrendered all within her power to give to answer the billowing passion she could feel racing through his body like a current of electricity. The sensations seared her until she and Shane were flesh absorbing flesh, moving as one essence, sharing inimitable pleasures that transcended all bounds.

The world careened around Calera in a swirl of darkness that twinkled like a thousand fireflies in the night. Calera held on for dear life as the wild crescendo built and exploded like a crash of cymbals . . .

"What the—?" Shane croaked.

Calera's breath came out in a rush when the bed slats shifted and the mattress plunged to the floor. Shane propped up on his elbows to stare over the wooden bed frame that now surrounded their mattress like a baby's crib. Though he had been burning in the throes of mindless passion a moment earlier, quiet laughter bubbled in his throat and he grinned down into Calera's startled expression.

"I don't think this wild brand of passion we share is made for beds, Irish. It belongs in the plush carpet of grass in the mountain meadows."

Calera felt her heart fill with excessive pleasure when she saw his smile burst loose, felt his laughter vibrating all the way through her.

"I think you may be right, Apache. Has this ever happened to you before?"

"Not even once, until there was you," he assured her on a chuckle.

Calera chastised herself for posing the curious question. She resented the thought of Shane sharing such intimacies with other women. This was too private, too personal. As for herself, she couldn't imagine sharing these sensations with any other man. But no man could be as skillful and tender as Shane without years of practice to his credit. He always knew where and how to touch her, taking her to the ultimate heights of ecstasy. It hurt to realize there had been plenty of somebody elses in his life.

A frown furrowed Shane's brow when he saw the shadows in her emerald eyes. "What's wrong, Irish?"

"Nothing."

His full lips quirked and he stared dubiously at her. "I know you too well to believe that."

"You don't know me at all," she insisted.

"Don't I?"

All right, so he could sense her moods, she reluctantly admitted. Thus far, he had been able to read her like a book. He always seemed to know what she needed before she figured it out for herself.

Calera watched her fingertips drift over the steel-honed muscles of his shoulders. "I was thinking about the others who have been in your arms."

"The others?" Shane queried cautiously.

"Yes, and don't bother denying it. You seem to know your way around a woman's anatomy better than a practicing physician."

"Like Lyle Broxton, for instance?" He frowned darkly at the thought of the doctor examining this lovely nymph for any reason!

Her gaze locked with his. "I don't like the thought of the other women who—"

"Cali? What the devil happened in there?"

Marsh's voice and the hammering at the door caused Calera

and Shane to flinch. Their gazes darted toward the door and then refocused on each other.

"Cali? What the hell's going on? It sounded as if the walls crashed in around you."

Calera couldn't take her eyes off the handsome giant who hovered above her. She suddenly found herself wanting to erase every other woman from Shane's memory, to brand her image on his mind. If she couldn't have his love, then she would at least become a lasting memory. She would become that quiet smile that settled on his chiseled features when there was no one around. She would be the burning thought that flared in his mind.

"I stumbled and fell on my way to quench my thirst," Calera replied to Marsh's question. "Go back to bed, Marsh."

"Well, if you're sure—"

"I'm sure," she insisted.

After a moment, the footsteps receded and Shane grinned in wry amusement. "Quenching your thirst?"

"What would you call it?" she challenged him.

"Feeding an insatiable hunger," he insisted before staring thoughtfully at the closed door. "I like your guard dragon when he's on the other side of your door, Irish. Keep him that way."

"Jealous, Apache?" One perfectly-arched brow lifted above a mischievous smile.

"Insanely," he said before he kissed away her smile and rekindled the flame that burned within them.

Calera promised herself, right then and there, that this would be a night Shane never forgot. She knew he would leave her again, just as he had before. But when he walked away, he would remember and he would go on remembering how she had loved him, body, heart, and soul. She plied him with caresses as soft as a butterfly's wing, as silent as the echo of thought. She worshipped his hirsute flesh with kisses as warm as sunrays. Hands, lips, and silky flesh ebbed and receded over his sleek body like a hypnotic tide caressing the shore, washing away all that had come before.

When Shane groaned in unholy torment, Calera smiled in

satisfaction. Perhaps she was not as insightful as the bronzed warrior who could decipher her moods and translate her private thoughts, but she had learned to make him a slave to his own raging passions. She could feel the fires blazing in the heat of his flesh, feel the pulsating hunger that channeled through him.

The long tendrils of her hair spilled over his rock-hard chest like a whisper and Shane wondered how any man could tolerate such exquisite torture and live to tell it. This imaginative vixen had the most incredible knack of using every method of erotic seduction to drive a man past the point of no return. She employed the silky cloud of red-gold hair to tease his ultrasensitive flesh. She utilized soft fingertips to make his taut body hum beneath her provocative touch. She used her satiny body in one long maddening caress that sent Shane over the crumbling edge of restraint.

"Dear God, Irish," Shane moaned hoarsely.

When Shane borrowed her favorite expression, Calera chortled in amusement. Her lips moved over the hard contours of his hips and she glided her tongue down the velvet length of him.

"I can't take much more, I swear it," Shane groaned when sensation after maddening sensation ricocheted through him.

"Ah, but you can and you will," Calera assured him before her kisses and caresses retraced their erotic path to drive him another mile closer to insane.

Shane could endure no more, he knew it for a fact. His body was racked with torturous pleasure that was about to explode. One lean arm shot out to hook around Calera's waist, dragging her supple body above his.

"You ignited this impossible fire, imp. Now put it out before I burn alive," he commanded hoarsely.

His eyes glowed with such intensity that Calera could no longer deny his need—a fiery, overwhelming need that *she* had instilled in him. His hands clamped around her hips, setting her exactly upon him. He arched upward, eager to become her possession. The feel of her breasts gliding over his chest while she moved upon him was almost more than Shane could bear. And when her petal-soft lips opened upon his in the climactic explosion of

unleashed passion, Shane felt as if some wild force of energy-
charged power was dragging the very life out of him. His mind
and body were numb, devoid of thought and feeling. He was
suspended in space, somewhere beyond the borders of reality. It
seemed an eternity before Shane could pry open heavily-lidded
eyes and breathe anywhere close to normally. When he did, that
green-eyed elf was staring down at him like an ornery leprechaun.

"I've decided to make you pay for all the times I hated you,
Apache," she said as she drew lazy circles around his male nipples. "I intend to torture you until you beg for mercy."

"I just did beg for mercy, as I recall." He heaved an exhausted
sigh. "You cannot torture a man who has already endured the
most fascinating brand of torment, a man who is too numb to
feel anything but paralyzing pleasure." He grinned up at her.
"Sorry, Irish. Men do have their limits."

"Nothing left to give, you say?" Her brow arched in teasing
challenge. "Oh, I think I know you better than that."

"I doubt it," he contradicted.

Uttering those words was a big mistake, as Shane soon found
out. Despite what he thought was beyond the realm of possibility,
Calera teased his body back to ardent awareness. She created
energy when there had been nothing left to give. She stoked the
fires of desire until they fed upon themselves, recoiling upon
him until he was begging for wild sweet release. Only when Shane
pressed her to her stomach and took her in a heated rush, did
he realize the full extent of his hungry passion for her. And
when he collapsed upon her, burying his head against the column of her neck, he knew this lively sorceress possessed absolute
power over him. He would never be free of her spell. No matter
what direction their lives took, she would be a living memory, a
fantasy that followed him like his own shadow. She owned his
soul and the impossible obstacles that stood between them could
never change that one enduring truth.

When Shane eased down and drew Calera possessively against
him, she surrendered to drowsiness, content where she lay. She
was more exhausted than she thought, for she didn't rouse from

sleep when Shane lifted her in his arms and lay her down on the pallet so he could repair the bed.

And much later, before the sun made its fiery ascent into the heavens, she felt whispering kisses and bone-melting caresses working subtle magic on her flesh. With a tenderness that tugged at her heartstrings, Shane brought her from the depths of sleep to the heights of rapture before she drifted off into another wild sweet dream.

Ever so quietly, Shane unfolded himself from the pallet to don his clothes. His gaze flooded over the angel who slept in a cloud of fiery hair and wrinkled sheets. A wry smile grazed Shane's lips as he padded silently toward the window to exit the same way he had entered. He wondered if Calera's recollections of this night would be as vivid as his, if the memories would reach across the distance that separated them and hold her until he returned to check on her. He had accomplished his purpose in coming to town, but he had obligations waiting at the ranch and Calera needed time to deal with her own tangled emotions.

Shane wasn't thrilled with the idea of leaving Calera in Marsh's all-too capable hands for the next few days, nor the practiced hands of the physician. He only hoped the night he and Calera shared would linger in her mind. He knew she was vulnerable after all the anguish and despair she had endured. He couldn't force her or influence her as he longed to do. Shane wanted this woman's love, despite everything. He knew that was asking a lot and he wasn't sure it was best for Calera. But the decision had to be hers alone.

Could she ever truly forgive him, except while they soared past the stars into a universe of splendor? Shane didn't know the answer to that question. Only time would tell the fate of Calera's feelings for him. She had loved him once in a hazy dream. Would she ever be able to love him in reality?

With the silence of a cat, Shane slipped away from the room like a shadow vanishing in the light of dawn . . .

Chapter Eighteen

Just as Shane predicted, Calera awakened to find him gone and cursed herself for surrendering to wanton desires of the flesh. She had never been able to trust herself with that darkly handsome giant, not even now, not even when she knew the gentle hands that seduced her had been deadly to her brother. Dear God! Had she no shame whatsoever?

Calera raked the tangled strands from her face and propped on her forearms to see that the bed had been repaired and that she lay on a pallet on the floor. Had she really thought the previous night would be so magical that Shane would never leave her, that he would beg forgiveness for taking her brother's life and pledge undying love to her?

"Right, Irish, and goats fly," Calera said to herself as she levered up to her feet.

Shane Stafford was as wild as prairie grass and clinging to him was like trying to grasp a fistful of fog. If she knew what was good for her, she wouldn't fall in love with that shiftless Apache warrior all over again so he could reject her a second time.

Calera had finally come to realize why Shane had dared to show his face in town. For that she thanked him. He had forced her to confront her frustrations. He had provided an outlet for the tangled emotions that hounded her. He had given her back her fighting spirit. While Doctor Broxton's gentle bedside manner, and Marsh's playful teasing had failed, Shane's unorthodox methods had succeeded. It had taken Shane's brand of medicine to get her back on her feet . . . and later, *off* of them. But their night of splendor was undoubtedly another lesson Shane wanted her to learn. He was always teaching her things about herself and then outwitting her. Too bad Keery hadn't learned his lesson, Calera thought ruefully. No man could match Shane Stafford, that was a fact. And loving him was as dangerous as crossing him.

Calera shook herself out of her pensive trance and set to work making her bed. She had just completed the task and wrestled with the stays on her gown when Marsh hammered on her door like a mad carpenter. Calera invited him in and watched his sky-blue gaze take inventory of the room.

"Judging by the racket I heard last night, I expected to find upturned furniture. What in heaven's name did you stumble over, Cali?"

Calera turned away to conceal her smile. She had stumbled over a brawny giant who could transport her to a mountain paradise in nothing flat. "I tripped over the chair that slammed into the commode," she said instead.

"Any bruises?"

"One." Her heart.

"How about breakfast?" Marsh suggested, watching Calera with a critical eye.

She had changed somehow in the past twenty-four hours, Marsh decided. The previous morning she had been sullen and lethargic. Now her movements suggested a new burst of energy. And who, Marsh wondered, was responsible for this amazing recovery? He didn't like the answer that quickly popped to mind. He and Lyle had been playing nursemaid, and in the course of one day, that half-breed who had destroyed her life had miraculously offered it back to her with his clever tactics. How had he known how to handle Cali?

"I'm ready to face the world," Calera announced as Marsh ushered her out the door.

"So I noticed. I'm sure I deserve all the credit for your miraculous recovery. A kiss of gratitude would suffice." He leaned down with lips puckered, only to receive an appreciative peck on the cheek. He heaved a disappointed sigh. "Do you enjoy seeing a man starve to death for the want of your affection, dear lady?"

Calera flashed him an impish smile. "You have my pity if that's any consolation."

"That is not at all what I wanted," he grumbled.

"My gratitude then?"

Marsh paused in the hall, suddenly very serious. "I think you know perfectly well what I want, don't you, Cali?"

Calera averted her gaze, refusing to meet that probing stare that might decipher more than she wanted him to detect. "I know, Marsh," she said with a sigh.

"And?" He waited a long moment for her to reply.

"And I will understand if you grow impatient, while I am trying to find myself."

"In other words, don't push," he paraphrased.

"I'm afraid so. Right now I'm not certain I know my own mind." Luminous green eyes, fanned by thick lashes, lifted to him. "I suffered an emotional blow that knocked me to my knees. I have to reorganize my goals in life without looking for a crutch to lean on. It would not be fair to you, or to me if we—"

He flung up a hand to interrupt her. "You're right. I shouldn't have asked for what you aren't ready to give. I promised to be a gentleman and I've already forgotten that vow. Damned restrictive, this noble suit of armor I've locked myself in," he muttered resentfully. "I don't do this sort of thing for just any woman, you know."

She graced him with a smile. "I appreciate that."

"Obviously, you don't appreciate it enough," Marsh said as he shepherded Calera down the stairs.

Marsh was a nice man, Calera thought to herself. She was

fortunate to have Marsh for a friend. Calera hadn't realized how rewarding it was to have a friend . . . until she endured the hours that followed!

"How come we gotta rush back to the ranch so fast?" Cactus grumbled as Shane hoisted him into the saddle, despite his hellish hangover.

"Lord, I can't ride in this condition," Sticker croaked as he clamped a hand on the pommel of the saddle to support himself.

Shane led the way out of town, employing the shortcut that veered through the mountain passes where only a surefooted horse and rider could go.

"Would you mind tellin' us why you made that mad dash to town in the first place, Shane?" Cactus shifted to find a comfortable position in the saddle that didn't jar his sensitive head. There wasn't one. "And don't tell us you needed a drink. There's a stockpile of whiskey in the bunkhouse an' you damned well know it."

"I had unfinished business to attend," Shane said evasively.

"Well, you should've joined us at The Cottage, especially since rumor has it that it will be shuttin' down. Royal asked about you," Sticker reported.

Shane said nothing. He wouldn't have traded the night in Calera's arms for ten tumbles at The Cottage. And if he didn't feel obliged to oversee the roundup and placement of the cattle, horse, and sheep herds in their summer meadows, he wouldn't be leaving now. He preferred to watch Irish fly into one of her amusing fits of temper than face Muriel's scorn any day.

Too bad Muriel didn't pack up and leave, thought Shane. She could be enjoying the social life of which she had been deprived all these years. But leaving would be admitting defeat to her half-breed stepson. Defying Shane had become Muriel's obsession in life. Shane and Muriel had spent years defying each other. Shane refused to let Muriel win, even if she put him through constant hell with her hatred and scorn.

Mentally preparing himself for another round of Muriel's scathing insults, Shane headed for the ranch. If he had known Muriel was traveling in the opposite direction to brew trouble for him, he would have retraced his tracks.

Calera frowned curiously when she passed a group of men on the street and found herself snubbed for the umpteenth time. She had endured enough cold shoulders during her jaunt to The Cottage to suffer frostbite. The male population of Globe City was giving her no measure of respect and treating her as if she had contracted leprosy. Even the manager of the lumber yard where she inquired about hiring carpenters and purchasing material for renovations had snapped answers to her questions. And come to think of it, the restaurant where she and Marsh had eaten breakfast had grown unusually quiet when Calera entered.

Dear God, were the menfolk of Globe so attached to The Cottage for their paid affection that they would shun Calera? Obviously she had made a passel of enemies when word spread that she was closing down The Cottage. Men! They cared nothing for respectability, only the appeasement of their lusts. Well, by damn, they would learn to care about propriety and nobility!

Calera froze in her tracks when she opened The Cottage door and came face-to-face with the two scalawags she had met on the stage before her abduction. She was still alive, no thanks to Ike Fuller and Grady Flax. She shouldn't be surprised to find them in the bordello. No respectable woman would have anything to do with foul-smelling hooligans like these. They would have to pay dearly for any affection they might receive.

"So you survived to prance into town and shut this place down, did you?" Ike smirked. "Of course, an ice maiden like you is too good to run a place like this."

"I'm sorry them Injuns didn't keep you," Grady sneered disrespectfully. "Truth is, them Injuns probably gave you back before they froze to death."

"Too bad those renegades didn't abduct the two of you,"

Calera retaliated, refusing to be intimidated by the likes of these scoundrels. "If they would have lifted your scalps, those two mops of unkempt hair might get the good washing and brushing they need."

On the wings of that insult, Calera sailed through the door to Keery's office. Grabbing paper and pen, Calera printed the announcement that The Cottage was closing down for renovations. That would fix those two rude galoots.

After Calera tacked the poster on the door, she pivoted to find Royal Winston glaring at her.

"So you are actually going through with this, are you?"

"Most assuredly. The carpenters will be arriving tomorrow to turn this parlor into a lobby and the upstairs rooms into comfortable suites for respectable citizens."

"If I were you, Calera, I would watch my back," Royal advised. "I have spoken with too many outraged patrons, many of whom hold positions in high places in Globe. This town consists of too many men who have very definite opinions about what kind of entertainment they prefer."

"Nonetheless, I intend to sort through my brother's belongings and begin remodeling," Calera insisted, tilting a determined chin.

"You are asking for trouble." Royal prophesied before she wheeled around and stalked off.

Calera had dealt with plenty of trouble of late. This was more than a business venture. It was therapy to distract her from tormented thoughts of Keery and the lingering image of the man who had disposed of him.

Determined of purpose, Calera sorted through the papers in the desk. She worked at accelerated speed until she opened the bottom drawer to find it brimming with empty whiskey bottles. There was a stockpile of full bottles in the bottom doors of the cabinet that set against the east wall.

Calera slouched back in her chair, trying to visualize Keery ingesting the incredible amount of spirits he had obviously consumed. Dear God, how and why had her brother turned into such a lush? It had undoubtedly happened when he dived headlong into this den of iniquity, she decided. Evil brewed evil. But try as she may, Calera could not envision the energetic young man who had left Philadelphia to seek his fortune as the same hard-drinking brothel owner who had clashed with Shane Stafford. Who would be that crazy . . . unless he was rip-roaring drunk?

Calera heaved a troubled sigh. Was she afraid to believe the truth about her brother after idolizing him all these years? Had Keery changed so drastically since he ventured West that she would not have recognized her own brother? Apparently he had. Keery *had* lied to her about the nature of his business investment . . .

"I hope you're happy, Miss O'Connell."

Calera glanced toward the door to see a flock of soiled doves staring down their noses at her.

"Any of you who wish employment as maids at the hotel are welcome to—"

"Maids?" One harlot snorted in disgust. "I make more money in one day than you could pay me in a week. And you are making a serious mistake. There are plenty of men hereabout who won't sit idly by while you close these doors."

Calera braced herself against the mutinous glowers that were tossed in her direction. "I am sorry I have upset you, but I am doing what I think is right."

"The last *respectable* female who tried to protest The Cottage got run clean out of town," somebody else reported. "You just might, too."

"I refuse to be threatened." Her chin lifted another determined notch.

"It's your neck, honey. But I'd wager we'll be in town long after you leave," a buxom blonde predicted.

When the colorfully-adorned flock of courtesans fluttered off, Calera muttered under her breath. She had no reason to regret her decision. This was her establishment now and she held the majority of interest. If the men of this community wished to associate with these harlots, then they could bed down in those dilapidated shacks on the opposite end of town in what was known as the red light district. The Cottage would become an estimable landmark. After the railroad arrived, there would be distinguished guests traveling through Globe. Calera could do a thriving business, she was sure of it. The townsfolk would learn to adjust. It was simply human nature to grumble at change. But respectability was definitely coming to Globe City. All towns underwent this kind of transformation when civilization caught up with them . . .

A muddled frown creased Calera's brow when she opened one of the closet doors to find a wooden crate heaping with dynamite sticks. She supposed the surplus of explosives had been left over from Keery's days as a prospector—one of the many professions he'd attempted during the past six years.

Calera picked up the crate and started down the hall to stash the sticks of dynamite in the back storage room until she had time to properly dispose of them. Why Keery kept such dangerous substances in his office, Calera could not imagine. Why, the man could have blown himself up if he accidentally knocked over a lantern.

"Big mistake," Royal muttered as she halted in front of Calera. "Closing these doors is as dangerous as setting a torch to that crate of dynamite."

Calera shouldered past Royal who was laden down with her luggage. "You will change your opinion when we start making money hand over fist," she assured the resentful madam.

"I was making money hand over fist the way it was," Royal grumbled before she continued on her way.

Calera inhaled a fortifying breath and marched toward the storage rooms that were attached to the back of The Cottage. The entire community had tried to twist her arm a dozen different ways to force her to change her mind about the bordello, but she didn't care how much opposition she met. The Cottage was going to become a reputable hotel and that was all there was to it!

Tiredly, Calera trudged back to her hotel room, having confronted the same dark scowls that greeted her that morning.

Those who had pitied her ordeals the past two weeks had changed their sentiments in one whale of a hurry. Calera was glad she wasn't running for public office. She would only have received one vote—her own. She was also beginning to understand how Shane felt when he ventured to town. Gossip obviously spread behind his back, too, making it impossible to keep a low profile.

"I suppose you are planning to shut down the cribs in the red light district while you're at it." Horace Baxter chuckled as he fell into step beside Calera on the boardwalk. "These Westerners are a mite backward in their thinking. Though I admit I am one to imbibe in the spirits, I have never seen so many saloons in one town as I have since we crossed the Mississippi."

"I hope that means you agree with me that The Cottage is meant for nobler endeavors," Calera said with a tired smile.

"Morality on the western frontier is shockingly relaxed. All the vices and sins condemned in Eastern aristocracy are not only tolerated out here, but enthusiastically practiced," Horace noted. "From what I've seen and heard, even the men who are considered pillars of this society make no bones about their visits to The Cottage. What this backward town needs is a few more decent women to upgrade its lowly standards. Why, I could make a fortune if I imported suitable wives for these love-starved miners. Then perhaps the nymphs du prairie wouldn't be in such great demand."

Horace tipped the hat that set cockeyed on his head and veered toward one of the saloons. "More power to you, Calera. I like to see a woman with determination and spirit."

Two votes, Calera encouraged herself. Of course, if she showed up at the saloons with banners waving, insisting on prohibition and citing the evils of alcohol, Horace would take instant offense. The man did love his nips of whiskey . . . just as Keery must have . . .

That depressing thought caused Calera to miss a step. No one in town would tell her exactly what her brother was like. That wasn't a good sign. Even if she didn't want to hear it, Calera needed to know the truth about Keery.

Calera had no time to dwell on her wandering thoughts. The minute she entered the hotel lobby, a fashionably-dressed woman who matched Calera's size and stature blocked her path.

"Miss O'Connell, I am Muriel Stafford, Shane's stepmother. I wonder if I might have a word with you."

Calera frowned curiously at the staunch older woman whose thin lips were pressed into a grim line. What, Calera wondered, did Muriel Stafford have to say to her? Calera couldn't imagine.

"We can speak privately in the room I have rented," Muriel said, leading the way.

Mutely, Calera followed the woman upstairs and sat down when requested to do so. Muriel removed her expensive bonnet and carefully laid it on the bed before facing Calera with a somber stare.

"I have spoken with Sheriff Nelson, who informed me that you have changed your mind about pressing charges against Shane. I think you are making a mistake."

Calera's eyes narrowed warily. Lyle had told Calera that there was no love lost between Muriel and Shane. It certainly seemed to be true.

"It is my firm conviction that Shane should be placed under arrest and convicted of his hideous crime against your dear departed brother," Muriel declared.

Calera stared at the older woman for a long, ponderous moment. "Then you do not believe your stepson was provoked into the attack?"

Muriel expelled a distasteful sniff. "You do not know my stepson, Miss O'Connell."

That's what Muriel thought. Calera didn't bother correcting her.

"Shane is half Apache, raised like the savage he is, and always will be. He is capable of anything, murder included. Just because he bears the name of Stafford does not give him the right to attack innocent victims to satisfy his demented rages. He has been an embarrassment to me for years, and you should not allow the status of the Stafford name to influence your decision."

It was one thing for Calera to criticize Shane, she suddenly realized, and it was another matter for this hateful woman to do so. Lyle Broxton was right. There was conflict, at least on Muriel's part. The woman seemed willing to go to any length to see her stepson tried for murder. Indeed, Calera rather suspected such a woman as this would stoop to bribing a jury to have her way. Muriel Stafford must have had a great deal to gain if she could remove her unwanted stepson from her life.

Calera could not begin to imagine what Shane's life had been like with Muriel lording over him, belittling him, insulting him each time she had the chance. Calera had been shuffled from one parent figure to another each time she lost a loved one, but she had been accepted and loved. Obviously Shane had been scorned and rejected. No wonder the man didn't smile often. No wonder he spent his time training the magnificent stallion to avoid clashing with this bitter woman.

"Fact is, I have met your stepson," Calera admitted. "I have not yet gotten to the bottom of the conflict that provoked the battle that left Keery dead. But I think there is more to Shane than the brutal savage you described."

Muriel's lips thinned to such extent that Calera wondered if they would split under the pressure. "All right, I can see what you are doing. How much money do you want to press charges. I am willing to pay for your cooperation. Name your price."

Calera stared at the woman in disbelief. "Do you hate him so much?" she dared to ask.

Muriel exploded in bad temper. "Hate him? Hatred does not begin to describe my feelings for my husband's bastard son. How would you feel if you learned your husband had betrayed you for a squaw and spawned a renegade? How well would you have tolerated the fact that each time your husband took beef to the Apaches he was with another woman? And how would you feel if your own son was taken from you and you had to spend ten years of your life under the same roof with a half-breed who never should have been born! Shane will never be anything except what he is—a killer by nature and by habit. The world is better off without that savage around, I assure

you. My God, how can you not press charges when he took your
brother's life? Will you let that half-breed live to kill again in
one of his spiteful rages?"

Shocked did not aptly describe Calera's reaction to Muriel's
emotional outburst. The woman was poisoned with hatred,
prejudice, and revenge. Composing herself as best she could,
Calera rose from her chair to confront Muriel face-to-face.

"Mrs. Stafford, did you ever once stop to think that your stepson did not ask to be brought into this world? Did he have a
part in the tragedy that has befallen you? Perhaps he had no
more desired to be taken from the people who raised him than
you desire to have him underfoot. It seems to me that, in your
grief of losing your own son, you have made an innocent man
the brunt of your despair. And seeing that for myself, I have
no desire to punish a man who seems to have been punished
every day of his life."

"Of all the nerve! How dare you speak to me like that!"
Muriel gasped, highly affronted. "I would have thought a God-
fearing woman like you would wish to see justice served. But if
you plan to be difficult then so will I. I intend to have your
cooperation, one way or the other."

"Are you threatening me?" Calera questioned point-blank.

"No, I am assuring you that I will have my way in this matter.
This is the opportunity I have waited for and I will not allow
it to pass me by. I can make life very unpleasant for you if you
do not agree to help me."

Muriel stamped toward the door and directed Calera out of
the room. "I will give you time to reconsider and name your
price." She looked down her nose at Calera. "I pity your
brother. You have forsaken him by refusing to bring his murderer to justice. I hope you can live with yourself, young lady."

Calera paused by the door, staring at the older woman whose
face was puckered in an unbecoming scowl. Another layer of
resentment had fallen away after Calera had the misfortune of
meeting Muriel Stafford. Shane did not deserve Calera's hatred,
no matter how much grief she had suffered over her brother's
death. She wondered if Shane even knew what love was, never

having been exposed to it, at least not in the last decade. Perhaps Shane had rejected Calera's love because he had not trusted what he didn't understand.

With chin held high, Calera swept down the hall. She would not become a tool for Muriel Stafford's cruel attempt at revenge. And ah, how she wished Shane would have been there waiting for her to return to her room. She would prove to him that there was such a thing as love in this world, even if she had spouted her hatred at him in her anguish. No doubt, Shane had endured the screeching of a madwoman many times in the past. Calera was dreadfully sorry she had stooped to Muriel's level.

To Calera's disappointment, Shane did not come to her that night, or the night after. Marsh was there to keep her company after her hectic days of overseeing the carpenters' renovations and tolerating the remarks of the disgruntled patrons of The Cottage.

Calera had stopped by Muriel's room the morning after their first encounter, declaring that she had thought it over and she would never be a party to any plot of revenge. Muriel had smiled a frosty smile and informed Calera that she would regret her decision.

Thereafter, Calera had found herself plagued with more enemies than friends in Globe City. She had the inescapable feeling Shane faced the same hostility she endured when he walked through town, which was probably why he didn't frequent the community very often. And Calera could not find many reasons to smile these days, either. In fact, she spent most of her time avoiding accidents. Twice, she barely managed to dodge falling timber and debris when she ambled through The Cottage, supervising the work of the carpenters. She had very nearly been squished as flat as a flounder by a drunken miner who had plowed into her on the street and, recognizing her, had demanded to know why she didn't pack up and go back East instead of upsetting the way of things in the West.

Calera was beginning to wonder if Muriel had bribed the townsfolk to provide scare tactics and fling insults. But Calera refused to be browbeaten. Although she had not completely forgiven Shane for what he had done to Keery, Muriel's attitude did more to convince Calera to side with Shane rather than against him.

Tiredly, Calera ambled into her darkened room after dining alone in a restaurant of patrons who had turned their backs on her the moment she arrived. The temperature had dropped a quick ten degrees and she nearly froze to death while she wolfed down a meal that was cold and overly spiced.

Fumbling her way across the hotel room, Calera reached for the lantern, only to hear an unidentified sound behind her. A groan gushed from her throat when a bulky, foul-smelling body plowed into her, forcing her to the floor. Her face was forcefully mashed into the rug and her arms were yanked behind her. The scrabble of feet indicated there were two unidentified persons in her room. And before Calera could open her mouth and scream the walls down, a cloth was pressed to her nose. The pungent smell of chloroform infiltrated her senses and she instinctively twisted away, but the strong hands held her fast. Try as she may, Calera could not battle her way through the drugging effects that claimed her mind and body. She slumped to the floor, oblivious to the world . . .

"Cali?" Marsh rapped on the door a second time and received no answer.

Curious, Marsh let himself in and lit the lantern. A muddled frown plowed his brow when he spied Calera's favorite bonnet lying on the floor beside a handkerchief. Marsh plucked up both objects and gasped for breath when he caught the redolent scent that filled his nostrils.

Frantic, he darted out of the room and down the hall. He had seen Shane Stafford ride into town after ambling from the saloon with the sizable winnings he had gained from his skills with cards. Marsh knew he wouldn't have to worry about the half-breed beating his time because neither man would be enjoying Calera's company that evening. Public opinion had turned against her and now her life was at risk. Marsh needed assistance to locate Cali and he knew where to find it. Rumor had it that Shane Stafford's tracking skills bordered on phenomenal. Now was the time for Shane to prove his abilities.

Heaving a weary sigh, Shane swung down from his stallion. His gaze automatically darted toward the hotel. He had arrived at the ranch to find that Muriel had left for town during his absence. At first, Shane had viewed the unexpected departure as a blessing and he had thrown himself into the task of separating the cattle and sheep that were gathered for sale at the reservations. But the longer Muriel was away from the ranch, the more suspicious Shane became. He had been plagued by an inexplicable uneasiness for the past few days, an intuition that Muriel's departure brewed trouble. As soon as the cattle had been penned up for the drive to the reservation, Shane had hightailed it back to town.

Before Shane could request a room at the hotel, Marsh bounded down the steps, glancing in every direction at once. The instant Marsh spotted Shane, he charged forward, thrusting out the hand that held Calera's bonnet and the chloroform-laced kerchief.

"Something has happened to Cali," Marsh declared. "She was working late at The Cottage and I was detained in a poker game. When I went to check on her, I received no answer at her door. I let myself in and found these on the floor."

Shane caught a whiff of the kerchief and recoiled from the offensive smell. He opened his mouth to pose a question and then snapped his jaw shut when he spotted Muriel sauntering toward him. His eyes darkened ominously at the gloating smile that hovered on Muriel's pinched features.

"What did you do to her?" Shane snarled at his stepmother.

"Do to whom?" she questioned innocently. "I'm sure I don't have the faintest idea what you are talking about."

Shane took a foreboding step forward to breathe the fire of dragons on Muriel. He waved the chloroform under her up-

turned nose, causing her to jerk away from the strong scent.
"I'm sure you know exactly what I'm talking about, Muriel."

Muriel nodded thoughtfully. "Ah yes, I see what you are trying to do. You are trying to lay blame on me since *you* are the
one who has dabbled in foul play again. How very shrewd of
you, Shane. What are you planning to do? Dispose of the be-
reaved sister of the man you viciously murdered to ensure she
doesn't press charges against you? Well, it won't work. Calera
has decided to press charges so you may as well set the poor girl
free before you are tried for two murders rather than one."

Shane cursed the fact that Muriel had drawn a curious crowd
from the restaurant that was attached to the hotel. Muriel took
full advantage of the gathering audience and turned to address
them.

"It seems my stepson has taken the law into his own hands a
second time this month. Do you intend to let him get away with
murder—again? Now he has dragged off Miss O'Connell!"

"Shut your lying mouth," Shane snapped, fighting for control
of emotions that bubbled all too near the surface.

Muriel paid him no heed. "I do not need to remind all of
you what kind of man Shane is. There are many among you
who have dealt with the Apache. You know how ruthless they
can be. First Shane killed Keery. Now he has disposed of Calera
and is trying to place the blame on me. And since we all know
that *I* am innocent, I expect he will try to point an accusing
finger at some of you."

"Nothing would make you happier than for me to become
the honored guest at a necktie party, would it?" Shane hissed
at her.

"And nothing would make you happier than to frame me for
your attempt to dispose of the one woman who could see you
punished for brutally murdering her brother, would it?" she
retaliated in a hateful tone.

Shane loomed over Muriel, his eyes like black pits of venom.
"You have pushed me to the very limits, woman. If Calera is
harmed in any way, you will pay dearly for it."

"How clever of you to say so. But you are the one who has proved himself capable of murder, not I."

Scowling at the scene Shane had foolishly allowed himself to be dragged into, he shouldered past Muriel on his way to the door. Marsh was one step behind him.

Shane had been too concerned about Calera's safety to keep the customary lid on his temper. He swore Muriel had arranged this abduction to set him up. Odd, wasn't it, that Calera wound up missing soon after Shane arrived in town? That witch had probably been waiting for him to make an appearance before setting her plan in motion.

"I'm not sure your stepmother is involved," Marsh said as he followed Shane around the corner to the alley. "Calera's unpopular decision to shut The Cottage down has turned everyone against her."

"If you believe Muriel is innocent of wrongdoing then you obviously don't know my stepmother." Shane paused to hold up the lantern he had plucked from its hook on the supporting beam of the hotel. "Seeing me dead has become Muriel's aspiration in life."

"I'm just briefing you on the events that have taken place the past few days," Marsh insisted. "When Cali's life is at stake, I don't want to overlook a single possibility . . . What the hell do you expect to find in the alley anyway, Stafford?"

"Tracks." Shane paused every few feet to survey the powdery dust. "Whoever carried Irish off could not have descended the steps without being spotted."

"There is a set of back steps," Marsh reminded him. "Someone could have—"

"There."

Marsh squinted at the smeared tracks. "There *what?*"

Shane directed Marsh's attention to the footprints that set beside a circular print that led to a second set of tracks. He then gestured toward the overhanging eaves. "My guess is that two men abducted Calera and carried her across the roof to descend at this spot since the prints appear out of nowhere. Judging by the tracks, Calera offered no resistance—"

"Thanks to a strong dose of chloroform," Marsh grumbled sourly. "Those bastards."

Shane inched forward, carefully studying the tracks in the lanternlight. "They tethered their horses here. The horse that threw a shoe is the one carrying Irish."

"How the hell do you know that?" Marsh questioned in astonishment.

"The same way I know the larger of the two men is carrying Irish," Shane informed him. "The depths of the tracks indicate excess weight. See how the footprints are distorted. Clear prints indicate a man's normal gait. These tracks are much closer together, balancing added weight. They cut deeper than the smaller man's boots."

"Anything else you can tell us about Cali's kidnappers?" Marsh inquired, annoyed that he lacked Shane's impressive skills.

"Yes." Shane followed the tracks down the alley. "One of the men has a hole in his boot."

"Now there's a fascinating clue," Marsh snorted sarcastically. "Half the down-on-their-luck miners in town have holes in their boots."

In the hours that followed Marsh became begrudgingly impressed with Shane's skills. There were scores of tracks in the streets and on the dusty path that led away from town. But Shane had the amazing knack of singling out the prints of the horse that carried Calera, even when Marsh couldn't distinguish the difference. He merely trailed behind Shane, feeling utterly useless in this phase of the search.

Marsh was ready to throw up his hands in defeat when the trail wound into the foothills where pebbles lined the path. "Are you sure you know where you're going? I don't see even one dammed print."

"They split up," Shane informed his dubious companion. "My guess is one of the men circled back to see if Calera's absence has been discovered—"

"Or to report in to whoever is responsible for the abduction,"

Marsh speculated. "Do you want me to double back to town? I'm not any use as a tracker, that's for damned sure."

Shane nodded agreeably. "Keep an eye on Muriel. She is probably awaiting contact from her hired henchman."

Marsh wheeled his steed around and trotted off, the clatter of hooves echoing in the night. In grim determination, Shane surveyed the trail that weaved around the mountains toward the shacks that set beside the copper mines. Dim lights dotted the hillsides and Shane expelled a frustrated breath. It could take hours to locate Calera. By the time he did, a half dozen disasters could have befallen her. Damn that Muriel! She wasn't satisfied making Shane's life hell. She had to drag an innocent victim into her feud. Shane vowed to deal with that hateful witch as soon as he located Calera. He and Muriel were going to have it out, once and for all!

Chapter Nineteen

Calera awakened to find herself lying in a tent on a smelly pallet, her wrists and ankles bound with rope. She squinted in the darkness and tried to inhale a breath that wasn't thick with the offensive smell of chloroform. Calera wasn't sure where she was. A mining camp was her guess. Whoever had drugged her and carried her off had obviously thought she would be unconscious a good long while. Although Calera didn't know who had abducted her or for what purpose, she didn't care at the moment. She had been granted the opportunity to escape and that was all that concerned her.

Propping upon an elbow, Calera reached for the jewel-handled dagger Shane had given her. She was thankful that her captors hadn't checked her for weapons. Their mistake was her good fortune.

Contorting her body, Calera retrieved the dagger from her high-top shoe and sawed through the rope. She rose, then moved quietly toward the tent flap to determine if a guard had been posted. Through the narrow slit, she saw only a few silhouettes milling around the campfire that was situated in the center of two rows of tents and dilapidated shacks. Wheeling about, Calera stabbed the blade through the canvas at the back of the tent. Thunder rumbled in the distance and she waited for the second drumroll before she slashed an opening large enough to crawl through. As easy as you please, she slipped out the back of the tent and tiptoed away.

The nicker of horses caught her attention. Calera veered toward the sound. Within two minutes she had located the horses that were tethered near one of the shacks on the edge of camp. Calera silently thanked Shane for teaching her to ride bareback and how to fashion a harness and reins from rope. Until that moment, Calera hadn't realized how often she depended on Shane's teachings to survive in the West.

A flash of lightning streaked across the sky like bony fingers spearing through the clouds. Calera tugged on her makeshift reins to lead her borrowed steed away before she was apprehended. When she was a safe distance from the mining camp, Calera found a boulder to serve as her ladder and climbed upon the steed. Smiling triumphantly, Calera trotted down the path, using the Apache's compass—the Big Dipper—to determine direction.

Calera allowed the horse to find its own way as they trotted along the winding path. She and the horse were both nervous. Darting shadows and flares of lightning danced beside them like disembodied spirits. Calera kept expecting someone or something to leap out at her every other second. And even though her self-preservation instincts were on full alert, she was ill prepared when an incongruous shadow bounded from the skirting of pines.

A startled shriek burst from Calera's lips, frightening her horse. Wild-eyed, the animal reared on its hind legs, sending Calera somersaulting over its rump. Her chin bounced off the back of the horse, causing it to wheel in alarm and bound off in the direction it had come. Calera hit the pebbled path with a thud and a groan. Before the stars finished revolving around her head, steely fingers clamped on her elbow, hauling her onto wobbly legs.

"What are you doing out here, Irish?"

Calera blinked and peered up at the looming form beside her. "What are *you* doing out here, Apache?"

Shane scooped her up in his brawny arms and set her in front of him atop Sultan. "I was looking for you. How did you escape your captors?"

Calera fished the dagger from her shoe and proudly displayed it in the illuminating flash of lightning. "Handy little thing. A friend of mine gave it to me."

Shane nuzzled his chin against the side of her neck and smiled to himself. For the past few hours, concern had been eating him alive. But the sight of Calera put the world back into perspective.

"Do you know who kidnapped you?"

"No, I didn't see either of them when they pounced on me and drugged me with chloroform. I woke up alone in a tent and cut my way out of the rope and canvas. I borrowed a horse and here I am."

When Shane curled his arm tightly around her and pulled her back against his chest, Calera snuggled up to his hard warmth. "I suppose someone decided to cart me off since I closed down the brothel. No one likes me much these days."

"I know the feeling," he murmured. "But I'm not certain disgruntled miners are responsible. My stepmother is in town. She accused me of having you abducted to ensure you didn't charge me with murder."

"What? That is ridiculous!" Calera spouted off. "Muriel knows perfectly well that I decided not to press charges. I told her so myself. The woman actually tried to bribe me into bringing the case to trial."

"And since you foiled her plans, I suspect she took it upon herself to stage your abduction so I would look the guilty party. She certainly went to great effort to announce that theory to the gathered audience in the hotel lobby."

Calera glanced up at Shane's shadowed profile. "Is there no way to rid yourself of that spiteful woman? Why don't you simply divide the ranch and livestock in half and be done with it."

"Muriel does not want half a ranch, not when I own the other half," Shane explained. "She is so bitter toward me that she cannot abide the thought of sharing anything with me. It infuriates her that I continue to sell livestock to the reservations and donate extra supplies, beef, and mutton to my mother's tribe, just as my father always did. Muriel would prefer to see the Apaches starve on the barren lands where the whites have confined them."

"I'm sorry you have to tolerate her hatred," Calera said.

Shane shrugged a broad shoulder. "Muriel's hatred I have learned to endure. It is yours that is difficult to accept."

Thick lashes swept up to focus on his chiseled features. "I don't hate you, Apache, especially not when your stepmother harbors so much animosity against you. Muriel has dealt you enough misery without my adding to it."

"And what of your brother, Irish?" Shane felt her flinch at the direction question.

"I cannot answer that."

"What was your brother like?"

"You know what he was like," Calera replied, feeling the inner pain uncoiling at the mention of the sensitive topic.

Shane rephrased the question. "How do *you* remember him?"

Calera looked back through the window of time, seeing the vibrant young man who was teeming with optimistic hopes and dreams. "Keery was rambunctious and full of exuberant spirit," she said reflectively. "When I stumbled he was always there to pick me up and help me through the tragedies that struck. He never let me give up when we lost our parents and our uncle. And when he came west, vowing to make a life for himself and for me, he continued to send money to support me until I completed my education. He was my inspiration and I idolized him."

Shane had been all set to paint a very different picture of the man Keery O'Connell had become. Hearing the adoring tone of Calera's voice caused the words to evaporate. Shane could no more bring himself to shatter the tender memory than Sheriff Nelson or Marsh Layton could.

"And how do *you* remember Keery?" Calera prodded.

"We did not know the same man, Irish," was all Shane would say.

Calera wasn't satisfied. She had to know the truth, no matter how much it hurt. Twisting around, she straddled Shane's legs to sit facing him on Sultan's back. "I am tired of being protected from the truth. I cannot fully accept the loss of my brother until I know exactly what happened between the two of you."

"Sometimes, Irish, one is better off not knowing what one doesn't really want to know," Shane insisted.

"Perhaps, but this is not one of those times." Her chin went up and her determined gaze locked with his. "I know Keery had fallen to drinking, maybe even to excess," she added in a tormented tone.

That was the understatement of the decade! Shane thought, but he kept his mouth shut.

"I found scores of empty bottles and full cases of Keery's private stock of liquor in the office. Now tell me what I want to know because I will badger you relentlessly until you do."

"I can't," Shane muttered.

"You will," she vowed.

"It won't bring him back and it will only destroy your memory of him."

"Curse it, will you let me live with a lie?"

"The lie is more pleasant than the truth."

"Damn it, Apache!"

"Damn it, Irish!"

Calera noted the frustration that claimed Shane's features when lightning knifed through the clouds. Obviously, her brother had changed drastically the past six years. If that were not so, she wouldn't have such difficulty prying the truth out of Shane or anyone else.

"I'm waiting . . ." Calera prompted.

Shane inhaled a determined breath. "And you will wait much longer. I have nothing more to say on the subject."

The patter of raindrops caused Shane to quicken his pace. The moment Sultan set foot on the well-trodden path that led to Globe, Shane urged the steed into a canter and let the conversation die a merciful death.

Calera curled herself around Shane and held on as the stallion galloped off like the gusty breeze that preceded the ap-

proaching storm. The rhythmic motion of their bodies gliding
with the steed incited memories of other times and other places.
Calera felt that old familiar coil of desire burning deep inside
her. She was far too aware of this magnificent giant who held
her protectively in his arms.

"Apache?" Calera murmured against his chest.

"Yes?"

"It doesn't matter anymore."

The quiet confession prompted Shane to gather her even more
closely in his arms. Dear God, he hadn't realized how he lived
for moments like these when he and Calera were pressed familiarly together. He had given this green-eyed elf time and space
to sort out her emotions, even when the last thing he wanted to
do was to leave her alone. He had asked great concessions from
her, and Shane would have given anything if her brother's death
would not always stand like a mountain between them.

"I'm sorry, Irish. If your brother and I could exchange—"

Calera pressed her forefinger to his lips to shush him. "Fate
did not allow me to choose one or the other." Her feathery kiss
grazed the hollow of his throat. "And if I could, I'm not sure
I could bear to make the choice. It would have been worse than
tearing myself in two—"

"Thank God!" Marsh's relieved voice brought Calera's head
around to see that they had arrived in town to face a waiting
crowd.

Calera's gaze swept past Marsh's concerned expression to see
Muriel Stafford poised on the boardwalk. The woman's features
reflected nothing but distaste. In fact, the woman appeared anything but pleased to see that Calera had returned unharmed.

While Marsh pulled Calera from the prancing stallion, Muriel
elbowed her way through the congregation of citizens who
didn't appear all that excited to see Calera, either. She was not
the most popular personality in town these days.

"How very shrewd you are, Shane," Muriel smirked. "I suppose your heroics have accomplished your purpose. But I, for
one, am certain you staged this whole incident to earn Miss

O'Connell's gratitude. There is no extent to which you will not go to save your neck."

Although Muriel relished these theatrics, Shane did not. He had allowed himself to be dragged into an incriminating scene earlier that evening, but not again. He dismounted and faced his stepmother, forcing him to speak quietly when he really wanted to strangle her for putting Calera's life in jeopardy.

"You are fortunate Calera was returned unscathed," he said through clenched teeth. "If she would have lost her life because of your spiteful scheme, I would have taken yours. Hanging would not dim my satisfaction of taking you with me."

Muriel stepped back apace at the deadly menace in Shane's tone. Her gaze darted from Shane to Calera. She had noticed the way the two of them had held onto each other on the back of that devil stallion. Shane's words suggested he held tender feelings for Calera. That would never do! The very thought of Shane enjoying one shred of happiness tied Muriel's mind in frustrated knots. This half-breed bastard had ruined her life and she wanted to ruin his!

Turning away in disgust, Muriel swept back into the hotel lobby before the heavens opened and drenched her. She had to find a way to rid herself of this Apache curse! Frustrated torment was driving her insane. Seething, she watched Shane escort Calera up the steps. To Muriel's further exasperation, she intercepted another intimate glance between Shane and Calera. Muriel had to put a stop to this obvious attraction! It would foil her plans. She should have known better than to hire those two besotted clowns to abduct Calera. They had botched up royally.

Muriel ascended the steps, her mind racing. She had to devise another plan—and quickly. Her attempt at forcing Shane back to his own people by spiting him at every turn and bombarding him with hateful insults had proved ineffective. Keery O'Connell's death was the only opportunity Muriel had at her disposal. Somehow, she would find a way to turn Calera completely against Shane. Muriel couldn't rest until that half-breed bastard was out of her life forever!

* * *

"Well, where did you find her?" Marsh demanded to know the second Shane closed the door to Calera's room.

"Her captors left her in a mining camp northeast of town," Shane informed him. "Irish managed to free herself and escape."

"All this enchanting beauty and keen wit to boot?" Marsh marveled. "Who taught you to be so self-reliant, Cali?"

Calera swallowed a wry smile and shrugged evasively.

"Well, whoever is responsible has my vote of appreciation. I was worried sick." Marsh crossed the room to press a fond kiss to Calera's brow. "Get some rest, love. You have had a harrowing night." To Shane, he said, "May I have a private word with you in my room?"

Shane pushed away from the wall upon which he had been leaning and followed in Marsh's wake. The instant they were inside Marsh's room, Shane closed the door and pivoted to find a doubled fist coming at him with lightning speed. Shane staggered back while Marsh cursed like a trooper and massaged his stinging knuckles.

"Damn you, Stafford!"

"What did I do?" Shane questioned incredulously.

"You know what you did. The very fact that you didn't hit me back tells me what I need to know," Marsh seethed. "Just how blind do you think I am anyway?"

"How would I know? I didn't even realize you had trouble with your eyesight," Shane replied dryly.

Scowling, Marsh threw another punch—one that connected with air.

"You *do* have a problem with your vision," Shane mocked.

"All the while that I have been portraying the gallant gentleman, bowing and scraping over Cali, you have been—" Marsh's voice trailed off into several unprintable oaths before he got himself in hand and continued, "You have been taking liberties with her. For how long, Stafford? And don't bother denying it. I have been around enough to decipher those glances the two of you exchanged. I ought to shoot you myself and save your stepmother the trouble. She seems in a great rush to dispose of you."

Shane discreetly tiptoed away from the sensitive topic of his liaison with Calera. "Did you return to town in time to see Muriel conferring with anyone?"

Marsh shook his blond head. "I didn't arrive much before you did. "I got—" He glanced away. ". . . lost."

"Then we have no proof to tie Muriel to the abduction?" Shane muttered.

"None whatsoever."

"Then we'll have to keep a close watch on Irish," Shane declared. "Muriel doesn't give up easily. I suspect she will try again."

"You can bed down with me," Marsh insisted. "That way I can keep track of *you* as well as Cali." He gave Shane the evil eye once more, for good measure.

Shane ignored the glare and nodded agreeably, even though he could think of another place he'd prefer to spend the night— like next door. Peeling off his doehide shirt, Shane prepared for bed. Marsh's stupefied gasp gave him pause.

"Who whipped you?" Marsh questioned, staring owlishly at the crisscrossed scars on Shane's back.

"Muriel," he said tonelessly. "Each time my father left the ranch, she found an excuse to take her vengeance out on me. She had me roped and tied up by some of the hired hands who despised the Apaches as much as she did."

"God Almighty, it's a wonder she didn't kill you!"

Shane reached over to douse the lantern and sank onto his side of the bed. "She tried. I survived just to spite her."

Marsh peeled off his clothes and plopped onto the mattress, inwardly cringing at the thought of being whipped until the hide had been stripped off his back. It was an unnerving thought.

"I want you to know that I am not in the habit of bedding down with men," Marsh announced in hopes of lightening the tone of their conversation.

"I never questioned that," Shane replied, settling comfortably on his back. "I had you pegged for a ladies' man the moment I met you, Layton."

"Too bad I didn't notice the same thing about you right off, Stafford," Marsh grunted.

Shane smiled quietly to himself, but he made no reply. There was much this gambler didn't know about him. Shane preferred to keep it that way.

The quiet rap at the door caused Calera to wheel around. Now what? she thought tiredly. It had been a trying evening and she was anxious to sprawl in bed.

"Who's there?"

"Muriel Stafford."

Calera frowned in wary trepidation, but she allowed the woman entrance, just to appease her curiosity.

Muriel swept inside and pivoted to face Calera. "I feel it only fair to warn you that if you are harboring any sort of infatuation for my stepson you are a fool."

Never let it be said that this spiteful woman did not get right to the point, Calera noted.

"I think Shane arranged this incident to win your favor and trust," Muriel declared. "In fact, I think your abduction was a clever scare tactic. Apaches are known for their cunning and deceit. They pride themselves in clever calculation. Don't you think it highly suspicious that Shane arrived in town shortly after you were discovered missing and that he was on hand to rescue you? And what tenderhearted woman would decry murder against the man who saved her from disaster?"

Calera smiled sardonically. "I find it far more suspicious that I was abducted after you tried to bribe me into bringing charges against a man you despise, and I refused you."

"Me? How utterly absurd," Muriel scoffed. "I'm sure my stepson is responsible for planting that thought in your head. Indeed, I expected as much from him. I also expect that he has been playing up to you to earn your affection. But, if you think for one minute that a savage like Shane has tender feelings for a woman, you are deceiving yourself. He takes women for his own pleasures and then discards them when he tires of them. Decent women won't have anything to do with him. He spends his time bedding the whores in the red light district on the far side of town. And more than a dozen times I have caught him sneaking off with the Mexican servants who work for me."

The thought cut Calera to the quick. She knew Shane had been with other women. He was too skilled in seduction not to have been. Yet, as much as the picture of Shane in other female's arms disturbed her, Calera was not about to be swayed by anything Muriel said. The woman had a personal vendetta against Shane. She would say and do anything to evict him from her life.

"Thank you for the advice," Calera said in a tone that was nowhere near appreciative. "Good night, Muriel."

Flashing Calera a sour glance, Muriel exited from the door that was being held open for her. "Mark my words, young woman, Shane will only bring you more anguish. Your brother's murder won't be the only heartache you suffer if you let yourself become bedeviled by that half-breed."

It was with admirable restraint that Calera did not kick Muriel on her way out the door. The woman was despicable. She was also obvious. Her hatred for Shane was so intense that it provoked the contrary side of Calera's nature. She would not agree with Muriel, even if her life depended on it. Calera couldn't be as hateful and vengeful for the simple reason that she didn't want to place herself in the same category with Muriel. Dear God, that woman was so obsessed with bitterness that she had ceased to enjoy life. She lived for nothing but revenge.

How Shane could have spent the last few years under the same roof with Muriel was a mystery to Calera. It was no wonder Shane considered the mountains a peaceful haven and refused to speak of the world below, while he was ambling through the panoramic wilderness. Ah, how Calera wished she could turn back the hands of time to the days of innocent splendor in those mountains. Life had not been so complicated then. She had lived and loved, oblivious to the despair that awaited her.

Lost in that wistful thought, Calera crawled into bed, listening to the impatient drumming of raindrops on the windowpane. She would have gone to Shane this night to cuddle up in his sinewy arms if that had been possible. But she imagined it would have been a mite crowded with all three of them in Marsh's bed.

Calera stared up at the ceiling, hearing the wailing wind and patter of rain. She reflected on the night Shane had taught her to depend on her other four senses to lead her when she couldn't see. She remembered those times when he had instructed her to reach outside herself, employing the powers of the mind over her injured body. She wondered if it truly was possible to communicate through the energy of telepathy. The Apaches seemed to have developed the knack because they were so attuned to the powers of nature.

Shane had informed her that Geronimo possessed precognition of the future. He mentioned other Apache prophets and medicine men who had harnessed the powers of thought. Shane had referred to "deep knowing"—the Apache's cherished secret. The keepers of wisdom had become sages among the tribe. Calera suspected Shane had learned to harness those phenomenal skills of intuition and reason since he depended strongly on self-reliance and individuality.

Calera recalled hearing of the vision Crazy Horse had seen before the Battle of the Little Big Horn five years past. In his dream, Crazy Horse had seen a bluff in the center of the battlefield. A ravine, hidden by underbrush, dissected the bluff. Trusting the vision, Crazy Horse and Sitting Bull had sent several hundred warriors to locate the arroyo. The Sioux found it exactly where Crazy Horse said it would be and the braves hid in the ravine to attack Custer from the rear, bringing him utter defeat.

Calera had also read the works of Ralph Waldo Emerson and his views on Transcendentalism. According to the literary philosopher, the physical world of experience and knowledge was secondary to the spiritual world that could only be reached by meditation and reason. She had given the theory considerable thought during her studies in school. Now seemed a perfect time to discover if there was something to the Apache's "deep knowing" and Emerson's power of reason.

Shane had told her that the Apache believed thunder and lightning possessed the greatest of all powers. The most omnipotent power was manifested in lightning—the arrows of the Thunder People. The thunder was said to be the shouts of the spiritual powers above. There were those in the white civilization who claimed that the so-called savages knew nothing of psychic powers, but Calera wasn't so skeptical. She had felt Shane working his magic on her mind and body. And now she was going to experiment with her own powers while the Thunder People were out in full force.

Calera closed her eyes and concentrated all her energy into one thought, just as she had those times when she had been forced to transcend the awful pain that racked her body while Shane cauterized her wound. She hoped Shane was in the habit of practicing what he preached when she called to him in a language that he could not *hear*, only *feel*. She willed him to come to her because there was something important she wanted to say to him, something that pride and grief could no longer deny.

Apache . . . The thought echoed through her mind as the thunder rolled.

Apache . . .

Chapter Twenty

Shane was jolted awake by something beyond the normal realm of his senses. He lay there, not moving a muscle, listening to the rumbling thunder, watching the flashes of silver illuminate the darkened room. Another nameless sensation touched him and he was on his feet in the time it took to inhale a breath. With only a backward glance at the sleeping form, Shane moved soundlessly toward the door. He didn't have to ask himself where he was going at this time of night; he knew intuitively.

Employing quiet caution, Shane eased open the door and slipped into the hall. When a shadow swept toward him, Shane froze in midstep.

"I was hoping to see you," Royal Winston whispered as she looped her hand around Shane's muscled arm. "Since I had to move into the hotel during the remodeling at The Cottage, I kept waiting the chance to speak with you."

The sultry brunette pressed closer, her breasts brushing wantonly against the wall of his chest. "Keery never would let me near you, the jealous scoundrel. You did me a great favor by removing him from my life. He had become intolerable the past year." Her lashes fluttered up to focus on Shane's bronzed face.

"I want to repay you for saving me from a dreary existence, and you can repay me for ensuring Eli didn't press charges . . ."

Her lips lifted to his and her hand anchored on the back of his raven head, bringing his mouth to hers. Royal offered him a kiss steamy enough to fog the windows.

Calera, hearing the voice in the hall, opened her door. She had been practicing her mental powers for a half hour, willing Shane to come to her. It seemed her experiment hadn't worked worth a damn. Shane hadn't been tuned into her thoughts at all. He was making time with the seductive madam! Curse him! Calera hadn't wanted to believe Muriel, but Shane's stepmother obviously knew what she was talking about in this instance. That virile Apache did like women—the more the better. Damn him to the nethermost reaches of hell!

Shane pulled himself away from Royal's scorching kiss when he heard the creak of the door. The wounded expression on Calera's face cut him to the bone. He knew what Calera was thinking. Hell, he could see her thinking it.

Royal swiveled her head around to see where Shane's attention had strayed and she smiled apologetically. "I'm sorry if we woke you."

Calera's temper burst loose in nothing flat. She had been on the verge of reaching out to Shane, despite the obstacles between them. She had become every bit the fool Muriel warned her not to be when she entrusted her heart to a man like Shane. Maybe he *had* been playing up to her to protect his handsome hide. And maybe he *had* staged her abduction to regain her favor.

Muttering epithets to Shane's name, Calera slammed her door and locked it. Men! No, *one man,* she furiously corrected. Why had she thought that midnight-haired rascal cared about her? Because she was not experienced with men, that's why. Calera would not have been surprised to learn that Royal was the ultimate reason Shane had disposed of Keery. Judging from what Calera had just witnessed, it would seem there was an attraction that Keery resented. No wondered Keery had battled Shane.

Still fuming, Calera flounced in bed and pummeled her pillow, wishing it was that magnificent giant's head. No wonder

Shane didn't want to tell Calera about the incident that took Keery's life. Shane and Keery had probably been fighting over a woman. *This* woman. And Royal Winston was an expert in beguiling men. She had experience galore and practice aplenty.

Well, this was the very last time Calera O'Connell fell beneath that cunning Apache warrior's wiles! And she would never again defend him, either. Muriel could insult Shane all she wanted and Calera wouldn't utter one word in his behalf. She hated him for tearing her heart into pieces time and time again!

Bleary-eyed, Marsh opened his door. After hearing voices and the slamming of the door, he expected to find Calera in dire straits. To his astonishment, there stood the bare-chested Shane with Royal wound around him like English ivy.

"I'm sorry," Royal said with a sigh. "We seem to be disturbing the entire hotel." She clutched Shane's arm, towing him with her. "My room is just down the hall."

Scowling at the incriminating situation Shane found himself in, he slipped free of Royal's grasp. She gave him the strangest look, as if she could not fathom why he would reject her generous offer.

"You know I have been attracted to you since I came to town. Now that I have the freedom to choose—"

"No." Shane stared into Royal's shocked countenance.

Royal glanced past Shane to peer questioningly at Marsh, who stood in the doorway with his breeches half-buttoned and his shirt gaping to reveal the thick matting of hair on his chest.

"Thanks but no, Royal. Another time perhaps. I don't like being offered the second invitation after the first one was declined. It offends my male pride," Marsh said with a wry smile.

Royal's gaze darted toward Calera's closed door. "It seems my new partner's respectability has rubbed off on both of you. Thankfully, the rest of the male population of Globe doesn't share your reformed attitude. I would be out of business."

With a good-natured smile that offered an invitation for a

later date, Royal sashayed down the hall and let herself into her room.

When Royal disappeared, Marsh chuckled and shook his disheveled head. "It looks as if Royal intends to keep her business in operation, even if Cali plans to turn the bordello into a fashionable boardinghouse and hotel."

At the moment, Shane didn't give a flying fig where Royal and the other prostitutes set up business. What infuriated him was the fact that Calera had instantly judged him guilty and slammed her door in his face.

"Irish," he growled at the closed door.

"I never want to see you again!" Calera's voice boomed around the cracks of the door.

Marsh lifted a blond brow and grinned, displaying pearly white teeth. "Cali saw you and the madam, did she? What a shame."

His tone was anything but sympathetic. Shane would have described it as a *mocking gloat.*

Muttering under his breath, Shane pivoted around and barreled past Marsh, to return to bed. He would give Irish time to simmer down before he confronted her. Although she did have an explosive temper, she had never been one to hold grudges as long as her brother had. By morning, Calera would be in a better frame of mind—he hoped!

Calera rose at the crack of dawn, having gotten no sleep whatsoever. When she had opened her door the previous night to find Shane and Royal in the clinch, her heart had broken in two. And to think she had intended to cast caution to the wind and let herself fall hopelessly in love with that damned Apache again. She must have had rocks in her head! Well, Calera was taking no more chances with her wounded heart. Shane had already dragged her through ten kinds of hell and taught her all the tortures of the damned. She was never going to let him close enough to hurt her ever again. She would avoid him the same way the male population of Globe City was avoiding her. She would give Shane the cold shoulder and hope he suffered frostbite. She would stick to Marsh Layton and Doctor Broxton like glue. At least they didn't put her emotions through a meat grinder.

After a breakfast that Calera had to force herself to eat, she marched toward The Cottage. She ignored the mutinous glances she received from the men on the street, unswervingly determined to pour her thoughts and energy into the renovations. The sooner The Cottage was remodeled, the sooner she could open for business. She would have no time to spare Shane a second thought. From this moment forward she would regard him as an unpleasant chapter from her past. She had survived one disappointment after another during her life. She could cope with rejection and betrayal as well as grief and despair.

She should be accustomed to losing those she loved by now, shouldn't she? It was obvious that she was to spend her life alone—like an island in the stream, so to speak. She would accept the hand Fate kept dealing her and get on with her life. She would become a successful businesswoman, and that would be more than enough gratification to make her happy. She needed no one. No one! Especially not that conniving Apache warrior who went through women like a squirrel through acorns! Shane Stafford was welcome to Royal. Calera didn't care anymore. She didn't really care about anything—period!

In grim determination, Shane strode toward The Cottage, listening to the whine of saws and the drum of hammers. Calera had managed to slip off without facing him, but Shane had every intention of discussing what had happened the previous night.

Shane stepped in the opened door to hear Calera barking orders like a military general, directing her troop of carpenters from one project to another. The Cottage had undergone enormous transformation since the last time Shane had visited. The red velvet wallpaper had been wadded up in the corner and the furniture was stacked under canvas for protection. The gaudy chandelier in the dining hall was being hoisted down. Crates of liquor bottles were being carted to the alley to be smashed to bits. The risque paintings had already been jerked from the walls, their canvas slashed to shreds. Obviously, Calera had found another use for the jewel-handled dagger Shane had given her.

When Calera wheeled around to spout another order, she spied the hulk of masculinity blocking the entrance. Her green eyes flashed fire as her arm shot toward the door like a bullet. "Get out!"

Shane experienced the feeling of *déjà vu*. He could visualize Keery standing there, glaring daggers at him, shouting him out of The Cottage. Shrugging off the unpleasant vision, Shane flagrantly defied Calera's order and deflected her furious glower.

"I came to speak with you, Irish, and I am not leaving until I do."

"We have nothing to say to each other—ever again."

She turned on her heels and zoomed toward the stairs. Stepping over the clutter as if it wasn't there, Shane caught up with her in four long strides. When Calera sensed his presence behind her, she lurched around, more determined than ever to make her point.

"I hate you as my brother hated you!" she burst out in bad temper. "I will never forgive you for what you did to him or to me." Calera inhaled a huge breath, fighting back the tears she refused to waste on a man who had a heart as cold as the Klondike.

"Irish—"

"No! I refuse to listen to more of your lies. All you wanted was to ensure I didn't press charges. Well, maybe I will after all. I'd like to see you hanging from the tallest tree in the Territory!"

When Calera spun around to sail up the steps like a flying carpet, Shane swore under his breath. All activity in The Cottage had ground to a halt. The carpenters were soaking up Calera's vocal outburst like sponges. But what was infinitely worse was seeing that Muriel had arrived on the scene to witness the angry display of temper. She was smiling at Shane in smug satisfaction.

"You do have a way of spoiling every life you touch," Muriel declared, staring down her nose at her stepson. "It is a wonder to me that you can live with yourself after you have destroyed the happiness of so many people. Or do you simply thrive on other people's misery?"

On the wings of that snide remark, Muriel sauntered off to spread gossip about the fiery confrontation between her stepson and the sister of the man Shane had murdered.

Royal Winston lifted her skirts and stepped over the debris that filled the dining room of The Cottage. She, too, had been on hand to hear Calera's livid outburst and witness her retreat upstairs. Royal flinched when lean fingers clamped around her arm, towing her around the maze of clutter and shoveling her into the office. Eyes like black ice glittered down at her, and Royal grimaced at the menace in that stare.

"I want to know what that little scene last night in the hall was all about," Shane demanded.

"I would appreciate it if you would give me back my arm," Royal insisted, staring at her pinched appendage.

Shane slackened the vise-grip on her elbow, but his eyes were still as hard as granite. "What were you trying to accomplish last night?"

"Accomplish?" Royal sniffed, offended. "Haven't you humiliated me enough already? I hardly need to suffer the third degree on top of all else."

Shane regarded her with a dubious frown.

Royal expelled a deep sigh, causing her ample bosom to strain against the scanty confines of her bodice. "Oh for heaven sake, you know I have been intrigued by you since the beginning. And I am not some coy maid who feels inclined to play coquettish games with the man she desires. If Keery hadn't thrown such tantrums when I cast you interested glances, we would have been lovers long before now."

Shane held his tongue. As far as he was concerned that was a matter of opinion—Royal's, not his.

Royal moved closer to trace the rugged lines of his tanned face. "All I wanted was to spend the night in your arms, to determine if you are as good in bed as I think you might be. Does that insult you, Shane, or does the thought arouse you—?"

Her voice trailed off when she heard an angry hiss in the doorway. She glanced back to see Calera standing in rigid fury.

Calera was hurting in ways that words could not appropriately express. Seeing Royal and Shane together the previous night had been a hard slap in the face. Catching them together a second time was like having a knife plunged clean through her heart.

Whirling about, Calera stamped off to find something to distract her from the tormenting vision of Shane and Royal making plans for their next tryst. And to think Calera had scoffed at Muriel's cruel declarations. The women knew Shane better than Calera wanted to admit. Calera had been all-too convenient while they were alone in the mountains. Now Shane had plenty of feminine distractions to occupy him. Damn him for turning her inside out and leaving her soul to bleed!

When Calera disappeared from sight, Shane's dark face puckered in a scowl. Royal glanced from the handsome giant to the abandoned doorway.

"Don't tell me you are interested in Keery's sister?" she said on an incredulous laugh. "Really, Shane. You have one strike against you from the onset. And besides, Marsh Layton and Lyle Broxton are both sweet on her. Calera seems a bit icy when it comes to men. Those Easterners are a different breed, to be sure. Don't waste your time with her." Her hand trailed up his arm in a familiar caress. "I can provide all the affection a man like you needs."

Swearing fluently, Shane disentangled himself from the aggressive madam and stalked back to the street. There was no sense inviting another scene with Calera while she was in a black mood. Shane's time would be better spent learning what kind of damage Muriel's vile tongue was doing. His stepmother kept popping up at the most unexpected places, and that made

Shane uneasy. He had the inescapable feeling that his long-standing conflict with Muriel was coming to a head like a festered boil.

Sure enough, Muriel was up to no good, Shane discovered a short time later. Muriel had kept her tongue wagging from both ends, relating Calera's hateful remarks. For some reason, Muriel wanted it known that Calera had changed her mind about pressing charges and was spouting about the possibility of Shane becoming the honored guest at a necktie party.

To Shane's further frustration, he received a visit from Muriel's lawyer. According to the attorney, Muriel had produced a will written by Robert, stating that all their joint holdings would be inherited by Muriel and their son Charles. Muriel requested that Shane be notified that she was no longer being generous in allowing him to live at the Bar "S" Ranch. Shane was instructed to gather his belongings and move out immediately.

What Muriel thought she could accomplish by that tactic Shane didn't know. His father had written a second will after Charles' death, leaving the ranch to his wife and his Apache son. Shane had the document tucked away for safekeeping, but he didn't relish making the long ride home to retrieve the updated will.

Muriel was definitely plotting, Shane grimly assured himself. She seemed determined to call as much attention to her stepson as possible.

Dear God, Shane thought as he sank down on the edge of the bed in the private room he had rented. How could his life keep becoming more entangled than it had been? Maybe he should return to the ranch to retrieve the latest will and make himself scarce for a few days. Calera would appreciate his absence, that was for sure and certain. Judging by the glares she had bestowed on him, she wished him as deep in perdition as a vulture could fly in a month.

Ah, how he wished he and Calera could return to the mountains and relive the memories of a less turbulent time in his life. But Calera was right. They could never go back, not with all the stumbling blocks between them now.

* * *

"You're awfully quiet this evening," Marsh observed, staring at Calera over the rim of his glass.

"Am I?"

Calera forced a smile that did nothing to erase the dull glaze in her eyes. There was a hint of sadness in her expression that all the pretense in the world couldn't conceal. She was hurting. Until the previous night, Calera had clung to that one source of security she had discovered in Shane's powerful arms. Even when everything went wrong, there was always that sense of right when they were creating magical dreams. She had allowed herself to believe that Shane had been faithful to only her the past few weeks. She had needed that sense of security while she was undergoing such a drastic transformation from one phase of her life to another. Knowing Shane had shared his passion with an experienced paramour like Royal cut all the way to the bone and destroyed that one shred of stability that kept Calera's spirits from plummeting to rock bottom . . .

"Cali?" Marsh reached across the dining table to jostle her from her silent reverie. "Are you sure you're all right, love?"

"Of course." She managed another smile for Marsh's benefit. "It's just that I have so much on my mind with the remodeling projects and all—"

"Or is your fiery confrontation with Shane Stafford bothering you?" Marsh asked perceptively. "Gossip has been flying all day, speculating that you intend to press charges, that you want to see Shane pay to the full extent of the law."

Her gaze dropped like a rock yielding to the force of gravity. Calera fiddled with her silverware, vowing that the tears that welled in her eyes would not betray her. "I hate him for everything he has done."

"Do you?" he asked pensively. "I wonder . . ."

Calera jerked up her head. "Wouldn't *you*, Marsh? Shouldn't *I*?"

Marsh eased back in his chair, watching those beguiling green eyes glisten with the evidence of unshed tears. "Before I turned out to be more of a gentleman than I ever planned to be, I would have listed all the reasons why you should forget about Stafford and concentrate your affection on me," he admitted. "I would have taken what I desired from you, Cali, playing to my advantage while you were vulnerable. And even now, I'm tempted to scorn that rascal for my own benefit." He smiled roguishly when Calera gaped at him. "At least I've become an honest scoundrel who can see himself for what he used to be."

Rising to full stature, Marsh walked around the table to assist Calera from her chair. "In fact," he said as he ushered her out the door, "I even considered settling into a respectable occupation, should you show the slightest inclination of accepting my courtship. And I thought there might be a chance for us . . . until that big brute burst into your room, as if he owned the whole damned place."

Marsh escorted Calera up the steps and down the hall to her room, pausing in front of her door to continue his colloquy. "And since that time, I have been plagued with the unshakable feeling that somehow and somewhere you have managed to fall in love with Stafford."

"I have not!" she vehemently denied.

His hand curled beneath her stubborn chin and he smiled wryly at her. "Are you trying to convince me or yourself, dear lady?" His blond head dipped toward hers, his full lips just a kiss away. "Shall we test my theory so we will both know for certain?"

Calera wrapped her arms around his neck and reached up on tiptoe to kiss Marsh until the taste of him burned away the lingering memories of another man, another time, another place. She leaned full length of him, pressing close enough to feel the accelerated beat of his heart. His arms came around her, crushing her to him, letting her feel his desire for her.

There was only one small problem, Calera discovered too late. The flame she willed to blaze in her soul would not ignite. Despite the fact that Marsh Layton had the kind of dashing good looks that could turn a lady's head, he was too fair complected to match the darkly handsome warrior who played havoc with her dreams. Despite the fact that Marsh was an expert at kissing a woman senseless, Calera realized disheartenedly that she had learned to respond only to that damned Apache's brand of kisses—the slow but tantalizing brush of his lips and hands over her flesh. And though Marsh was tall and muscular, he couldn't begin to equal Shane's phenomenal size and strength. The feel of Marsh's body molded to hers just wasn't quite right. The scent of his cologne was pleasing, to be sure, but it just wasn't quite right, either. Damn!

Calera vowed to make all things right, to adjust to the feel of Marsh's masculine contours. She longed to find affection for a man who had been kind and caring and had not betrayed her. And she could have if this idiotic heart of hers would cooperate. She wanted to fall in love with Marsh, or even Lyle Broxton— anyone but that infuriating half-breed. But she may as well have tried to hold a handful of moonbeams.

As much as Calera hated to admit it, *wanted* it to happen, she could not fall in love with one man while she was helplessly in love with another. Kissing Marsh was like trying on a shoe that didn't fit. She could walk all over creation, trying to adjust, but nothing could alter the fact that she was clomping around in the wrong shoes, feeling a constant pinch . . .

A movement close beside her brought her from her pensive deliberations. Calera pulled away to see Shane's swarthy form slipping soundlessly past her toward his own room. She was instantly reminded of the first time she had seen Shane. His bronze face had been a mask of cool indifference, revealing none of his thoughts. If he was the least bit jealous about find- ing Calera and Marsh in the clinch, it didn't show. He simply ambled down the hall and closed the door behind him.

He didn't even care, Calera thought dispiritedly. When she had seen Shane and Royal together, she had slammed her door so hard that the entire structure shook like rattling teeth. Dear God, why was she wasting so much emotion on a man who had used her for his own lust and selfish purpose? Muriel Stafford was right. Shane was barely more than a savage who felt none of the human emotions normal people experienced. He could say *anything* and mean *nothing!*

Marsh heaved a defeated sigh and reached around Calera to open her door. "I suggest you decide what you are going to do about the man," he advised. "Either love him or hate him, Cali, but quit trying to do both at the same time. You'll make yourself crazy. Though I have prided myself in being good-natured and easygoing, there is a limit to what I can tolerate. These eternal triangles are worse than bluffing my way through a bad poker hand."

"Marsh, I—"

His forefinger grazed her lips. "You tried, I know. Problem was, you had to try a mite too hard," He dropped a kiss to her puckered brow. "I was hoping you wouldn't have to try at all, that the feelings would come naturally."

"I'm sorry."

"Don't be," Marsh consoled her. "Not every hand is a winner, no matter how shrewdly you play your cards. And I hope you will understand if I take my affection elsewhere."

Calera felt the whole world crumbling around her. "Does that mean we can't be friends?" Dear God, she wouldn't even have one friend left to her name. Honestly, there were times when she wanted to throw up her hands in resignation and leap off the nearest cliff!

Marsh's soft laughter echoed around her. He helped himself to another taste of honeyed lips. "We will always remain friends, my lovely lady. And if the time should ever come when you have a change of heart, then perhaps . . ."

He let his voice trail off, leaving Calera to deduce what might come between them, *if that time ever came.*

When Marsh walked away, Calera heaved a cathartic sigh. She had to get a grip on herself. But damn it, she was so tired of being strong, pretending her emotions weren't in a tailspin. She was going to have to make some decisions and stick by them. And if she didn't do it quickly, she was going to lose her ever-loving mind!

Chapter Twenty-one

Sitting alone in his room, Shane polished off his third drink and brooded some more. The whiskey was supposed to take the edge off his frustration, but his method wasn't even mildly effective. In fact, the strategy wasn't working worth a damn. Considering the fire that burned inside him, it probably wasn't wise to ingest so much liquor. He might blow himself up. But then who would care? Muriel would have celebrated his death. Calera would have been relieved. Marsh and Lyle Broxton would be rubbing their hands together in gleeful anticipation of having Calera all to themselves.

Watching Calera kiss Marsh in the hall had ignited Shane's temper. He had wanted to tear that blond-haired Casanova limb from limb and curse Calera up one side and down the other. Instead, he had stalked to his room to do hand-to-glass combat, hoping he could drink himself blind so he couldn't see the image that tortured him.

Curse it, he should have grown accustomed to never having what he wanted in life. He had been born under a black cloud and left to wander on the border between two worlds, never finding himself at home in either of them. Even that one bright glimpse he'd had of paradise was now blanketed with foreboding shadows. His affair with Calera was just another something else that had gone wrong with his life.

A muddled frown creased Shane's brow when he saw an envelope magically glide under the door and slide across the wooden floor. Shane downed the last of his drink in one swallow and staggered toward the note. His head swam when he doubled to pluck the envelope off the floor. Damn, he shouldn't have consumed so much whiskey on an empty stomach—one that was already churning with frustration.

Without his usual coordination, Shane stumbled back to his chair and plopped into it. Squinting through the fuzzy haze that glazed his vision, Shane unfolded the letter with all the coordination of a man with ten thumbs. The note was from Calera. It was brief and to the point, requesting that he meet her at The Cottage at his earliest convenience.

Shane tossed the letter aside and stared at the blank wall. He could guess why Calera wanted to see him. She wanted to continue their morning discussion—one-sided though it had turned out to be. Shane rather expected to hear the announcement that Calera was going to be seeing a great deal more of her other two beaus, and that she was going to press charges for murder. That should make Muriel immensely happy. She wouldn't have to waste her time scheming with that outdated will she had produced. The Bar "S" Ranch would be Muriel's by default. The hated half-breed would be swinging from a rope, compliments of Calera O'Connell.

Dear God, did his life ever change? Ah, but there *was* a change, he reminded himself dispiritedly. *From bad to worse.*

"At my earliest convenience?" Shane questioned the room at large. He grabbed the bottle and guzzled another drink. "When has any event in my life been convenient? And who, I wonder, feels anything except regret that I was born?"

At the moment, with an excess of whiskey acting as a depressant, Shane wondered why he hadn't done the world a great favor years earlier by simply walking off a mountain and plunging into infinity. Even spiting Muriel's attempt to force him off the ranch didn't provide much motivation for surviving in a world where he wasn't wanted.

Calera had just learned what it was like to be all alone, Shane reminded himself, but he had coped with those feelings for a lifetime. Now it was even worse after that emerald-eyed elf had taught him to smile again, taught him the joy of laughter, of contentment, of unbridled passion. He had been tempted by an impossible dream that had evolved into an atrocious nightmare. Ah yes, hell did have a few more lessons to teach him after all, didn't it?

Setting the empty bottle aside, Shane staggered out the door and ricocheted off the walls of the hall. He hoped the whiskey would numb him to the upcoming torment of listening to Calera condemn him to the furthermost reaches of Hades. He hoped he wouldn't feel a damned thing when she announced she was offering her affection to Marsh—the ever-present Marsh, who had always been around to pick Calera up each time she stumbled over life's latest pitfall. Good ole Marsh and his gambler's luck, Shane thought sourly. That suave blond rake had the kind of charm and refinement Shane could never acquire, even after Robert Stafford pounded etiquette into his son's head and forced him to behave like a white man. Shane could not have become a gentleman if his life depended on it. He was a half-breed, an unwanted person in the world, nothing more.

"Are you finished feeling sorry for yourself, Apache?" Shane slurred out as he wobbled down the street.

Not quite, came a sullen whisper from deep inside him.

After inhaling a fortifying breath, Shane stepped upon the porch of The Cottage and grasped the supporting beam to maintain his balance. His head was spinning like a carousel and his belly was rolling like waves on a storm-tossed sea. He *definitely* had too much to drink. Cursing his lack of agility, Shane tripped over the clutter the carpenters had left on the floor. He was making enough racket to raise the dead—of which he was sure he was one. *The living dead,* thought Shane. That described him perfectly.

Shane located the wall and leaned heavily upon it. He heard

approaching footsteps. From what direction? He couldn't say
for certain. Footfalls echoed around his head as if it were a
fathomless chasm that amplified sound.

His foggy gaze swerved toward the shadow that drifted in
front of the opened door. The street lamp framed the petite
form of the woman who appeared before him. Shane smiled to
himself as the golden light flooded over the wide-brimmed bonnet with its decorative plumes and flowing sash. It was Calera's
favorite and she wore it often. The matching emerald gown
accentuated the vivid color of Irish's eyes.

Of course, Shane couldn't see her eyes at the moment. Her
face was concealed by the oversize bonnet. But Shane didn't
really want to stare into those expressive green pools, knowing
they were brimming with hatred and contempt. He preferred
to remember those days when Irish eyes sparkled with love,
glowed up at him in the sunlight that blazed through their
mountain paradise . . .

It took a moment for Shane's dulled senses to register the
gleam of silver that appeared from the folds of Calera's gown.
Suddenly, Shane found himself staring down the barrel of a
Colt .45. He didn't even flinch at the threat to his life because
he no longer gave a damn. Nothing mattered anymore. Nothing
had mattered before Calera had stumbled into his life and nothing would matter so much again.

"So it has finally come to this, has it, Irish?"

The barrel lifted another notch and Shane heard the click of
the trigger sliding into firing position. Vaguely, Shane became
aware of muffled sounds coming from the direction of the dining room, but his attention was on the woman who had uttered
not one word and didn't have to. Her actions spoke for themselves. It was glaringly apparent that Calera had decided she
would like him a whole lot better dead than alive.

"Go ahead, Irish," he slurred out. "But I want you to know
that I—"

Shane wasn't allowed to finish his sentence. Sparks spit from
the pistol barrel. The vicious bark of the weapon shattered the
silence. Another shot rang out, but Shane was on his way to the

floor, stunned by the searing pain that exploded in his skull. Faint sound penetrated the fading consciousness of his mind and he thought he heard the scrambling of feet. The clatter of fallen debris thrummed in rhythm with his own pulse. He wasn't sure if the crashing sounds were the result of his own fall into the pile of clutter, or if they had come for somewhere in the near distance. But it didn't matter. Nothing mattered anymore. Calera wanted him dead. That was the only truth Shane knew.

With a groan, Shane yielded to the sickening darkness that swirled around him. He could smell the blood seeping from him, but he was too numb to battle his way out of the black abyss that swallowed him. And to be honest, Shane wasn't sure he wanted to rescue himself. He simply wanted to find peace, to dream that impossible dream that had once collided with reality before wrapping itself in the dark thundercloud his life had become . . .

Marsh Layton bounded out of his chair at the saloon when he heard the shots echoing in the night. Shouts penetrated the darkness as bodies flooded from every door on main street.

"Miss O'Connell and Shane Stafford shot each other in The Cottage!" someone blurted out.

"Are they both dead?" somebody else questioned over the sound of stampeding footsteps.

Marsh's mind reeled at the appalling thought. He was pounding a path to The Cottage as fast as his legs would carry him, shoving bodies out of the way to reach Calera. Sweet mercy! This was all his fault. He had ordered Calera to decide if she loved or hated the half-breed Apache. Hell and damnation! Marsh hadn't meant for her to go out and kill the man in order to decide what to do about him!

Panting for breath, Marsh plowed through the rubble inside The Cottage to see two shadowed forms lying face down in the debris. Someone behind him had raised a lantern to shed light on the disaster. Marsh swallowed hard and his stomach somersaulted around his belly like a crazed acrobat when he stared at Calera's lifeless body.

"Get the doctor!" Marsh demanded hoarsely.

"I already sent someone to fetch Broxton and the sheriff," came another voice from behind him.

With sickening dread, Marsh stared at the bloodstains on the back of the green velvet gown. Gritting his teeth, he reached out to ease Calera onto her back. A startled squawk erupted from his lips when the broad-brimmed bonnet tumbled to the floor and glassy eyes stared sightlessly up at him.

The congregation of onlookers gasped collectively at the ashen face that was cradled in the crook of Marsh's arm.

"Muriel?" Marsh croaked. His astonished gaze lifted to the surrounding crowd, seeing the reflection of his own disbelief.

"What the devil is going on here?" Lyle Broxton demanded as he elbowed his way through the crowd.

No one responded. They simply stared at the woman who was garbed in Calera O'Connell's familiar bonnet and gown. Muriel's head was tilted to an unnatural angle and the Colt still tangled in her blue-tinged fingers.

"Give me room," Lyle ordered as he shoved the onlookers back apace. Squatting down, he felt for a pulse in Muriel's neck. Grimly, he stared at Marsh. "She's dead." His gaze darted to the sprawled form of the other body on the far side of the room. "What happened?"

"Nobody seems to know," Marsh replied. "At first we thought it was Cali who had been involved in the shooting."

"I saw Miss O'Connell marching out of the hotel a few minutes ago," a bystander spoke up. "Of course, I pretended to ignore her the way I've been doing since she decided to shut The Cottage down. I thought it was Miss O'Connell in that dress and matching bonnet."

"So did I," someone else chimed in. "I caught a glimpse of her, but I was busy ignoring her, too."

"Muriel must have wanted the whole town to think she was Cali," Marsh mused aloud.

"What the hell is going on?" Sheriff Nelson's voice boomed

in the silence. The crowd parted to let him pass. "Sweet Mother of God!" he gasped. "What is Muriel doing in Miss O'Connell's clothes?"

"Good question," Marsh muttered. "Too bad no one has an answer." Rising, Marsh surged toward Shane's lifeless body which was draped over a pile of lumber and wads of red velvet wallpaper.

"Is Shane dead, too?" Sheriff Nelson questioned bleakly.

"That has yet to be determined." Lyle unfolded himself and stepped over the rubble.

"Do you suppose Muriel tried to kill her stepson, hoping we would think Cali was responsible?" Marsh asked The Cottage at large.

"Or maybe Miss O'Connell talked Muriel into doing her dirty work for her," the sheriff speculated. "I heard Miss O'Connell flew into a rage this morning, vowing to see Shane dead for murdering her brother. I also heard she had planned to press charges. Maybe she decided the justice system wasn't expedient enough to suit her."

Eli Nelson surveyed the scene with a critical eye. "I guess no one counted on Shane firing back. Muriel must have thought her disguise would give her the edge she needed."

He ambled over to pluck up the pistol that lay at Shane's fingertips. The warm barrel indicated the weapon had recently been fired. And everybody in the room knew where the bullet had lodged itself. Muriel's condition testified to that.

Gloomily, Marsh helped Doctor Broxton shove Shane's bulky body over to inspect his wound. Blood caked Shane's raven hair and streamed down the left side of his face. Quickly, Lyle felt for a pulse.

"He's still alive. Help me get him to my office so I can determine the severity of the wound."

Within a few minutes, Shane was toted to the physician's office and placed in bed. Lyle set to work cleansing the wound.

"Fortunately, his injury isn't as bad as it looks," Lyle announced to Marsh and Sheriff Nelson. "The bullet grazed his skull and put a new part in his hair. He should be all right in a few days, but he is going to have one heck of a headache when he rouses."

Since Shane was in good hands, Marsh ambled back to the street. He was faced with the bleak task of informing Calera that Shane had been injured in a shoot-out with his stepmother. Despite Eli's speculation, Marsh suspected Muriel had somehow managed to swipe one of Calera's gowns and employed it as a disguise. He wondered how Calera was going to react. She had faced one calamity after another since she arrived in Arizona.

Rehearsing his soliloquy, Marsh walked back to the hotel, listening to all the speculations that were buzzing along the street. Marsh rather thought Muriel could have carried out her attempt at murder if she hadn't faced such formidable opposition. No doubt, Muriel had carefully plotted her scheme, planting seeds of gossip pertaining to the argument Shane and Calera had earlier that morning. Marsh did wonder, however, how Muriel had lured Shane out into the darkness.

That curious thought prompted Marsh to whiz past Calera's door to enter Shane's room. The empty whiskey bottle suggested Shane had been drinking heavily that evening. The note Marsh found in the chair answered his question. Muriel had apparently forged Calera's signature to the letter and waited her chance to dispose of her unwanted stepson. Lord, with a family like Shane had, he didn't need enemies!

Tucking the letter in his pocket, Marsh reversed direction to take the bleak news to Calera. He rapped on the door and was greeted by silence. Poking his head inside the room, Marsh was met with more silence. Obviously, Calera had heard the commotion and went to investigate. Marsh must have missed seeing her while he was in Broxton's office.

Whirling about, Marsh strode down the hall. By now, Calera was probably in Broxton's office, checking out the rumors for herself. Good. Marsh hadn't relished the thought of delivering the information to Calera.

Marsh detoured into Sheriff Nelson's office and extracted the note from his pocket. "I found this letter in Shane's hotel room.

It looks as if Muriel plotted murder, using Calera not only as bait but also for a disguise."

Eli read the note and frowned ponderously. "True, there has been bad blood between Shane and Muriel for years, but I can't overlook the fact that Miss O'Connell might have had a part in this shooting. She may have plotted the incident and convinced Muriel to dispose of Shane without bothering with a court trial."

"That is the most preposterous theory I have ever heard!" Marsh exploded.

"Maybe to you," Eli countered. "But you're sweet on Calera. Everybody in town knows that because you never bothered to hide the fact."

"And how do you think Cali could have talked Muriel into wearing that bonnet and gown?" Marsh muttered in question.

Eli shrugged a thick-bladed shoulder. "I don't know. I was only plodding through all the possibilities. All I know is that Calera was visibly distressed by her brother's death and collapsed right here in my office. She debated about filing charges, even when I advised against it. Nobody wanted to tell her what a bastard Keery had turned out to be. Maybe Calera thought we were trying to protect Shane and decided to take the law into her own hands—with Muriel's help."

Marsh bit his tongue before he blurted out the fact that he suspected Calera of being in love with Shane. Marsh decided that imparting that tidbit of information would do more to damage Calera's credibility than restore it. Calera had seen Shane and Royal in the clinch the previous night. The theory of a jealous lover striking down her unfaithful beau might appeal to Sheriff Nelson since he was known to be infatuated with Royal Winston. For all Marsh knew, Eli might be out for a little revenge himself.

"I still think this was all Muriel's doing," Marsh said with great certainty. "Muriel saw the chance to acquire the ranch for herself. I heard she registered her husband's will with a lawyer this afternoon—a will whose authenticity Shane protested.

Muriel must have been planning this incident since she arrived in town."

"And I think you are taking sides with Calera because your feelings for her are influencing you," Eli insisted. "*I* heard that Calera was in a fine temper this morning when she confronted Shane. There are all sorts of witnesses to corroborate that story."

"Oh hell, Sheriff, that was—"

Eli flung up a hand to forestall another of Marsh's objections. "We'll see what Shane has to say when he regains consciousness. In the meantime, I plan to hear Calera's version of the story—"

The clatter of footsteps had Eli wheeling toward the door. Two dusty ranch hands trooped into the office, wearing concerned frowns.

"Is Shane okay?" Cactus questioned point-blank. "We rode into town an' heard Muriel an' Shane shot each other."

"What about Muriel?" Sticker inquired.

"She didn't survive," Eli reported gravely. "Shane is unconscious, but he is recovering in Doc Broxton's office."

Like two dust devils, Cactus and Sticker whirled around and blew off down the street.

Marsh set his Stetson atop his head and ambled off. He had yet to locate Calera. Marsh preferred to find her before the sheriff did. She needed to know that Eli Nelson harbored suspicions about her involvement in the tragic incident.

Calera could not possibly be involved, Marsh assured himself. Yes, Calera had been in a bit of a temper, but she wasn't homicidal and she couldn't possibly have influenced Muriel into garbing herself in the familiar gown and marching off to shoot Shane. That was absurd! The sheriff would realize that after he had time to analyze his preposterous theory . . . wouldn't he?

Well, just in case, Marsh planned to intercept Calera and make certain she had her story straight.

Chapter Twenty-two

To Marsh's dismay, he found Sheriff Nelson following in his wake as he strode back to the physician's office. To Marsh's further dismay, Calera had not arrived to check on Shane. Cactus and Sticker were on hand, however, pumping Doc Broxton about the patient's condition and the tragic incident.

"No one knows for certain what actually happened," Lyle was saying when Marsh and Eli walked inside. "We're hoping Shane can supply some answers when he rouses."

A quiet groan erupted from the bed and all five men tried to push through the door that led to the back room. Marsh squirted through the blockade like a cork popping from a bottle to hover over Shane's sprawled form.

"Dear God . . ." Shane mumbled groggily.

Cactus and Sticker glanced curiously at each other.

"How come he says that all the time these days?" Sticker asked.

Marsh knew where Shane had picked up that expression, but he wasn't about to say a word, not with Eli underfoot. The sheriff had already become suspicious of Calera's intentions toward Shane.

Damn, wasn't it ironic that Marsh was forced to protect his own competition in his futile pursuit of the most desirable woman he'd ever met? Marsh had become so damned noble of late it was making him nauseous! The next thing he knew he would be settling down in Globe City to open a butcher shop, cutting meat instead of cards. *Dear God* was right! And just listen to him. Now he had borrowed Cali's favorite expression, too!

"Shane, it's me—Cactus." He wedged past Marsh to poke his stubbled face into Shane's. "Are you okay?"

"No, my head feels like it exploded," Shane moaned. Ever so slowly, he pried open one eye to see the whisker-faced and leather-skinned Cactus Linnox staring at him. Above Cactus was another weather-beaten face—Sticker's. "Where the hell am I?"

"In Doc Broxton's office," Cactus supplied. "Do you remember what happened?"

"No, am I supposed to?"

All eyes swung to Lyle Broxton in unspoken question. The doctor shrugged noncommittally. "It may just be the excess whiskey clouding his brain," he diagnosed. "That and the hellish headache he's bound to be having. However, it is possible that the head injury caused amnesia. It's too soon to tell."

It was sooner than the physician thought. After the initial fog parted, the incident erupted in Shane's mind like a discharging cannon, shooting him straight up in bed.

"Irish!" Shane choked out.

Marsh clamped his hand on Shane's shoulder and urged him to his back. "Are you beginning to remember what happened? Would you mind sharing it with the rest of us?"

Shane slumped back and closed his eyes against the sharp stab of pain caused by the flickering lantern. He was hesitant to elaborate. The last thing Shane wanted was to see Calera behind bars for shooting him. He knew what it was like to be confined to a cell—infuriating, restricting. Besides, he deserved to be shot after the torment he had put Calera through.

Sheriff Nelson unfolded the note and held it under Shane's nose to prompt his memory. "Do you remember this letter?

Marsh found it in your room." He cast Marsh a dubious glance. "Or at least he *says* he did."

"Of course I found it in Shane's room," Marsh muttered resentfully. "Do you think I wrote it myself?"

"The idea did cross my mind," Eli said frankly. "You seem all-too eager to protect the lady who has been receiving all your affection since the two of you arrived in town together."

"Geezus!" Marsh snorted disdainfully. "That's hardly the kind of evidence a law official should be relying on!"

Since Shane didn't have the foggiest notion that Muriel had disguised herself in Calera's clothes, he was reluctant to acknowledge the letter for fear of incriminating Calera. For all he knew, his would-be assassin was at large. If she was, she was going to stay that way.

Marsh was growing more apprehensive by the second. Shane refused to explain and he was doing more to implicate Calera than he knew. It occurred to Marsh that Shane didn't know it was his stepmother who had shot him, or that he had killed her. But why Shane would take Calera's measure over his pistol and fire the fatal shot was even more shocking. Marsh was in a state of panic. He decided he had better change the subject before Eli leaped to another of his ridiculous conclusions.

"It seems we are assuming Shane knows more about the incident that he actually does." Marsh sank down on the edge of the bed and snatched the letter from Eli's stubby fingers. "It was not Calera who shot you; it was Muriel dressed in Calera's gown."

"What!" Shane bolted upright, only to be shoved back down.

"You didn't know?" Eli frowned bemusedly before glaring at Marsh for interceding in the questioning. That sly gambler. He had purposely imparted that information—to protect Calera, no doubt.

"It was Muriel you shot," Marsh grimly continued. "She's dead."

"What!" Shane's head exploded at the sound of his own roaring voice.

"There, you see, Sheriff, Shane didn't know of Muriel's charade—" Marsh's voice evaporated and he carefully chose his words. "But if you didn't know it was Muriel who faced you with a pistol, why would you take aim at the woman you assumed to be Calera? Are you crazy!"

Shane grimaced at the throbbing pain in his head. Suddenly everyone was talking at once, each man trying to gain control of the conversation by shouting louder than the others. Shane grabbed his pounding skull and held onto it before the upraised voices launched his head into orbit.

"For God's sake!" Lyle shouted. "My patient is being put through torture. Clam up, all of you!"

Silence dropped like an anchor and Shane sighed in relief. "I didn't shoot anybody," he said quietly. "I wasn't even carrying a gun."

Five pairs of eyes bulged from their sockets and five sets of jaws dropped open.

"But we found a pistol lying by your outstretched hand," Eli said. "It had been fired."

"It didn't belong to me and I didn't fire it," Shane insisted firmly but softly. His head couldn't take another beating, not when it was thumping like a tom-tom. "I did receive the letter in my room. Someone slipped it under my door while I was sitting there drinking. I arrived at The Cottage first and waited inside for Calera. It was dark when she stepped in the doorway. I wasn't close enough to realize it was Muriel in that bonnet and gown. When I saw the gleam of the pistol barrel I did nothing to stop the attack. I saw the flames spitting from the Colt and that's the last thing I remember."

"Well, someone sure as hell shot Muriel," Eli scowled. "If it wasn't you, who was it? As if I can't guess!"

"Now hold on a minute, Sheriff," Marsh protested. "If you're thinking what I think you're thinking, you can stop thinking it."

"What is he thinking?" Shane questioned. "My brain broke down and this headache is killing me."

Marsh shot Eli a black look. "Our suspicious sheriff keeps trying to link unrelated facts together, indicting Cali. You and

I both know Cali isn't capable of violence. Hot tempered, maybe, but definitely not homicidal."

"Damn it, quit stuffing thoughts in Shane's head while he can't think straight," Eli objected.

"You're the one with the preposterous theories and outlandish suppositions," Marsh accused. "Has it occurred to you that perhaps whoever abducted Cali this past week might have been hired by Muriel. Maybe the two men disposed of Muriel for reasons unknown?"

"No, it has not!" Eli blustered.

"Well, maybe it should occur to you," Shane spoke up. "I suspect my stepmother was responsible for having Calera kidnapped from her room. Muriel tried to lay the blame on me, if you recall. You were there the night I brought Calera back to town. Muriel was quick to point an accusing finger at me. She claimed I arranged the scheme to draw Calera's gratitude so she wouldn't have me arrested for murder. I wouldn't be surprised if Muriel *did* hire the kidnappers and had not expected Calera to escape by her own clever devices. Muriel was prepared to accuse me, hoping that I *would be* arrested."

"God, all this speculation is giving *me* a headache," Eli groaned.

"Believe me, Sheriff, you have no idea what a headache is," Shane guaranteed.

"I think this conversation has gone far enough for the night," Doctor Broxton insisted. "My patient needs his rest." He shook his finger in Shane's face. "I could have given you laudanum to relieve that headache and help you sleep, but you overindulged in whiskey. The combination of medication and liquor could kill you. Now you have to suffer until the whiskey wears off."

As much as Shane would have liked to wade through the tangled thoughts that formed a jungle in his mind, he simply could not. His head was hurting something fierce and the side effects of too much whiskey made him nauseous. Indeed, he had lapsed into a restless sleep before the last man filed out the door.

"I think I'll go have a talk with Calera," Eli announced.

"I'll go with you," Marsh volunteered.

"No thanks." Eli's gray eyes homed in on Marsh. "You have a nasty habit of intervening in the judicial process. Go shuffle your cards and leave me to do the job I'm being paid to do."

"Just don't *overdo* your job," Marsh muttered darkly. "Sometimes an officer of the law can bend over so far backward ensuring he hasn't overlooked a single clue that he winds up seeing the world upside down."

"Like I said, Layton, go shuffle your damned cards and stay out of my way," Eli grumbled before stalking out the door.

Somewhere between the vibrating gong that measured time by thumping against Shane's sensitive skull and the throb of his pulse, a hand clamped on his shoulder, jostling him awake.

"Now what?" Shane groaned miserably. "Can't I even die in peace?"

Marsh Layton sank down on the bed. "I know you feel like death warmed over, Stafford, but we've got a problem."

"Another one?" Shane exhaled an enormous sigh.

"Yes, I'm afraid so."

Shane's tangled lashes swept up to see Marsh's face swimming in shadows. "What's wrong?"

Marsh swallowed hard, causing his Adam's apple to bob in his throat. "Cali is missing. Sheriff Nelson went to her room to question her and she was nowhere to be found, neither were all her belongings. Then Eli turned the whole town upside down. No one has seen Cali since I walked her to her room earlier this evening. Now the sheriff thinks she *was* involved in the shooting, and that she planned to let you take the blame for Muriel's death. The sheriff has this crazy notion that Cali didn't expect Muriel to be capable of killing you with one shot. And since you didn't try to defend yourself against Muriel, the sheriff figures Cali blasted Muriel so you could take the blame."

"That man does entirely too much thinking, considering the pea-sized brain he has to work with," Shane muttered.

"My sentiments exactly." Marsh handed Shane his shirt. "I

know you aren't up to this and I wouldn't ask if I was worth damn at tracking, but we've got to find Cali before the sheriff does. He's forming a posse at this very moment. And since public opinion turned against Cali when she closed the doors to the brothel, I'm afraid her newly-acquired enemies might try to take advantage of the situation."

Shane outstretched an arm, silently requesting that Marsh haul him upright. When Marsh complied, the world spun furiously around Shane. His stomach flip-flopped and his skull struck up with another chorus of killing agony.

"Can you stand up?" Marsh asked in concern.

"Do I have a choice?"

Marsh wrapped a supporting arm around Shane's midsection and helped him stab his arms into the shirt.

"I hope you appreciate what I'm doing for the two of you," Shane murmured weakly.

Marsh chuckled at his ailing companion. "I think you have that exactly backward, Stafford. It's not what you are doing for me; it's what I'm doing for you. I never stood a chance with Cali."

Shane scowled. "You looked as if you had all the chances you needed last night."

"This is still *last* night," Marsh corrected with a wry grin. "But what you saw was me trying to kiss every haunting thought of you right out of Cali's lovely head. I'm sad to report that I wasn't the least bit successful. I've certainly been around enough to know when a woman doesn't feel a fire burning. You probably know what it's like to have a woman kiss you, knowing she wished it were someone else." He cut Shane a sharp glance. "And don't you dare tell me every female you have seduced has been hopelessly infatuated with you or I'll resent your power over women more than I already do."

"I—"

"Save your breath, Stafford." Marsh shepherded Shane toward the door. "We don't have time for a long-winded dissertation on your feminine conquests. I don't have a clue what happened to Cali, and finding her before the sheriff does is all that matters."

Numbly, Shane allowed himself to be led outside and herded toward the alley of the hotel. Although he was concerned about Calera's disappearance, it was difficult to orient himself with a splitting headache that drained his energy. Shane battled for mind over lethargic body, even when his brain wasn't cooperating. *Will* over mind and body, Shane told himself fiercely. Calera's life was at stake and he had to rise to the occasion.

Marsh held up the lantern and gestured toward the conglomeration of tracks in the dirt. "Can you tell me something about these prints that might give us a clue?"

Shane sank down on his haunches, forcing himself to concentrate, despite his blurred vision. "This hombre never did have his boots re-soled and none of the three horses are shod. That will make tracking easier."

"There are three men this time?" Marsh questioned.

Shane shook his head—carefully. "Only two, the same two who kidnapped Irish last time. One of the horses is carrying Irish and no one else." He gestured toward the clear track in the dirt. "The steed with the cracked hoof is carrying the lightest weight."

Marsh marveled at Shane's ability to read footprints. The man's skills bordered on phenomenal!

"Obviously Muriel was dissatisfied with her henchman the first time. They are paying closer attention to details this time," Marsh said. "When I checked Cali's room, I noticed the faint smell of chloroform, but there was no saturated kerchief lying around as evidence, and her bonnet had been set on the nightstand beside the bed."

Shane staggered to his feet and followed the tracks that led down the alley. "These men are dangerous," he mused aloud.

"You can tell that by the tracks?" Marsh questioned, astounded.

"No."

"Then how do you know they're dangerous?"

Shane's dark eyes swung to Marsh. "They must have killed

Muriel and were clever enough to toss the pistol at my fingertips. I shudder to think what they have in mind for Irish."

Bleakly, Shane followed the prints that trailed to the end of
the alley, circled, and then doubled back in the direction they
had come. When Shane's knees very nearly folded beneath him,
Marsh led him to a stack of crates and planted him on one.

"You stay here and rest while I fetch the horses."

"Go find Cactus and Sticker and have them bring my stallion," Shane instructed. "Sultan may object to having you lead
him away."

Marsh scurried off to organize their own private rescue bri-
gade, one that would be more sympathetic to Cali's plight than
Sheriff Nelson's posse.

Shane leaned his aching head against the rough-hewned wall
and inhaled a reinforcing breath. He felt awful, and worse, he
could not focus his energy on Cali as he had been able to do
the night he had awakened, feeling as if she were calling out
to him. Shane couldn't hear the echo of her sultry voice when
his skull was thumping like the tympanic section of an orches-
tra. And why, he wondered, couldn't calamity come at a more
convenient time? He could have used one-night's rest to reju-
venate his strength. But no, this latest disaster followed on the
heels of another, leaving him weak and disoriented. Dear God,
Irish needed him and he was floundering about like a witless
moron, barely capable of holding his head in a position that
didn't throb quite so much.

"Where are you, Irish?" Shane whispered to the hazy image
that floated across his mind.

Calera was incapable of mental communication at that moment. She had awakened in pitch blackness, her senses permeated with that all-too familiar scent of chloroform. She cursed
herself for falling into the same trap a second time in a week.

After Marsh had left her at the door to her room, Calera had
fumbled her way to the bed and lay down upon it. She had
dozed off, only to be awakened by the creak of the door. Before

she could get her bearings, she was pounced on from two directions at once. She had been unable to let loose with a bloodcurdling scream before a chloroform-soaked cloth had been clamped over the lower portion of her face. This time, however, Calera had managed to catch a whiff of the men who attacked her. She would have known that rank odor anywhere. Indeed, she had spent a week cooped up in a stagecoach with these two foul-smelling hooligans who never bathed of their own free will.

Calera couldn't swear that these two men were the same ones who had attacked her before, because she had been too terrified to do anything except panic the first time. Though she had been no more prepared this time, she was more aware of her captors. The men had employed the same tactics, and Calera had succumbed to the groggy effects of the anesthetic, assuming the same men were making a second attempt to dispose of her after their first ploy failed.

That had been the last thought to filter into her mind before she collapsed. And to be honest, she hadn't fought as hard as she should have to remain conscious. She had reached the point that she didn't care what became of her. She was sick of battling her way through life, coping with one heartache and disappointment after another, pulling herself up by her boot straps and struggling to survive.

Everyone Calera had ever loved was hopelessly out of reach. It seemed to her that the O'Connells bore some kind of legendary curse that followed the immigrants across the sea from their native Ireland. Destiny seemed to be calling to her, just as it had summoned the rest of her misfortunate family.

Inhaling a breath to clear her senses, Calera scanned the inky darkness, wondering where she was and why she even cared. She was bound up like a mummy, but she was able to contort her body this way and that to reach the jewel-handled dagger. Obviously her captors hadn't determined how she escaped the first time. Otherwise, they would have searched her for weapons.

After a few minutes, Calera had cut her way through the ropes and rose from the cot where she had been staked. Employing the technique Shane had taught her, she negotiated across the dark room, relying upon her sense of feel to guide her when she couldn't see her hand in front of her face. Every step was silent inching, testing her path and determining the identity of the objects that surrounded her. Calera concluded she had been confined in a storeroom, judging from the crates and shelves that lined the walls.

When she finally located the door and twisted the knob, she cursed under her breath. Her captors had locked her inside. Part of her wanted to throw up her hands in defeat and accept her fate, but the survival instincts that had brought her this far in life refused to knuckle under. Not that anybody cared what became of her, Calera thought disheartedly, but self-preservation forced her to care enough to fight back against the endless string of vicissitudes that hampered her life.

Dropping to her knees, Calera inserted the tip of the dagger into the keyhole. Holding her tongue just so, she managed to turn the lock. The door creaked open and Calera swallowed her breath. The sound echoed in the darkness. Calera waited, listening for footfalls. With her dagger clenched in her fist, she slipped out the door to find herself in yet another storage room. Moonlight splintered through the small window on the far side of the chamber and Calera finally realized where she was—The Cottage. She had been in this room that very morning, tossing out crates of whiskey bottles.

Hardly daring to breathe for fear of alerting her captors to her presence, Calera tiptoed around the maze of boxes toward the door that led to the alley. The portal whined and Calera cursed the betraying sound. When she stepped outside, she found herself face-to-face with the two men who had abducted her. But what held Calera immobilized at that crucial moment was the sight of the third person in the alley—one Calera had never expected to see. The shock of realization cost Calera valuable time in an already precarious situation.

Dear God! thought Calera. She had more dangerous enemies out to get her than she had believed possible!

Chapter Twenty-three

Calera gave herself a mental slap and wheeled with dagger in hand when Ike Fuller charged at her. Wielding the blade, as she had seen Shane do when he confronted the Tonto braves, Calera girded herself up for battle. Ike snaked out an arm to swipe her dagger and Calera lunged, catching him on the arm. With a muffled curse, Ike recoiled, grabbing his bloody wound.

"Get her, Grady," Royal Winston ordered.

Grady Flax took a cautious step forward while Calera shifted position, keeping her attention focused on both men. She thought she was doing a splendid job of defending herself until both men ganged up on her. Calera stabbed at Grady, but Ike grabbed her wrist, wresting the dagger from her fingertips. Calera found herself trapped in Grady's arms. Before she could scream her head off, his grimy hand clamped over her face.

Calera bit savagely at him, causing Grady to snatch his hand away before she bit off his fingers. This time Grady was careful to smash her lips against her teeth so she couldn't sink them into his flesh. The pressure exerted, when he covered Calera's mouth, made it impossible for her to bite a few chunks out of his hide. She did manage to kick his shins to splinters when he tried to pick her up and tote her back inside under Royal's explicit orders.

"Ouch! Damn it, you little bitch!" Grady snarled when Calera's heels hammered at his knee caps. "Help me with her, Ike. She's worse than tangling with a wildcat."

"I'm bleeding all over myself," Ike snapped. "You're bigger than she is. *You* take care of her."

Royal surged through the door to retrieve the rope Calera had cut loose. Although Ike was still grumbling about his wound, he scurried over to hold Calera down when Royal brusquely commanded him to do so.

Despite Calera's valiant attempt to escape, she found herself tied in a chair. Royal lit the lantern and set it on the table, staring thoughtfully at her captive.

Calera was not about to give the madam time to devise a way to dispose of her. "I demand to know what this is all about."

Royal smiled nastily. "I thought perhaps you had figured it out by now, Calera. I suppose your are not as witty as you have given yourself credit."

Perhaps Calera *had* given herself too much credit, but she had most certainly been deceived by Royal's duplicity. Now, Calera had her suspicions about Royal's involvement, but she wanted to hear the truth from this horse's mouth. "I assume I have something you desperately want."

Royal nodded her dark head. "The Cottage, of course. And I had control until you showed up and spoiled everything." She looked down her nose at Calera and sniffed derisively. "For weeks you have been trying to drag information about Keery out of everyone in town. They were all being polite. The fact is that Keery was a mean-tempered, obnoxious bully who was drunk more than he was sober. I had tolerated him since I arrived in town. When he took me in as his partner, he expected me to cater to him and only him. It made the situation all the more unpleasant when I became intrigued by Shane Stafford. Keery was so jealous and prejudiced that he made Shane's life hell."

Calera looked away. It hurt to think of Shane and Royal together, even when Calera had vowed never to give that deceitful half-breed another thought.

"How convenient that Shane disposed of my brother for you," Calera muttered bitterly.

"*In*convenient, actually," Royal contradicted. "Shane merely knocked that boorish drunkard silly. In all the commotion, everyone followed Shane to the street and I had to finish the deed myself."

Calera stared owl-eyed at Royal. "*You* killed my brother? *You* let Shane take the blame?"

"Why not?" Royal shrugged carelessly. "I had no intention of pressing charges against Shane. Since the sheriff was one of my regular customers—one who had to sneak around to prevent clashing with your insanely jealous brother—my wishes were granted . . . until you showed up to stir trouble. Suddenly I found myself with another partner who wanted to turn my brothel into a hotel—of all things!"

"And so you had Ike and Grady kidnap me," Calera assumed. "Unfortunately, they were unsuccessful the first time."

"The first time?" Royal chortled before glancing over to see how Grady was coming along with his efforts to treat and bandage Ike's wound. "Your first abduction was Muriel's scheme to throw suspicion on Shane and get him hanged." Royal shook her head and sighed. "Such a spiteful woman. She even threatened to shoot Ike and Grady herself after they botched up her original plans for you. I hoped Muriel would succeed, but it seems I am left to tend the matter myself."

Calera digested the information and darted a glance around the storeroom, desperately trying to conjure up a method of escape. She had to keep Royal talking, to stall for time.

"In fact," Royal went on to say, "Muriel paid me to seduce Shane. She tried to turn you against him so you would despise him as much as she did. Not that I had any complaints about seducing him, mind you. I find Shane to be a wildly fascinating man." Royal smiled craftily, taking fiendish pleasure in leading Calera to believe Shane preferred the experienced courtesan to this naive Easterner. "I cannot imagine how you thought you could be woman enough for a virile man like Shane when he has me. He was only toying with you for his own amusement, you know. I'm sure you provided plenty of entertainment for him until he tired of you."

Calera was forming a most distressing picture of the situation. The way Calera figured it, Shane and Royal had plotted to dispose of Keery. When Shane failed, Royal completed the dastardly deed. The two of them had been in cahoots from the beginning. Their lust for each other, and Royal's greed, had cost Keery his life. Now that Calera stood in the way, she would also meet with an untimely death.

"And what of Muriel? Do you plan to dispose of her so Shane will have sole title to the Bar "S" Ranch?"

Royal cast Calera a puzzled glance before it dawned on her that her captive was unaware of the evening's events. "Muriel is already out of the picture. She's dead, quite by accident, I'm afraid."

When Calera frowned, bemused, Royal explained, "Muriel garbed herself in one of your bonnets and gowns and met Shane at The Cottage. Ike, Grady, and I were under the mistaken impression that it was you and that you were about to shoot Shane down."

"What!" Calera gasped in stupefied astonishment.

"I had Ike fire at you—or rather at Muriel—since Shane was surprised to find himself staring down the barrel of a loaded pistol. Ike's well-aimed bullet found its mark. When Shane fell to the floor, I tossed Ike's pistol at Shane's fingertips, thinking things had worked out splendidly. Unfortunately, you were not the target, as we hoped. It was Muriel instead of you who had been killed. I had to send Ike and Grady to abduct you, using the same technique Muriel had ordered the men to use the first time."

Calera's mind was whirling, trying to fit all the pieces of the puzzle together. Muriel had tried to murder Shane by disguising herself as Calera? Royal and her henchmen had tried to ambush Calera and killed Muriel by mistake? No doubt, Royal had every intention of correcting the oversight as soon as possible. That's why Royal sent Ike and Grady to kidnap her. They weren't giving this night up for lost.

"What about Shane?" Calera questioned.

"Muriel's bullet grazed his skull," Royal reported. "He is still alive and recuperating in Doc Broxton's office."

Naturally Royal was relieved that her lover was still alive, thought Calera. And while Shane was recovering from his injury, Royal had taken it upon herself to dispose of Calera, just as she had disposed of Keery.

The worst mistake Calera had ever made was leaving Philadelphia. This whole affair had been a one-way trip to hell. She had not even arrived in time to attend Keery's funeral, and she had met with disaster. Dear God, if only she could rewind the hands of time and pretend this past month never existed!

"Hurry up, Grady," Royal snapped. "We have arrangements to make. Sooner or later Marsh Layton will come looking for Calera. The last thing we need is a search party linking us with Calera's disappearance."

"I'm almost finished," Grady assured her.

"Ouch! Not so tight," Ike hissed when Grady wrapped the bandage around his arm like a tourniquet.

"Hold still," Grady demanded.

In that instant, Calera made a crucial decision. As she saw it, her chances of surviving this latest ordeal were slim, if nonexistent. But for damned certain, Calera was going to do everything humanly possible to foil their plans. While Royal was watching Grady put the finishing touches on Ike's bandage, Calera gave the table a mighty heave. The lantern slid toward Royal, forcing her to grab the object before it set the storeroom ablaze.

Calera's actions were so unexpected that Royal and her henchmen were too occupied trying to prevent a fire to give Calera a thought. Ike and Grady dashed forward to stamp out the flames that smoldered in the hem of Royal's gown. In the meantime, Calera bounded up like a jackrabbit and hopped toward the door. With her legs bound at the ankles she couldn't exit with as much speed as she preferred, but a small head start was better than nothing at all, she reckoned.

Curses flew from Royal's lips when she saw Calera jumping toward the door. "You stupid bitch! You will pay dearly for this," Royal screeched.

Frantic, Calera vaulted into the alley, hoping to latch onto one of the horses. When Grady launched himself forward, Calera saw the ground fly up at her with astonishing speed. She landed with a thud and a whoosh. Before she could worm loose, Grady hoisted her to her feet and tossed her over his horse. Wildly, Calera hammered her bound fists against the steed's flanks. The horse balked and lunged forward, but not before Grady jerked down hard on the bit.

"Stand still, you damned nag," Grady snarled at the wild-eyed steed.

Despite Calera's attempts to fling herself off the horse, Grady clamped onto her and swung into the saddle. Royal stomped outside, her gown saturated with kerosene, her petticoats singed. Ah, what Calera wouldn't have given for a dancing spark to set this wicked woman aflame!

Royal flashed Calera a murderous glare and then focused on her henchmen. "Take this troublesome chit into the mountains and dispose of her. I am going to enjoy ridding myself of her, more than I delighted in removing that bastard brother of hers from my life!"

Calera's breath came out in a pained groan when the steed bounded off in a bone-jarring trot. From where Calera lay, viewing the world from her upside down position on the steed, it looked as if the O'Connell curse had caught up with her. Of course, Shane probably wouldn't give her disappearance a second thought. He and his lover would have everything going their way, especially since Muriel had met her bad end.

Calera slumped defeatedly, her chin bumping against the steed's ribs. It was achingly clear that while some folks were watched over by guardian angels, others were circled by faithful buzzards. Calera had obviously gathered the latter. A sense of fatalism engulfed her, knowing she was doomed to destruction.

No one was going to rescue her because no one really cared what became of her. Oh, Marsh might attempt to locate her. And Horace Baxter would wonder what became of her, but theirs would be a futile search. Calera would be long dead by the time Marsh found her. She had been such a fool, but Shane was an ever bigger one, Calera thought to herself. Royal had been using Shane, letting him shoulder all the blame for two premeditated murders.

Why fight the inevitable? Calera asked herself despondently. She was as good as dead. And may Shane Stafford burn in the fiery pits of hell! He and his paramour had disposed of Keery. Now Calera would go to her grave, cursing her ill-fated affection for a cold, heartless, deceitful man who had used her and discarded her because of his lust for this provocative madam.

And to think Calera had believed Shane when he fed her all those lies! Muriel was right about her stepson. He was a bastard of the worst sort. Calera despised Shane with every part of her being. It was a shame Shane couldn't read her mind at the moment. He would feel the eerie tingles snaking down his spine and he would know he was being cursed with each breath.

Shane jerked up his throbbing head when an odd sensation skittered down his backbone. He wasn't sure if his ears were burning from vicious thoughts that were being directed at him, or if it was the side effects of his hellish headache. Struggling to his feet, Shane wobbled toward the street. He was very nearly run down by Cactus, Sticker, and Marsh who thundered around the corner, sending him spinning like a top.

Only Shane's wobbly shout—one that came at great expense to his aching head—caught the threesome's attention.

Sticker wheeled around and leaned out to hand Shane the reins to the prancing stallion. "Are you sure you're up to this?"

Shane didn't respond; he simply dragged himself onto Sultan's back. Studying the tracks in the dirt, Shane led the way down the alley, following a trail that circled to the edge of town. Shane halted his steed and stared at the dark silhouette of The

Cottage. Nudging Sultan, he trailed the prints to the door located behind the one-time brothel.

"You think she's in there?" Marsh questioned.

Gingerly, Shane eased to the ground and squatted on his haunches. His hand brushed over the indentation in the dirt, frowning at the implications of what might have happened.

"What's wrong?" Cactus quizzed him.

"There was a struggle before Irish was hoisted onto the back of the horse."

"How the devil can you tell that?" Marsh inquired.

Shane was too preoccupied studying another set of tracks to reply. He had the unshakable feeling that the next leg of Calera's journey was going to be a perilous one. If time had not been of the essence, Shane would have followed the single set of prints that trailed off in the opposite direction from the horses. Unfortunately, he didn't have that much time, not when Calera's life was in danger.

"I'll follow Irish alone," he insisted, unfolding himself from the ground.

"But—"

Shane flung up a hand to silence Marsh's protest. "Too many riders will draw too much attention," he said reasonably. "Cactus and Sticker are needed at the ranch. I need you to stay in town, Layton, to keep abreast of the developments. I have the feeling some changes are about to be made."

"And how in heaven's name can you tell *that* from a half-dozen sets of smeared footprints, I'd like to know!" Marsh erupted in frustration. "I swear, Stafford, I think your head wound has caused you to hallucinate. No one could read that much in those damned tracks."

When Shane stepped into the stirrup and rode off, Marsh expelled an audible sigh. "I don't think we should let him go alone."

"You think you could keep up with him, even on a bad day?" Cactus chuckled at the gambler's naivete. "I've known Shane for ten years an' I'm here to tell you that he could track a bird across a desert—no problem. He knows this country better than you can imagine. We would only slow him down. Believe me, I know what I'm talkin' about. Me an' Sticker tried to keep up with him a few years back while he was roundin' up mustangs in the mountain meadows. Shane may be half-white, but he is all Indian when it comes to negotiatin' these mountains an' followin' tracks."

"But he isn't trailing horses," Marsh grumbled. "He's following a woman who might be in grave danger and there are two men."

"Only two?" Sticker snickered and glanced at his brother. "Why hell, that ain't enough to give Shane much of a challenge. You can bet them two hooligans will be damned sorry they crossed paths with Shane Stafford."

Marsh wasn't certain if Cactus and Sticker were trying to reassure him, or if they honestly believed that half-breed could work miracles. Marsh was still ill at ease and he wasn't going to feel one bit better until he knew exactly what had become of Cali and why. And if Stafford didn't locate Cali in time to save her from calamity, Marsh was going to hold it over the man's head for the rest of his natural life!

On that spiteful thought, Marsh trotted back to the hotel, wondering what *interesting development* Shane anticipated. He rather suspected Shane had conjured up the excuse not to take Marsh along because of his lack of tracking skills. That rankled. Even though Cali couldn't return Marsh's affection, he did not appreciate being outdone by any man. His pride was smarting.

A devilish smile pursed Royal's lips as she scurried to her room. At long last she could put her business back in proper working order. She would simply commandeer the carpenters' renovations according to *her* specifications with the cash Calera had designated for the laborers. *The Royal Cottage* could use a face lift, she decided. Now that Keery was out of the way, she could give the bordello a touch of class.

Royal could envision the new parlor—elegant, expensively furnished. Business would increase without Keery turning away potential customers for one flimsy reason or another. The parlor house would prosper as it never had, now that Royal was in control. She had Sheriff Nelson in her pocket and Calera O'Connell was about to be launched into eternity.

Ah yes, Royal mused while she checked to ensure that Calera's belongings were safely concealed in the closet. Within the week, all her girls would be reinstated at The Royal Cottage. The carpenters would work twice as fast, knowing they would enjoy one free night of hospitality with the ladies of their choosing. No one would miss Calera O'Connell and her ridiculous notion of a boardinghouse to replace the brothel. As Royal saw it, she had done the town and its surrounding mining camps a tremendous favor. Calera had been out of place since the day she arrived in Globe City. Her absence would not be missed, certainly not by Royal or the patrons of The Royal Cottage!

Part Three

O God! Put back Thy universe and give me yesterday.

Henry Arthur Jones—*Silver King*

Chapter Twenty-four

Try as she may, Calera could not remain conscious for more than a few minutes at a time while she lay jackknifed over the steed. The blood ran to her head until she swore her skull would explode under the pressure. Calera had hung upside down for so long that she couldn't measure time or determine which direction they had been traveling. With her upturned view of the darkness, one mountain peak looked pretty much the same as another.

Sometime during the night Calera remembered being dumped on the ground while her captors took time to sleep. There was no food or water forthcoming, only the gnawing of tight ropes that rubbed the flesh on her wrists and ankles raw. Somehow or another, Calera vowed to return from the dead to torment Royal and Shane. She would haunt The Cottage's halls forevermore, so help her she would! And she would hurl a few curses at Ike Fuller and Grady Flax while she was at it.

"Get up, woman, we've got more traveling to do," Ike nudged her with the toe of his boot.

"I'm not in that great of a hurry, if it's all the same to you," Calera sassed him.

"It ain't all the same to me," Ike snorted. "The sooner we get rid of you, the sooner we can return to town."

"I'm hungry," Calera declared.

Grady bent at the waist to stuff a strip of dried beef in her mouth, more to shut Calera up than to appease her appetite, she decided. Before she could chew and swallow her meager portion, Grady jerked her upright and tossed her over the horse. Calera was positively certain she would spend eternity doubled over in this uncomfortable position. Part of the O'Connell curse, no doubt.

"You got any idea where we are?" Ike questioned, peering at the rising peaks that were spotlighted by the first rays of dawn.

"Not a clue," Grady replied. "We'll ride toward the sun and find some remote region in the mountains to leave our unwanted baggage."

Calera envisioned all sorts of unpleasant endings to her life. She might be left to starve to death, if some wild beast didn't make a meal of her first. Or perhaps Grady and Ike would simply toss her off a cliff. No, on second thought, these two scoundrels wouldn't be that merciful. Too bad she had ignored these two galoots while they shared a coach. Maybe they would have treated her kindly if she had been more tolerant of them. And then again, maybe not. Oh, what difference did it make now? Calera asked herself dully. These men were loyal to Royal who probably promised them money and sexual favors when the deadly deed had been accomplished.

That was the last thought to surge through Calera's mind before unconsciousness overtook her. She hung over the saddle like a carcass of beef, certain she had nothing to live for. She had been forsaken and betrayed by a man she thought she loved. There was no reason to survive . . .

Employing a makeshift torch, Shane had followed the tracks along Pinto Creek toward Rockingstraw Mountain. Although Shane had pushed himself to the very limits and demanded more of his body, exhaustion had caught up with him. Shane had been forced to bed down for a few hours. His head had been throbbing something fierce and his vision was blurred more often than not.

Leaving Sultan as a posted sentinel, Shane collapsed on his pallet and slept every bit as hard as he had been pushing himself. The sun had long been perched in the sky, playing hide and seek with fleeting clouds when Shane came to. He felt the urgency to begin his search, but his lethargic body was reluctant to cooperate.

"Too damned much whiskey," Shane muttered at himself as he climbed onto Sultan's back. And too much spirited horse with which to contend, thought he. Sultan was prancing around like a ballerina, tossing his cream-colored mane, anxious to run. Even after several sharp scoldings, Sultan had not adjusted to the slow pace. Shane was beginning to wish the blood-red stallion was a mule. The horse wouldn't cooperate. Sultan was as jumpy as a grasshopper, darting glances one direction and then the other.

"What's the matter with you?" Shane asked several miles later. The horse, of course, said nothing. Shane exhaled a heavy sigh. His senses were fuzzy, but obviously Sultan detected trouble. Of what nature Shane didn't have a clue. But for certain Sultan was apprehensive. Since Shane's mental faculties weren't what they should have been, he depended on Sultan's keen senses, letting the stallion veer away from the meandering tracks that indicated the men who had taken Calera captive didn't know exactly where they were going.

When Sultan paused on the banks of Salt River to help himself to a drink, Shane *kerplopped* in the water, desperately seeking a cure for his sluggishness. Again, Sultan jerked up his head, his nostrils flared, his eyes wide and alert. Shane slowly rose from the river to scan the thick underbrush and stony face of the cliff that overlooked the river.

Shane was thoroughly convinced that he had been in civilization too long. He had lost touch with nature, had lost that necessary edge on his senses which all Apaches prided themselves in possessing. Until Shane became the man he had once been, he would be useless to Calera and to himself.

Determined of purpose, Shane plodded ashore to retrieve his breechclout from his saddlebag. He had to dress like an Apache, think like an Apache, behave like an Apache. There were too many dangers lurking in this labyrinth of mountains and canyons to be wandering around without completely dedicating himself to his mission. He called to *Holos,* the sun, for renewed energy and strength. He chanted to the powers of the Earth Mother and lifted his arms to *Usen,* requesting the return of the Apache life-way. He gave himself to the blue-violet mountains, reaching past the towering pines and firs to absorb the omnipotent forces of the spirit world.

Although Shane had lingered beside the river, he emerged a different man, invigorated by the reclamation of the Apache spirit. He had overcome the physical weakness that had hounded his keen senses. Once again, he was all Apache and he, too, felt the presence that had set Sultan's nerves on edge. Riders were approaching. Shane could sense it and he went to investigate . . .

Calera was so weary from traveling in an unnatural position that she could no longer raise her head to view her surroundings. It felt as if every ounce of her energy had been drained from her aching body through a spigot that had been implanted in the top of her head. Muscles knotted and throbbed. Nausea had become her ever-constant companion. This journey into hell had her begging to shed the confines of the flesh and find peace in a higher sphere. Dear God, how much more torture did she have to endure to cleanse her wicked soul? Hadn't she suffered enough yet?

"This should do it," Grady announced, pausing his steed to stare back in the direction they had come.

Ike massaged his injured arm and surveyed the obscure canyon with its looming granite walls. "I hope the hell we can find our way back to Globe," he grumbled tiredly. His disposition improved considerably when his gaze landed on Calera's shapely backside. He darted Grady a quick glance and grinned slyly. "I don't know about you, but I plan to be repaid for all my trouble."

Grady returned the diabolical smile. "I never intended for it to be any other way, Ike."

Dazed, Calera felt herself being hauled from the horse. The blood drained from her head and the world spun furiously around her. When the supporting arms fell away, her knees folded beneath her and she collapsed like a boneless jellyfish. Calera offered no protest when her arms were lifted over her head and lashed to whatever was behind her. She didn't know and cared less. There was only blessed relief from the constant jarring motions of the horse. Her mouth was dry as cotton and her lips were chapped. Even her eyebrows ached.

Vaguely, she became aware of the rustling noises beside her, heard the rasp of a knife cutting away the rope that rubbed her ankles raw. When her legs were roughly jerked apart, her tangled lashes swept up to see the burly silhouette framed by the blinding sun. The realization of what her captors intended in their next phase of torture brought a feeble protest from her lips.

Grady chuckled at the once-feisty hellion who lay sluggishly before him. Her red-gold tresses cascaded around her ashen face like a river of fire. "I pictured myself buried inside you since the day we boarded the stage," he told Calera bluntly. "Now I'm gonna to see those fantasies come true."

Calera made a futile attempt to kick at Grady when he dropped to his knees between her legs. "No!" she burst out when his grimy hand groped at her breast.

The nausea she experienced earlier did not begin to compare to the sickening revulsion that riveted her body. Calera tried to heave herself away from Grady's disgusting touch and quell the awful apprehension of what was to come, but her efforts were a waste of energy. She had been staked to a tree and Grady's hands punished her for attempting to fight him.

"Hurry up, Grady," Ike snapped. "I don't want to wait all day to have my turn."

"Hold her legs," Grady ordered, and then to Calera he barked, "Hold still, bitch. You're gonna enjoy this as much as I do."

Dull green eyes focused on the homely face that boasted several day's growth of whiskers. Enjoy being molested by the likes of these two repulsive ruffians? Never! Difficult though it was, Calera moistened her lips and spit in Grady's sneering face. His outraged growl exploded in the afternoon air and he reared up to backhand her across the cheek. Calera ignored the stinging pain and dug her heels into the grass to push backward before Grady flung himself down upon her. She called upon every last smidgen of energy to fight back, refusing to surrender to such degrading humiliation.

"Hell's fire, Ike! Hold her down!" Grady growled as he clutched a handful of skirt and shoved the garment up to Calera's waist. "I'm gonna love this—"

A startled gasp gushed from Grady's throat when he felt the stabbing pain plunge between his shoulder blades.

"Holy Hell!" Ike staggered back, staring incredulously at the end of the dagger that protruded from Grady's back. The knife had appeared from nowhere, hissing like a rattlesnake before it penetrated Grady's flesh.

Wild-eyed, Calera watched Grady teeter above her like a boulder about to tumble downhill. His glassy-eyed stare focused somewhere behind her as he pitched forward. Calera jerked herself sideways to prevent taking the full impact of his falling body. The air surged from her lungs when Grady collapsed half on, half off of her. Calera stared at the dagger and the blood-soaked shirt before glancing at Ike who had turned white as flour. Calera watched him stare in every direction at once before he spun around to dash toward his horse.

Another missile soared through the air, catching Ike squarely between the eyes. A pained squawk exploded from his lips when the momentum of the cantaloupe-size stone sent him cartwheeling off his horse. His boot heel tangled in the stirrup, flipping him upside down. The alarmed steed bolted sideways, jerking Ike with it. Ike thrashed about trying to free his foot, but he only succeeded in startling his horse again.

Stark fear paralyzed Ike when a foreboding shadow fell over him, eclipsing the sunlight like a cloud of doom. He stared up at the towering mass of copper flesh and rippling muscle, seeing the expression on Shane Stafford's face that was as fatal as the grave. Wild with terror, Ike grabbed his pistol, only to have his fingers crushed beneath a moccasined foot. He blinked the blood from his eyes when it tumbled from the wound on his head and then swallowed audibly. There was no mercy in those fathomless obsidian pools that bore down upon him. Ike could see and taste death.

"Don't kill me!" he yowled.

A hard smile stretched across Shane's lips as he squatted down to retrieve Ike's Colt. "I won't have to. After you endure the Apache's brand of torture for what you have done, you will gladly kill yourself."

Never taking his eyes off his captive, Shane removed the cartridges from the pistol's chamber—save one.

Ike grew very still. "What are you going to do?"

"The same thing you did to Calera," Shane told him in a tone that carried such deadly menace that Ike blanched. "But you will be screaming for mercy when she did not."

"This was Royal's idea," Ike insisted. "All we did was—" His words died in silence when he looked past Shane to see an infantry of shadows silently inching closer.

"Dear God!" Calera gasped when she spied the stalking, bronze-skinned warriors who were closing around them. There must have been twenty heavily-armed braves converging on the campsite. They all looked exactly like Shane—dark and deadly. Eyes like chips of black diamonds swung from her to Ike and back again.

When Shane spoke in his native tongue, three bare-chested young warriors descended on Ike. He squealed like a stuck pig when he was yanked to his feet and shepherded off behind one of the monolithic boulders that lined the chasm. Even when

Ike disappeared from sight, Calera could still hear him bellowing at the top of his lungs, promising Shane anything if it would spare his life.

Shane leaned over to retrieve his dagger from Grady's back. Another clipped command from Shane prompted two more somber-faced warriors to hoist Grady's limp body off Calera. She, of course, would be saved for last, she reasoned. Shane had obviously trailed after her captives to ensure the deed was done according to Royal's specifications. Ike and Grady would not return to Globe to blackmail Royal or Shane. And Calera would be disposed of by Shane himself. He probably showed up to have the last laugh, to remind her what an idiotic fool she had been to believe he was more of a man than his stepmother claimed him to be. Shane Stafford was as ruthless as they came. Calera had discovered that the hard way. He had used her, deceived her, betrayed her. But by damned, he would not defeat her! She would curse his black soul with her last dying breath and she *would* come back to haunt him and his deadly whore. They deserved each other, deserved every curse Calera placed on them.

A stony-faced warrior, who looked to be in his mid-forties and stood five-foot-seven-inches tall, strode toward Calera. His thick chest would have done a buffalo proud. His hawk's beak of a nose, the pronounced cheekbones, and the straight thin mouth gave the Apache warlord a formidable appearance.

While Shane and the older warrior loomed over Calera's prostrate body, she uplifted her chin, defying both ominous looking men. They would not hear *her* begging for mercy as Ike was still doing. She would utilize the powers Shane had taught her to overcome whatever physical pain they inflicted on her. She would project her soul and spirit away from the torture, and she would die with the kind of dignity no man could ever strip from her.

Geronimo very nearly cracked a smile when he peered down into the bruised but bewitching face that was surrounded by strands of living fire. "This is your woman?" he asked Shane.

"If looks could kill, you would be as dead as the White-Eyes who planned to defile her."

For the life of him, Shane could not imagine why Calera was glowering at him as if he were a slimy serpent that had slithered out from under a rock. He had saved her from rape and certain death. He had expected at least one smile of gratitude. Women! Who could understand them? He knew Calera had been furious with him after she had seen him and Royal together, but . . .

"How nice of you to invite your friends to accompany me to my own funeral. What do you plan to do, Apache? Let them watch while you chop me into bite-size pieces to serve to the vultures?" Calera spat in question. "Why don't you quit dilly-dallying and finish the deed? I much prefer to die than to lie here looking at you!"

"What did the white woman say?" Geronimo queried curiously.

"Nothing her eyes haven't already told you," Shane replied.

Geronimo nodded thoughtfully. "There is much power in the color of her eyes, much inner strength. And there is fire in her hair—"

"And thunder on her tongue," Shane added dryly.

Geronimo was amused, though he had very little reason to smile these past years after he had lost his wife and family in a massacre by Mexicans at Janos. He had become overwhelmed by bitterness and the need for revenge, not to mention his outraged cry for freedom against his oppressors. Five years earlier, Geronimo had been tricked and captured during what was supposed to have been a parley with Indian Agent John Crum. In chains, and surrounded by almost a hundred soldiers, Geronimo had been conveyed to the San Carlos Reservation near the Gila River.

The area consisted mostly of low-lying desert, where summer temperatures reached one-hundred-ten degrees—a miserable climate compared to the forests and mountains Geronimo had once freely roamed. The vegetation consisted of cactus, mesquite, and cottonwoods. Sandstorms were frequent and rattlesnakes and centipedes were common nuisances. And worse, civilian contractors, who were to provide supplies of beef for the tribe, charged the government for thousands of pounds of meat that were never delivered, along with half-rations of water that never reached the reservation. After a few months of demeaning reservation life, Geronimo had escaped, preferring flight to the wretched conditions he had been forced to endure.

Despite all the unpleasant memories and the turmoil in his life, Geronimo chuckled at Shane's remark and at the feisty belligerence displayed by the white woman. Geronimo stared down at the spirited female who reminded him of a cornered mountain lion with claws and teeth bared. He did not offer the woman a hand of friendship and good will for fear she would bite off his fingers and spit them back at him.

"Laugh if you will," Calera spluttered at the sniggering warlord. "But you will never intimidate me, for I have already been intimidated by the devil himself! But beware that you do not stand too close to this viper. He will poison you with his deceitful lies and then he will betray you!"

"What did she say?" Geronimo questioned, thick brows knitted over his onyx eyes.

"She warns you not to doubt her ability to defy all of us until her death," Shane translated. "She also advises you to keep your distance from me because I am an evil curse."

One dark brow elevated. Geronimo's gimlet-eyed gaze bounced back and forth between Shane and Calera. "You would keep this woman alive when she has nothing but hatred to offer you?"

Shane stared at the hard-bitten chief for a long moment. "Would you destroy such strength of spirit, my brother? Considering all the cruel injustices that have befallen The People, would you object to her fierce will when you possess so much of it yourself? This white woman knows the anguish that you yourself have suffered. She understands the pain of great loss, knows how it feels to be forsaken and betrayed. She will fight to the death for her own free spirit, just as we have scorned the white men's lies when they leave their trail of broken promises for the Apaches."

When Geronimo nodded thoughtfully, his coal-black hair rippled around his sharp, angular features. "I, too, will fight for my freedom. I will roam this land that has been ours since our ancestors fled the Fire Dragon to the south and came to the mountains where *Usen* rules." His dark eyes focused on Calera's defiant features and he nodded before glancing at Shane. "We will leave you to tame this spirited tigress as you tamed that blood-red stallion. My braves yearn to see their families again before the hounding Army comes to dog our footsteps."

Geronimo stared at the gargantuan half-breed for a long moment before he continued, "Be careful, *Si-ha-ney*. Do not become like the White-Eyes. You may have been sired by a white father we came to call our friend, but you are Apache. Breathe the life-giving air and walk in the presence of *Usen*. Never forget who you are."

Shane grasped Geronimo's forearm in the customary gesture of friendship. "And never forget that you are my brother," he solemnly reminded the chief. "When your warriors grow hungry and weary, what is mine is yours. The cattle that graze the valley below the Mogollon Rim, as well as the horses and sheep, are yours for the taking. May your journey be a safe one."

Geronimo spared Calera one last glance before pivoting away. "And may you have the presence of mind never to turn your back on this lioness. She might eat you alive."

Calera lifted her head to stare after the departing chief. "Aren't you going to take me with you? Don't leave me with this monster!"

Geronimo swiveled his head around, silently requesting translation.

"She wants to go with you instead of being stuck with me," Shane interpreted with a faint grin.

"I have too much trouble with the Army hounding my heels," Geronimo grunted. "You keep her. If you manage to tame this wildcat, perhaps she will become as devoted to you as the stallion." He paused to flash Shane a scant smile. "And then again, maybe not."

To Calera's dismay, the bronze-skinned warriors disappeared

into the dense thicket of pines. The sound of Ike screaming in the distance absorbed the silence of the Apache's retreating footsteps, leaving Calera alone with the last man she ever wanted to see.

"Why don't you go away and leave me alone," Calera muttered, chin in the air. "I'll take my chances with the buzzards—relatives of yours, no doubt."

"Damn it, Irish, I saved your life," Shane said irritably. "A little appreciation and a display of respect in front of Geronimo would have been nice."

"Dear God! Geronimo?" Calera blinked, bewildered. "Was that who that was?"

"None other," Shane confirmed. "When I crossed paths with him this morning, he was in favor of scalping all three of you before roasting you at the stake, just to make another point with the White-Eyes who have betrayed him more times than he cares to count."

"You should have let him. Then I would have been out of your hair *and* mine."

Shane put his hands on his hips and stared down into Calera's battered features. "What devil has gotten into you, Irish? I hauled myself out of bed with a splitting headache to track you down and this is the thanks I get."

Calera could not believe the man's audacity! Didn't he realize his lover had told Calera how the two of them had arranged Keery's death? Didn't he recall that Muriel had warned Calera that Shane was deceitful and heartless? Well, maybe it was time she reminded this gargantuan Apache of all his transgressions against her.

"I hate you!" Calera burst out bitterly. "You and Royal plotted to kill Keery and then you tried to sweet talk me into forgiving you, insisting my brother was to blame. Of course, you wouldn't bother with the details of the incident so you could protect your greedy lover who was dying to get her hands on the deed to The Cottage so the two of you could come and go from her bed as you pleased. And then when Muriel tried to kill you,

Royal came to your rescue by ordering Ike to gun her down and—"

"What?" Shane gaped at Calera as if she had tree branches protruding from her head.

Calera glared him down—or rather she glared him *up*. She was still flat on her back. "Don't deny it, you insufferable snake. If I have to listen to another round of your lies, I'll kill myself with no help from you!"

Shane heaved an exasperated sigh and squatted down to untie Calera's hands. She recoiled as if she had been snakebit.

"Don't touch me, you bastard."

"Perhaps I am that in the white man's eyes," he agreed. "But no more than that, Irish."

Ah yes, this was where Shane tried to convince her that he was guiltless. Well, it wouldn't work—not again, not *ever* again! Before Shane could say one word in his defense, Calera whacked him on his tender forehead and rolled to her feet. Her knees immediately gave out and she collapsed. She had been jack-knifed over a horse so long that her appendages had forgotten how to function properly.

Before Calera could crawl away, a pistol blast echoed around the towering walls of the chasm and died into eerie silence. Her gaze flew toward the boulder behind which the Apaches had taken Ike a half hour earlier. She knew without asking what had happened. The unspeakable torture Ike had endured was over. He had managed to reach his pistol and end his agony.

When Shane scooped her up in his arms, Calera squirmed for release. "Put me down!"

Shane obliged, watching her legs wobble before she collapsed a second time. Again, he gathered her to his chest and called to Sultan. Upon command, Sultan bowed down so Shane could seat himself and his squirming bundle on the saddle blanket. Using his knees to guide the blood-red stallion, Shane veered around the outthrusting stone wall and rode toward a location where a mineral spring gushed from the side of the rocky preci-pices, leaping from cliff to cliff in a breathtaking cascade of falls. Shane passed beneath the first waterfall to enter a small, open-ended cave of stalactites that led to a pool that was surrounded by tangled vines and thick bushes that were teeming with red berries.

"You're going to drown me, I presume." Calera smirked. "How very inconvenient that I never learned to swim."

Shane expelled a long-suffering sigh. "Will you get it through that chunk of rock you call your skull that I did not come here to kill you, but rather to rescue you."

"Fine." She fumed like a steaming clam. "You saved me. Now go away and leave me alone."

"Irish—"

His voice held a rumble of warning that indicated he was on the verge of losing his temper. Not that Calera cared one whit. She didn't care about anything anymore. "Just toss me in the water. If it makes you feel better, you can hang around to watch me drown—"

Thoroughly out of patience, Shane complied. He swung Calera out of his arms, launching her clean over the miniature waterfall and into the pool below. Calera sank like a rock and then, with arms flailing, she surged to the surface, gurgling and gasping for breath. Shane sank down on the rocks and reached out to clutch the soggy sleeve of her gown.

"Just as I thought," he concluded. "You are too much of a survivor to die on your own accord. You're still fighting to live, Irish. Sometimes a person simply cannot overcome their stubborn instinct, no matter how much one tries to defy it."

When Calera tried to open her mouth to spout like a geyser, Shane dunked her. Self-preservation brought her sputtering back to the surface. Shane was instantly reminded of a panther cub he had once seen floundering in a stream, its eyes flared, its coat glistening with water droplets. Then, as now, he plucked up the feisty creature, avoiding bared teeth and sharp claws.

"Damn you, Apache!" Calera spumed when he set her beside him.

"Now that you have cooled off, we'll talk."

"I have nothing more to say to you."

"Good. I'll do the talking and you can do the listening."

Calera opened her mouth to protest, but her teeth were chattering ninety miles a minute and she couldn't utter another word. But that was the whole point of the dunking, wasn't it? Shane wanted the opportunity to speak his piece and he swore to have it—here and now! Calera had no other choice but to let him.

Chapter Twenty-five

While Calera shivered in her skin, Shane stared at the glistening walls of the cavern and carefully formulated his thoughts. "I had vowed not to tell you about your brother to spare your feelings, Irish, but I have to break my promise to myself. He was not the man you once knew. He had become a harsh, vindictive man. He let the wealth he acquired go to his head and he became so addicted to whiskey that drinking became his occupation.

"Keery had come to view himself as a member of a superior race and he lorded over everyone he knew," Shane reluctantly informed Calera. "He developed a fierce dislike of the Chinese after working on the railroad crews with them. He treated them like second-class citizens, refusing to associate with them in Globe. Because of my Indian heritage, Keery also held a grudge against me. When he served in the Army of the West, he battled my people. Friendships were lost and enemies were made in war. He, like many whites in Arizona Territory, came to despise the Apaches as fiercely as warriors like Cochise and Geronimo hate Mexicans and whites. Last month when I entered The Cottage to fetch Cactus and Sticker—"

"Who?" Calera asked through chattering teeth.

"Two men who work at the Bar "S" Ranch," Shane elaborated. "They were enjoying the favors of the soiled doves who inhabited The Cottage. Keery met me at the door and ordered me out. He had been drinking to excess, as usual. When I informed him I wasn't leaving without my friends, he threw a punch. Furniture was demolished during the fracas and Keery saw to it that I landed in jail. He told Sheriff Nelson that I had instigated the argument and destroyed his property."

Try as she might, Calera could not picture the spiteful man Shane described, even after Royal had bluntly declared Keery to be a loud, bigoted bully. Calera didn't want to relinquish her cherished memories of her brother. It was like losing him all over again.

"While I was locked in jail for the night, Keery decided to confiscate Sultan to pay the damages. He sold my stallion to the Army officers from Fort McDowell."

Calera reflected on that time when she had aided Shane in retrieving the stallion. Had Keery swiped Shane's horse as a spiteful act of revenge? Dear God, that was worse than issuing a declaration of war. She knew how much Sultan meant to Shane.

"When I discovered what Keery had done, I rode the piebald into The Cottage, without the slightest concern for the amount of damage I was doing to the brothel." Shane paused to heave an audible sigh. "Yes, I went there with every intention of releasing my fury and retrieving the cash Keery acquired from the sale. I was ready to kill your brother for his spiteful deed, as well as all the cruel remarks I tolerated while Keery was in his drunken moods—"

"But you didn't accomplish the deed, so Royal did it for you," Calera inserted. When Shane glanced at her and frowned, her head jerked up. "I know perfectly well that Royal entered the office after you left. She disposed of Keery so she could have control of The Cottage. She told me so herself. She let *you* take the blame and then defended you so there would be no charges filed."

"She committed the murder?" Shane questioned, bewildered.

"Didn't I just say that? Or is there an echo in here?" Calera smarted off, green eyes flashing. "The point is you and Royal both wanted to dispose of my brother so the two of you could wallow in your lust for each other. And of course, when I showed up in town, you took advantage of the fact that I had fallen in love with you like an idiotic fool."

Shane was seriously considering dunking Calera again to keep her quiet. Once her teeth had stopped chattering she was rattling nonstop. *He* had intended to do all the talking and there was still a mouthful left to say!

"I did *not* conspire with Royal," Shane declared emphatically. "And she is *not* my lover!"

Calera sent him a withering glance. Shane obviously believed her to be an imbecile. "No? You certainly didn't appear dismayed to have her in your arms in front of my hotel room and again in the office of The Cottage." Let him try to talk his way out of that!

"I was neither pleased nor dismayed," Shane insisted. "I felt nothing at all because Royal means absolutely nothing to me."

"Doesn't she just!" Calera said flippantly. "Well, I have news for you, Apache, you are wasting emotion on Royal. She has affection only for herself. She is using you as you used me. She even accepted money from Muriel to corner you in the hall to put on that amorous performance for my benefit, not that she minded, of course!"

That certainly explained *that,* thought Shane. He had wondered why Royal had made the overt gesture at that particular time and place. He should have known Muriel was involved. Shane was finally beginning to understand why Calera was so peeved at him. Royal had gone out of her way to drive wedges between Calera and Shane, to imply that Royal and Shane had been intimate.

Shane had been distressed by the presence of the fourth set of footprints he had seen in the alley behind The Cottage. He had realized that Royal was somehow involved, but he never dreamed she had gone to such extremes to satisfy her greed and flaunt the nonexistent affair in Calera's face.

"I have never made love to Royal," Shane said simply and truthfully.

Calera didn't call him a liar, but her glare suggested as much.

"I haven't!" Shane declared in a voice that echoed around the cavern to come at Calera from all directions.

"Maybe you should tell that to Royal," Calera sniffed. "She doesn't seem to know it."

"She lied."

"I wonder where she picked up *that* habit?"

Shane clamped his hands on Calera's quivering shoulders and gave her a firm shake. "I swear to you that I have never touched Royal."

Calera shrank away and very nearly fell off her rock. "Curse it, Apache, I don't want to hear any more of your poisonous lies! You have told enough of them to earn yourself a century in Purgatory!"

His arms snaked around her waist, dragging her resisting body against his until his full lips were only a hairbreadth away. His black eyes bore into hers. "I will tell you true, Irish. There has been no other woman but you. Perhaps some men find shame in admitting to a woman that she was his first real kiss, and his very first time, but—"

Calera's wild screech and glancing blow caused Shane to unhand her. That was a mistake. Calera had thrown herself so far off balance to escape his arms that she plopped into the icy pool and was a long time in coming up for air. Shane stabbed his arm into the clear water and hoisted her back to the surface.

"You lie!" Calera choked out.

"Do I?" Amusement glistened in his eyes while he surveyed the incredulous expression on her face and the mop of tangled hair that was plastered against her ears.

"No man could have been so gentle and skillful unless he—"

"On what are you basing your comparisons, Irish?" he quizzed her. "I know for a fact that you were a virgin. How can you detect experience *without* experience?"

"Isn't that the crux of your outrageous lie?" Calera muttered in question. "How very convenient for you that I cannot contest what I do not know."

Gently, Shane drew her out of the water and onto his lap, despite her objections—and she had plenty of them. His fingers curled beneath her chin, holding her wide-eyed gaze. "When I told you I wanted you in ways I had wanted no other woman, I meant exactly that, Irish," he said softly. "You were the sweet, cherished memory of my fantasy come true. For once in my life I wanted to cling to a precious treasure—one given and also received from no others.

"Cactus and Sticker often taunted me for refusing to enjoy the favors of the whores they visited at The Cottage and elsewhere. I wanted more than physical satisfaction, more than a chance to boast of my conquests, as if that could make a man more of a man. I earned my manhood as a competent warrior among the Apaches. And I watched in disgust at times when I could not prevent the degradation of female captives by some of my vengeful brothers. The deeds were swift and cruel, serving spiteful lust. And I have seen white men perform the same vile deeds at too many women's expense—Indian, Mexican, and White. In my eyes, each man who stooped so low became less a man, not more of one."

His hand lifted to examine the purplish bruise on Calera's cheek. "You came dangerously close to discovering the difference between rape and lovemaking with Grady Flax. In my own vindictive fury, I sentenced him to instant death instead of the agonizing torture he deserved." The anger evaporated from his eyes and he stared solemnly at Calera. "We gave ourselves to each other, Irish, and we created magic. It was the first time for both of us, and each time thereafter I reminded myself that my abstinence had been well worth the wait. For once in my life, I knew what it was like to feel whole and alive, to fill the missing void with emotions I have never before experienced."

"But Muriel said she had seen you with the servants—"

His index finger grazed her lips, shushing her. "Muriel wanted your cooperation," he reminded her. "She was willing to go to any length to see me hanged, to rout me from her life. I don't suppose she bothered to tell you that the servants who worked for her were old enough to be my mother, did she?"

Calera glanced away, cursing herself soundly for falling prey to Muriel's wicked scheme. "No, she didn't mention that."

"I thought not. Muriel wanted you to think the worst, to despise me as she did. She could never bear the thought that I survived when her own son died. It infuriated her that I was allowed to keep Sultan after he trampled her son to death for resorting to the whip to subdue the steed's spirit. She took the whip to me to have her revenge. There is no doubt that bitterness and hatred motivated Muriel as strongly as the greed that drives Royal."

His hand dropped away and he peered into the distance, watching the sunlight dance on the river that flowed from the far end of the cavern. "When you pledged your love to me in our world of dreams, I silently returned it, wishing I was not who I was, wishing I could take you into my life. You had my heart even then, Irish. But for your sake, I had to let you go. I could not ask you to live between two worlds, not with Muriel's hatred, not with so many prejudices in the white man's society." His gaze locked with hers. "And even if I was never to see you again, there would have been no one else, no substitute for perfection."

Calera desperately wanted to believe him, to believe *in* him. She had almost forgotten how to believe in anything after the turmoil her life had become. It humbled her to know that such a remarkable man as this held such high ideals, that he had denied himself the lust other men craved to obsession. How many other men would take pride in discretion, finding honor in the purity of body and spirit? Very few, Calera imagined. Men seemed to have a need to boast of their prowess, but this Apache knight was confident of his masculinity and had no need to prove anything to anyone. He possessed the kind of honor and nobility that lesser men could not comprehend.

When Calera peered into the depths of his coal-black eyes, she felt her very soul rising from deep inside her. Entranced, she reached out to him, just as she had when he had commanded her to transcend the pain of her wound. He was calling to her again. The unspoken words whispered through her mind and her heart, making her believe in something so rare and special that it overshadowed the hurt, the despair, the prejudices of all civilizations.

"I love you, Irish, as I have loved nothing else in life," Shane assured her huskily. "When you were hurt, I bled. When I learned you were Keery's sister, I died inside, knowing I had taken something precious from you, something I could never give back. You had taught me to smile again and I had brought you tears. You were my faith that life held wondrous pleasures and I destroyed *your* faith, *your* dreams."

Calera well remembered that day Shane had barged into her room to become the scapegoat for her despair. She had struck out at him in broken-hearted anguish, but Shane had refused to defend his actions against Keery by berating him. This wild Apache knight was a rare breed of man who possessed great strength of character and depths of insight. He was aware of her moods and he understood her needs before she realized them herself. And knowing that, Calera also understood why Shane had let her go when she would have eagerly remained with him in the mountains. This magnificent giant had lived a lonely, miserable existence that he would wish on no one else. He had suffered in ways she wondered if she would ever fully comprehend. And through all the torment his life had become, he was more man—inch for inch—than anyone Calera had ever known.

How could she not fall in love with him all over again? He was generous of heart, wise beyond his years, gentle in his ominous strength, and fierce in tender devotion. His loyalty touched her heart and brought sentimental tears to her eyes, clouding her vision. But even if Calera were struck blind this very second, she still could have seen this muscular giant poised beside her. Wasn't he the one who taught her to see without her eyes? Wasn't he the one who had absorbed all her pain and lifted her spirits to pinnacles no human hand could touch? How could she not believe in the way he held her protectively against him, the way he was always prepared to fight her battles for her, if only she asked it of him? How could any man offer a woman more than the priceless gift of a love he had saved only for her? Wasn't that the greatest commitment and compliment a woman could receive from a man?

The surge of overwhelming emotion caused Calera to fling her arms around Shane's bare shoulders and hug him. She regretted every harsh word, each spiteful thought. She promised herself, there and then, that no one's lies and deceptions would ever come between the two of them again. She would match this phenomenal man's unfaltering loyalty and devotion and she would never *ever* doubt him again so long as she lived! He was the one truth she had discovered in life.

Shane rested his chin atop her head and wrapped her as tightly in his arms as she held him in hers. "Irish, I cannot ask you to walk in my footsteps on the border of two civilizations that will never truly be at peace. I am trapped by my heritage, but in your happiness I will find my own freedom. And no matter what you decide to do or where you decide to go, my heart will go with you, for it is no longer mine to command."

Calera leaned back as far as his encircling arms would allow, her eyes sparkling with a mist of tears. "And where would I go without you, Apache?" she asked him.

"Back from whence you came," he suggested. "The East is far more civilized, or so I am told."

"And leave my heart behind?" Calera gave her red-gold head a shake, sending corkscrew curls dangling around her oval face. "I tried that, you know. Leaving you was like venturing into hell. I became an empty shell, searching for what I had already found and could not recover again. Apache, don't you realize that all I am is *you*?"

Shane frowned, trying to decipher what she meant by that last remark. When he realized what she was trying to say, a wry smile quirked his lips. She implied she was nothing without him, but nothing was farther from the truth.

"No," he contradicted. "I only taught you to channel your

fiery spirit and make it work to your advantage, as The People have learned to do. It was your strength and determination that drew me to you. You have always been a rare breed unto yourself. It is you who gave me a special touch of elegance that I could never acquire." He paused to toss her a teasing grin. "And the next time you call out to me in the dark of night, no one will ever stand in my way. That was one invitation I would have given anything to accept, Irish."

Calera blinked owlishly, remembering the night she had lain abed, willing Shane to come to her, thinking he had desired Royal instead. "You heard me calling to you?"

He nodded affirmatively. "I also felt my ears burning two nights past. At first I thought it was my head wound and too much whiskey. But I think perhaps I was being soundly cursed for something I didn't do."

Calera smiled guiltily. "I thought you had betrayed me. I even swore to return from the grave to haunt you and Royal."

Her hand uplifted to limn the handsome bronzed face that formed the perimeters of all her dreams. "You seem very adept at reading my mind, Apache? Have you any idea what I'm thinking now?"

Shane peered into those lustrous eyes that twinkled like emerald starlight. A roguish grin claimed his rugged features. "I hear every word, Irish," he assured her huskily.

With catlike grace he rose from the rim of rock and carried Calera to the thick carpet of grass that rippled like waves upon the sea. Ever so gently he lay her down and propped himself up beside her. When his sensuous lips slanted over hers, Calera felt her weary body magically come to life. His kiss was like a thirst-quenching sip from the Apache spirit springs. Calera felt herself sinking in a pool of inimitable pleasure, surrendering her very breath for a love that could last long past forever.

"Do you mind too much that all my experience in lovemaking begins and ends with you?" Shane whispered against her lush lips. "I'm sure Marsh Layton has many amorous skills to his credit and he has developed quite an attachment for you."

"Mind?" Calera chortled as her fingertips coasted over the

whipcord muscles of his chest, marveling at the incredible amount of potential strength beneath her wandering hand. "I can think of nothing more pleasing than knowing you are only mine, Apache, just as I am only yours."

"And what of Marsh?" Shane asked her, his voice noticeably altered by the tantalizing sweep of her hands over his hypersensitive flesh.

"Marsh is a good man," Calera replied, more interested in caressing every inch of Shane's steel-honed body than in conversation. "But Marsh isn't you."

"And when you kissed Marsh that day in the hall?" Shane prodded.

Calera grinned impishly and her hand trailed lower, making Shane's breath catch in his throat. "Oh, that."

"Yes, *oh that,*" he wheezed.

Feathery kisses flooded over his male nipples, following the faint shadow of hair that descended over the washboarded planes of his belly. "That was my attempt to forget this incredible hold you have on me." Her roaming hand glided over his hip to unfasten the breechcloth that prevented her from rediscovering every magnificent inch of his masculine body. "I was most unsuccessful, by the way. The instant I closed my eyes, I was transported back to that wild mountain fantasy to make the most eye-opening comparisons."

A groan of unholy torment bubbled in Shane's chest when the warm rush of her breath whispered over his flesh. Her caresses became bolder, causing his passions to rise like high tide. All thought and conversation escaped Shane. He couldn't breathe much less speak. When Calera's moist lips and velvet fingertips glided over his swollen manhood, Shane felt the pulsating throb of desire pounding at his mind, body, and soul. She cherished him as if he were her most treasured possession. She spun an intricate web that entranced him, aroused him until his every breath was the sound of her name. Shane was certain he was about to explode with the aching want of this woman. And yet, the pleasure she bestowed on him was so intense that it demanded to be returned—kiss for tender kiss, caress for gentle caress.

Calera found her hands set away from his muscular body, saw the sun eclipse when the powerfully-built giant rolled to his knees, lifting her to her feet. With maddening deliberateness, Shane unfastened each tiny button on the front of her gown, greeting every inch of flesh he exposed with whispered kisses. His lips were like satin gliding over her skin, his hands as gentle as a breath of wind. The garments fell away, as if they had dissolved at the seams, leaving her standing before him, watching him savor the sight of her as if she were a work of art that had been stashed from his sight for years on end.

"Do you know how very beautiful you are, Irish?" he murmured as his hands swept from her collarbone, over the rose-tipped crests of her breasts to swirl around the trim indentation of her waist. "You're like a princess from a fairy-tale—breathtaking, utterly enchanting, incredibly exquisite. You are perfection . . ."

Calera couldn't speak. His tender touch and quiet compliments had robbed her of breath and sent her mind reeling.

"I have waited a lifetime to find you," he rasped as he knelt in front of her.

A tiny moan wobbled from her throat when he suckled at her breasts, causing a burning coil of desire to knot in the very core of her being. Her knees threatened to fold beneath her when his hands and lips kneaded her breasts, savoring the taste and feel of her until she cried out to him in tortuous pleasure. For a man who claimed to have limited experience in passion, Shane had the most remarkable knack of knowing how and where she liked to be touched, how to boil her body down to the consistency of marmalade. She could barely stand when he was doing such delicious things to her, and doing them so well!

"Apache—" Calera gasped and swayed beneath the onslaught of riveting sensations that engulfed her.

"You taste like heaven." His lips drifted over the ladder of her ribs and fluttered over her belly like velvety butterfly wings. "I could survive on you and you alone, Irish. You're my feast."

"Apache!" Calera braced her hands on his massive shoulders when his thumbs trailed over the ultrasensitive flesh of her inner thighs. Calera swore she was burning alive when his fingertips stole deeper into her, teasing her, exciting her beyond bearing. Flames seared her very essence when his kisses followed in the wake of his fingertips. She clung to him in wild shuddering pleasure that sizzled through her like repetitive lightning bolts.

Touching her so intimately was like exploring the dewy petals of a flower that opened for him, filling his senses with the taste and scent of the woman who had come to mean everything to him. Caressing her was like gliding through silken fire, feeling the flames that were burning her and then burning him. Shane levered her quaking body to the grass and hovered over her, watching the ardent passion he had aroused in her glow like emerald fire in her thick-lashed eyes. His devouring gaze flowed over her satiny flesh, committing the delicate picture to everlasting memory. Confessing his love to Calera had granted him a special kind of peace and freedom he had never known. The words had unlocked the vault of emotion that he had concealed inside him to protect himself from the cruelties and injustices of the world in which he lived. But confessing to love and knowing Calera returned his affection healed all wounds, consumed all emotion.

When Calera uplifted her arms to him, love shone in the depths of her eyes and a welcoming smile curved her heart-shaped lips. Shane felt humbled by the gesture, mystified by her enchanting smile, aroused by the unspoken promise of the pleasures to come.

"Come here, Apache." Her sultry voice was like a whisper of the Apache spirit wind, chanting sweet incantations for him and him alone. "I need you as I need nothing else. Let me show you how much I love you . . ."

Shane couldn't bite back the rumbling purr that trickled from his lips when he looked down at the exquisite beauty who offered herself to him, uncaring who he was to all the world, caring only what he was to her, wanting him for no other reason than to love and be loved in return.

Without hesitation or one ounce of inhibition, Shane came to her, not as the overpowering possessor but as her possession, wanting to give all of himself to pleasure her. And in her pleasure he could attain his own sublime satisfaction. She was the spark that could ignite him into a raging flame—one that burned *only* for her, *because* of her.

The moment his sinewy body glided upon hers, Calera was lost to a need so wild and intense that nothing seemed so desperately important as appeasing it. She felt the bold evidence of his desire inflaming her, felt his entire body tremble as he gathered her to him. She heard him whisper her name before his sensuous lips claimed hers. He made love to her like the dawn burning away the darkness of night, like the sunbeams dancing on dewdrops. Calera could feel the warmth of his powerful body penetrating hers, only to recede and return again, setting a hypnotic cadence of passion so overwhelming that she arched up to consume him as completely as he consumed her.

Calera felt herself being lifted from one heady plateau to another like a kite gliding upon drafts of wind. Sweet flames engulfed her, feeding a fire that burned brighter than a hundred suns. Sparks leaped from her hungry body to his and back again like a breeze spreading wildfire across every fiber of her being. A kaleidoscope of vivid colors burst in her mind's eye before the world turned black, pierced only by flickering pinpoints of blinding light. Calera found herself suspended in a dimension of time where body became soul and spirit became as tangible as flesh. Ineffable sensations pulsated through her—expanding, rising, inflaming her until her body shuddered with such indescribable pleasure that mere words could never do the maelstrom of sensations justice.

These feelings Calera experienced reminded her of the many times Shane had commanded her to step outside the limitations of the flesh, to transcend all pain, to see through visions the eyes could not comprehend. But all the lessons Shane had taught her in the past could never compare to the knowledge that she was loved and cherished as she had never been by any other man.

The very beat of her heart tapped out Shane's name and every thought of him became synonymous with paradise. All she was *was* what he had taught her to become, whether he believed it to be true or not. She *was* all that he had made of her. He taught her soul to sing, taught her to reach beyond herself, to employ every power in the universe, to hear the whispering voice that spoke of things far greater than the eyes could behold and the ears could hear. Shane had taught her to believe in him and in herself. He had offered her a glimpse of heaven. When she was in the protective circle of his arms, she could *feel* forever and she knew she was there, sharing her very existence as if she and Shane were one.

"I love you, Apache," Calera murmured, her moist lips grazing his shoulder.

Shane levered upon his forearm and grinned down at her. "I know. You just told me so in the most pleasurable ways imaginable." His index finger traced her kiss-swollen lips. "But I do enjoy hearing the words."

"Do you know that the first time I saw you sitting upon your steed in midstream, waiting to pluck me out of the river like a half-drowned kitten, I envisioned you as my dark knight," Calera confided as her fingertips trailed over the rippling muscles of his arm. "I thought you were the most magnificent creature I had ever seen."

Deep, resonant laughter reverberated in his chest and obsidian eyes twinkled down at her. "And do you know that when I saw you launch yourself away from the Tonto brave to plunge into the river and chance the rapids, I knew you possessed the kind of remarkable courage that every Apache warrior envies?"

"Courage?" Calera parroted. "That was the necessity of desperation hard at work. I even forgot that I didn't know how to swim until I was plummeting through infinity. I could just as easily have missed the river and landed on the rocks."

"And if you had landed on the rocks, I would have missed

the greatest love of my life, Irish. I'm ever so glad your aim was good. I like you much better in one piece."

Calera uplifted her hand to investigate the mending wound on Shane's forehead, her expression pensive. "Why didn't you defend yourself when Muriel tried to gun you down in The Cottage? She could have killed you."

His full lips brushed over her honeyed mouth. "Because I thought Muriel was you. I would never hurt you, even at the expense of my own life, even if you despised me for what you thought I had done to betray you. I would do anything for you, Irish. Don't you realize that?"

When Calera peered up at him in utter disbelief, Shane smiled tenderly. "I thought I had lost you to Marsh. I had reached the point that I didn't care what happened to me after I lost you to another man. I even resorted to guzzling whiskey in hopes of drowning my torment, but all I received was a hellish hangover."

"And I thought I had lost you to another woman. It tore me in two to see Royal draped all over you like Spanish moss. I seem to have a jealous nature that riles my Irish temper," she admitted.

It must have been an inherited trait, Shane decided. Keery had always become unbearable when any man glanced in Royal's direction. Royal, unfortunately, was like the deadly black widow and Keery had lost his life because of her. But even if this green-eyed beauty with flaming red-gold hair was possessive in her love, Shane didn't mind one bit. Indeed, he was flattered! No one had ever cared enough to be jealous. He rather liked knowing Calera's Irish temper flared when he ventured too close to another woman, for his disposition had certainly turned sour each time Marsh touched this lovely nymph. Several times Shane had battled the urge to break both of Marsh's arms and bury a fist in the man's handsome face for hovering around Calera like a honeybee.

"I don't want to go back," Calera said abruptly, emphatically. "There's nothing below these mountains but trials and torment. Nobody likes me."

Shane chuckled out loud. "I'm familiar with the feeling, Irish." He dropped a kiss to her lush lips. "These mountains have been my sanctuary each time life becomes unbearable. I come here to renew my spirit." He stared pointedly at Calera. "But we have to go back. There is unfinished business to attend. Royal has killed twice in her greed. You were to have been her victim. For that she will pay. As soon as you have had time to rest, we are going back to see justice served."

"Can't we just—"

His hungry kiss silenced her. "No, Irish, we can't. But we will worry about that later. Right now, I feel like loving you again . . ."

Calera stared up into those craggy features and felt the hot rush of desire sweep through her. She didn't want to fret over what might happen when they confronted Royal. Knowing how devious, pretentious, and deadly Royal could be, something might go wrong, as it had so often in the past. Calera had tripped over so many of life's stumbling blocks already that she found herself clinging to each precious moment with Shane as if it were her last. If she lost him now . . .

Shane became very still when Calera flung her arms around him and held on as tightly as if she were drowning in a churning sea. "It's all right, Irish," he reassured her. "I'll be there with you. I'll always be with you in soul and spirit."

The man had the most remarkable knack of reading her moods. "How can you say everything will be all right, given our past track records?" she questioned, cuddling closer to his hard contours. "I'm afraid . . . that . . . I'll lose you, too . . ."

His hands framed her face, forcing her to meet his piercing gaze. "You'll never lose my love. It is yours until the end of eternity." A crooked smile dangled on the corner of his sensuous mouth. "And if you will quit strangling me for a moment, I'll show you how long *forever* is."

When Calera eased her fierce grasp on him, Shane set about to rekindle the flame of passion and chase her fears away. Calera gave herself up to the potent magic of his touch, savoring each scintillating sensation, hoping beyond hope that, this time, she wouldn't lose the one she loved most. She wanted to believe that dreams came true. She wanted to believe that she had not been cursed to love and lose again and again. But in the back of her mind there were still lingering doubts—ones that even Shane's solemn promises couldn't dissolve. She had known grief and despair too often to deny their gloomy existence.

"Irish," Shane whispered against her satiny flesh. "Just love me until nothing else matters. I need all of you, not just your willing body, but your mind and spirit as well. Look at me . . ."

Her tangled lashes swept up at his husky command, lost to the mystical glitter of his onyx eyes. When she felt herself drawn into those dark depths, her fears evaporated like tear drops in sunshine and summer winds.

"That's better," Shane murmured as his caresses drifted over her shapely contours, setting fires that fried them both alive. "Now kiss me until neither of us can tell where your love ends and mine begins."

It was a wild, breathless merging of bodies, hearts, and souls, a communion of passion so ardent and intense that gentleness fell away in a savage rush of ungovernable need. Calera matched each driving thrust of his masculine body, absorbing him as if his every movement, his every breath were her own. And for that cherished moment in time, there was no yesterday or tomorrow, only the sweet ecstasy of love blossoming and growing until it engulfed her and filled her world to overflowing. No matter what tomorrow might bring, there was nothing to compare to this wild, wondrous moment. There were only the two of them, gliding like eagles in graceful flight, scaling the lofty precipices and winging across the high mountain meadows to disappear into the crimson horizon of forever . . .

Chapter Twenty-six

Shane grunted when Calera playfully plopped down on his belly while he lay sprawled in the grass. He opened one eye to view the enchanting face that was surrounded by billows of flame-colored ringlets. An elfin smile pursed Calera's lips and her eyes sparkled with deviltry.

Since he and Calera had come to an understanding two days past, she had cast caution to the wind, living each moment and reaping each pleasure. Calera was as uninhibited as Shane had ever seen her. She had become an adventuress, scaling the swirling shelves of granite to perch like a bird above the sparkling rivers and pine forests. Watching her flittering around the lofty precipices and running through the meadows, her voice lifted in laughter, made his spirits soar. Shane had shown Calera all the panoramic beauties of the majestic mountains and she had marveled at Mother Nature's handiwork. The fact that she was as awe-inspired by this wilderness pleased Shane to no end.

They had lived and loved without the shadows of the past or future to tarnish their paradise. Shane had never felt so content, so utterly complete, so—

"Ouch! Watch where you're sitting, imp!" Shane yelped when

Calera scooted backward, her hips slamming into the private parts of his anatomy.

Calera glided seductively over the rousing evidence of his desire, making him suck in his breath when pain transformed into the hard throb of hungry need. "I think you rather like where I'm sitting," she contradicted, smiling at her power over his virile body—the same fascinating power he held over hers. "And I also think you have slept long enough."

One black brow arched and his entire body flinched when her roaming hand trailed over the muscled wall of his chest. She bent over him, her thick hair teasing his belly, his ribs. Her alluring scent saturated his acute senses. Her lips brushed his cheek and her breasts caressed his chest through the sheer fabric of her chemise.

"What have you got in mind, Irish?" he asked, his baritone voice rumbling with heightened awareness.

"I thought you would know without asking, Apache," she purred provocatively.

When his hand settled familiarly on her hips, pressing her closer to the hard pressure of his desire, Calera bounded to her feet. Shane gaped at her while she stood straddling him, watching her grin down at him with teasing mockery. His gaze flooded over her luscious body, memorizing each lovely inch of her.

Dear God, thought Shane. *The woman has become an expert at driving me to utter distraction.* She had become such a skillful seductress these past few days that the very thought of their splendorous lovemaking could melt him down like wax. Now she had taken to tormenting him and then withdrawing. But he had to admit that he enjoyed her impish games, the light-hearted camaraderie between them. It was like nothing he had ever experienced, and he was bewitched by everything she said and did.

"What I would like, at the moment, is for you to teach me to dive and swim," she requested, reaching down to draw him to his feet.

"Is that all?" Disappointed, Shane unfolded himself from the ground.

Grasping his hand, Calera led him to the river's edge. "If your instructions prove satisfactory, you will be rewarded later—" She tossed him another one of those heart-jarring smiles that suggested he would find no complaint with her method of compensation. "Now teach me to swim as expertly as you do."

"In one afternoon?" He chuckled. "I don't think that's possible."

"I'm a willing student. I'll learn quickly," she said with great confidence. "If fish can do it, so can I."

Shane admired her optimism, he really did. But he well-remembered the panic that overcame Calera each time she had found herself in over her head. Peeling off her garments, Shane lifted her in his arms and carried her into the river until the water level reached his shoulders. His excessive height allowed him to stand while Calera had to cling to him to keep her face above water.

"First you will learn to float, and then to swim," he said matter-of-factly. "Just lie back and relax. Let the river hold you."

Calera felt none of the fear she had previously experienced when she was left floundering. With Shane's capable presence, and her explicit trust in him, she arched back to let the river cradle her like a feather mattress. "Mmm . . . this isn't bad, not bad a-tall."

Wasn't that the truth! Shane thought with a rakish leer. He was granted a delicious view of satiny flesh and rose-tipped breasts tempting him in a visual feast. This was going to be a lot more fun than he first thought. Swimming was taking on an altogether different perspective.

"Now kick your feet, Irish—No, not like that!" Shane wiped the water from his eyes when Calera's overenthusiastic thrashings doused him. "Keep your legs straight."

"How's that?"

"Much better," he complimented, allowing her to propel them in a circle. "You're doing fine, Irish."

While Calera concentrated on her newly-acquired skills,

Shane admired the delicious view of water droplets dancing on
her skin. He could have spent the remainder of the day staring
at perfection—or maybe not. It was a mite too arousing to have
this lovely nymph floating in his arms while he stared down at
her voluptuous body and those dewy pink lips without actually
touching her. In fact, this swimming lesson was turning out to
be a form of torture. Shane was going to have to proceed to
other aquatic skills before he became so sidetracked that Calera
learned nothing except to float.

Reining in the hot desire to take her there and then, Shane
flipped Calera over on the cradle of his arms. But that didn't
help matters one whit. He was forced to stare at the flawless
contours of her back and the mesmerizing flare of her hips.
And worse, her breasts were pressed against his arms. He could
feel every movement of her body as she paddled around, apparently oblivious to his growing discomfort. Damn! Even the
cool water couldn't squelch the slow burning fire of watching
her, holding her, wanting her.

When Shane stopped—stock still—Calera glanced over her
shoulder to see his eyes transfixed on her derriere. Calera bit
back an ornery smile. Somewhere along the way, Shane's noble
restraint had crumbled. "Pay attention, Apache. I have things
to learn. Are you going to tutor me or stand there staring like
a gargoyle?"

Shane snapped to attention and grinned wolfishly. "Sorry."

"I'm not." Calera rolled over in the cradle of his arms to lace
her fingers behind his neck. "In fact, I find it flattering that
you haven't tired of me after you have had your way with me
more times than I can count the past two days."

"Five."

One delicately arched brow lifted in pretended innocence.
"Five what?"

A raking grin caused the smile lines to etch deeply into his
bronzed features. "I made love to you five times, not counting
the two times you had your way with me. I'm surprised either
of us can still walk."

Calera was feeling giddy and reckless while she lay against

the massive width of Shane's chest. The river's currents washed over her flesh like a caress—one as tender as the one this gentled giant bestowed on her. "I wonder if it's possible to make love in the river."

The very thought put Shane's already aroused body on full alert. He could picture—and quite vividly—the two of them making wild sweet love in midstream, consumed by a fire that all the water in the Seven Seas couldn't put out.

"I thought you had your heart set on learning to swim," he croaked, his vocal cords locking up when desire clenched his body.

Calera slid her legs around his waist and lifted inviting lips to his. "Suddenly I find that I don't want to learn to swim as much as I thought I did . . ."

When her soft lips melted against his and her lush body pressed closer, Shane forgot everything except the taste and feel of her, everything except the exquisite pleasure that awaited him. His tongue thrust into her mouth, stealing her breath and then generously returning it. He nipped at her bottom lip while his hands wandered as freely over her flesh as the water that surrounded them. He felt the taut peaks of her breasts boring into his chest. He felt the pulsating throb of desire surge through his loins until the ache became unbearable.

"I think I'll leave swimming to the fish," Calera whispered when Shane allowed her to come up for air.

"Someday I'll teach you to swim," he promised her. "But not now. I can't keep my mind on anything except the business at *hand*."

A quiet gasp broke from her lips when his lean fingers splayed across her hips, gliding her against the hard length of him. Her eyes locked with his, watching the coal-black pools burn into her, feeling their bodies brush intimately together and then apart.

When his left hand slid beneath her hips to hold her in front of him while his right hand swirled over her breasts, Calera struggled to breathe over the furious pounding of her pulse. The lapping water and feel of his slick body were so wildly arousing that she began to burn from inside out. The touch of his fingertips kneading her breasts ignited another flame that burned back upon itself. When his dark head dipped down and his tongue flicked at the tight buds, Calera shivered in erotic pleasure.

"Cold?" Shane questioned while he caressed her with his lips.

"On fire," she moaned in response.

His quiet rumble of laughter echoed through her sensitive body. "On fire in all this water, Irish? How that could be—?"

Shane forgot how to speak when Calera's hand knifed into the water and her fingers closed around him, gliding up and down until the wanting became such a pronounced ache that it hammered in rhythm with his accelerated pulse.

Emerald eyes twinkled at him when he panted for breath and found none forthcoming. "You were saying, Apache?"

Shane said nothing more. He couldn't have formulated a word, even if his life depended on it. Her imaginative caresses were driving him wild. He swore his body had condensed into a cloud of steam. His hand dropped away from her breast to clamp onto her hips. His heart slammed against his ribs when she opened to him, guiding him to her, caressing him until he was buried deep inside her. The silky heat of femininity closed around him like the petals of a rose consuming a honeybee. Every muscle in his body quivered as he stood in midstream, moving with the heated current that rippled through him.

When Calera closed her eyes to the wild riveting sensations that claimed her, Shane's husky voice came to her through a sea of hazy pleasure.

"Open your eyes, Irish," he commanded. "I want to watch you find fulfillment. I want you to watch me find it with you."

The request seemed too intimate. It was enough that they were so close that she could breathe him, feel him moving inside her. But for him to see her composure shatter in *broad daylight* was almost too personal.

"No," Calera gasped. She squeezed her eyes shut when he drove into her, sending her senses into orbit.

"Yes," he demanded as he drew her hips away from him, letting her feel only the tip of his passion brushing against her.

Having him so close and yet so tormentingly far away while passion seared her was more than she could bear. Her dewy lashes fluttered up to see the ravenous hunger that claimed him. "Apache—"

Her voice evaporated when he guided her hips back to his, only to push her away, leaving her quaking with the want of him. When his gaze dropped to watch their bodies merge into the ultimate depths of intimacy, Calera felt the uncontrollable shudder of passion rivet her. A cry of desperation tumbled from her lips, bringing Shane's gaze back to her face. In triumphant fascination he watched ecstasy claim her, watched her eyes darken, her lips part on a ragged breath. He felt the very core of her femininity burning around him.

Intrigued, he withdrew ever so slowly, maddeningly, until her body arched toward his in helpless abandon. Her nails dug into his shoulders and she cried out his name when another wave of rapture swamped and buffeted her.

In that most intimate of all moments, he watched her succumb over and over to the overwhelming effects of his brand of passion. He watched Calera surrender her all to him. With a sense of wonder and pride, he felt her body convulsing around him. He had learned to make her want him to such extremes that he could enjoy this splendorous brand of pleasure *through* her, experiencing what she felt, starkly aware of each moment when passion consumed, ebbed, and rose to engulf her again.

The silent plea in her heavily-lidded eyes, the raspy whisper of his name on her lips called to Shane like a siren's song. He felt his taut body driving into hers, answering her request to share the quintessence of pleasure that remained incomplete without him. Shane caught his breath when the bullet-like sensations pelted him. He could no longer restrain his own urgent desires, couldn't bite back the low groan that tumbled from his lips when he shuddered deep inside her.

In bewildered fascination, Calera watched his sleek body flex, his jaw clench, his dark eyes explode with unleashed passion.

She felt the last spasmodic surge of passion rippling through him to whisper into her. Only then, when she found ultimate fulfillment with him, did she collapse against him, her head resting against his shoulder, her lips pressed lovingly against the throbbing veins of his throat.

All the walls between her and Shane had tumbled down. Each time they made love he explored new boundaries of intimacy and then extended them until there were no limits to the pleasure they could offer each other. Now there was not one secret between them. They had been through each other until they knew each other in ways Calera never believed possible. She had seen Shane shamelessly succumb in the most vulnerable of all moments, and he had watched her dissolve in his arms, uncaring if there was life after such divine lovemaking. She had seen his dark eyes catch fire and burn, reflecting the intense sensations that coursed through him. In those glorious moments they became one another—one loving essence that beat heart for heart, sharing soul with soul.

And even when the flame of desire dwindled and Calera could breathe normally once again, she still felt that phenomenal closeness that transcended the physical intimacy they shared. She had given him all of herself, baring her very heart and soul. In return, Shane had shed his own protective armor, letting her watch him become crippled by emotions so fierce and demanding that he lost all control . . .

A disconcerting thought intruded in her mind. Despite Calera's attempt to block out the nagging concerns, she felt a sliver of desperation stabbing at the contentment that enshrouded her. She couldn't bear the thought of losing Shane as she had lost everyone else—not now, *especially* not now. She had died a little inside each time she lost those near and dear to her heart. But losing this wild Apache knight would be like losing the ability to breathe. How could she exist without him when he had become her sun and moon?

"Irish? What's wrong?" Shane questioned when he felt her shiver against him.

"I'm getting cold," she lied. She couldn't reveal her fears

because she didn't want to confront them now. She wanted to
cling to each loving memory, just in case . . .

"We have to return to Globe City tomorrow," Shane told her
as he carried her ashore. "If we tarry much longer, Royal will
become suspicious about her henchmen's long absence. We will
settle this once and for all."

Would they? Calera wondered. What if something went
wrong? What if—? Calera forced that pessimistic thought aside.
No matter what happened, she was not going to spoil paradise
lost and *found*. Her hours alone with Shane were numbered.
Each one was as precious as a nugget of gold.

When Shane ambled off to hunt game for their evening meal,
Calera clutched her arms tightly around herself and stared at
the majestic mountains that towered above her. Ah, if only she
could be as immovable and invincible as these craggy peaks that
weathered every storm. If only she possessed Shane's tremendous courage.

Why return to civilization? There was nothing there that
meant as much to Calera as Shane did. If she had him and the
love they shared, she needed nothing else. Nothing matched
her need for him, nothing!

It was with great reluctance that Calera prepared herself for
her descent from paradise. Oh, she projected a lighthearted air
for Shane's benefit, but she suspected he knew she was apprehensive. He could not help but know that night when she made
love to him with such reverence, savoring every second, every
delicious sensation. And when she kissed him—as if she wanted
him to commit that moment to everlasting memory, in case there
was never another—and held him to her long after passion had
run its fiery course, he must have known that she dreaded the
coming of tomorrow. She lived with the fear that all her tomorrows would become as unkind as the yesterdays had been.

That night, while Calera slept in Shane's arms, he peered up
at the dome of twinkling stars, listening to the sounds of darkness. He knew of Calera's reluctance to leave the mountains.

He had felt that same hesitation each time he returned to the ranch to endure Muriel's blatant contempt. But he and Calera had to make a place for themselves down below. Running away was not the answer. Despite what the citizens of Globe City thought of either of them, justice had to be served. But whatever difficulties they faced, Shane vowed to protect Calera. She was his everything.

True, it would be no small feat convincing Sheriff Nelson that the woman who had bewitched him was guilty of murder. Eli preferred to let Calera shoulder the blame for what had happened to Muriel. And Royal Winston was shrewd, no doubt about that. She preyed on Eli's affection for her, using it to her advantage. But this time Royal would be held accountable for her sins, Shane promised himself. She was not going to sweet talk her way out of Eli's jail and Eli could not look the other way to spare her. Royal had killed for her own selfish greed, in order to take what rightfully belonged to the O'Connells. She had Calera thinking her life had been cursed to gloom and destruction. Shane would find a way to restore Calera's faith in justice, and hopefully, he would restore his own faith as well.

On that positive thought, Shane roused Calera from the depths of sleep to convey his love for her once more before they confronted the world below the mountains. She responded to him as she always did, sharing his passion until his mind blurred and wild fierce pleasure consumed both of them.

And so help him, he would find a way to make all their tomorrows one long, contented dream . . .

Chapter Twenty-seven

"*Royal* Cottage! Why, that—"

Calera would have shot right out of the saddle the moment she saw the new sign hanging above The Cottage if Shane had not shoved her back into her seat.

"Be still," Shane snapped, glancing around the darkened streets. "Don't draw any more attention to yourself than necessary. We don't know what kind of greeting awaits us in Globe City."

Calera plastered herself behind Shane as the blood-red stallion trotted through town, avoiding street lights: Shane had insisted they return to Globe in the cover of darkness to bypass trouble. Calera had told herself she cared nothing for public opinion of her, but she did take quick offense to the fact that Royal Winston had been hard at work, remodeling Calera's hotel back into a cursed brothel! That cunning madam had taken advantage of Calera's absence and her bank account. No doubt, Royal was making preparations to open business as soon as possible. The blazing lantern that shined in the window of the office indicated Royal was working into the night to reorganize and reopen The Cottage under new management.

"I have a few choice words to say to that murdering harlot," Calera muttered acrimoniously.

"A few?" Shane chuckled, feeling Calera's seething body pressed tautly against his back. Her fingers were digging into his ribs as if they were clenched around Royal's throat. "You'll have your chance to give Royal *what for,* but not until we speak with Marsh. He'll know what has been going on since we left."

"It's obvious what's been going on." Calera stared irritably at The Cottage, cursing Royal with every breath. "That witch has assumed control of my inheritance and denied my wish to make The Cottage a respectable place of business!"

"Your temper is showing again, Irish," Shane cautioned her.

"I'm sorry, but that makes me furious," she hissed against his neck.

"Really? I never would have guessed."

"You don't understand—"

"Don't I?" Shane's head swiveled around to peer into her irate features. "Now you know how the Apaches felt when the whites waltzed in and took over their land, as if it were their own. If there was profit to be made in the property, the white men staked their claim, shoving the Apaches onto worthless land, accusing them of committing bloodthirsty atrocities. Before this matter with Royal is resolved, you will probably understand exactly how my people feel. Knowing Royal, I expect she has done everything in her power to turn the town completely against you. It seems to be a favorite tactic in the white man's world."

When Shane drew the stallion to a halt and ambled into the hotel to locate Marsh, Calera made herself as inconspicuous as possible. She waited in the alley for five minutes before Shane returned. Wearing the oversize garments Shane had given her to conceal her identity, Calera circled around the hotel and ascended the back steps to reach Marsh's room. Shane followed shortly thereafter.

"Cali?" Marsh bolted out of his chair when Calera ambled into his room. "Are you all right?" His concerned gaze focused on her face, noting the purple bruise that marred her cheek.

"Damn those bastards. I hope Shane punished them for daring to lay a hand on you."

"They won't touch her again," Shane inserted as he ambled inside and shut the door behind him.

Marsh darted Shane a quick glance, noting the grim set of his mouth. Although Marsh asked no questions, he had a pretty good idea what had become of Ike Fuller and Grady Flax. Shane had obviously launched them into hell, where they belonged.

"If you don't mind, I would like to change into my own clothes before I confront Royal," Calera declared.

"That's not possible," Marsh replied.

Calera frowned, bemused. "Why not?"

Marsh shifted awkwardly from one foot to the other. "Things have changed since you were abducted, Cali."

"Obviously. But what has that to do with wearing my own clothes?" Calera demanded impatiently.

"You tell her, Shane," Marsh insisted.

"You tell her, Marsh," Shane countered. "You're the one who knows all the details."

"Well somebody better tell me and quickly!" Calera erupted.

"Why don't you sit down," Marsh suggested.

Calera eyed him apprehensively. "That bad?"

"It isn't good," Marsh said gloomily.

Calera sank down in the chair Marsh vacated and waited with bated breath.

"Your partner has been very busy while you were away," Marsh began.

"I noticed."

"According to *her* testimony, you schemed to have Shane shot down by his stepmother while she was disguised in your clothes."

"What!" Calera blurted out incredulously. "Is that the story she gave Eli? Did he believe her?"

Marsh nodded affirmatively. "According to Royal, you confided your plot to her, vowing revenge against Shane for killing your brother. Also according to Royal, *you* had *yourself* kidnapped two weeks past by the two men you had previously met

on the stage, planning to lay the blame on Shane. But since he
was the one who brought you back, the first ploy backfired."

"That is the most ridiculous—"

"Quiet, Irish, there's more," Shane interrupted her.

Calera was afraid that was going to be the case. Damn that
conniving woman! Royal had twisted the truth until no one
recognized it.

"Royal maintains that after Muriel wound up dead, you feared
your part in the would-be assassination might be discovered so
you high-tailed it out of town to save yourself. You gathered all
your belongings before you left. Sheriff Nelson checked your
room and, sure enough, everything was gone. He sent out a
warrant for your arrest and delegated full control of The Cottage to Royal."

"You mean to say l have nothing left except Shane's clothes
on my back?" Calera chirped in disbelief.

Marsh nodded bleakly. "I'm afraid so, Cali. I don't know what
became of your belongings. I suspect Royal confiscated them
to lend credence to her story, but I haven't been able to sneak
into her room. She keeps it locked."

"But how can anyone believe I persuaded Muriel to gun
Shane down while she was wearing my clothes?" Calera quizzed
him. "That makes no sense."

"It does if you hear Royal's embellishments," Marsh replied.
"Royal claims you were so bitter and vindictive that you were
willing to do anything to see Shane pay for Keery's death. You
used Muriel's fanatical hatred for her stepson to your own advantage. You were going to have Muriel claim self-defense when
she killed Shane and *you* were waiting in the wings to make
certain that if her shot didn't cut Shane down, *yours* would. But
you betrayed Muriel by killing her so she couldn't speak against
you, and then you tossed your weapon at Shane's fingertips to
suggest he had shot Muriel. You wanted Muriel to dress in your
garments so there would be two of *you* to ensure Shane met
with disaster."

"That is madness!" Calera erupted.

"That is exactly what Royal contends." Marsh sighed heavily.

"Royal convinced Eli that your brother's death drove you over the brink and your mind snapped. She also claims she tried to dissuade you from your fiendish scheme, but you refused to listen. She says your mind was so twisted with revenge that you were no longer capable of sane thought and that your scheme to kill Shane, using Muriel, testifies to that."

Calera slumped in her chair, glancing first at Marsh and then at Shane, who had propped himself against the wall. "I told you I didn't want to come back here to face another of the crises my life has become," she grumbled.

"You are accepting defeat at Royal's hands?" Shane challenged shrewdly.

"No—yes! I don't know!" Calera flung up her arms in frustration and stared helplessly at Shane. "I can't very well go around town with a reward on my head. Royal has convinced Eli that I'm a lunatic. The way that woman operates, she'll claim I seduced you to gain your loyalty in order to corroborate my own story of innocence—"

Calera groaned when she noticed the bleak expression on Marsh's face. "Don't tell me Royal has already suggested that possibility to Eli."

"She most certainly did. When Shane turned up missing from Doc Broxton's office—"

"You didn't tell anyone where I went, did you?" Shane cut in.

Marsh puffed up with offended dignity. "Hell no. Give me a little credit, Stafford. I may not be able to track as well as you can, but I do have the presence of mind to keep my mouth shut and my ears open!"

Having spouted his indignation, Marsh circled back to the matter at hand. "Royal must have considered the possibility that you went after Cali. Royal suggested that you might have wanted a little revenge for yourself." His blue eyes darted to Calera's fuming face and then settled on Shane's. "But of course, Royal is ever-so concerned that Calera might work her feminine charm on you, using you to save herself, even if she has to postpone her vendetta until later."

Marsh sighed heavily as he surveyed Calera's disgruntled expression. "Royal has painted a very incriminating picture of you, Cali. She has made you out to be a madwoman who will go to drastic extremes to save yourself and to exact revenge."

"Dear God!" Calera half-collapsed in her chair to stare dispiritedly at Shane.

Marsh paced from wall to wall, speaking more to himself than to anyone else. "I swear that conniving female has stayed up nights concocting her explanations that cover every possibility. You cannot imagine what an accomplished liar she is. She has an answer for everything, and she can project an air of sincere concern that you wouldn't believe! When I told Eli that Royal was feeding him a pack of lies, he looked at me as if *I* were the crazy one. I have never met a more calculating chameleon."

"*Deadly* is nearer the mark," Shane inserted, bringing Marsh's frustrated pacing to a halt. "Royal is the one who hired Ike Fuller and Grady Flax to abduct Calera after her henchmen mistakingly shot Muriel instead of their intended victim. Royal is also the one who walked in to murder Keery after my blows left him unconscious. Royal admitted the truth to Calera before Ike and Grady toted her away."

"What?" Marsh's blue eyes bulged from their sockets.

"Royal wanted control of The Cottage and the O'Connells stood in her way," Shane explained.

"What am I going to do?" Calera questioned in exasperation.

"What we *cannot* do is break into Royal's room to search for your belongings," Shane said thoughtfully. "I suggest you confront Royal, dressed as you are, to verify your claim that you were abducted and left with nothing. Marsh and I will handle Eli."

Shane drew the dagger from his moccasin and strode over to place the weapon in Calera's hand. "Do not take Royal for granted for even a second, Irish," he warned her. "And do not enter Royal's office until I signal you."

"But—"

"Make Royal condemn herself with her own words while Eli is outside listening to her," Shane instructed. "There is nothing more gratifying than to use the kind of cunning that allows your enemy to cut her own throat."

Calera stared at the dagger for a long moment before stuffing it into her shoe. She realized just then that she *did* want to confront that clever witch and see Royal pay restitution for her crimes. She also wanted to ensure that whatever happened, Shane's life would not be in danger. This was her private battle, her chance to bring Keery's murderer to justice.

Shane studied Calera warily, noting the sudden calm that overcame her. The firm acceptance in Calera's demeanor worried Shane. He had experienced these same feelings himself, before battle—that quiet but devil-may-care resolve that made Apache warriors deadly and utterly dangerous.

"No unnecessary heroics," Shane ordered. "I will be close at hand if trouble arises."

There were times when Calera resented the fact that Shane could read her moods so clearly. This was one of those times. She didn't want him rushing in to save her at the risk of his own life. She would rather die than lose him. She had lost too many loved ones already! No, Calera promised herself, whatever else happened, Shane would survive. She would make certain of that. He would not become the sacrifice she made to bring Royal Winston to justice.

"Irish—" Shane's deep voice held a note of warning. "Did you hear me? *No daring heroics.*"

Calera ambled over to retrieve Marsh's hat and tucked her hair inside it to conceal her identity. "I heard you, Apache."

But was she *listening?* Shane asked himself.

Marsh stood aside, watching the brawny giant stare down at the petite beauty who was garbed in oversize buckskin clothes. Shane's face was no longer a mask of well-schooled indifference. What he felt for Cali was written in every chiseled feature, billowing in his onyx eyes like an Apache smoke signal. Marsh knew right there and then that any lingering hope of winning Cali's affection no longer existed. There was a mystical presence about Shane and Cali that signified a union of heart and mind.

It was almost tangible and Marsh resented the fact that he had never experienced that kind of devotion in his life.

Indeed, Marsh had never even considered such commitment until he found himself infatuated by this lovely nymph with dazzling green eyes and red-gold hair. And worst of all, Marsh understood why Cali was so intrigued by this man of formidable strength and unrivaled skills. Too bad Cali hadn't been fascinated enough to tame Marsh. He would have knelt at her feet with just one come-hither glance.

"Remember, Irish, Royal wants you dead," Shane said gravely. "See that she does not succeed."

Following Shane's instructions—and he had plenty of them—Calera made her inconspicuous departure from the hotel and aimed herself toward The Cottage—the newly-established *Royal* Cottage, to be specific. Calera mentally rehearsed what she intended to say to the deceptive madam. However, she would have preferred to claw out Royal's eyes after that cunning witch had caused her so much grief and torment.

Clinging to the shadows, Calera positioned herself outside the front door. With tense anticipation she waited for Shane's signal before she approached the deadly madam.

Sheriff Nelson jerked his feet off the edge of his desk and bolted up when Shane and Marsh burst into the office.

"Where the hell have you been, Stafford?" Eli demanded without preamble.

"Where I've been is not as important as where you are going." Shane grabbed Eli by one arm and Marsh latched onto the other. "Don't say one word, now or later. Just listen."

"What in the—" Eli set his feet, only to be uprooted from the spot and shuffled out of his office.

"Not another word," Shane growled in a tone that would have sent a snarling panther slinking to its den.

While Eli was being ushered down the street toward Royal Cottage, he glanced puzzledly from one stony face to the other. He didn't have the foggiest notion what was going on, or why this errand demanded silence and secrecy. It didn't look as if he was going to find out anytime soon, either.

Before the threesome reached their destination, Shane raised his arm, giving a silent command to the silhouette who hovered outside the door. A muddled frown puckered Eli's features when the silhouette in baggy clothes slipped through the door. Bookended by Shane and Marsh, Eli was escorted into the parlor and ordered to remain as quiet as a mouse.

When Calera found the office empty, she muttered several unladylike curses and veered down the hall. She had prepared herself for this confrontation and she had no intention of postponing it until Royal returned from whatever errand had taken her from the office.

Faint light speared from the partially opened door that led into the double storerooms that were attached to the back of The Cottage. Determined of purpose, Calera eased around the door to see a lantern on the table. Royal was doubled over the crates in the corner, rummaging to locate some misplaced object.

"Looking for something that I stashed away, Royal?" Calera questioned.

Royal jerked upright and wheeled toward the silhouette that tarried beside the door. Her blue eyes widened in disbelief when Calera tugged the hat from her head, allowing the red-gold curls to tumble over her shoulders. The tendrils caught fire in the lanternlight and Royal automatically stepped back apace.

"How—?" Royal chirped.

Calera remembered what Shane had said about letting Royal cut her own throat. She also knew that Shane and Marsh were holding the sheriff captive in the hall, forcing him to listen to this conversation. Calera vowed to make it a most incriminating one.

"How *what*, Royal?" she baited her nemesis.

"How did you escape Ike and Grady?" Royal blurted out without thinking.

Calera smiled sardonically. "Your paid assassins were not as competent as you had hoped, and I seem to have been blessed with the nine lives of a cat. You have tried to kill me twice, Royal. Would you like to try again? Perhaps the third time will be the charm."

Damnation, Calera's return was going to cause serious difficulty, despite the lies Royal had concocted. She debated utilizing the derringer she kept stashed in her garter. She was confident she could devise an explanation to feed Eli after she shot Calera where she stood. It would be in self-defense, of course. But what Royal did not need was for Calera to survive and contradict the testimony. Royal had to move into point-blank range to ensure accuracy with her weapon.

"You do seem to have the most annoying knack of surviving when others do not," Royal declared, taking a casual step forward.

"Unlike my brother." Calera watched the cunning madam like a hawk. "Too bad Keery wasn't immune to your fatal charm. Then perhaps he would have realized how deadly and deceitful you are, Royal. You used Keery as you have used everyone else to get what you want. I only regret that Keery didn't see you coming at him to deliver the deadly blow after his battle with Shane. Then he would have known you were the one who disposed of him. He could have cursed you with his last dying breath." A pensive smile pursed Calera's lips. "But then, maybe Keery *did* know it was you who killed him. Perhaps it is *his* curse that keeps bringing me back each time you try to dispose of me."

Royal eyed Calera warily. "What do you intend to do?"

"I intend to tell Eli Nelson about your deadly schemes, of course."

Mocking laughter bubbled from Royal's lips. "You think Eli will believe you? You are very much mistaken. He is quite fond of me."

"He is also an elected officer, bound to uphold the law," Calera contended.

"I have already told Eli that you are vindictive and deranged."

Royal smiled craftily. "In fact, I have explained your disappearance to him and he accepted the story without blinking an eye."

"Has he?" Calera frowned in feigned deliberation. "And how did you explain the fact that Ike and Grady haven't been around the past few days?"

"Who would question the disappearance of worthless drifters like Ike and Grady?" Royal parried. "There are dozens of men like them who come and go from Globe City."

"You are very shrewd, aren't you, Royal? And calculating, too."

Royal smiled nastily. "Too clever for the likes of you, I assure you. In fact, I will have a perfectly logical explanation for your death by the time Eli finds you."

"Ah, let me guess. Self-defense?" Calera chortled.

"Exactly." Royal reached down to retrieve her weapon from her garter and trained her derringer on Calera's chest.

Calera glanced toward the partially opened door, knowing full well that Shane couldn't see the weapon that had magically appeared in Royal's hand. Calera also knew that she couldn't get her hands on the dagger before Royal squeezed the trigger. Calera had every intention of drawing Royal's fire. She was *not* going to risk having Shane burst through the door to catch a bullet with her name on it. If she mentioned the pistol, Shane would dart in the storeroom lickety-split.

All Calera had for protection was the hat she held in her hand. It would have to be enough to distract Royal for a moment. A split second was all Calera asked, that and half a chance to dash from the path of the oncoming bullet.

With a quick flick of her wrist, Calera sent the hat sailing toward the pistol and then she dived beneath the table. The unexpected flight of the hat caught Royal off guard. She automatically dodged the object and fired at the moving target. To Calera's dismay, Royal was a better shot than anticipated. Calera felt the searing pain slash her forearm. Frantic, she huddled against the leg of the table, taking advantage of the small amount of protection it offered.

A wild roar exploded from the hall immediately after the

pistol discharged. Afraid Shane was about to draw Royal's fire, Calera jerked upright, intending to claim the madam's undivided attention. The pistol swung from the door to Calera's uplifted head. Just as Shane barged inside, looking positively murderous, Calera shoved the heels of her hands against the table. The lantern plunged to the floor, sending a stream of kerosene and flames stretching toward Royal like a lighted wick.

Horrified, Calera watched the flames flow like a river, splashing against the crate in the corner. Disaster had already struck, but it was worse than anyone except Calera could imagine! Calera knew exactly what that crate contained—dynamite. She had removed that particular box from Keery's office herself and she had stashed it in the storeroom to be disposed of in a proper manner. Unfortunately, Calera had not been granted time to remove the explosives that had been left over from Keery's days as a prospector.

When Shane tried to launch himself toward Royal to tear her limb from limb, Calera blocked his path. There was no time to deal with Royal or contain the fire. There was only time to run! The storeroom was like a ticking time bomb waiting to go off.

"Explosives!" Calera railed, clutching at Shane's arm to turn him around.

His startled gaze met her alarmed expression. Shane watched Calera stab her arm toward the crate. In less than a heartbeat, Shane caught Calera around the waist and whirled toward the door that led to the hall. Behind them, Royal's furious screeches damned them both to hell. Wildly, Royal scrambled away from the crate and the scorching flames that were climbing the wall.

The foursome stampeded down the hall toward the front door of The Cottage, attempting to escape catastrophe. They had just reached the newly decorated parlor when a deafening roar exploded behind them. Calera felt herself jerked off her feet and carried out the door. Flying debris and leaping flames belched from the doors and windows of The Cottage. The force of the explosion knocked the foursome to their knees on the boardwalk. A steely hand clamped around Calera's waist, hoisting her up and away from the shattering glass, smoke, and flames.

The Cottage blazed like an inferno, glowing against the night sky. In grim silence, Shane, Calera, Marsh, and Eli watched the structure collapse inside itself, engulfed by orange flames. The dreams Calera had once held for a fine hotel to replace the disreputable bordello went up in smoke. But oddly enough, Calera was not distressed over the loss. She and Shane had managed to emerge from this latest disaster with their lives. Royal, however, had not been so fortunate. She had been unable to escape before the devastating explosion blew The Cottage to smithereens.

Bleakly, Eli stared at the burning debris. "I'm sorry, Miss O'Connell. It seems I owe you an apology."

"Indeed you do," Marsh snapped. "I told you Cali was innocent."

Calera's sympathetic gaze focused on Eli whose thick shoulders had slumped deflatedly. He had developed a fond attachment for Royal the past few years. Calera could see the despair and disillusionment on his weather-beaten features and she remembered how tormented she had been when she believed Shane had betrayed her. Eli was experiencing that same sense of loss and torment. He had believed Royal because he had allowed himself to see what he wanted to see in her, just as Calera had relied upon past memories of her brother. Royal had employed subterfuge for her own selfish purposes, playing on Eli's affection for her.

While the crowd gathered outside the fiery remains of The Cottage, Calera found herself swept off her feet and cradled in Shane's powerful arms. In swift strides he carried her toward Doctor Broxton's office. As of yet, Shane had said not one word. His expression was as hard as rock and he hadn't glanced at Calera for even a second. Calera was too lost in thought to gauge his mood. It was as black, as she was about to find out—very black indeed!

Chapter Twenty-eight

"Let's have a look at that arm," Lyle Broxton insisted, cutting away the sleeve of Calera's doehide shirt.

So much had happened since Calera sustained the wound that she had almost forgotten about being shot. When she glanced down at the bloody fabric and saw the raw flesh, she very nearly fainted. The pain returned in full force, and Calera had to brace her good arm on the examination table to prevent toppling from her perch.

"You are lucky, young lady," Lyle assured her as he dabbed a clean cloth against the wound. "The bullet grazed the flesh rather than penetrating bone."

Calera said nothing. She was battling down a sudden case of nausea. When Lyle soaked the wound with antiseptic, Calera nearly came unglued. She had barely escaped being blown to kingdom come and then charred beyond recognition. Now her arm was on fire. Unfortunately, she received no sympathy from Shane, who was lounging in the chair watching the physician administer first aid.

While Calera hissed at the pain, Lyle kept speaking in a calm, controlled voice, reassuring her that the tender wound would heal nicely if she applied the salve for a week and frequently changed bandages.

"Would you like a dose of laudanum to help you sleep?" Lyle inquired. "You have had another terrible day."

Calera nodded sickly and blinked back the tears brought on by the agonizing throb in her arm. Before she could ease off the examining table, Shane strode across the room to pluck her up in his arms. Still, he hadn't spoken to Calera and did not intend to until they were in the privacy of a rented hotel room.

With her arm in a sling and her wound burning like hell on fire, Calera laid her head against Shane's shoulder. The muscles beneath her cheek were as hard as granite. However, Calera was too busy trying to ignore the pain, as Shane had taught her to do, to notice the tension that vibrated through his brawny body.

Once Shane had ordered a room for the night and ascended the steps, he laid Calera on the bed. He had just drawn himself up in front of her, prepared to read her the first paragraph of the riot act when Marsh and Eli breezed in, carrying armloads of satchels.

"We found Calera's belongings crammed in the closet of Royal's room," Marsh announced.

Eli still could not meet Calera's gaze. "She told me you had taken your belongings with you when you skedaddled out of town to save your hide. I-I didn't contest her. I'm sorry." With head downcast, he added, "I believed what she wanted me to believe."

"I bear no ill feelings," Calera assured him. She managed a smile when he finally raised his head to meet her gaze.

After the sheriff apologized all over himself again and promised to send out the word to remove the reward from Calera's head, he made his meek departure.

Still Shane said nothing. He simply lingered on the perimeters of the room like a shadow while Marsh fussed over Calera.

"Can I get you anything, Cali?" Marsh cooed into her peaked face.

"Supper would be nice," she answered with a wobbly smile.

"Done, my lady. Your wish is my command."

Marsh's blond head dipped toward her lush mouth. His gaze darted toward Shane who had practically made himself invisible—almost but not quite. Marsh was met by a disapproving frown that warned him not to do what he looked as if he intended to do. Instead of targeting Calera's lips, Marsh kissed her on the forehead. After executing a courtly bow, Marsh pivoted on his heels and strode toward the door. There he paused to cast Calera a parting glance.

"I hope you realize that you scared ten years off my life when I heard that shot ring out in the storeroom. Don't ever do that again, Cali."

When Marsh closed the door behind him, Calera glanced toward Shane who was swathed in shadows. Eyes as black as midnight glowed at her, making her flinch at the intensity of his expression. The only way to describe the look directed at her was *silent fury*. Calera swallowed hard when Shane's foreboding form emerged from the corner to tower over the foot of the bed. Shane looked like a black thundercloud that could spawn tornadoes. His body was so taut with barely restrained control that Calera wondered if he might pop.

"I told you no daring heroics, Irish," Shane growled down at her with such distinct menace that Calera jumped, causing the bed to vibrate. "You should have called out to me when Royal pulled a pistol."

Calera had faced many of Shane's moods the past month. She had experienced exquisite tenderness, enjoyed his bright, ringing laughter, consoled herself in his sympathy. But *never* had she seen him quite so furious. He was glaring at her as if she had committed a horrendous sin that he could not, and would not, forgive.

She swallowed with a gulp. "I—"

In angry jerks Shane retrieved his dagger from her shoe and plunged it into his moccasin, very nearly slicing the tendon of his leg in the process. "You could have gotten yourself killed!" He exploded like blasting powder. "Damn it, Irish. I nearly suffered heart seizure when I burst in the storeroom, expecting to find you lying in a pool of your own blood!"

His harsh words bounded off the walls to come at her from all directions. Calera shrank back against her pillow when Shane circled the bed and braced his arms on either side of her shoulders. When he stuck his face into hers, Calera got an unhindered view of his teeth before he proceeded to bite off her head and chew up a few pieces of her hide.

"I thought you loved me. I thought there was one person in this world who cared what *I* thought and how *I* felt."

"I do," she assured him.

"No, you don't!" Shane jerked upright and thrashed around the room before wheeling to glower at her for the umpteenth time. "If you cared, you would know that what affects you also affects me. I could have lost you! You threw yourself in harm's way in your compulsive need for revenge against Royal. Restitution meant more to you than I do!"

"Will you kindly keep your voice down," Calera snapped. "This is supposed to be a private conversation. I wouldn't be surprised if every citizen in Globe City can hear you."

"I don't give a damn if they do!" Shane roared loud enough to drowned out a booming cannon.

He stood there in a towering rage, pinning her to the headboard of the bed with a look that could have melted rock. It struck her just then why he was so furious with her, why he was reading her every paragraph of the riot act with such a vengeance. *He* was striking out at her for the very same reason *she* hadn't called out to him when Royal pulled her pistol. Calera could not bear the thought of having Shane catch the bullet meant for her. The thought of losing one so loved and cherished had terrified her and now it had terrified him. That realization caused a smile to purse her lips.

"And what, I'd like to know, do you find so damned amusing?" Shane snarled at her.

Calera suddenly became immune to his lightning glares and thundering voice. Her smile broadened and her green eyes twinkled up at him.

"Curse it, Irish!" Shane scowled at her mischievous grin. She wasn't taking him seriously, not seriously a-tall!

"Curse it, Apache, hasn't it occurred to you that I didn't call for your assistance because *I* would have preferred to die than risk losing you? I could accept no other alternatives." Her eyes took on an emerald sheen that very nearly brought Shane to his knees. "I placed your life above my own because, without you, I would have no reason to go on living. I couldn't sacrifice you when you are every breath I take. You *are* my life. Don't you know that?"

The frustration seeped out of his body like floodwaters. Oh yes, he still wanted to wring this daring tigress's neck for scaring the pants off him, but what man could refuse the love that glistened in those heavily-lashed eyes? And what man alive could resist that impish smile that could turn him into sentimental mush?

"Humor me, Apache," Calera entreated. "I'm injured. Instead of raving at me, come kiss me until I forget where it hurts."

Shane had been completely humbled by her admission of love that proclaimed no sacrifice too great to spare his life. And after he got over being furious, he realized he would have reacted exactly the same way Calera had. He had wanted to draw Royal's fire to save Calera. He would have gladly taken the bullet to spare her.

"Well?" Calera prompted when he continued to stand there staring at her. "Do you want to kiss and make up or go on fighting?" she teased him affectionately.

His massive shoulders dropped another notch and he breathed a rough sigh. "To tell the truth, if I touch you I'm afraid I'll kiss you to death, among other things. It might prove embarrassing if your faithful puppy comes trotting back with your supper tray—"

Speak of the devil and he appeared. Shane didn't even have time to punctuate his last sentence before Marsh buzzed into the room with a heaping tray of food.

"Here you are, Cali." Marsh set the tray on her lap. "A feast fit for a queen. And you will be pleased to know that I bumped into your friend Horace Baxter. He sends his regards. He plans to check on you first thing in the morning. But at the moment he is spreading your story all over town to counter Royal's lies. He has every intention of making you the heroine of his tale. By the time he's through, I suspect you will be forgiven for the shameful sin of wanting to turn The Cottage into a boarding-house."

"It would be nice if somebody around here liked me," Calera replied, darting Shane a sly smile.

Shane caught her intended meaning and managed to return the grin. "Since you seem to be in good hands, I'll go tend to Sultan. With all the excitement, he's probably wearing a trench in front of his hitching post."

In hurried strides, Shane moved down the hall, thankful for an excuse to flee the room. Damn it, he was still shaking. *Shaking! Him,* mind you! Once his frustration wore off, the fear he had experienced when he heard that shot ring out went all through him like a lightning bolt. Shane could not remember being so terrified in all his thirty years. Danger he could handle unafraid, as it pertained to himself. He was accustomed to that. But being frightened for someone that he loved so deeply unhinged him. Damnation, for a man who always prided himself in masking his emotions, he wasn't coping well with Calera's latest flirtation with disaster.

When Shane stepped outside, he noticed that Sultan wasn't coping well, either. Humanity was still flooding down the streets with buckets of water, ensuring the smoldering Cottage didn't ignite nearby structures. Sultan was skittish with everyone bustling around him, dipping water from his trough. The spirited stallion was anxious to make his departure, so much so that Sultan nearly dragged Shane to the livery stable. Other horses Sultan could tolerate. Two-legged creatures, however, were another matter entirely. The steed had his preferences in the human race. He tolerated only a select few.

"Easy, my friend," Shane cooed in Apache while Sultan wore ruts in his stall. The steed quieted, but every unidentified sound caused his ears to prick and his nostrils to flare.

Once Shane had his own emotions in check and saw that Sultan

was fed and brushed, he ambled back to the street to stare at the
glowing embers of what had once been The Cottage. He had
been too upset with Calera to consider how she felt about the
loss of the property into which she had sunk her savings. Did
she regret the explosion that destroyed the building? And what,
he wondered, did she plan to do now? What Shane wanted her
to do was come to his ranch, to fill the house with love and laughter after years of icy hatred and frigid contempt. Would Calera
be content on an obscure ranch after living in a bustling city in
the East? Or would the seclusion make her restless? Did she have
her heart set on rebuilding The Cottage to fit her expectations?

Calera had declared a few days earlier that she never wanted
to return to Globe, that she simply wanted to forget the torment
and anguish. But now that her name had been cleared and her
enemy had been defeated, she might have a change of heart
about her future. Well, he and Calera would discuss the matter
later. But not tonight. All Shane wanted was to lie beside her,
to thank the Powers that Be that she had been spared from
calamity. And for damned certain, he was not going to leave
her alone for a minute.

Shane strode past the smoldering remains of The Cottage
and headed toward the hotel. A faint smile brimmed his lips.
As soon as he routed the lovesick Marsh Layton from the room,
Shane was going to make Calera forget the pain in her arm in
a much different manner than he had employed when he
treated the festering wound on her shoulder. He was also going
to make *himself* forget the torment he endured when he heard
the gunshot that felt as if it had lodged in his heart. Dear God,
the sound of that barking pistol had made his blood run cold!

Calera munched on her ham and fried potatoes while Marsh
sat attentively at her side. Now that the worst was over and Calera
could think clearly, she was ready to get on with her life and
forget the haunting events that had turned her world upside
down. She remembered that day she and Shane had come to
terms with their feelings for each other, when he had informed

her that he would not ask her to step into his world, which bordered on two contrasting civilizations. She also recalled the complete and total eruption of his emotions when she risked her life to ensure he remained safely outside the storeroom.

Shane had been downright amusing while he stamped around, raging at her. She imagined it was the first time Shane had completely lost that well-controlled temper of his. She bit back a grin and swallowed her mouthful of potatoes. Knowing Shane and his fierce vow to let her make her own decisions—unlike so many men of his time—Calera predicted that, if she was going to have a husband, she would have to do the asking. And before she ruined her reputation completely, she had better make the arrangements for a ceremony—posthaste!

"Marsh, I wonder if I might ask a favor of you," Calera requested.

"Anything, Cali," he said generously.

"Would you fetch the justice of the peace for me?"

His smile turned upside down. "Is someone getting married?"

"I am."

"I was afraid of that." His tone was deflated.

Calera stared at the handsome gambler who had been loyal and caring throughout her many ordeals. "I'm sorry if I—"

He flung up a hand to forestall her. "No need to apologize, princess. I think I knew the first time that big brute powered into your room and ordered me out that I didn't stand a chance with you." Reluctantly, Marsh rose to his feet. "I'll round up the justice of the peace, but don't expect me to give you away. I'm not that good a sport."

"But you're a good man," she said sincerely.

"But not the best," he grumbled. "Ah well, maybe I'll find another certain someone another time and another place."

When Marsh exited, Calera set the tray aside and flung her legs over the edge of the bed. She was not going to be married in Shane's oversized clothes with one sleeve ripped off the baggy garment. Rummaging through the pile of satchels, Calera made a one-armed attempt to retrieve a fashionable gown. Tossing

Shane's clothes aside, she struggled into the mint green dress. Hurriedly she ran a brush though the wild tangle of hair and cleaned the smudges off her face.

Calera slumped dejectedly when she stared at her reflection in the mirror. Shane, if he chose to accept her proposal, was going to get a bedraggled-looking bride.

A disconcerted thought picked that moment to trip across Calera's mind. She wondered if she was being too presumptuous in sending for the justice of the peace. Perhaps marriage was not what Shane intended at all, since he had never mentioned the subject *per se*. Calera shook off the thought and pinched her cheeks to enhance the color in her face. If Shane didn't want to marry her, he could say so. She had no intention of holding him at gunpoint and forcing him to repeat the vows.

When the door creaked open, Calera pivoted, expecting to see Shane. Her anticipatory smile vanished and an astounded gasp burst from her lips. The unidentified intruder pointed a Colt .45 at her chest. Calera stumbled back against the dresser when a shadowed gaze focused on her from beneath the wide brim of the hat. Eyes as fatal as the grave bore into Calera, leaving her with the inescapable feeling that this wasn't going to be her wedding night, after all, but rather the eve of her funeral.

"Surprised to see me?" the intruder questioned with a diabolical sneer.

Surprised did not aptly describe the depth and extent of Calera's shock.

"It seems you are not the only one with the nine lives of a cat," Royal jeered. "Nor are you the only one who can employ disguises when you return from the dead."

Calera swallowed the lump that clogged her throat and stared grimly at Royal. There was no question what Royal intended— quick and fatal revenge. And, of course, no one would know who was responsible for this latest murder because Royal was presumed dead. Royal would simply turn up in some other mining town under an assumed name and wheedle her way into another brothel. Dear God, this vampish woman was worse than a boomerang that kept coming back!

Royal smiled in wicked triumph while she stared at Calera over the silver barrel of the pistol. At long last she would have her revenge on this troublesome female. It was this same obsessive craving for vindication that had allowed Royal to flee out the back door of The Cottage before the devastating explosion blew the building to smithereens. She had purposely aimed herself in Calera and Shane's direction to convince them that she had perished before she could follow the route they had taken. But the instant Shane and Calera were out of sight, Royal had spun around, covering her face with the hem of her gown, and plunged through the billowing smoke to reach the back door. She had been safely outside when the blast resounded. Diving to the ground, she had covered her head to protect herself from falling debris.

While the flames engulfed the Cottage, she had scurried away. It had been a simple matter to swipe a set of men's clothes from the cribs on the east end of town. Melody Bright, the calico queen who had worked at the Cottage for her, had readily handed over the garments when Royal requested assistance. Of course, Melody had been sworn to secrecy and Royal had promised to send for her and the other prostitutes after establishing herself in another community.

With vengeful anticipation, Royal had sneaked up the back steps, waiting to hide out in her hotel room after Eli and Marsh confiscated Calera's clothes from the closet. Keeping watch at the door, Royal had seen Shane exit a few minutes earlier and then waited for Marsh to take his leave. When Calera was alone, Royal had crept down the hall to pay that meddlesome bitch her last call. The time of reckoning had come and Royal could taste sweet revenge.

"Come with me," Royal ordered with a demonic smile. "We have unfinished business . . ."

A muddled frown furrowed Shane's dark brow when he returned to the hotel room to find it evacuated. His perceptive gaze scanned the room, noting the supper tray that had been set aside, the opened satchels on the floor, and the buckskin clothes Calera had left draped over the back of the chair.

An unfamiliar scent permeated the room. The fragrance was that of cheap cologne, near as Shane could tell. His keen sense of smell assured him that it wasn't Marsh's cologne and it certainly wasn't Calera's perfume. He would know her scent anywhere.

Concerned, Shane lurched around and hurried down the hall. He was halfway down the steps when Marsh ambled through the lobby. "Where's Irish?" Shane demanded.

"In the room." Marsh frowned at the grave expression on Shane's bronzed face. "Or at least she was when she sent me on an errand."

"What kind of errand?"

"I'm not sure it's my place to say." Marsh spun on his heels to follow Shane out the door. When Shane stopped short, Marsh plowed into his backside.

"What kind of errand, Layton?" Shane repeated with emphasis.

Marsh hesitated for only a moment before replying. "I think it was to be a surprise for you, and I doubt I'll put it as delicately as Cali, but she wanted me to fetch the justice of the peace."

"What!" Shane gaped at him.

"I think she planned to propose to you and marry you on the spot." Marsh noted Shane's shocked expression. "Just as I thought, it was to be a surprise." His blue eyes narrowed meaningfully. "And you damned well better be planning to accept, Stafford. If you think you can trifle with a woman like Cali, then you are sorely mistaken. And believe me, if it is not marriage you have in mind, then *I* will gladly stand in your stead. I may have bowed out gracefully, but I can bow back in because I care one helluva lot about her!"

Shane blinked at the intensity of Marsh's statement and at the information he had been given. Calera was planning to propose to him? If she did, where had she gone without leaving a message?

"The justice of the peace will be along in a few minutes. He was indisposed when I finally located him in one of the cribs on the far side of town," Marsh explained. "It seems that while he was dallying with one of the harlots, someone stole his clothes—"

Shane spun around and darted out the door, glancing in every direction at once. Something was wrong; he could sense it. He didn't know exactly what, but Marsh's explanation struck a chord of alarm. Shane was prepared to swear that the strange scent that clung to the hotel room bode ill for Calera. With a sense of frantic urgency, Shane darted off, with Marsh one step behind him.

Chapter Twenty-nine

"That's far enough," Royal declared.

Calera pivoted around to face Royal in the dark alley behind the bakery. Every step of the way, Calera had conjured up and discarded a half-dozen possible solutions to her problem. She had been nudged down the back steps of the hotel with a pistol indented in her spine. One false move and it would be her last. Royal was trigger happy, no doubt about that! Even now, Calera could see Royal's fingers flexing and relaxing, yet constantly clinging to the Colt in case Calera attempted to bolt and run.

"You are such a stupid little fool," Royal insulted her. "Did you really think you could defeat me?"

"I think"—Calera said with perfect certainty—"that no matter where you go, no matter what alias you employ, Shane will hunt you down and destroy you." Calera smiled, relishing the sense of quiet calm she had developed after such close association with Shane and so many encounters with disaster.

In the face of danger, and even at a serious disadvantage, Shane possessed an unnerving presence that exuded confidence and refused even the slightest possibility of defeat. That was what gave Apache warriors the cutting edge in battle, Calera had come to realize. Shane had been taught to defy death and employ cunning. Fear was a crippling emotion that a warrior learned to overcome. Thanks to Shane, Calera was able to control apprehensions that clouded rational thinking.

Calera instantly recalled the day Shane had squared off against the three Tonto braves. Shane had lunged and attacked rather than remaining on defense. The Apache warrior always fought to win, never to prevent being defeated. It was that mental attitude, that air of overpowering confidence, that gave him the psychological advantage.

The thought prompted Calera to raise her chin a notch higher to counter Royal's malicious sneer. Even though Calera was at a disadvantage with her left arm in a sling, she was not admitting defeat.

"I didn't have the chance to tell you what became of Ike and Grady after Shane caught up with them," Calera said in an astonishingly calm voice. "Grady was the more fortunate of the two. Shane sentenced him to quick, immediate hell with the hiss of his dagger. Ike, I'm afraid, was not so lucky."

She paused to smile triumphantly when Royal's expression faltered. "Have you, perchance, witnessed the Apache's brand of torture, Royal? Can you imagine so much physical pain and torment that you would turn your last bullet on yourself to end the unbearable suffering? Can you envision what it would be like to be skinned alive and be forced to see yourself in that horrifying condition—?"

"Shut up!" Royal hissed.

"Ike couldn't tolerate the pain. He screamed until he was hoarse," Calera continued. "Then I heard the shot echo through the canyon—"

"I said shut up—!" Royal screeched.

It was at that moment when Calera launched her attack, defying the pistol, defying death, defying all odds. She came uncoiled like a cobra to spring at Royal. Her gaze was transfixed on the barrel of the pistol. Her good arm shot upward to misdirect the bullet that exploded from the chamber and echoed in the silence like a crash of thunder.

Wildly, Royal slashed her arm through the air to knock Calera's hand away. Calera skidded on her knees in the dirt, battling for control of the weapon. Vaguely, Calera heard approaching footsteps, but she was too intent on her purpose to glance up.

Royal heard the ferocious growl behind her and swiveled her head around to see the gigantic silhouette that loomed like a shadow of doom. Calera's words had struck unnerving fear in Royal and she instinctively swung her pistol toward Shane.

When Calera focused on the swerving pistol and saw Shane darting into the path of oncoming disaster, horror clutched her throat. "No!" Her shoulder rammed into Royal's knees in attempt to knock her off balance. The pistol exploded, sending sparks dancing against the silver barrel.

In a blur of swift motion and hazy shadows, Calera saw Shane double over into a somersault. His hand suddenly held the dagger he kept in his moccasin. Even before Calera's brain could register the lightning-quick action, the knife sailed end-over-end toward its target. Calera heard the deadly thud, felt the shudder pass through Royal's body. Another pistol shot danced in the dirt beside Calera's head before Royal collapsed atop of her.

Terrorized with a fear she could not begin to express, Calera glanced up to see Shane sprawled facedown in the dirt, his body motionless. What Calera had willed not to happen had happened! It was obvious that Royal's bullet had brought Shane down, even though he had managed to hurl his dagger.

"Dear God!" Calera wailed as she wormed out from under Royal's lifeless body. "Apache!" On one hand and two knees, Calera crawled toward him, swearing she had aged a year for every tormenting second that ticked by. "Apache!" Her hysterical sobs echoed down the alley, amplifying and returning to haunt her.

Panting for breath over the bone-jarring hammer of her heart, Calera sank down to cradle Shane's head in her lap. "Don't you dare die, for I'll never forgive you if you do!" She showered him with kisses that mingled with salty tears. She clutched him to her, willing him to survive.

Thick lashes fluttered up and twinkling black eyes sparkled in the starlight. "Damned unnerving, isn't it, Irish?"

Calera jerked upright, her hand groping at his chest. She found no bullet wound or seeping blood, only the vibrations of silent laughter. "How? I thought—" When she realized that Shane had agilely dodged the bullet, staged the dramatic scene, and allowed her to believe the worst, she whacked him on the shoulder. "Damn your ornery hide! That wasn't the least bit funny. If I could get my hands on a pistol I would shoot you myself!"

"Are you angry, Irish?" he questioned while he lay there, perfectly content with his head in her lap.

"I am livid, if you want to know!" Calera spluttered.

"And frightened within an inch of your life?"

"A half inch, maybe less," she muttered into his wry grin.

"Then you understand how I felt when you refused to call out to me for protection and drew Royal's attention away from me in the storeroom, just as I drew your captor's attention away from you here in the alley."

Calera was not enjoying the lesson Shane felt obliged to teach her. Even after the worst was over, she still couldn't stop shaking. Her body was wracked with indescribable fear, not for herself but for *him!* Is that what he had experienced when he barged into the storeroom, thinking Calera had suffered a fatal wound? Dear God!

Tears trickled down her cheeks, forming mud. Shane uplifted his hand to tilt her face down to his. "Marsh claims there is something you wanted to ask me, Irish. What is it?"

"Marsh?" Calera parroted, still too overwhelmed with emotion to think straight.

"Yes, Marsh. You remember him, don't you?" he teasingly prompted. "The handsome blond gambler who half-collapsed against the hotel wall because he thought you were a goner—"

"I know who he is," Calera snapped when she finally regained her senses.

"Good. I'm glad to know you're beginning to recover. It takes awhile, doesn't it, Irish?" White teeth gleamed in the faint light.

"Stop badgering me," Calera said grouchily. "I'm still furious with you."

Shane glanced toward the fallen form that lay facedown in the dirt. "Who the hell was that anyway?"

"Royal."

Shane jerked up his head to stare incredulously at his victim.

"Royal wasn't as dead as she led us to believe," Calera explained. "She escaped through the back door of The Cottage while we were making a mad dash through the front door."

"And when you turned up dead, no one would have thought to suspect her," Shane mused aloud.

"That's the way Royal had it figured," Calera assured him.

When a flood of humanity spilled into the alley, Calera found herself hoisted to her feet by Marsh, who was as shaky as a leaf in a cyclone, even after the danger had passed. Murmurs rippled through the gathering crowd like waves on a wind-tossed sea when the citizens of Globe City recognized Royal. While Sheriff Nelson assumed the grim task of removing the body, Calera, bookended by Shane and Marsh, adjourned to the hotel. Once there, Calera found herself the recipient of Marsh's scathing soliloquy.

"Confound it, Cali! How could you have thrust yourself at Royal without one care for your own safety?" Marsh ended in exasperated question.

"It is the way of the Apache warrior," she informed him. "The best defense is a surprise attack."

Marsh's rounded blue eyes flicked from Calera to Shane, who was propped negligently against the wall smiling in amusement. After an astounded moment, Marsh shook his head and expelled a sigh. "Perhaps the two of you *do* deserve each other. You are both hopeless daredevils who have tendencies toward self-destruction." He whirled toward the door. "I'll go fetch the justice of the peace before you two find another way to put your lives at risk. Surely by now the official has located his missing clothes."

When Marsh whizzed out, Calera glanced apprehensively at Shane. Would he be offended by the fact that she had taken it upon herself to summon the justice of the peace to marry them without consulting him first?

"Marsh told me what you had planned," Shane said, pushing away from the wall. "Are you certain this is what you want, Irish?"

"I'm certain," she said without hesitation. "I'm just not sure that is what you intended. Perhaps I have been too presumptuous."

When Calera's gaze dropped self-consciously toward the floor, Shane strode over to curl his forefinger beneath her smudged chin. "In the eyes of the Apache, we are already married. We are one in body and spirit. But if the formality of a ceremony seems proper and necessary to you, then so be it."

Calera sighed audibly and glanced down at her soiled gown. "I wanted to look presentable for the ceremony, to make you proud of whom you would be acquiring for a wife. Instead, I look like a bedraggled puppy."

"To be honest, Irish, it doesn't matter what you wear. I have been looking through those concealing garments since the first time I dragged you from the river," he admitted with a rakish grin. "I have never been in love with your clothes, but rather with the intriguing woman inside them."

Her lashes fluttered up, feeling her heart swell at the sight of his charismatic grin. Calera remembered the first time she had met this Goliath of a man whose well-schooled expression revealed no emotion whatsoever. Ah, how Shane had changed these past two months. He was no longer self-contained, and Calera basked in the warmth of his dazzling smiles—lived for them.

Her good arm settled over his broad shoulder and she pushed up on tiptoe to press a kiss to his sensuous lips. "And to be honest, Apache, I delight in seeing you wear nothing but that blinding smile."

Shane clutched her to him, uplifting her petite body from the floor to nibble at the curve of her neck. "Where is that damned justice of the peace anyway?" he muttered, his voice thick with hungry longing. "I want to strip you down to your gorgeous hide and make love to you until I forget how many times the past two months that I came within a hairbreadth of losing you. Dear God, Irish, I love you so much that the thought of living without you unnerves me!"

"Then I suggest that, after the wedding, we find a *safe,* secluded spot to live out our lives together so we don't have to scare each other to death," she murmured, her soft lips skimming his flesh in a promise of pleasures to come. "Don't ever leave me, Apache. I have lost so many others in my life that I can't bear the thought of losing my greatest love."

Her words, and the sincere tone in which she conveyed them, very nearly buckled Shane at the knees. He had never felt so pleased, so proud, or so humbled. "I've never belonged anywhere in this world," he whispered before his lips reverently skimmed hers. "And I never felt as if anyone truly belonged to me until there was you . . ."

Belonging. Calera breathed the word, breathed in the masculine scent that was so much a part of Shane, so very much a part of her. It had been ages since she had felt as if she belonged anywhere herself. She had been shuffled from one place to another since the age of five, struggling to cope with one loss after another. She had been an extra person in the world, striving to make a place for herself. Now she had found her place in Shane's generous heart. There was nowhere on earth she preferred to be.

When Shane's lips reclaimed hers in a kiss that savored and devoured, all in the same moment, Calera gave herself up to the emotions that sizzled through her. She ached to absorb every inch of him, to communicate this magnanimous love she felt for him. Unfortunately, the door swung open, forcing them apart.

Shane's brows elevated when he peered at the plump man who waddled into the room, his scent preceding him. Now Shane knew what had become of the justice of the peace's clothes. Royal had confiscated them. It was that same sticky sweet fragrance that had clung to this room when Calera disappeared.

"Cali, this is Gunther Farkleberry," Marsh introduced.

Calera smiled wryly. "I believe we have already met, in a roundabout way."

Shane leaned close to pose a confidential question. "You recognized that scent, too, did you? The man must wash his clothes and himself in that offensive cologne."

When Gunther frowned at Calera's odd remark and the twosome who looked as it they were about to burst into snickers, Marsh dismissed their foolishness with a flick of his wrist. "Don't mind them, Gunther, they are giddy and in love. Shall we get on with this?"

Gunther opened the law book he had brought with him and rattled off the words in a drab monotone. After Calera and Shane supplied the necessary *I dos*, Gunther snapped the book shut, wigwagged his stubby arms like a fairy godfather waving a wand, and decreed the couple to be man and wife.

Calera should have been appalled at the simplified ceremony, but she was merely thankful to have it concluded, so she could get on to more tantalizing matters. As Shane had said—and it was true—they had spoken their vows to each other days ago in the chapel of panoramic valleys beneath the spectacular steeples of mountains, while the greatest powers of all civilizations stood as witnesses.

When Marsh ambled over to present the bride with a congratulatory kiss, Shane touched Calera's cheek, indicating where he wanted the peck delivered. Disappointed, Marsh complied and then stepped back apace.

"Don't you ever cut anyone any slack, Stafford?" he questioned.

Glistening black eyes dropped to Calera's streaked face. "Only Irish, always Irish."

"Amen to that." Marsh sauntered over to scoop up his hat and set it on his head at a jaunty angle. "I'll be leaving on the stage tomorrow."

"Where are you going, Marsh?" Calera inquired as she curled her hand around Shane's sinewy arm.

"Wherever the stagecoach takes me," he replied. The easy

smile faded from his handsome features. "And maybe that certain someone will be waiting for me." He regained his suave smile and winked at her. "I wish you love, Cali, but I'll keep the *luck* for myself, if you don't mind."

Marsh strode toward the door, halting only when Shane's rich baritone voice flowed across the room. He turned back to see the solemn expression that settled into Shane's craggy features.

"Thank you, my friend."

"No need to thank me, Stafford," Marsh insisted. "Thank your bewitching wife. She's the one who made a gentleman out of me." He chuckled at the thought. "Dear God, a gentleman gambler! I almost lost my bad reputation because of this Irish leprechaun."

"She has a knack for ruining everyone's bad reputation," Shane agreed. *His and Sultan's,* to name another two.

Marsh's gaze darted back to Calera and lingered for a long moment. "Be happy, Cali," he said quietly before he disappeared into the hall.

"I thought he'd never leave," Shane grumbled as he gathered Calera close.

"He really is a nice man, Apache," Calera insisted as she rested her head on his broad chest. "A better man than he would like to be, I think."

"I think you're right, but I'm thankful he wasn't the *best* man for you. I wouldn't like having to hate him for taking you away from me."

Shane scooped Calera up in his swarthy arms and carried her to bed. There he paused to frown thoughtfully. The last time he and Calera had made love in a bed, the slats had given way in their ardent passion for each other.

Calera smiled, knowing without asking what he was thinking. "I believe a pallet is the best solution," she suggested.

Returning her grin, Shane set her to her feet. In record time, the mattress, sheets, and quilts lay invitingly on the floor and the two of them were upon it, answering kiss with breathless kiss, caress with bone-melting caress. Calera wasn't certain that even physical communication could fully express her love for this man who had come to mean all things to her. Though she spelled out her affection by embroidering her love with each adoring touch, it wasn't enough. Only a lifetime of loving him with her body, heart, and soul would satisfy this yearning inside her . . .

All thought vanished when Shane's warm lips skimmed her cheeks, her throat, her collarbone. Every ounce of tension that had claimed her during the frightening events of the night washed away like the tide smoothing footprints from a sandy shore. She felt his moist breath whispering over her pliant flesh like a warm summer wind. She arched upward when his fingertips teased the throbbing peaks of her breasts, when his mouth tenderly suckled.

A soft sigh escaped Calera's lips when his kisses and caresses streamed over her body like a masterful musician playing an enchanting rhapsody. Calera felt the compelling melody filling her soul and she became mesmerized by the mystical sounds that vibrated through every nerve and muscle.

When Shane's questing fingers drifted lower, stroking her, teasing her, Calera felt the familiar flame burning in the very core of her being, expanding until it consumed her. Her body burst into sweet flames as his kisses fluttered over her belly and his hands swirled over the ultrasensitive flesh of her inner thighs.

"Open to me, my wild Irish rose," Shane whispered huskily. "I want to pleasure you until my touch is all you require to exist."

When his fingertips glided into the silken warmth of her, Shane shuddered with her, feeling her intense pleasure echo through him. He longed to arouse her in the most intimate ways imaginable. He yearned to create inventive techniques that would compensate for his own lack of experience.

There was a part of Shane that envied Marsh's Layton's expertise with women. And yet, another part of him was ever-so thankful that he had waited to explore the dimensions of passion with this one bewitching beauty who had captured his heart and stolen his soul. He wanted to be the most attentive lover

Calera could ever wish for. He wanted to see her succumb to
the splendor he could offer, to feel her luscious body calling
out to him. And when she was in the throes of wild sweet ecstasy,
he wanted to embark on the most remarkable of all journeys
with her, feeling the fiery warmth of her closing around him
until they melted into one loving essence.

"Please . . . no!" Calera gasped when his kisses and caresses
sent tremors undulating through every fiber of her being. Frantic, she reached for him, dragging his lips back to hers, enfold-
ing the throbbing length of him to guide him to her.

"No more, Irish?" Shane teased her, for he knew exactly what
she meant. He could feel her lush body crying out to him, but
he wanted to hear the words that conveyed her need for him.

"Come here before I die with the want of you," Calera rasped.

"Only when you die with wanting will I come to you," Shane
whispered before his lips trailed over the beaded peaks and
descended over her flat stomach.

"I already died twice—" Calera choked when his feathery
kisses and pulse-jarring caresses worked their maddening magic
on her body once again.

Shane took tremendous pleasure in sending Calera's senses
reeling, in touching her so intimately that she cried out in pleasure, so consumed that her body contracted around his fingertips, burning him with the heat of her ardent need. When she
trembled and dug her nails into his shoulders, whispering his
name with each ragged breath, his sinewy body slid upon hers
and he buried himself deep within her. Shane's hard-fought
control dissolved when Calera's tears of pleasure flooded over
his chest, when she arched toward him, demanding all he had
to give. Her frantic need unleashed his passions like a sword
slashing through fragile thread.

A muffled groan echoed in his throat when he felt his muscles
clench and his body move upon its own accord, matching the
rapid pulsations of his heartbeat. The intense pressure of wanting consumed him, sending him plummeting into mindless
abandon. He drove into her, afraid he was hurting her in his

ravenous need for her and yet helpless to contain the ungovernable passion that wracked his body.

"Calera!" Shane gasped for air and clung desperately to her when shudder after soul-shattering shudder converged on him. It was like being struck by a lightning bolt that sent aftershocks rippling through him with such fierce rapidity that he couldn't tell where one sweet, torturous sensation ended and another began. Shane, who knew his own formidable strength and had learned to leash it, felt totally out of control and completely drained of energy. The battle of noble restraint had cost him dearly. There was nothing left but a shell of a man who had given Calera all he had to give. When he sagged in absolute exhaustion, he feared he would not only crush her but smother her as well.

Dear God, he could barely breathe, much less move! How could loving a woman consume a man so? It demanded all he had and still he did not feel as if he had given enough in return for the ecstasy she unselfishly offered him.

When Shane braced upon both elbows to peer down at Calera, while he was still buried deeply inside her, she squirmed seductively beneath him. Shane shook his head in disbelief. Each time they made wild love it damned near killed him! He had just gathered enough strength to lever himself up to give her space to breathe and she wanted more of him? There was nothing left.

"I can't," he admitted hoarsely. "This time I swear it, Irish. You wore me out."

"Liar," she playfully teased him.

"I have never lied to you."

"It's true. You haven't," she concurred. "But there have been times when you have refused to offer me the whole truth. Like the time you let me believe you couldn't speak English, for instance." Her smile broadened and her eyes sparkled like polished emeralds. "But this time I intend to *make* a liar out of you . . ."

And damned if she didn't! Calera urged him to his knees, granting herself access to every inch of his masculine body, provocatively stroking and tantalizing every muscled plane and sleek contour. Her hands and lips' whispered and swirled, creating energy, igniting his desire. She held him; she tasted him. She savored him; she excited him until his breathing became so altered that even his tormented groans sounded like gasps.

"Irish, don't!" Shane croaked and shuddered in barely controlled restraint. "You're tearing my willpower to shreds."

She smiled mischievously against the pulsating length of him, her tongue flicking at the velvet tip before she took him into her lips and suckled him.

"Ir—" Shane not only couldn't breathe, he forgot *how* to breathe. When she shifted, her breasts gliding over his laboring chest like silk, Shane felt his body quavering like a jellyfish. Her thumb brushed against his swollen heat before her fingertips contracted around him. Still holding his burning gaze, Calera slid her knees along the hard columns of his hips. When she felt him tremble and instinctively press closer, she smiled in satisfaction.

"Liar. Your lips say you cannot, but your body says you can. Come love me 'til dawn, Apache . . . We'll greet the sun . . ."

With a sigh and a moan, Shane settled exactly upon her, gliding into the silken fire to burn alive all over again. She had proved to him that loving her so completely was his weakness, his strength, and his life. Shane gathered her to him, feeling her moist breath upon his seared flesh, feeling her supple curves blend perfectly into his. He plunged into her, driven by needs that had engulfed and ebbed and crested to consume again.

And later, when the touch of her hand and the whisper of her kiss called to him, he came to her like the stars glowing in the night, reaffirming the love he felt for her, marveling at the unconditional love she offered back to him.

Shane no longer regretted the years of loneliness and misery he had endured while he lived on the boundary between two civilizations. Perhaps he had profited from his trials and torments. Perhaps the miserable life he had known made him more appreciative of life's greatest treasure. Now he beheld the glorious reward of his suffering in the exquisite face that rested so trustingly against his shoulder. Knowing emptiness, he understood the abundance of love. Where there had been the absence of a smile, there was echoing laughter. Calera had brought him life after he had merely endured and existed. He loved her for that awakened awareness to life. But most of all, he loved this green-eyed nymph for loving him back . . .

Chapter Thirty

"Do you think when folks smile too much it gives them wrinkles?" Cactus questioned his brother, who was draped against the rails of the corral.

Sticker spit an arc of tobacco and stared into the distance, watching Calera ride off on Sultan's back. "Nope. I think it causes people to puff up with so much air that they float. An' if you ask me, Shane's head is filled with air, too. He's been back at the ranch with his bride for two weeks an' he don't even know where the hell he is most of the time. Every time I ask him a question, while his new wife is underfoot, I have to repeat myself to gain his attention."

Cactus spit an arc of tobacco to outdistance his brother and then nodded his wiry head. "Lovesick," he diagnosed. "Terminal case, I'd say."

"Brain dead," was Sticker's opinion.

One brother looked at the other and they cackled like nesting hens.

While the Linnox brothers were having a good laugh at Shane's expense, amused by the transformation in the owner of the Bar "S" Ranch, Calera walked Sultan along the path that led to the open meadow. Shane was in the process of training the sleek blood-red stud colt that Sultan had sired three summers past. Calera had returned from her jaunt into town and had immediately questioned Cactus and Sticker as to her husband's whereabouts. It had been a week since she had laid eyes on her wild Apache knight and she had missed him like crazy. Although she had enjoyed the feminine companionship of Neva Sanchez and Solana Muella, who had been thrilled by the invitation to venture into town, there was no substitute for that brawny giant whom she loved to distraction. Calera had not been able to wait for Shane to return to the house. She had requested that Sultan be saddled and she had gone in search of Shane.

A marveling smile curved the corners of Calera's lips upward as she paused in the shadow of the towering pines to survey the sunlit meadow. The pasture was bordered by the steep stone walls of the Mogollon Rim, nurtured by the stream that stretched out like a shiny silver ribbon. Wearing nothing but a breechcloth, Shane sat upon the prancing stud colt, putting him through the rigorous paces, teaching him obedience and guiding him only with his knees and heels. The colt bore many of his sire's characteristics—that same proud tilt of his head, that same alertness, that same confident stride.

Calera would have given most anything if she could master Shane's equestrian skills. But she wouldn't be doing much riding the next few months. Her visit to Doctor Broxton's office had confirmed her suspicions. She carried Shane's child and she hoped he was as thrilled at the prospect of parenthood as she was. They had not discussed children, but it was definitely time they did.

When Calera emerged from the shadows, Shane pulled the stud colt to a halt. His gaze settled on the spirited stallion whose glossy coat burned like fire in the sunlight. Immediately, Shane sensed a difference in the steed's gait. Sultan approached in an uncharacteristic manner, as if he were walking on ice and guarding every step. There was no arrogant toss of his head, no sideways prance that indicated his need for a faster pace.

Indeed, Sultan plowed forward like a nag that carried an inexperienced child on its back . . .

Shane's eyes widened as he stared at the lovely nymph who approached him. "Dear God!" he whispered before gouging his heels into the colt, forcing him to lunge into a gallop. Shane skidded the colt to a halt a safe distance away and dismounted in a single bound. His gaze never left Calera's enchanting face as he strode forward to lift her from the saddle and cradle her in his arms.

"I missed you, Irish," he murmured before he took her lips under his and savored the taste, scent, and feel of her after a week-long drought of loneliness.

A contented sigh escaped Calera's lips as she traced her fingertips over the padded muscles of his chest. "Next time I decide to venture into town, I hope you'll come with me. A week without you seems like a lifetime . . . And Apache, I have something I wish to discuss—"

Her gaze followed Shane's when he stared over her shoulder. Calera watched in silence while a cavalcade of warriors descended from the lofty rim, disappearing and reappearing from the wild cascade of rocks and thick timber.

Still holding Calera in the circle of his arms, Shane turned to study the proud Chiricahua chief who led the procession of braves. Geronimo lifted a dark brow as he studied the oversize half-breed who clung possessively to the flame-haired woman. The faintest hint of a smile quirked Geronimo's lips.

"I see that the wild one has been tamed," Geronimo observed in wry amusement.

Shane glanced down into Calera's flawless face and nodded. But he jerked up his head in puzzlement when Geronimo barked a laugh.

"I do not speak of the white woman, *Si-ha-ney Das-ay-go*. I speak of *you*." Geronimo broke into a teasing grin. "I think you were inappropriately named by The People. *Swift Killer* has made a *Swift Surrender*. I hope she is worth it, my brother."

"What is he saying?" Calera demanded when Geronimo cast her a glance and then burst into a chuckle.

"The great chief is mocking me because he thinks you tamed me rather than the other way around," Shane translated, smiling in spite of himself. "The old rascal is right, of course, and he is gloating because he knows it."

"Tamed you? Don't be absurd." Calera stared levelly at Geronimo. "No man tames my husband. He knows no master."

"What did the sassy squaw say?" Geronimo wanted to know when Calera tilted that rebellious chin at him.

"She disagrees with you, Geronimo," Shane replied, smiling rather smugly.

"And of course, being her devoted slave, you believe her," Geronimo noted with taunting amusement.

Calera wormed loose to position herself in front of Shane like a shield, even though he was head and shoulders taller than she was. "I will not have you poking fun at my husband, even if you are the God Almighty chief of the Apaches."

Two black brows jackknifed at Calera's defiant tone. From his lofty perch atop his paint pony, Geronimo surveyed the spirited young beauty, who looked as if she meant to do battle with him for his playful teasing. "Call off your guard dragon, my brother, before she breathes her fire on me. Have you no control over this flame-haired woman with the fiery tongue?"

"None whatsoever." Shane produced a wide grin. "I would no more attempt to chain her spirit than I would leash an eagle and restrain its natural instinct to fly. I am happiest when this wild bird soars."

When Shane slipped his arm around Calera's waist, holding her possessively against him, the teasing laughter died from Geronimo's obsidian eyes. He succumbed to a memory of those days gone by when he had known great happiness, before tragedy struck its devastating blow to his heart. "Cherish every moment, my brother. I hope your happiness will last until the end of time, even if mine could not. Never take for granted what you have."

Geronimo reined his steed close and reached down to trail his lean finger over the soft texture of Calera's cheek. He smiled ruefully, reflecting on the days when he had experienced the contentment Shane now enjoyed. Briefly touching this young, vibrant beauty put him back in touch with those years of serenity, in touch with the gentle pleasure of life before the intrusion of the white men who led the Apache down a path paved with broken promises.

Calera was stirred by the sadness reflected in the chief's dark eyes. She knew his life had become one of constant flight, that his steps were dogged. Her hand closed around his fingers, giving them a squeeze, silently offering sympathy for his plight and wishing him well on his journey into the Dragoon Mountains to elude the ever-present patrols that searched for him.

Geronimo blinked in surprise at the compassionate gesture. His gaze lifted over Calera's red-gold head to meet Shane's twinkling eyes.

"She is an iron clad rose with a heart as wide and free as the *Apacheria*," Shane murmured to the chief. "Do you think I would ever take such a priceless treasure for granted?"

"Not unless you are a fool, which I do not believe you to be," Geronimo replied as he pulled into an upright position on his steed.

Shane left Calera for a moment and strode over to grasp the stud colt's reins. Leading the steed forward, he presented the gift to Geronimo. "I have trained him for you. He has Sultan's endurance, his spirit, and his generous heart."

"We have already cut three head from your cattle herd to feed us," Geronimo informed him. "I will accept no more of your generosity."

Calera picked up the gist of the conversation from Shane's actions and Geronimo's firm tone. She knew the chief had declined the offer. Taking the reins from Shane, she placed them in Geronimo's hand. He stared down at her before focusing on the muscular steed. After a moment, he nodded appreciatively.

"I will take the colt to remind me of the woman with fire in her hair and jewels in her eyes. If the colt possesses the same brand of spirit, I will be as well protected as you are, my brother."

Geronimo lifted the beaded necklace from his throat and handed it to Calera in exchange for the steed. With a nod and a stare that conveyed what words could not, he led the procession of warriors away, bound for the stone mountains to the south that offered much protection from the dragoons who sought to confine him to the reservation.

When the Apaches disappeared into the pine forest, Calera pivoted to face Shane. "Now, as I was saying before I was interrupted—"

"I already know."

Calera did a double take. "How?"

"Sultan told me."

Calera gaped at the stallion and then stared bewilderedly at Shane.

"He carried you to me with a cautiousness nothing could mistake, Irish. Did you not notice Sultan's careful reserve? No toss of his head, no sideways prance to remind you that he only allows you to be his mistress for the duration of your ride."

Calera grumbled under her breath. "I can't keep a secret around here, not with you and that confounded stallion reading my every thought and mood." Her lashes fluttered down to shield her eyes and stared at the grass beneath her feet, as if something there demanded her attention. "Do you mind, Apache?" she asked hesitantly.

"Mind?" Shane threw back his head and laughed. "Dear God, Irish, how could you think I would mind?"

"Well, I wasn't sure . . ."

Her voice trailed off when Shane got down on his knees in front of her to rest his cheek on her belly while his arms looped familiarly around her hips. "Never doubt that I want this child and the others who will follow. Our children will have what I never had, what you lost so long ago—a true family. Our children will grow like the wildflowers, basking in the warmth of my love for you. And I will look at them and see a part of me entwined with a part of you. They will be the personification of what I feel each time I hold you. They will be the living extension of my love for you."

Calera was overwhelmed by his words. She was humbled by the way this powerful giant knelt before her, honoring her as if she were precious and special to him. Never once, even in the beginning, had Shane attempted to prove his dominance over her or tried to impress her with his unrivaled strength and courage. He merely accepted her as he wished to be accepted—freely, completely. When Calera paused to consider the blessing that had been bestowed on her, she was consumed by tender emotion.

Biting back the sentimental tears, she knelt down to him. Her hands linked behind his neck and her lips parted in invitation. "Oh, Apache, do you have any idea how much I adore you? Each time I think of all you have done *for* me and *because* of me, my heart very nearly bursts."

Shane framed her exquisite face in his hands, his thumbs brushing away the tears that spilled from her eyes. "Everything I do, I do because I love you to the depths of my very soul." His lips brushed hers in a reverent whisper of a kiss. "You are not just my link with paradise, Irish. You *are* my paradise—"

Shane was not allowed to speak his piece, for Calera was so overcome with emotion that she kissed the breath out of him. A week of wanting unfurled inside her. She longed to recapture the paradise he had unveiled to her. In the depths of those midnight-black eyes she could see forever. In Shane's muscular strength she could feel the radiance of fierce and yet gentle power. In his kiss there was life-giving breath and the communion of spirit. Her wild Apache knight, who could strike terror in the hearts of men, brought indescribable contentment to her soul. Here, beneath the stone mountains and tall pines, was a world of dreams that had become her reality. This was where Calera belonged. This was life in its purest, sweetest essence.

"Love me, Apache," she whispered to him. "That is all I will ever ask of you."

Shane stared down into that beguiling face that was alive with emotions and he felt his heart melt on his ribs. How could a man who had been so lonely and tormented have found such a lovely treasure? What had he done to deserve such happiness? Shane didn't know the answer to those questions, but he wasn't going to argue about his good fortune. He only wanted to plumb the depths of this love that could span eternity.

"I do love you and I always will," he told her in a voice thick with passionate promise. "I yearn to make love to you until you have no doubt that you are my whole world."

"Make love *with* me," she corrected in the most provocative voice imaginable. "You, my wild Apache knight, will always have my eager and *everlasting* participation . . ."

And sure enough, he did . . .